Praise for

Warming Up
(She Writes Press, Berkeley 2013)

- Illinois Library Association, "Soon to be Famous" Author Project Finalist
- Top Ten, *Writers Digest* Self-Published Book Awards, Mainstream Fiction
- Finalist, Book of the Year Awards, *ForeWord Reviews*
- Finalist, Eric Hoffer Book Awards, Mainstream Fiction
- Short List Finalist, William Wisdom-William Faulkner Prize for an Unpublished Novel, 2011

Courting Kathleen Hannigan
(Ampersand, Inc., Chicago 2007)

"**Wonderfully intelligent and revealing. In brisk yet thoughtful prose, Mary Hutchings Reed has wrought a juicy tale of a brilliant woman lawyer facing the toughest challenge of her career: another woman lawyer.**"
Lucia Blinn, *Passing for Normal; Navigating the Night; We Called It the Country*

Fairways
(World Premiere 2006, Steel Beam Theatre, St. Charles, IL)

"The production is a solid gold nugget that sparkles and shines in all of its many facets. ★★★ a musical that is funny and thought provoking."
Jill Orr, *The Kane County Chronicle*

© 2015 Mary Hutchings Reed. All rights reserved. No part of this book may be reproduced in any form or by any electronic or mechanical means, including information storage and retrieval systems, without permission in writing from the publisher, except by a reviewer who may quote brief passages in a review.

The names of people, characters, companies and/or events mentioned herein are fictitious and are in no way intended to represent any real individual, company or event unless otherwise noted.

ISBN 978-0990560340

Design
David Robson, Robson Design

Published by
AMPERSAND, INC.
1050 North State Street
Chicago, Illinois 60610

203 Finland Place
New Orleans, Louisiana 70131

www.ampersandworks.com

Ten percent of revenue from sales of this book will be donated to the **Legal Assistance Foundation**, the largest provider of *pro bono* civil legal services to the poor and underserved of metropolitan Chicago.

Saluting the Sun

MARY HUTCHINGS REED

To Paula —
Thank you for
all your support
throughout the years —
All the best
Mary Hutchings Reed
April 2015

AMP&RSAND, INC.
Chicago • New Orleans

Acknowledgements

Next to Chicago, New Orleans is my favorite city in the United States. I made my first visit with a childhood friend, Barbara Lachenmaier, who was then in the travel business, and during that short weekend, she met her husband of 31 years, Robert Spangenberg. Barb has been a first reader of all of my work, and I am grateful for her and Rob's friendship, hospitality and insights. While they were dating, I visited for Mardi Gras, and later for their wedding. Since then, I've visited several times for the Words and Music Writing Festival, on a post-Katrina week-long mission trip, and several times with my husband, Bill, both for a health policy conference, and for fun. *Saluting the Sun* was written before Katrina, but I was happy on a recent visit to see the French Quarter as vibrant as ever. We still love all that is New Orleans: the music, the architecture, the lush gardens and bougainvillea, the sweet smell of beignets and coffee, the French market, and especially the street musicians, artists and entertainers.

Contrary to many stereotypes of the hermit-writer isolated in her study, writing is for me a collaborative effort. I am grateful for my writing coach, Enid Powell, whose weekly writing workshop has always nurtured my writing, and to the members of her workshop who commented on the very first drafts of these pages. I am also grateful to Fred Shafer and the writers in his novel-writing workshop, who read and commented on more polished, but not yet final, drafts, and whose commitment to making work as good as it can be is unfailing. Marjie Rynearson was an early teacher who emphasized story structure, helping me to tackle a twin-chambered narrative such as this. Anne Mini, whom I met at Words and Music in New Orleans in 2001, has been a steady long-distance writing companion, and was good enough to read and comment on early drafts of this book. My weekly writing sessions with poet Lucia Blinn help keep me on my "page a day" program, and my sister, actress Donna Steele, reminds me constantly of the critical importance of art and creativity in our lives.

Based on *Saluting the Sun,* April Eberhardt, literary change agent and author advocate, accepted me as her client in 2007 and has guided my writing career ever since; her belief in me and my stories has kept me going in the rapidly changing publishing industry. Finally, as this book goes to print, I am particularly grateful to editor David Bloom, a tough critic and a true friend.

Suzie Isaacs and Ampersand, Inc. have been pioneers in indie publishing since before we even knew what that was. I am privileged to again be her client, and to have the services of her colleague David Robson of Robson Design.

As always, I am grateful for the love of my life, William R. Reed.

Mary Hutchings Reed
April, 2015

1

When Nevaeh Thera woke up that Sunday in her tree house 10 feet up in an aging oak on Farmer Jones' back 40, she peeled back the clear plastic door, looked down, and saw that her boyfriend, Tray Ashley, was gone. The previous night, after one too many tequila sunrises, he'd tarzanned off the tree house's rope ladder and landed in a soft heap next to their outdoor shower. He wasn't hurt, but she couldn't wake him, so she'd tossed a sleeping bag over him and left him, a curiosity for the raccoons and other night critters. Now, assuming he was down at the creek answering nature's call, she yodeled his name, "Oh, Tray-ay," and it carried so far into the open Iowa fields that it didn't come back to her.

Despite the early hour, she poured herself two shots of cheap tequila and downed them in one gulp, angry to be left alone. Then she grabbed the bottle and lifted it directly to her lips—to hell with shots, glasses, and false measures—but as the liquid spilled onto her chin, she saw her pet white rat's glassine eyes fixed on hers.

"You don't know," she said to the rat and tipped the tequila back. It burned her throat and rumbled in her empty stomach. Tara, the pet, stood her ground. "Okay," Nevaeh said. "Okay." She had responsibilities and she was a responsible person. For the sake of her rat, she set the bottle aside.

She wandered through her day, expecting Tray to show up, apologetic. Once before he'd left for a single night, but that had been early on, and he'd returned with a couple hundred dollars. She hadn't asked how.

That very Sunday night she started to dream again, which was both a good thing and a bad sign. Whenever she didn't have a man in her life, she had busy, colorful dreams, which she liked to think of as direct instructions from whatever divine spirit ran the universe. Monday morning, after a fitful and unfamiliar night without Tray, she woke up with a gut feeling that he wasn't coming back, but with an odd word in mind, a word she'd actually seen written in an elaborate script in her dream, and had heard repeated over and over: "Pulchritude."

She didn't know the word, which seemed an especially cruel joke, and so, dream in hand, but unsolved, she started that "first day of the rest of her life" like any other day. She saluted the sun: actually, most mornings she shortened the yoga exercise from a series of prone positions to only the final, standing stretch to the sun, arms straight over her head, hugging her shoulders, palms in, chin up. Then, she poured two handfuls of dry cereal into an oversized coffee mug and ate while sitting in the lotus position, facing east. Then she showered with lemon-scented dish-washing liquid under a plastic camp shower she'd filled from Farmer Jones' garden hose, humming a tune from "South Pacific" for its parodic value, and tried, unsuccessfully, to wash Tray Ashley right out of her hair. Determined to resume her normal life, she put Tara in her pocket and walked as usual the two and a half miles to The Bluffs, the family resort overlooking the Mississippi where she worked as a housekeeper.

As she changed sheets and scrubbed tubs and toilets, she pondered her dream, and the possible meanings of "pulchritude," and, since she couldn't help herself, how long it would take Tray to come to his senses and come home to her. How could he give up his tree house—built with their own hands—and Prairie du Chien and the almost five years of their relationship? Had he finally given in to his father's demands that he go to law school? He'd taken the law boards only to strike a bargain with his dad, a man he claimed he had no desire to emulate. He'd deferred his admission last year when she'd reminded him that his father, a wealthy corporate lawyer, was so bored by the routine of his practice that it took three extra-dry martinis, every night, just to crank up enough enthusiasm to greet the next day. But his father had a big house and steady money, and knew, at least, what to do the next day.

She finished her 24 rooms at The Bluffs by shortly after three, and headed for Prairie du Chien's two-room public library to look up her dream word. While she was there, she figured she'd apply for a library card, to help pass the time without Tray.

"Your address?" librarian Judith Scott asked, friendly enough at first.

"Tree house, Third Oak Up from the Second Downstream Bend in Farmer Jones' Creek, Prairie du Chien," she said proudly.

Judith eyed her up and down the way she might've inspected a potential boarder, as if waiting for her to say she was just joking. Enduring the woman's inspection, Nevaeh stood very still. She was wearing her good blue jean skirt, which she'd fashioned out of oversized overalls and filled out with bright triangles of flowered fabric remnants pilfered from the old-fashioned dime store on the town square. Her white tube socks were clean, and her tennis shoes relatively new, from the Goodwill over in Muenster. Even though Tara was asleep at the back of her neck, under her long and kinky brown hair, she was feeling highly presentable.

"How old are you?" the librarian asked.

"Old enough to read," Nevaeh wanted to say, but there was a thick growth of dark hair on the woman's upper lip and, out of sympathy, Nevaeh was struck civil. The librarian probably lived in a real house—but alone, obviously. "Twenty-five," Nevaeh lied. She was really 23.

"How long have you been at this—" The woman worked her lips. "This address?"

"A few months," she said. She felt Tara shift her position.

"What about the winter?" the librarian asked, leaning over her desk, her voice more concerned than stern.

"Last year, we went to Mexico." Sort of true. Nevaeh tried to sound casual; she was hoping that she wouldn't have to face the coming cold, that Tray would come back and together they would figure how what to do.

The librarian straightened. "Oh."

Nevaeh knew what she was thinking: how could someone who lived in a tree house afford a Mexican vacation? Though surrounded by thousands of volumes describing the entire world and every sort of experience one could have in it, the woman probably had ventured out of Prairie du Chien only long enough to get her library degree over in Champaign. Most likely, she'd never hitch-hiked anywhere, never conned anyone out of bus-fare, never begged at a church's food pantry, never played blues harp on a corner or camped on a beach for a week until the *policia* asked her to move on. It was surprising, really, how wonderful people had been to Nevaeh. It nourished her belief in the goodness of the universe, in a heaven here on earth. It was her birthright and her name: "Heaven" spelled backwards.

The librarian began typing up a library card with a little metal strip on it. While she waited, Nevaeh made her way to the big dictionary sitting on an oak stand with a little brass plaque stating that it was given in memory of the Travis and Violet Johnson family. She turned to the Ps, found "pulchritude" spelled exactly as in her dream, and was profoundly disappointed at how little guidance this word offered on her future. Beauty. Why did the English language need an obscure word like "pulchritude?" Could anyone use it in a sentence with a straight face? What good was a word even the college-educated had to look up? What was the DS trying to tell her?

The librarian called her over when she was done and handed her the card with her first two books. "Don't let them get wet," the librarian said, but, since it was bright outside and there wasn't a single cloud in the royal blue sky, Nevaeh didn't quite get her meaning. "If it rains," the librarian said. "What do you do when it rains?"

"Oh," Nevaeh said, "we—I—have a roof, and walls—like a regular house! But I'll put them in my pack. It's waterproof." She felt Tara wiggle and resisted the urge to sit down and tell the woman that the tree house was built with old barn wood Tray had scavenged on Farmer Jones' property, had glassless windows that she draped with clear shower curtains with Donald Duck borders from the Goodwill, and was crammed with furniture. They owned two plastic lawn chairs that had been on sale for six dollars each which Tray had managed to finagle the salesgirl into selling him for the price of one, a small round white plastic outdoor table with a crack in it that someone had condemned to the trash and a six-by-nine orange shag rug, same source. People threw out some of the best, most useful stuff for no reason other than their boredom with things. Her own mother had been motivated—if that was the word for it—only by the ennui that often plagues the well-to-do and causes them to want to add a little drama—or, in her mother's case, a lot of drama—to their ordinary, well-to-do-lives.

Nevaeh hadn't spoken to her mother in two years, since the day the woman ruined her college graduation by getting stumbling drunk at the English Department's post-ceremony reception and making a pass at the chairman. When the chairman's wife tried to guide him away, Mrs. Thera shoved her, and the wife had, remarkably, shoved back. Tray intervened, and they'd dragged Nevaeh's mother across campus, people watching and shaking their heads. They dumped her on the bed in her hotel room, leaving an angry note from Nevaeh not to call her or ever contact her again. Even before Nevaeh had given up her cell phone, her mother, isolated on the snooty North Shore of suburban Chicago, had honored her wishes.

After grad school, Nevaeh (creative writing) and Tray (film) moved to San Francisco together, taking all summer to coax his 20-year-old Ford 150 across the country. They both had escaped the university with respectable grades and almost no debt, and they each had a little stash of graduation money from aunts and uncles and a few extra dollars saved from jobs around campus. They were going to look for jobs, but they weren't in any hurry. In state and national parks where they'd stay for a week or so at a time, men and women, usually wistful people in their 40s, would invite them to their family campsites for dinner, enchanted by the romance of being on the road for a summer without three kids and a mortgage or the need to be clear-headed in the morning.

Tray, with his patrician features—straight nose, chiseled jaw line, perfect white teeth—immediately earned the trust these families would otherwise have withheld from someone in raggedy jeans, a long-sleeved cotton shirt open nearly to the waist and an auburn pony tail half-way down his back. He opened his mouth and lyrics came out: funny words, kind words, college words. Just the right words at the right time. He was like a hypnotist, and Nevaeh was in heart-stopping love. Tray was pulchritudinous. He also happened to be a pretty skillful pickpocket.

In San Francisco neither of them found work. Nevaeh wanted to be an editor, Tray a television producer. They had liberal arts degrees from the Midwest and no connections to the San Fran aristocracy.

In the winter they headed south, but they found LA too big, too expensive, and too glitzy, so they headed further south to Tijuana. Tray made friends with the locals and they smoked a lot of dope and drank a lot of wine. The old pick-up didn't move for six, maybe eight weeks. Then Tray got to feeling tied down, and in the middle of the night on a Tuesday in late February, they fired her up and left. Nevaeh had looked over her shoulder for the first hundred miles, worried that Tray had picked the wrong pocket.

She ducked when he shouted, too frightened to scream when the trailer park gatekeeper from their last week in Tijuana leaned out of the window of his Isuzu Trooper and aimed his rifle at them as if they were a couple of prairie dogs. Just as he removed his hand from the wheel to shoot, the Isuzu hit a bump, slipped onto the gravel of the right shoulder and skidded into a 360 in the middle of the interstate. A semi swerved around and jack-knifed in the middle of the southern California highway, fencing off the angry, swearing rifle-man and saving Tray's and Nevaeh's lives.

After the Tijuana terrors, they'd spent a few months searching along the river for just the right town. Tray wanted a town where the police would know him as a local and not harass him because of his ponytail. He said he'd learned his lesson in Mexico and swore he'd never again prey on his neighbors. When they simultaneously noticed the billboard for The Bluffs, a family resort in Prairie du Chien, Nevaeh saw the possibility of employment, and Tray saw a welcoming port in a storm. City folk would come to The Bluffs, overlooking the river, and, weak with bucolia, let down their guard, consigning their wallets to their rear pockets. With the tourists in town, Tray didn't have to feed off his neighbors.

Almost immediately, Nevaeh'd found her housekeeping job at the resort, and developed a sideline of her own. She never lifted more than five dollars, usually in ones, from any given room, and never from anyone with more than two kids. Most people failed to leave a tip in the room, even though the etiquette books suggested it, and she was sure it was because in their last-minute muddle to get out by 11:00 a.m., they simply forgot, not because they didn't want to.

She didn't give them a chance to forget.

Back at the tree house with her two library books—*Best American Short Stories, 2000* and, *Making Your Own Music*—Nevaeh put Tara in her wicker dog basket and sat on the curved plastic chair. She reached in her backpack for her Bible and opened it to Luke, 12:22, where she kept her money. On top of her wad, she found a page torn from a college-ruled spiral notebook with a twenty dollar bill attached. In Tray's large and confident scrawl, it read, "Going legal. Will also try to change my ways. It's probably best if we go it alone for a while—you'll be a better person without me." It was dated August 23, 5:45 a.m. At the end of the note, he'd drawn a little diagram, and added that if she continued to live at Chez Nay Tray, she should anchor the rope ladder at the bottom.

How dare he leave her a note! They'd been together all through their last two years of college and a year of grad school and another on the road before landing in Prairie du Chien. At the least, he should've talked to her sober and in person; she was sure she could've talked him out of it—both law school and leaving her behind.

Sighing, she took a can of Five Aces Blend down from its shelf above her bed. A package of Zig Zags lay on top of the tobacco. She held the can to her face like an airplane mask and sucked in the sweet raw smell, good enough to eat. She rolled a cigarette, lit it and took a long drag, holding the smoke in her lungs like dope. She lay back on the double air mattress and, for the first time in the 30 hours since Tray had left, cried. She let herself cry for seven minutes, and then stubbornly wiped the tears from her eyes and flicked her ashes in a Chock Full O'Nuts coffee can that was chock full of butts.

She picked up her Bible, and the words "lilies of the field" caught her eye. Setting her jaw, she resumed counting her money. Three-hundred-eighty-seven dollars, including Tray's twenty. It was remarkable how long that much money could last, if one didn't have to pay rent and car installments and taxes, and if you didn't smoke store-bought cigarettes or drink fancy liquor. She took a deep breath, feeling like a veritable lily of the field. She had to trust that she'd be taken care of.

Then she poured herself a glass of wine and opened her library book, a teacher's guide to instruments that could be made out of old fashioned cigar boxes and rubber bands, tin cans and beans, glass bottles, washboards, washtubs, and other relics once but no longer commonly found around ordinary households. Idly, she ran her finger around the rim of the glass, and was noticing the sweet sound of a middle C when she turned the page to "Musical Glasses."

She'd been fascinated with the sound of musical glasses ever since their meandering trip to the West coast, when she and Tray had heard a bearded, ageless man playing an extensive collection of stemmed wine glasses on Jackson Square in New Orleans. He'd had a wooden cart with three rows of glasses, each filled with water at different levels. He ran his wet index fingers around the rims of the glasses, producing natural, almost haunted tones. The man had played "Amazing Grace" and told the story of the instrument in a voice as soothing as his wind-like music. He called himself a glass harmonicist, and said the music went back as far as 1492, the date of an Italian woodcut that showed a musician striking glass bells with a stick. At every diner where she and Tray stopped after that, they remembered New Orleans and played two-note duets with their water glasses while they waited for their food. Tray said she was better at it than he and that if she wanted to, she could be a star. She'd thought it was just because he loved her.

Nevaeh put the book down, dipped her finger in her wine, and ran it around the rim of the goblet. Nothing happened. She drank a little and wet her finger and tried it again. Still nothing. She consulted the book, irritated that the magic had stopped working for her. The book said to make sure her finger was clean and to apply pressure until the glass produced a sound. She pressed down, at first concerned that she might break the glass and cut her finger, but she was rewarded with a high, sweet note. She filled the glass to the top, producing a lower pitch.

She only had five stemmed glasses, and none of them matched. She filled them from the round red insulated jug in which she stored her drinking water and started sipping. Do re mi fa so. She played "Doe, a deer, a female deer, ray, a drop of golden sun, me, a name I call myself," and ran out of notes. She dipped both index fingers in glasses and played a two-note chord, one note clock-wise, one counter-clockwise. It felt as if she were patting her head and tickling her stomach at the same time, but she liked the sound. It blended seamlessly with the open air of the tree house.

Nevaeh adjusted the water in her fifth glass and wet the little finger of her right hand to see if she could play three notes at once, a C-major chord, do, mi, so. She played until her fingers tingled, and then she slept. When she woke up Tuesday morning, she tried to fish her dream from the great pool of the universe's sub-conscious instructions, and remembered only the image of a book. It had two glossy pages, without words, but with brightly colored shapes, including a squarish circle constructed out of many straight lines, to make whatever an octagon would be called if it had eight times the number of sides. She hadn't a clue to its meaning. But she had a job, she had five-eighths of a beautiful octave for her new musical hobby, and she knew, as surely as she knew anything, that someday, somehow, Tray would come back to her.

Still, she had to live as if he were lost to law school, and to act as if she were in charge of the rest of her life.

Not knowing what else to do, she rose and saluted the sun.

2

One night in early November, the water in Nevaeh's glass harmonica froze. By then, she had an instrument of 15 stemmed glasses which she'd gathered one by one at that fall's last round of really good garage sales, and a couple of special, deeply colored cobalt blue and ruby ones from the DollarDaze, each a treat to herself for not getting laid off until October 21, the last weekend for fall foliage crowds to fill The Bluffs. She was hoping to create an instrument of all colored glasses.

Also that morning, the water in her Farmer's Insurance two-quart cooler was crusted on top but punctured easily. She boiled some in a pot on her two-burner propane camping stove, grateful Tray had left it for her. He obviously wouldn't need it in Iowa City, if that's where he still was. She hadn't heard from him in the nearly three months since he'd split.

She dropped the boiling water by teaspoonful by teaspoonful onto the ice in each glass until a rounded cube slipped out. Remarkably, none of the glasses broke, but it took the better part of the day to unfreeze, dry and label each one. Already two inches of snow blanketed the ground. The natives wore spring jackets, sometimes only wool shirts, but at the Goodwill, Nevaeh had spent 60 of her precious dollars for a parka, a pair of long underwear, a second pair of wool socks, another sweater, and laced-up boots, like hiking boots. Still, when the winds shot over 20, the Donald Duck shower curtain on the north window bulged and flapped, and Nevaeh shivered with a cold she'd never felt before. This wasn't a waiting-for-the-school-bus cold, a run-across-the-yard-to-the-mailbox cold, not even a half-hour-at-the-ice-rink cold. Those colds were for kids whose mothers would warm them in front of roaring fires with hot chocolate and sugar cookies. This cold was different because she lived in a plywood tree house. She taped the shower curtain taut over the window with duct tape and slept in all her clothes in her sleeping bag, a top-of-the-line, high school graduation present rated to 40 degrees. If Tray had been there, they would've zipped their bags together, generating extra heat. Instead, Tara crawled up under her sweater and stayed there.

On the third morning of the early winter, with the temperature in the 20s, Nevaeh lay in her sleeping bag, imagining Tray in law school, learning to be his own defense attorney. He was an exquisite liar. Always had been. Knew how to pick out the detail that made the most outlandish of his stories true: a finger cut off at the second joint, a shaved eyebrow, a three-legged dog. In a place like Prairie du Chien, someone like Tray stood out so boldly that he was above suspicion, but Nevaeh had no reason to think that he'd changed his stripes in Iowa City. Even as she huddled in the tree house, he was probably hustling in the law library, flirting with the wrong girl while he picked the right one's pockets. The thought inspired her. She put Tara in her parka pocket and jogged, as fast as her booted feet would take her, to the Prairie du Chien Public Library.

At one o'clock, Judith Scott seemed surprised to find Nevaeh waiting for her to open the building.

"Good morning, Nevaeh," Judith chirped.

Her nose numb with cold, Nevaeh couldn't bring herself either to chirp back or let her know that it was past morning and she'd been waiting not for one hour but for three, having forgotten that two mornings a week the library was closed due to budget constraints. She'd walked around the block five times, had slipped into Herb and Grace's for a small, fifty-nine-cent coffee, worn out her welcome there when the place began to fill up with farmers coming into town for their morning gossip, and finally dodged into Nellie's for a grilled cheese and water, $2.75 plus tip. Nellie had thrown in some potato chips, and after an hour and 15 minutes in the same booth, Nevaeh had left her $3.50.

At this rate, Nevaeh thought, she should try to find herself a place to live: surely there would be a room with heat someplace in the county for $300 a month. Nevaeh tried to picture such a room, a radiator hissing under a window overlooking a backyard patch of dry grass with four children running wild and a part-German Shepherd patrolling on a long leash running the length of a clothesline. The thought of sharing a bathroom with strangers was not nearly as distasteful as being hawked by such a suspicious landlady and her curious children. It would probably take $400 to get even a one-room apartment of her own, and she was short the cash for the security deposit. Besides, Tray always said that small landlords cheated their tenants on heat and rigged the electricity meters. He knew because his stepdad owned a few apartments. More to the point, she didn't make $400 a month. She didn't have a job. She didn't have Tray.

"Looking for something in particular?" Judith asked, opening the inside door of the library.

"Heat," Nevaeh was tempted to say. "Just some research," she said evenly, hoping Judith would not pursue it. From her own experience, she should've known better: librarians are nosy and ask questions until they've gotten to Dewey's fourth decimal.

Judith turned on the lights and headed towards her small, glassed office at the rear of the library. To the right was the children's room, four square tables, walls lined with book cases not more than four feet high and a brightly-colored globe. Cut-out turkeys, pilgrims and horns of plenty were pasted to the cement block walls. To the left of the entrance was the adult reading room, larger, but still modest. Across the back of the room, there were three cubicles with computers and free internet access. To the side, there were rows of books, and in the middle, four shiny blond six-person tables.

Nevaeh put her backpack down at the table at the front because it was the furthest from Judith's office. Facing out a large picture window that overlooked the town square, she turned her back to the librarian and skillfully transferred Tara from the pocket of her parka to the pocket of her oversized cable-knit sweater. She rubbed her hands together, as if anxious to get to work. She'd forgotten her notebook, so she walked back to the computer carrels and took a couple of sheets from a recycled scratch pad. She sat at her table, too cold still, to think.

"What are you researching, Nevaeh? Can I help you?" Judith was standing over her, eager to assist.

Tray and Nevaeh had been kicked out of libraries before, in larger cities where they'd been mistaken for homeless folks—potential olfactory nuisances. Those librarians were not as committed to the "Freedom to Read" as their public relations folks proclaimed.

Nevaeh eyed Judith with suspicion. Did she really want to help or was she testing Nevaeh's motives for visiting the library? Nevaeh wasn't homeless; she lived at Tree house, Third Oak Up from the Second Downstream Bend in Farmer Jones' Creek. Still, Judith might suspect Nevaeh of seeking shelter, not knowledge. Nevaeh couldn't take a chance. "Glass harmonica?" she said.

"Again?" Judith asked. "Seems to me I gave you everything I had last August."

"Wow, what a memory!" Nevaeh said, thinking how creepy it was that Judith would remember what each of her patrons researched, thought about, dreamt about. The woman really needed to get a life. "Well, let me read a little, then, just to get started, and I'll get back to you, okay?"

Left with nothing to do, Judith frowned, but Nevaeh smiled sweetly.

Tara wiggled in Nevaeh's pocket, then scrambled up the side of her sweater and around to the back of Nevaeh's neck, burrowing in her hair. Nevaeh felt her move but didn't flinch. Unable to breathe, she held Judith's gaze. The slightest crease appeared between Judith's untweezed brown eyebrows. Then she rubbed her hands together and turned, as if preparing to start her work day over.

"Alright, then," she said.

Over the next few hours, Nevaeh was amazed at how many of the local citizenry visited the library. Two farmers exchanging mysteries, the real estate agent asking for a book on the American Craft movement, a couple of mothers with their youngsters looking for books with pop-up dinosaurs. For them, the library was a destination, not a hideout from the cold. They'd probably been first to the post office, the drug store, the grocery store, and the Ace Hardware, and had saved the last stop as a reward, as if it were summer, and the library served cool treats like the Dairy Mart. They came in radiating the cold like an open freezer door, hung their coats over chairs to thaw while they browsed and chatted with Judith, and then bundled up again and were on their way. Only Farmer Lundgren stayed, hunkered down in a computer carrel.

Nevaeh grew desperate about the night to come. She studied the heavy down coats, their pockets stuffed with gloves and mittens, and wished that Tray was there. Rummaging through those coats for spare change—even dollars—was a two-person operation, she could appreciate that.

"Anyone sitting here?" a thirtyish woman asked her, and before she could answer, put her parka on the chair opposite Nevaeh, her back to the window.

"Great day for jambalaya!" the woman said, and went off in search of a recipe.

Nevaeh considered her options. She rolled a pen under the table in the direction of the parka.

"Oh," she said out loud, to emphasize for whoever might be watching the accidental nature of this incident, and crawled on her hands and knees to the other side of the table. The parka drooped heavily, skimming the indoor-outdoor-carpeting and teasing her with promises, like a Megamillions lottery ticket. She put one hand on the pen and one arm on the back of the chair, as if to steady herself. Without looking, she slipped a hand in the pocket closest to her, and, fingering some paper, lifted it out, hope singing in her heart. She put her fist again on the carpet, and peeked at her winnings. A dollar and a shopping list. She heard Judith's whisper approaching her table and brushed the list under the chair with the parka, where one could conclude it had fallen out of the jacket on its own accord. She crawled back to her side of the table, her right hand clutching the pen, like a treasure harvested from the bottom of the sea. Her heart was racing as if she'd finished a marathon. Against the wall, Judith was showing the woman cookbooks, and interrupted herself long enough to say, "Try to stay on top of your subject matters, Ms. Thera!"

Nevaeh laughed louder than the poor librarian's joke was funny. She held up the pen. "It's one of those new rollers," she said, and Judith put her fingers to her lips. Nevaeh looked around. The only other person in the room was a large man with his nose pressed against a computer screen, who didn't seem to have been disturbed. She nodded to Judith. Tara wiggled. Tickled, Nevaeh bobbled her head again in Judith's direction, and quickly sat down. She yawned and put her hands behind her head, elbows akimbo, searching for Tara in her hair. Still clutching the dollar in her left hand, she closed her right around the rat, but Tara scooted away, scurrying down her arm, down her leg and across the room in front of Judith and the gourmet cook books to the front corner, near the window. Nevaeh didn't move a muscle. She couldn't be sure that Judith had seen Tara. The librarian hadn't screamed, even though she seemed to be both the meticulous and the hyper-observant type.

The rat had never done such a thing, but then again, never had she been subjected to the extremes of weather they'd experienced these past few days. Nevaeh let out a little cry that drew a sharp look from Judith. The jambalaya lady had her hands full of Judith's selections and was totally preoccupied with her own mission. Neither she nor Judith seemed to have noticed Tara. Nevaeh couldn't look at Tara's corner without giving her away, and she couldn't be sure, with only her peripheral vision that Tara was still in the corner. Again, Nevaeh wished Tray was there, to cause a distraction, to rescue Tara, to come up with the big idea that would save them both.

Feigning boredom, she stood, stretched her arms out straight over her head, slipped the dollar from her left fist into her pocket and shuffled towards the stacks. She pulled down a book at random and opened it. It was a book on weather. Interesting. She had a cousin in Chicago, Dawnie, who broadcast the weather on TV. But she had no time for such distractions: she had to save Tara. Pretending to read the book, she surreptitiously studied the corner where Tara had run. The rat wasn't stupid. She wasn't sitting there staring back. She'd disappeared without a trace, and although Nevaeh tried to get inside Tara's rat mind, Nevaeh could not fathom where she'd gone next. If Tray'd been there, he'd have her calling, "Here, ratty, ratty!" Why was she laughing? This was a terrible situation, really. Tara was lost in the library, and it would be closing in 45 minutes. She could hear Judith finishing up with the jambalaya patron. Soon, she would be onto her.

"A new interest, Nevaeh?" There she was.

"Not new. Necessary," Nevaeh said. She didn't think the ACLU would approve of her having to discuss her every interest with Judith the librarian.

"It says here," she said, searching the page in front of her, "that winter doesn't start until December 21. Could've fooled me."

"I hope you find someplace to stay by then," Judith said, her tone more in the way of a warning than a consolation.

Nevaeh thought briefly of Chicago, although it was no doubt much colder there, but just then a white flash streaked between their feet and the bookcase. Judith screamed, a shrill, little girl scream the frequency of the weekly emergency siren that blared from the yellow speaker atop the village's volunteer firehouse. Tara froze in her tracks. Farmer Lundgren, Stephen King's *Cycle of the Werewolf* in one hand, grabbed the rat with the other and pressed his oversized thumb against her throat. Nevaeh stood stricken dumb, staring at her pet's pure white, motionless body. Lundgren grinned at Judith with a vaguely lascivious satisfaction and strode outside, where, through the picture window, Nevaeh watched him toss Tara's body in the bushes at the edge of the library's lot. She dropped to her knees, buried her face in the weather book and wailed.

At first, the cold off of Farmer Lundgren's work boots, like smelling salts, roused her from her misery to remind her where she was. Then the lady from whom she'd pilfered the dollar, unaware, apparently, of the reason for Nevaeh's outburst, put her arm on her back to comfort her.

Only inches from Nevaeh's face, Judith's tightly-laced, sensible shoe tapped. The weather book said that winter officially lasted 88.99 days, Nevaeh was freezing even if winter wasn't yet official and now some lout she didn't know had squeezed her pet to death before her very eyes. Why?

Nevaeh sucked in a heavy sob. She felt like a childless widow, utterly alone. She pounded her fists against the hard tiled floor. She wasn't meant to be a loner, but she couldn't—wouldn't—chase after Tray, he would come after her someday. When she finally looked up and saw Judith's temporal vein pumping purple and furious like a downed power line, she knew, too, that she wasn't welcome anymore in Prairie du Chien. Chicago could be an option; maybe her cousin would take her in for a while. Dawn Ann McKnight was beautiful and smart and popular and always said and did the right things. Nevaeh had been in awe of her, but she hadn't seen Dawn Ann since college. It wouldn't be right to suddenly call her and ask for help, as if she couldn't take care of herself.

"Is there something I can do?" the jambalaya lady offered.

"I'm cold," she whimpered.

"She lives in a tree house on Farmer Jones' place," Judith Scott said, her upper lip curling in outright contempt. "Apparently, with rats!"

"And hungry," Nevaeh added loudly, ignoring Judith and thinking, as Tray would if he were there, that exaggeration could help to make the most of this terrible, terrible situation. "I haven't any money."

"You must be freezing to death!" the woman said. With a flash of her eyes, she gave the farmer a swift kick. "Come, let me take you home and get you something to eat. You can stay with us tonight, and tomorrow we'll call the county and figure out where you can go."

Nevaeh pulled a red bandanna that she used as a handkerchief from her pocket and the crumpled dollar came with it. It wasn't enough to make a liar out of her. She blew her nose louder than library regulations allowed, and scurried like the late Tara past a sputtering Judith Scott. She threw her things in her pack and left all her borrowed books on the table, due or not.

"Neither a borrower nor a lender be," she said, her voice quivering, and walked out, her savior right behind her, clutching an inspirational copy of *Cookin' in N'awlins*.

3

Although she'd been broadcasting the weather for nine years, today Dawn Ann McKnight was as nervous as Punxsutawney Phil on Groundhog Day. This was her first broadcast in a major market. With fog, wind, torrential rains, city-crippling snow, a month of 95 and a month of minus 10, a 20-degree swing from the lakefront to the collar counties, Chicago television was Dawn Ann's dream come true. Dawn Ann's mother had been a famous psychiatrist, and had been disappointed that her daughter would choose a career as "common" as television. She'd been particularly disappointed that Dawn Ann would eschew hard news for something as frivolous as the weather. Dawn Ann had told herself that while forecasting wasn't like curing cancer or restoring the mentally ill or something highly intellectual that her mother could approve of, it was what she was good at, and honestly, so many of her parents' patients didn't get all that much better. Who was to say that what they did in psychology was any more important than what she wanted to do?

Dawn Ann had promised her mother that she'd be a star someday, and here she was, back home, and almost a star. She'd be leaving for the station in less than an hour. She dialed her mother's number, hoping the woman would be lucid enough to share the moment with her, perhaps, but not very likely, even say how proud she was of her.

"This is Dr. McKnight," her mother answered after the sixth ring.

"Hi, Mother, this is Dawn Ann," she said, smiling into the receiver as if her mother could see her.

"What?"

"Mother, this is your daughter, Dawn Ann," she said more firmly. "Hope I didn't wake you."

"I've been up for hours," Dr. McKnight said. "So much to do. Can't get it all done. And they line up outside to see me, but I don't let them in. I tell them to go away but they won't."

"Didn't Rosie come today?" At Dawn Ann's expense, Rosie came every day for a few hours to help her mother shower, prepare a nutritious lunch, and stay somewhat anchored in reality.

Her mother hesitated. "She's no good. She doesn't even see them there, lining up to see me." Rosie was the fourth such helper Dawn Ann had hired; her mother had refused the first three, all younger, two with foreign accents, one with crooked teeth. Rosie was in her 50s, and dressed not like a cleaning lady but an administrative assistant, which apparently had been the key to earning Dr. McKnight's trust, such as it was. Dr. McKnight had always had a reputation at the hospital as the kind of tough taskmaster who not only set impossibly high standards, but was also unwilling to admit anyone had ever met them. Dawn Ann herself felt she'd never quite measured up.

"I'm sure she's doing her best," Dawn Ann said, although she knew "trying" had never been sufficient for her mother, for whom *being* "the" best was the only thing that mattered. "Say, I called to remind you to watch me tonight on the TV," she said.

"What?" her mother asked. "You have to speak up. Don't mumble. You always mumble."

Dawn Ann knew she wasn't mumbling; asking her to repeat herself was her mother's way of trying to hide that she didn't comprehend what she was being told.

"Channel Three, ten o'clock tonight. Also tomorrow night, Sunday night, at ten o'clock. I want you to be sure to watch me, okay, Mom?" She sounded to herself as if she were begging, as if she were back in grade school and her mother couldn't promise to be at her piano recital, or her first speaking role in a school play, or once, even, her birthday party at the Children's Museum, which her favorite babysitter had helped plan for a dozen friends. Teachers always gave Dawn Ann special attention, assuring her that they would tell her parents what a fine performance they'd missed because of Mrs. McKnight's "emergencies." Sometime during high school, Dawn Ann had finally understood how few true "emergencies" psychiatrists actually had.

"Why would I watch TV?" Dr. McKnight scoffed. "How could I possibly have time?"

"I know you're so busy," Dawn Ann agreed. "Affirm and redirect," Rosie had advised her, so she went on. "If you do have a little extra time, I thought you'd like to see me on TV. Not every mother gets to see her daughter on TV, you know. So, if you have a chance, I thought you might enjoy it."

"I can't be bothered enjoying," Dr. McKnight said. Dawn Ann quietly agreed and hung up. She shook her head, gathered up her things and knocked on her husband's darkroom door.

"Don't come in," Derek said. "I'm in the middle of something."

"Just wanted you to know I'm leaving now. Wish me luck," she said.

"Of course," he said back.

At the station, she reviewed the computer model for this last week in November—cold and clear skies. In place a few minutes before airtime, Dawn Ann smoothed her hair, which was parted in the middle and pulled back in a gentle ponytail, and checked her smile on the monitor. She was struck, as she always was, by how much she looked not like her mother, but like her father. A man of science, he, at least, would've been proud of her. Dr. Kenneth McKnight, also a psychiatrist, had been an avid student of the weather, putting his knowledge to use in competitive sailing and, when he could, sport fishing. With his encouragement, she'd earned her bachelor's degree in meteorology, studying differential equations and atmospheric dynamics, with a minor in broadcasting, including three credits each in voice and diction and in acting for the camera. Now, with her initial Chicago assignment of Saturdays, Sundays and three mornings a week, Dawn Ann was close to her ultimate goal, the ten o'clock weeknight spot, currently the domain of Susan Stevens. Susan was the diva of Channel Three Weather Central, having reigned there for 15 years, nearly half of Dawn Ann's life. Susan's days were numbered, Dawn Ann thought. Anyone could see that the 45-year-old Stevens needed a little nip and tuck work to have any hope of retaining her time slot. That was, no doubt, one aspect of the business that her mother objected to, that looks trumped experience. It wasn't just looks, Dawn Ann assured herself; her hard work and meteorology degree should clinch it for her.

Finally, the director pointed at her and she was on. Fair skies tonight and average temperatures. Nothing her audience could blame her for. She smiled, dipped her chin, rotated her shoulders in an intentionally flirty three-quarters profile, and, in 90 seconds, told her share of 3.4 million households the current temperatures, winds and barometric pressures, the overnights and the five-day forecast. Over the course of her career in Cedar Rapids, Rockford, Madison and Milwaukee, Dawn Ann had confirmed that the shorter the horizon of the forecast, the more accurate it was. "Observation forecasting" was extremely accurate the minute before the thunderhead burst, if you knew what to look for. Still, as her father used to say, most people had trouble seeing what was plainly in front of them. By way of example, he'd taught her to calculate the temperature by counting the chirps of a cricket: add 37 to the number of chirps in a 15-second interval and you'd have your temperature. He'd taught her that insects were good predictors of weather, at least in the short term; that spiders weave their webs in improving weather and that bees won't swarm before a storm. When she'd asked why insects were so reliable, he told her it was because insects couldn't think for themselves. He'd said they were mini-computers, programmed to react in certain ways, unlike humans, who were, as a species, notoriously inconsistent and unpredictable. As a child, unpredictability, like a surprise, seemed to her a good thing. Predictably, her father would usually make it to her recitals and important games, but "unpredictability" gave her the hope that this would be the time she'd look out and see her mother in the audience.

Dawn Ann beamed at the camera, a bittersweet pride swelling within her. Even though it was a Sunday night, it was probably her largest audience ever. She guessed her mother hadn't remembered to watch, and, reminded of her father's lessons, she was also convinced the computer model was wrong. At lunch, her cat, Bernard, had sneezed, a sure sign of rain.

So, her first broadcast was wrong, but Dawn Ann had learned that, despite what she'd thought as a child, being wrong was no big deal. Unlike her mother, who'd cared a great deal, most people were really quite forgiving. Especially about the weather. Not much bad happened if you were wrong as a weathercaster, and even if you failed to predict a tornado or something, who could really blame you? In fact, half the people expected you to be wrong at least half the time, and a good fraction of those *hoped* you'd be wrong because they needed a weather-related excuse to get them out of cutting the grass, washing the windows, going to school, shampooing the dog.

With a friendly wave, she threw it back to the news anchors as if they were her best friends, and then, off-camera, joined the evening team at one end of the four-person news desk (the sports anchor had the other end). At 10:29:30, the director cut to her for one last look at the weather, and she repeated her uninspired forecast.

"Clear," the director said and those on the set relaxed. Dawn Ann smiled warmly at the anchors, Alberto Beltran and Felicity O'Neal, but they were flirting with each other, removing each other's mics as if they were clothes, and paying her no attention. She smiled at Ed Page, the sports guy, a former NFL offensive lineman who boasted that he'd spent most of his time in the hot tub safely soaking a lower back injury and who was also new to the station, but he turned his attention to the director, clearly seeking reassurance. This might be the best weather market in the whole world, Dawn Ann thought, a bit of the wind luffing out of her sails, but at this station, no one seemed much interested in her performance. She felt herself blush, a mixture of anger and embarrassment to be so ignored, and took off her microphone.

"My cat sneezed," she said, and Alberto and Felicity stopped their chatter long enough to cast an inquisitive glance.

"When my cat sneezes, it means it's going to rain," she said. "I think my first forecast for Chicago was wrong."

"Great," Felicity said. "We're already number two in the ratings. Now we've got a weather girl who is not only wrong, but relies on her cat."

Alberto laughed dismissively, a trill of r's. "My cat spat up a hairball four inches in diameter!" he said, stroking Felicity's hand. "What do you think that means?"

"I think it means we better call our agents," Felicity said, as if Dawn Ann's appearance on her newscast was going to be her downfall.

Dawn Ann bristled, shocked by the dismissiveness of their reception. She knew that everyone who pulled weekends was looking to move up, but in Iowa and in Milwaukee, she'd sensed a certain camaraderie and mutual ambition on the part of the weekenders.

Chicago was clearly going to be an every-person-for-his-or-her-self kind of place, and, although she wouldn't use it for some time, right then and there she had a brainstorm that she hoped would become the trademark of her career, one that would make her the reason people watched the Channel Three News. It had something to do with her cat.

No one at the station asked the "new girl" out for a celebratory drink, so she took a cab home, imagining the champagne on ice and shrimp cocktail Derek would have set out for her arrival. She'd told him not to send flowers to the station, that it would make her look amateurish and although he'd seemed surprised, he'd honored her wishes. This was their third city together, their second as a married couple. She intended Chicago to be home.

When she arrived at her building at 11:15 p.m., she had to remind James, the doorman, that she lived in apartment 2503.

"Of course. My apologies, madam. It must be the hour. You look lovely this evening. Again, I'm sorry. I usually don't forget a beautiful face." Despite his litany of apologies and the fact that he opened the door for her rather than simply buzzing her in, it rankled. She would've thought he'd recognize her. Derek had made a point of telling him when they moved in that his wife was famous and that he should be watchful for stalkers. (Once, back in Cedar Rapids, she'd been hounded by a middle-aged guy who fell hopelessly in love with her, and, even though that was before Derek's time, he was jealous when she'd told him and often overly protective.) James assured her that he was a professional, that she could call on him at any time and that "it would be a pleasure" to be of service. He promised not to forget again. "Your husband's name is Derek Baldwin," he said, as if to reassure himself.

One elevator came and went while she accepted his apology, and it occurred to her that perhaps he was delaying her on purpose, that perhaps—wouldn't that be sweet?—Derek had planned a surprise party for her. There would be just a few people he could invite, a couple of friends from college, perhaps their neighbors on their floor, and maybe Terry, her agent, but it would be a wonderfully thoughtful thing to do. It would boost her spirits. Although she'd just taken a gigantic stride in the forward trajectory of her career, they were beginning to sag just the slightest, the way a rainbow inevitably washes out and leaves an oblivious sky.

The hallway on her floor seemed abnormally quiet, the calm before the storm, confirming her suspicions. She stopped outside of her own door and quickly applied a fresh coat of Pink Lizard lipstick. She always kept her lipstick in a pocket, and often had a couple shades in her purse as well. In a pinch, she'd use it high on her cheek bones, where a little extra pink or rose would accent her green eyes.

She put her key in the door and braced herself. Inside it was completely dark. She waited, jingled her keys and stepped in.

"Hi, honey!" she sang. She rarely called Derek "honey," but it sounded like the right signal to trigger shouts of "surprise!"

Dead silence.

"Derek, you home?"

She turned on the hall light then, and without hanging up her coat walked into the living room. Bernard was curled up on the couch and didn't bother to lift his head—cats can be so fickle—but she went over and patted his furry belly anyway. Bernard stretched and purred in appreciation, leaving Dawn Ann to feel sorry for herself. How dare Derek trick her! Bitterly, she charged to the opposite end of the apartment to their bedroom, also empty. She skipped her study and knocked on the master bedroom door as she opened it. They used the room as Derek's studio and its windowless bathroom as his darkroom. The studio was dark, although she could hear the hum of his computer. Lights from neighboring buildings filtered through the blinds and sparked off the aluminum rolling tool chests Derek used for his negatives and prints. She banged on the darkroom door.

"Hey! You're home. Give me a minute, huh?" Derek sounded genuinely happy.

A minute? She wanted him to drop everything and fling open the door even if it meant ruining his night's work. She should blast him for not planning a celebration, but it was her own fault. She was the one who'd said opening night flowers would be amateur. But that was because that would have been a public display, not an intimate affair like a party for close friends! Was that so much to ask? Who wouldn't want to celebrate a promotion with her best friends?

Still, standing outside the darkroom, waiting to be let in, she felt foolish. His disinterest made her feel that wanting to be a weather woman on Channel Three news was a lame excuse for a goal.

Derek opened the door. In the butcher's apron he always wore for his developing work, a lazy smile stretched like a hammock across his round face. For a split second, he looked as if he'd been caught catnapping.

"How'd it go?" he asked.

A surge of adrenaline attacked her heart. "You didn't watch?" she said in disbelief. "I ..." Derek nodded towards the darkroom. "I got stuck. In the middle of something. Time got away from me."

"And?" she demanded, looking up at him. At six foot one, he towered a good eight inches over her.

"And ..." he winced, his transgression apparently occurring to him. With his fingers, he combed back his straight brown shoulder-length hair. "And time got away from me. I mean, I just forgot."

"Forgot? About your wife?" She sometimes wondered what it was that had made her choose him when magazines in Madison had put her picture on the cover and any number of men had been calling the station and sending roses and singing telegrams and trying every which way to get her attention.

"I got busy."

"But it was my first broadcast!" she said.

He looked perplexed. "You've been on TV for years," he said. "I was in the darkroom."

She'd heard his explanations before. She'd done her first broadcast. He'd produced a photographic image. These two things had happened roughly simultaneously. She'd been with him long enough to know his purported philosophy: there was no right or wrong here, their activities were not mutually exclusive. She was the one who was always vying for the world's undivided attention, and she was never going to get it, so she better get over it. How could he be expected to apologize for being in his own flow? Wasn't that where he was supposed to be? He wasn't begging her to look at his new image, was he? How could she possibly expect him to interrupt his own creative surge to watch electrons buzz across their 48 inch TV? He had her in person, higher than high-definition. He didn't need to see her on TV!

"What masterpiece was it this time?" she asked, but not too sarcastically.

"Not yet a masterpiece," he said, almost apologetic. "You know I never show work-in-process," he said lightly, as if she'd truly forgotten that.

"It's never out of pro-cess," she said, hitting the "o" as in "professional." As she said it, she realized how much she detested the word. "Pro-cess," along with "appropriate," had been favorite professional words of her mother's. In truth, her mother honored the concept of "pro-cess" more in theoretical reference to third-party lives than in practical application to her own. With 42 professional papers published, she'd been ruthlessly ambitious and achievement-oriented. When Dawn Ann introduced Derek to her parents, her mother expressed concern, in her own sideways fashion, about his character. "Do you think he's ambitious enough for you?" she'd asked. Before Dawn Ann could answer, her father had scolded her mother. "One star per family is enough," he'd said, and when Jacqueline McKnight scowled, he'd hastened to add, "and in my experience, that would be the woman's prerogative."

"It's all about the process, you know that," Derek said.

"No!" she said, her frustration threatening to overtake her self-control. "I don't know that, and I don't know that I agree. What about results?"

"Re-sults," he said flatly. "How Philistine."

"Don't," she said. "Just finish your pro-cess,"

Leaving him standing in the darkroom doorway, she marched to their room, kicked off her plain black heels and flopped on her side of their queen size bed. She didn't want to see his work in process—even when they were arrangements of screws or fruits or bottles, they were always abstract images of women, and when she was feeling insecure in any way, they made her crazy. He hadn't taken the time to see her Chicago debut—how self-absorbed! "Narcissistic," if she wanted to apply the proper psychological term. Even now, he was probably putting things away in the darkroom rather than wrapping his arms around her, apologizing, trying to make it up to her. He could at least have said that he'd recorded the broadcast, and they could watch it now, or soon. She wanted to crawl under the covers and feign sleep so that she wouldn't have to deal with him when he came to bed—in fact, she probably wouldn't talk to him for the rest of the night. Still, she had her make-up on, and since her complexion was an important professional asset, she forced herself up and to the john, where she spent the next 15 minutes in a ritual of smoothing and cleansing of her pores. She peeled away her light brown false eyelashes, tissued off her foundation with a cleansing cream and washed her face with a mild soap. She massaged her face for a full five minutes, exfoliated the cells that had died under the bright lights of the television studio, and clarified her skin with an aromatic toner that filled the bathroom with the exotic and calming essence of bay. Then she applied a light oil, a heavy night cream and an age-defying neck cream. Unlike Derek's, hers was what her parents called a "healthy" narcissism. When it came right down to it, no matter whom you married or who your boss was, you had to take care of yourself. No one else would do that for you. And if you didn't, you wouldn't last long in her business.

4

One month into Dawn Ann's new job, Alberto Beltran and Felicity O'Neal had cemented their relationship, both on-camera and off. While weekend ratings had jumped a couple tenths of a point, Channel Three was still solidly number two in the Chicago market. As Bernard had predicted with a sneeze, Dawn Ann's first weather forecast for Chicago was wrong, but no one at the station seemed to notice or care. Two weeks later, Bernard sneezed again just as Dawn Ann was giving herself one last splash of Samsara. Although she considered writing it off to the cat's allergies, when the computer model that evening said the city was facing another cold, dry day ahead, she'd closed her forecast with a coquettish, "but, my cat Bernard sneezed today, and you know what that means."

No one at the station asked her what it meant until Monday morning, when the station received 100 emails from curious viewers, asking what she meant, what kind of cat Bernard was, and could she please send a picture of herself—with the cat.

The weekend producer was beside himself. The station's General Manager, Stanley Watkins, had called him, wanting to know what the weather bimbo—the strawberry blond one—meant, and couldn't somebody do something about her hair? Why was it pulled back in a ponytail? It made her look like she was a gym teacher, or a physics teacher, going out for a jog in inclement weather. On high-definitions sets, it looked fuzzy. Couldn't Make-Up give her a more distinct, sharper look? The producer told her that otherwise, Watkins thought she had a great on-camera persona. Susan Stevens was going to the Caribbean for two weeks and Dawn Ann would get to substitute. And, they were to figure out this Bernard thing. Watkins wanted to know: Does it sell?

She was tickled by the attention, but deeply troubled by the General Manager's desire to change her looks. Her appearance had always been a strong point, never criticized by any of her former employers or by any of the television reviewers in the local markets where she'd been a minor celebrity. In Milwaukee, a city magazine had done a cover story about her, an over-the-top ode to the girl-next-door-you'd-most-like-to-bed. The Milwaukee writer even had said he liked her hair pulled back; it gave the impression that her face was "but the beguiling surface of beautiful and mysterious depths, like ocean waters over vibrant reefs." Though she wanted to be flattered, she found herself worried about what the reviewer didn't say. He'd complimented her eyes and her skin and her smile, but said nothing about her nose. Was it too big? She studied the cover photo and a couple of profile shots inside, but couldn't decide. What was a nose supposed to look like? She'd always thought hers was straight and inoffensive. Why hadn't he mentioned it? The cover story boosted the ratings of her evening newscast in Milwaukee, and probably was responsible for bringing her to the attention of Channel Three in the first place, but that gnat of insecurity still scratched at her self-confidence whenever she needed it most.

Now Channel Three's Stanley Watkins was finding fault. Why had he hired her, if her looks were so awful? Monday night, over a chef's salad at Walter's Round-the-Clock restaurant, Derek told her she was over-reacting.

"Lowest common denominator," he said, as if that should help.

"What's that supposed to mean?" she countered, stabbing a perfect white cube of chicken.

"He's just going for the look that most people will least object to," Derek said. "It's nothing personal."

"It's my *face*!" she protested. "What's wrong with the way it is?"

He gave her a pious look, as if she'd never understand the plane on which he operated, the enlightened strata where "Right" and "Wrong" were value-laden judgment calls, not realities. He reached over and touched her hair. "Haven't you, my little strawberry, juiced up your hair just a squeeze for your beloved camera?"

"Don't ridicule me."

"What ridicule? All I'm saying is, it doesn't matter that much. If the guy wants you to curl your hair or shave it off, who cares? If you want the job, you'll do it, and if you don't, you won't."

"Like a whore who needs the money," she mumbled, and was

furious when he didn't disagree. She limited herself to monosyllables for the rest of dinner, and when they were done, she'd left most of the chicken and ham cubes in a heap at the bottom of the bowl. The last thing she needed now was for someone to comment on her weight. She'd gained two pounds in the past couple months and didn't want that to flare out of control as well. For a photographer, Derek had no appreciation for how things should look, or the effort it took to keep them picture-perfect.

The next day, after three hours of color enhancement, cut and blow-dry, Dawn Ann emerged with a fluffy, curly disarrangement that was supposed to make her look windswept and sporting but instead looked as if she'd been walloped in a wind tunnel. The logic to her hair's disarray escaped her, and would now require a daily stylist to repeat the look with any consistency. Color that once passed in natural light for genuine was now so pronounced that the intensity of the studio lights couldn't hide its *faux* tone. She knew that at least a third of the time, women who went to salons for new hair-dos thanked their stylists with stiff upper lips, and cried all the way home. She'd always thought that vain and foolish, but then again, she'd never given a hair-stylist free reign. Never. Until now. And this hadn't been an act of free will, it had been mandated by a General Manager as the price of success.

She stopped at the station to show Watkins, but he barely acknowledged her as he bustled past her in the hall, not stopping to notice or approve her new look. Still, she paraded around the newsroom, collecting those lukewarm reviews—"Wow, that's different!"—that made her want to stand under a cold shower until every strand of hair was straightened and bleached to its original, if unnatural, color. She stomped home and asked Derek to do some quick headshots so she could show the stylist tomorrow what she was supposed to look like.

"I like it, honey, I really do," Derek said, cuddling up to her as she studied herself in the mirror. "I'll take your beautiful face, if I can also take your beautiful body." She laughed and playfully peeled her clothing for him, pink angora sweater, short purple skirt, high leather boots, pink lace bra and panties. Just last month, before she'd started working at Channel Three, she'd posed nude for him for the first time since they'd gotten married, and that had led to an afternoon of love-making. With her new schedule, and Derek's work re-establishing his darkroom in their apartment, they hadn't made love since. She was feeling warm with anticipation when he threw her a robe.

"Don't freeze your little titties," he said. He busied himself with the lights and a screen, teasing her with his professional and disinterested demeanor. "It'll take me a few more minutes."

She shivered as if she'd opened the window to the December cold, but stood away from the lights, so as not to melt her makeup or wilt her new hair-do.

"Hurry," she coaxed, pitching her voice to the urgent and breathless side of sexy, but he took his sweet time adjusting the tripod. Finally, he positioned her on a little stool for the headshot, letting his hands brush against her breasts in an absent-minded way. She nipped at his wrists as he lifted her chin and he snapped his hand away as if from fire. She found herself short of breath and pleaded, "Oh, that's enough for the stylist. Let's …"

"Shhhh," he said, and rearranged his camera and her body with a cool detachment that she thought stepped over the line from tease to turn-off. As he worked, it occurred to her that he was photographing her body without her head. Sometimes, she had to wonder why she'd been so desperate for Derek Baldwin, why, in Madison, she'd even turned down Louisville when it was offered, to give him time to commit. Only when she gave the Milwaukee ultimatum did he agree to move with her, and then she'd been the one to say she wouldn't live with him there unless he married her, and he'd said yes and they'd used her money to buy a condo. At the wedding he'd been a compliant and charming groom, escorting aunts and flirting with teenage cousins who took him to be their latest idol, but even then she'd been slightly unsettled by his "ho-hum, it's all the same" attitude. Still, while he professed not to care about wedding rituals, Wedgewood china and Ralph Lauren linen selections, Derek had developed, perhaps as a result of proximity to Dawn Ann, very definite, high-brow, and expensive tastes, like thirty dollar briefs from Brooks Brothers. While she could afford a lot, her income wasn't so high that there were no limitations, and Derek's attitude suggested that he lived in just the slightest state of disappointment that his imperviously high standards were not being met.

The thing about Derek Baldwin was that he was in many ways what her parents had defined as a successful professional outcome: unworried, autonomous, marching to his own drummer. He wouldn't care if he never sold a photograph (and he'd only sold two in the entire time she'd known him) or if she took a job as a greeter at Walmart. You didn't have to worry about Derek Baldwin being too demanding, or being jealous of your job or your friends or your fans. He'd let you be, and you could be with him on whatever terms suited you. There were, however, days when she found this attitude, even if enlightened, annoying. She wanted, perhaps more than was responsibly adult, *to be wanted*. She wanted him to act a little more human and a lot less Buddha.

"Okay, that's it," he said finally, as if she were a paid model and not his wife. He tossed her her robe and began to break down the lights and screens. Having been kept on tenterhooks for half an hour, the last of her waning desire drained out of her.

No sooner had she sashed her robe than he was on her, wrestling her to the floor right there in the middle of the studio, unzipping his slacks, shoving himself into her with a grunt of relief as if she'd been the one playing hard to get. She pounded her fists against his shoulders but that excited him even more. He came with a thrust so hard and swollen that she cried out in pain. Only then did he kiss her, sucking the breath from her so that she felt taken against her will.

He rolled off and she pulled her robe around her, shivering with a cold she hadn't felt under the lights. Without a word, she stood up and went down the hall to their bathroom.

"You're the best, sweetheart," he yawned after her.

She stood in the shower for a quarter of an hour, and let the water beat on the small of her back, up her spine, between her shoulder blades, and finally, over her head. She stared at the beige tiles beneath her toes, half expecting to see the water leeching both the fluff and the reddish stain out of her hair. She tried to make sense out of what had just happened. Derek usually was tender and loving, even adoring. His turn towards this roughness had to be a phase, an exaggerated aggression to show the fierceness of his love, an exploration of a darker side, which, like the phases of the moon, would pass. Perhaps she'd been unavailable, given her odd working hours. Maybe he was frustrated by that, or by her success, and had unintentionally been more aggressive than usual.

Sex was, she understood, a completely selfish act. They weren't trying to make a child; there wasn't that kind of mutuality in it. If she wanted a child—and she wasn't sure yet that she did—Derek would probably go along, assuming she could continue to work. It wouldn't occur to him to change his professional direction in order to support a child. That wouldn't occur to him, even if they were drowning in debt, and she'd never let that happen.

She wrapped a heavy bath sheet around herself and twisted a towel into a turban on her wet head. She slid her hand down her nose. Did it need to be fixed? If Stanley asked, would she have it done? If she did, would Derek care? What was the word he'd used? *Whore?* He hadn't actually said the word, but that's what he meant. If you want the money, you'll do it, like a whore. She couldn't begin to fathom the male psyche, but somehow, that explained Derek's behavior enough so that she could, if not forgive him, at least excuse him.

The steam was so dense in the bathroom she couldn't see her nose or her own complexion, so she opened the door and turned on the noisy overhead fan. The fog dripped away from the mirror, and turning full face to it, she saw herself, her complexion flawless, her light brown eyebrows neat, her teeth as white as her dentist could realistically manage. She wasn't being vain, she told herself. She was being professional, taking a realistic inventory of her business assets. She could hardly be expected to achieve success without the capacity to objectively assess herself, her appearance, and the potential for change. Thirty-two wasn't old, but it was a dangerous precipice. She would have to be on guard.

The trick in her business was not to change, at least not to age relative to your demographic. It would be okay to change a hairstyle to keep current, but only for the purpose of *not* changing, relative to the televised image the public knew and trusted. She would always conceive of herself as 32, and her job was not to change in any way that would force a viewer to recognize in her the passage of their own time. She could manage that kind of change. She would have to. It was the change in Derek—if that's what it was—that was harder to accept.

5

Hope Abels threw a plush purple dinosaur and a box of vanilla wafers from the front seat of her minivan into the back and drove Nevaeh home from the library. Hope said her husband was out of town on a sales trip, and she'd like the company. Nevaeh, still in shock from Tara's untimely demise, was grateful.

She stood on the stoop of Hope's modest three-bedroom ranch on the far side of town, away from the river, while Hope fiddled with her keys. They could hear the five o'clock news loud and clear. Inside, Hope introduced her to her mother, Ginger, who nodded as if Nevaeh were just another in a long string of strays Hope had brought home. Ginger's thinning gray hair was queued in tight, permanent-induced curls, and she slumped in an easy chair, staring impassively at a giant TV. Two toddlers, perhaps four and six years old, played hand-held computer games, oblivious to the thunderous rant of the day's top headlines: A double murder in a trailer park upriver and a homeless man frozen to death in Iowa City, the first fatality of a season that hadn't started yet. Hope gestured to Nevaeh to sit, and Nevaeh cleared two more plush toys from a brown corduroy La-Z-Boy, folded last week's *Prairie du Chien Crier*, and sat down.

"Loud enough for ya?" Hope's mother asked, pointing to the TV.

Just in time, Nevaeh realized the question was meant to be polite, not facetious, and smiled demurely. "Yes, it's fine," she said quietly, and Hope's mother nodded, as if she'd heard. She fixed her attention on more bad news and the teaser for the weather. Nevaeh shivered. Hope's home was not much warmer than her own tree house and it smelled ever so slightly of menthol or eucalyptus, like a muscle ointment. Nevaeh realized she'd hoped for the cayenne, onion and thyme of jambalaya.

Hope brought her a cold Rolling Rock and handed her mother a brown liquid in a stubby glass with a cherry, no ice.

"Ma," Hope began, "Nevaeh here lives in a tree house!"

"How's that?" Ginger said.

"It's very peaceful, really," Nevaeh said, "but right now it's cold—very cold. Colder than I expected."

"I expect," Ginger said, nodding.

"I mean, we have walls, and an orange shag rug, and I have a good sleeping bag," Nevaeh added.

"Bad," Ginger said, and Nevaeh finally understood that Ginger was in fact as deaf as the decibel level of the TV suggested.

Hope stood up. "You two talk some more, Ne—Nevah," she giggled at the nickname she'd picked for her guest. "I'll get us something to eat. But first things first." She took her mom's glass, went out to the kitchen and came back with another drink for her mother and another bottle of Rolling Rock for Nevaeh.

"Hey, thanks," Nevaeh said.

The television blared, and it seemed impossible to carry on a conversation, but Nevaeh wanted to repay Hope's kindness by entertaining her mother, so she decided just to ask questions. She hoped that like other old people she'd known, Ginger's answers would stretch the conversation out like a strand of rubber cement. The effort distracted her from her grief.

"Have you lived in Prairie du Chien long?" Nevaeh asked.

"Lungs fine," Ginger said. "Ankles swollen." She pointed to the ottoman where she rested her feet, in black-soled, librarian shoes like Judith Scott's, and tugged at her maroon polyester slacks to reveal her swollen ankles, dry and scaly, the size of tulip bulbs.

Before Nevaeh could compose another question which might elicit a more positive response, the toddlers started a commotion and the old woman, drink in hand, nodded off. On the television, the weather man blared the temperatures up and down the Mississippi. It was a relatively balmy 60 degrees in New Orleans. It was so loud, she couldn't miss the message: for the second time that day, the world was pointing her south. Or maybe the third time—the charm—if you considered that this all started because her glass harmonica had frozen. So she decided that New Orleans would be the next stop on what she was beginning to imagine would be a great adventure. She told herself she could work there and gather material for her writing and live a free and independent life, alone if need be.

On the back of an envelope from the phone company, she left a thank you note for Hope's hospitality, then stretched out in the brown corduroy La-Z-Boy and timed herself to sleep until just before dawn, at which point she intended to be gone. That morning at the tree house she'd boxed up her harmonica. Everything else she owned of any value (except her sleeping bag) was already in her backpack and always by her side.

• • •

It was still dark at the tree house when Nevaeh hoisted herself up the rope ladder, hearing it creak as it eased and gave way like a swim ladder thrown over the side of a boat. With her flashlight she surveyed her home, saying a silent good-bye and thank-you to the things she'd have to leave behind: a printed, fake-patchwork quilt, a rocking chair missing only a row or two of caning on the seat, an orange crate filled with paperback books, many yet unread. She realized then both that she was richer than she'd imagined and that there were only a couple of really important things she'd need to take with her for survival on the road, like the stove and her plastic camp shower. There were also some more things she would like to throw in if she had room, her coffee pot, her stash of tobacco, and her summer clothes, two scoop-necked cotton tees, a one-piece tank suit, and a pair of velcroed sandals that matched Tray's. He'd called them his Jesus sneakers, and sometimes wore them, like an old man, with white cotton socks and Bermuda shorts. He said they gave him credibility. Since Tray'd left, the realization that she was alone in the world had descended on her at odd times, triggered by the most ordinary of events. Now, the sandals taunted her, turning her great adventure lonely. Without Tray to share it with, traveling wouldn't be as easy or as interesting. She shut her eyes tightly, hoping to squeeze them dry.

She tied the sleeping bag and camp shower to the bottom of her backpack, double-bagged the stove and coffeepot in heavy black plastic, and after three careful trips up and down the ladder, left a note, a kinder one, she hoped, than the one Tray had left her, "To whom it may concern," reminding "whom" to anchor the ropes at the bottom, and with her box of 25 glasses in one hand and the awkward plastic bag in the other, she set out for Highway 22 and warmer climes. It was so cold, if she blew soap bubbles they would splinter into bits of instant ice, but the sun had flowered like a Florida orange and she stopped, as she did every morning, dropped her packages, and, yoga-style, saluted it, her arms reaching over her head into the sky.

It took Nevaeh 45 minutes to walk to the highway, stopping frequently to move the box from her left hand to her right, to shift the backpack up or down, sideways. A couple times, out of habit, Nevaeh reached in her jeans-skirt pocket to check on Tara. She knew tears wouldn't freeze, but they would chap, and while she wanted to cry for Tara and for Tray, it was not a luxury she could permit herself. She would need all her wits and charm to make New Orleans, a couple hundred miles down the Mighty River.

A middle-aged farmer with a rounder face than Farmer Lundgren's picked her up in a Dodge Ram as soon as she stuck out her thumb.

"I'm Hank," he said, his smile pleasant, but contained.

"I'm Nevaeh," she said, and when he raised an eyebrow she spelled it. "Heaven, backwards," she explained, and he sighed. Her mother could've been a little tipsy when she chose the name, although she'd once told Nevaeh she liked the juxtaposition of heaven and earth, especially since her own name was Star and unusual names ran along the maternal side of the family. The exception was Nevaeh's mother's sister, Dawnie's mother, a crazy psychologist, who'd ended up with the relatively ordinary, but still beautiful name, Jacqueline. Still, Nevaeh liked her name, and, Hank's sigh notwithstanding, her explanation brought a smile to many, like an unexpected bit of good luck.

Hank cracked the window slightly and lit a Camel. "Where ya headed?"

"Way down yonder," she said, unable to stop herself. He blew out the smoke, apparently sorry he'd picked up a wise ass. "In New Orleans," she finished the song and flashed him her most charming smile.

He took a long drag of his cigarette, as if struggling not to say what he wanted to say. Then he poked a fat finger at her nose and said, in a stern and father-like tone, "That's a bad town."

"I've been there before," she said. When she'd been there with Tray, it had been fun. They'd listened to music on the streets, watched performers of all sorts make a living entertaining tourists in the parks, walked along the Mississippi, even treated themselves to a swamp tour where they learned "alligator tastes like chicken." They city had seemed to them friendly, relaxed, easy, not "bad," but she didn't want to argue with her driver. Even with the window cracked and the heater barely keeping up with the cold, she was grateful not to be stranded on the side of the road. She opened her gloved hands.

"It'll be warmer," she answered. Even if the temperatures there were only 50 or 55, that would be 30 or 40 or even 50 degrees warmer than Iowa! And she could always move from there, if she had to.

"Girls your age can get old real fast there," he said. "Traveling alone ain't no good either."

"I'll be careful," she said lightly. Of course the farmer was being overly protective. He'd probably not traveled beyond the Midwest, hadn't seen the country like she had. Even though she wouldn't have Tray with her this time, she had experience on the road, and the universe had pointed her in the direction of New Orleans.

"Don't compromise yourself," he said. "Don't go dancing in no clubs or nothing." She liked to dance, and it took her a few seconds to understand that he didn't object to "dancing" dancing, but to show dancing, pole dancing, lap dancing.

"I'd never do that!" she cried.

He looked at her thoughtfully, tossed his cigarette butt out the window, and said, with the first humor he'd shown since picking her up, "Never say never."

• • •

The bravado Nevaeh'd felt in the farmer's pick-up wavered when he dropped her near a trucker's motel in Mt. Pleasant and she realized that during all of their time on the road, Tray had handled the logistics of renting camping lots and rooms. Waiting for someone to come to the barred window at the check-in counter, Nevaeh positioned her head three-quarters to the front, so she could see the door behind her. She only released her grip on her things when a woman came to the desk and asked her to fill in a form and said the charge was thirty-five dollars. Nevaeh stepped away from the counter and turned her back while she dug in her backpack for her Bible and the money. Inside her clean but spare room, she locked the door, fastened the flimsy chain, and dragged the room's one green Naugahyde chair in front of it. Without changing, she flung herself on the bed, closed her eyes, and tried to sleep, leaving the lights on as if she were afraid of the dark. She told herself she wasn't, that she'd slept alone for months in a tree house without electricity, for god sakes, and the woman at the desk, all shoulder and thick neck, would keep a good look-out. Fear wasn't useful: it would only interfere with sleep, and without Tray she needed to have all her wits about her for whatever was to come.

The next day, she took the once-a-day bus to Champaign, Illinois, and transferred for Hattiesburg, Mississippi. There would be only three scheduled stops between Hattiesburg and New Orleans, two in Mississippi, Poplarville and Picayune, and then Slidell, Louisiana. As the towns rolled by, the excitement of her adventure melted away and a new terror took hold. Where to stay? Should she try to find a job? Well, maybe not a real job, not yet. She didn't have the right wardrobe for a person with a bachelor's degree and half a master's, and her job skills were limited. Cleaning rooms at The Bluffs had combined the right amount of responsibility, just enough money, and not too many hours. Plenty of time to hang out and gather material for what she might write someday. Plenty of time to be with Tray, to get a little high, make a little love, get down tonight. She moved her shoulders to the song from K.C. and The Sunshine Band, in serendipitous sync with the vibrations of the bus on the interstate. She would give herself some time before graduating to what her mother used to call "the real world, young lady." Not that her mother, even before she'd sunk into the sodden depths of her suburban alcoholism, had had very real interactions with the world outside her daily bottle.

Arriving at the New Orleans bus station, she picked up her glass harmonica box and her garbage bag, the two items she'd been required to check, and, shouldering her backpack, hiked across the great expanse of the oddly quiet waiting room to the women's restroom. She dragged all her stuff into the stall and sat. She turned her head to the right, half-expecting to see the countryside rushing past her before she could take it all in. Beneath her, the commode was cool, steady, firmly placed in the cement floor. The stall didn't vibrate. It was lovely. It was safe.

Obviously she couldn't stay there, so she flushed and moved herself and her stuff to the row of sinks, stashing the glasses and the garbage bag under the ledge. Since the hot water wasn't working, she washed her face with cold and dried it by squatting in front of the hot air blower. Standing up, her face warm, she saw a woman with matted gray hair at the sink furthest away from her, sorting through a plastic shopping bag. The woman had two other bags strapped with raw string to a two-wheel luggage cart.

Nevaeh studied the backpack, harmonica box and garbage bag of cooking equipment piled at her feet. She'd always prided herself on traveling light. Now, after only half an hour in New Orleans, she realized she was, in fact, overburdened with even these minimal things.

"Pardon me," she said, walking towards the woman with the luggage cart. "That's a great cart you've got there. Can I ask you where you got it?"

The woman turned to her, hissing like a cat. She had tiny eyes like Tara's, but black and hollow, as if she understood only sound, not words.

"I'm sorry," Nevaeh continued, "I didn't mean to startle you." She took a step backwards.

The woman hissed again, grinning so widely Nevaeh imagined whiskers protruding from her lips like wire filaments, piercing the air like fine needles. The cat woman stepped in front of the cart, hiding it from view. Signaling retreat, Nevaeh held up two empty palms, slid backwards and, without taking her eyes off the woman, shouldered her backpack and picked up her two bundles. She nodded, smiling without teeth so as not to threaten the woman further and backed out. In the waiting room, she sat on a molded tan chair in a long empty linked row, her soles flat on the floor, spine straight, arms loose at her side, thumbs out. She stared at the blue, busy mural that edged the entire room and scoffed at the first image that caught her eye, a knight embracing a young woman, obviously newly saved, while a trio of nuns and an angel looked on. Waiting for her breathing to return to normal, she closed her eyes and started chanting silently, "Hello, Let Go."

"Hello, young lady," a voice startled her. "Hello?" Blinking to fix her eyes again in working mode, Nevaeh caught a glimpse of a tall figure to her left, and turned towards it.

"My name is Harold Hummer and this is my wife Cheryl. Are you new to N'awlins, young lady?"

"I am," she said, in a voice she hoped sounded determined. She'd been mistaken for a vagrant before, but Tray had always managed for them in these situations. He'd construct an identity, piling lie upon lie like Lincoln Logs: One day they were undercover journalists, another, doctoral students working at the U of C. Yes, Chicago. And, of course, Tray had sounded like his lies, big words and all.

"A musician?" Cheryl asked, her lips stretched in what Nevaeh judged to be an insincere smile. Cheryl had blond bouffant hair, decades out of style; pasty-white makeup; light blue eye-shadow, a lovely shade, actually, but far too much of it. She and Harold wore matching blue oxford shirts, and khakis—hers a skirt and his pressed pants.

"Yeah," Nevaeh said, and tried to picture what Tray would do: lecture the woman with more than she would ever want to know about the history of the glass harmonica and its place in early music, boring her away with his erudition, or clam up totally, copping an attitude like "it's a free country and none of your business, lady." Neither style suited Nevaeh. She wasn't Tray. "As a hobby, not a profession," she said. "My name is Jane Shane."

"Well, welcome to N'awlins, Jane," Cheryl said in a drawl that reeked of the deep South. "Mind if we sit down?" She did mind, but with her backpack, the box and the plastic bag blocking her path, she could neither extricate herself nor stop these two from bookending her. She reached out and grabbed the strap of her backpack.

"Listen, honey, a lot of young people like yourself move down here to N'awlins to play music and they find there's just not that much work. There's a lot of competition and there's a lot of—well, sin and all manner of temptation on the streets. Harold and I have been sent here to save your soul." Nevaeh gripped her pack harder. "We're here to help!" Cheryl beamed. "If you believe in Jesus," she added, placing her right hand over her heart.

What's not to believe in? Nevaeh thought. She read her Bible for comfort and inspiration, and she'd grown up on the North Shore, where every other suburb believed in Jesus, and the rest were waiting for Him. Still, like the tzitzits of the orthodox Jews in Skokie, Harold and Cheryl seemed to have some strings attached to their Jesus, and what they were offering in exchange for belief was not yet clear to her. Nevaeh didn't have Tray's flair for spoken words, so she reverted to silence. She looked at Cheryl's right hand; its peppermint pink manicure was badly chipped.

"Do you?" Cheryl swung her hand from her heart to Nevaeh's shoulder and Nevaeh nearly jumped out of her seat. Cheryl withdrew her hand as if she'd touched fire. Nevaeh disliked being touched by strangers.

Harold intervened, as if to suggest that his wife had gotten carried away. "Do you have a place to stay here?" he asked Nevaeh.

Nevaeh considered the implications of his question. No, she'd be living on the streets. No, she'd accept an offer to live with them. No, they'd call the police.

"Yes," she said. And then, in a stroke of genius—surely inspired by Tray—she added, "Thank you for your concern."

"Oh, we're, uh, sorry," Cheryl said. "You just looked as if you might not ... the plastic bag and all."

"Well," said Harold, apparently not convinced but perhaps in need of saving face, "here's our card, if you need anything."

"Good-bye, Jane," Cheryl said, and, taking Harold's hand, the two of them strolled towards the exit, where Nevaeh saw them approach another woman, much younger than herself, who sat on an overstuffed backpack, studying some kind of brochure.

It was only early afternoon. She had a few hours before she'd have to find a place to stay. Again, she wished Tray were there, that this was a few years ago and they were still together, Tray in charge. She glanced at the card Harold had given her, "Lilies of the Field, TLC, a Transitional Living Center providing shelter and guidance for women." She thought about Hank's warning back in the truck, and in a moment of over-reaction, she wondered whether dancers made enough to save themselves from the clutches of the Hummers.

She stretched her hands over her head, then stood up, reached for her backpack, and balanced her load. "Nevah say nevah," she said out loud.

At the exit, a wiry young man with a long, oily pony tail approached her. At first she thought he was a bus-station equivalent of a valet. She tried to look past him while keeping an eye out in case he was a pickpocket.

"You need wheels, girl!" he said, and immediately her feet halted in agreement. He held up a hand as if he were stopping traffic, and seemingly from out of nowhere, produced a battered rolling cart like the cat lady's. "Five dollars," he said.

Without hesitation, she answered, "Okay." Maybe she could get a new one for that, but she didn't know where, and five bucks was a small price to pay to avoid living at Lilies of the Field, TLC.

6

Weekends were grueling. Dawn Ann was close enough to her goal to redouble her efforts, studying charts, forecasting, rehearsing, practically living at the station from first thing in the morning to way after Linda Livingston's final sign-off. Linda was substituting for the lovebirds, who'd let it be known on air that they might sneak away and get married over the holidays, and that Channel Three would have the scoop and the first pictures if they did. By the end of that week, the potential for marriage on Channel Three was as tired a teaser as the number of shopping days left until Christmas. It was not, despite the station's frenetic hype, of great interest to the thousands of Chicagoans who were either preoccupied with their own behind-schedule holiday preparations or capable of ignoring altogether the Thanksgiving-Christmas-New Year's gauntlet. By Dawn Ann's reckoning, if there was a slight increase in ratings that week and the next, she was in line, along with Linda, for some of the credit. She'd reach out and grab it and the more she was present at the station those two weeks, the more legitimate her claim.

There was a natural interest in the weather, both for travel and for aesthetic purposes, and, starting five days before Christmas, the additional teaser for the news was, of course, "Will we have a White Christmas? Tune in at ten for the latest from Dawn Ann McKnight." If there was hope for snow, she donned her black mink pillbox and ventured outside for a live shot. Like an astrologer reading the night skies, she made a show of looking up and predicting light flurries, about which she'd just learned from the computer inside. In truth, the lights of Michigan Avenue, just a few blocks away, obliterated all of the heavens' tell-tale signs.

Sometimes during the day, she would walk an extra two blocks to the lake to try and detect a bluish tint to the winter storm clouds. Comparing them to delicate white flowers, her father, a seasoned weather-watcher, had called them "Snow blossoms." So far, there was little hope that Chicago's Christmas would bloom, meteorologically speaking, but Dawn Ann McKnight was doing her damnedest to heat up the station's ratings.

Derek was most understanding of her rationale for spending 12 hours a day at the station. A night-owl himself, he'd usually wait up for her, even when she went out for drinks with her new best friend, Linda Livingston, with whom she'd talk and wind down until after midnight. She'd be happy to see him, but exhausted, and he'd give her a kiss good night and go into his darkroom to work. A certain calmness fell over their life together, the incident in the studio not repeated nor spoken of, so that she dismissed it entirely as an aberration. Most days, she'd be up at nine, and at ten, and so as not to wake him, she'd tiptoe out of the apartment. What if her spouse had a normal job and had to catch the 6:30 a.m. train? They'd never see each other! She had some appreciation then for the stresses of two-career marriages and was grateful for her own arrangement. She just wished that Derek, with no need to conform to any particular schedule, would conform a little more closely to hers. It would be nice to have some time in the morning when they both were fresh, even if only for an hour.

On the 23rd, she came home a little early—11:30 p.m.—and found Derek stretched out on the daybed in the studio, a forest green wool throw tucked under his chin. The red light stood its watch in the darkroom while an empty glass waited on the floor. Had there been a box of Kleenex and a pile of wadded-up tissues next to the glass, she would've felt sorry for him, but there was nothing there to indicate anything but sloth. She stepped over to the darkroom. Two prints were swimming—probably drowning—in their final baths. She wanted to think "poor guy, exhausted by this work, art a demanding mistress," but her gut told her differently. She left the wet prints, walked back over to the daybed, stood over Derek and sniffed. Something woodsy. Sharp, but sweet. Not a flowery smell, but a strong scent. She could almost taste it.

Derek was not exhausted. He was drunk. On gin.

Ignoring the photographs—ruined surely—she turned off the red light and went to bed.

The next morning was Christmas Eve, and she left their apartment before he managed to get himself off the couch. They had no plans for the holiday. She had to work, and Derek was feeling sorry for himself—at Thanksgiving at a friend's house, he'd complained that her career was interfering with his dream of spending the holiday on St. Thomas.

"You sell a print?" she'd asked then. He'd given her an ugly look, and she'd passed him the sweet potatoes. She hadn't meant for it to sound snide; she'd be truly happy for him if he sold a work. She'd be happy if he even tried.

Technically, she was the one whose holidays were being "ruined." She was working on Christmas Eve, and she had to work again on Christmas Day, both in the morning and again at ten. In between, they'd invited three other childless couples without nearby family for a Christmas dinner. Derek wanted to cook a Christmas goose, an expression he'd heard all his life although his family usually served turkey. Since he'd never cooked a goose, and wasn't much of a cook to begin with, Dawn Ann hired a caterer, who would arrive at noon and serve at three. The guests would come at two. To her, Christmas wasn't being "ruined," it was giving her unanticipated gifts, like the chance to splurge on a special dinner party and showcase her best work in prime-time.

Just after the noon report on Christmas Eve she called Derek to remind him to buy the wine and other beverages for the Christmas dinner. She could tell when he answered that she'd woken him.

She lowered her voice into the phone. "You've been asleep for more than 12 hours!"

"Aw, honey," he mumbled.

"Don't honey me," she slapped back. "Get off your duff and go buy the wine for tomorrow. And try not to drink it on the way home!" She wouldn't be drinking, of course, because she'd be between shows, but their guests would want something, and it would be a lot cheaper than having the caterer choose the wines. She hadn't said so, but they were, after all, a one-income family. They couldn't afford to be frivolous.

"Oh, honey," he yawned. "Wine. Anything else?" He sounded

rational, anyway, as if he comprehended the request.

"There's a list in the kitchen," she said. "Why don't you go to Bob's, have them deliver, and then come by and take me to Walter's for a Christmas Eve hamburger between shows? Six thirty?" It wasn't much to ask.

"Yeah, I can do that," he said.

She wished he'd thought of it himself, but at least he'd agreed. "And Derek," she said, "Don't forget to buy me a present."

When he didn't say anything right away, she could picture the immediate flinch-or-freeze panic on his face: his forehead collapsing over his wild eyebrows, the pupils of his eyes swelling. In the next split second, Derek Baldwin, in charge of the world, would calculate which way to go with this: he could give her his lecture on crass commercialism and not being told when, why, and for whom to buy presents, or he could go for the smug and self-serving, "I bought your present weeks ago. Want a hint?"

She knew he was hung-over, and she knew that he knew that she knew. He should also know that he owed her something—she was supporting his art, and for the most part ignoring the ups and downs of his artistic temperament. She cradled the phone before he could respond.

At 6:40 p.m., she was trying to get Derek on the cell phone when he walked into Walter's, bringing her a miniature poinsettia plant in red foil with a white ribbon, its five red double blooms each the size of her thumb, smaller even than her on-camera weather clicker. He arranged it in the middle of the booth table and gave her a kiss on the top of her head. "Merry Christmas Eve, my sweet," he purred.

"Darling!" she said.

He beamed.

She never called him darling—so affected—and hadn't meant to now. She was referring to the plant. "It's the cutest thing I've ever seen! Wherever did you get it?"

He grinned a grin as innocent as the Dalai Lama's. "When the soil is ready, the flower will appear," he said.

She gave him a look. She should know better than to ask questions about logistics. Derek never took responsibility for how things happened, they just did.

Even though it was Christmas Eve and she wanted a hamburger, she ordered the whitefish and an iceberg lettuce salad with a lemon wedge, no dressing. The waitress, perhaps in her late 20s, had short frizzy red-brown hair and wore a white plastic badge with the name Trudy on it just at the level of her left nipple. In a deeply scooped tight green sweater, she flirted shamelessly with Derek, spilling herself over his raised menu to point out the "turkey dinner-with-all-the-trimmings" special. Trudy must have recognized Dawn Ann McKnight—all the folks from the station ate at least one meal or snack or cup of coffee a day at Walter's, and not one, but four different TVs were all tuned to Channel Three, but she didn't acknowledge that she did, even her second time at the table, when she brought Derek his beer and Dawn Ann a cup of coffee.

When Trudy left, Derek climbed on the offensive. "You weren't very nice to her," he said, his tone even.

"What?" she cried. "I didn't say anything to her, I just ordered."

"You looked annoyed."

"Please," she said, raising her coffee cup to her lips and blowing over the top. It was too hot to drink, and she put it down with a tremble. "I'm not annoyed. And I'm not annoyed at her."

"You're annoyed she was flirting with me and didn't recognize you." He took a swig of his beer. "She probably didn't want to bother you is all."

"Oh, come on, Derek, why are you taking her side?"

"Sides? What's the competition? I concede, darling, that you are more famous than I—and deservedly so."

Dawn Ann looked away, searching the restaurant for the offending waitress, but not finding her. Derek always had a way of making her feelings somehow her fault, as if *she* were the one behaving poorly, not, in this case, like that hussy of a waitress. She had every right to be annoyed at Trudy, who'd had the nerve to call her "hon," and at him, too, for his behavior last night, getting drunk and passing out, but somehow Derek had switched the focus of their conversation to her personality defects. She squirmed. No one knew her like he did. No one loved her like he did. And no one could hurt her like he could. He knew her most vulnerable spots, her nose, her ambition, and how much she always wanted to be liked. All the psychology with which she'd been raised couldn't save her from him.

"People always flirt with you," she countered. "It's nothing personal." She tried her coffee again.

"Touché!" Derek held up his bottle of beer as if to toast the end of the argument. She understood that Derek protected his own ego by putting down hers. She also understood from her mother that some men didn't deal well with successful women, but she'd always thought that artists were different. They didn't measure themselves by the same crass standards as commercial television, so, in a sense, artists weren't really competing with ordinary business people. Still, when he watched her broadcasts, he could isolate with uncanny precision her one otherwise imperceptible moment of hesitation or missed inflection, the inevitable imperfection of live TV. If she took offense at something he observed, he'd say, "don't shoot the messenger," or "it is what it is." There was always just enough truth in what he'd said that she would turn her anger inwards, embarrassed at being found out, as if she cared whether a horny waitress in a 24 hour restaurant recognized her or not. The ratings would speak for themselves. It was going to be hard for anyone in this town not to know of Dawn Ann McKnight, it was just a matter of time.

Comforted by a vision of her future success, when she'd wear sunglasses and welcome being ignored, Dawn Ann accepted the end of their argument, even though no apology was offered and none would be. When Trudy brought their dinners, Dawn Ann smiled her most charming, most camera-ready smile, and Trudy called her "hon" again. When the waitress came back to remove their dirty plates, Derek asked her what perfume she was wearing, and before Dawn Ann could guess, Trudy replied "Giorgio" and bent towards him to prove it.

"You should get some of that, honey," he said to Dawn Ann.

"Maybe, hon, Santa will bring me some," she smiled sarcastically at him. "If I'm real nice."

"You'd have a better shot at it if you were naughty," Trudy said, and winked provocatively at Derek.

"I don't need your marital advice," Dawn Ann said, icing her words.

"You'll have to forgive my wife," Derek hurried, his eyes as soft as a spaniel's. "Sometimes the rich and famous are just plain rude. TV stars can be just as temperamental as true artists."

Dawn Ann had had enough. "I'm due back in the studio," she said, getting up and pushing past Trudy. "Don't wait up. And thanks for my poinsettia. Don't forget to take it home for me." It would be just like Derek to leave the plant there.

"Have a good one," he called after her, signaling Trudy for another beer.

The Christmas Eve show went well, the world was calm and Dawn Ann predicted only scenic flurries: perfect for the spirit of the season but not enough to interrupt anyone's plans. Still, Derek's flirtation with that brash waitress and calling her temperamental annoyed her. It wasn't that she was jealous of him, but that he would ridicule her—saying she wasn't an artist—in front of a stranger. Even if she wasn't trying to be an artist, she had some aesthetic sensibilities, some standards of performance applicable to her own art of broadcasting. How dare he! She hurried out of the studio as soon as the director hollered "clear."

Two other couples were in the elevator when she arrived home. Both got out before her, one on 10 and one on 17. On 17, the apartment opposite the elevator door had a small poinsettia plant in front of it. When she got out on her own floor, she saw similar small poinsettias outside the three other apartments, but not hers.

Did he really think she wouldn't find out? Or did he simply not care?

"How stupid do you think I am?" she muttered to herself, and rattled her keys in the door. She headed straight for their bedroom, hoping to strip the bedcovers off him and give him a piece of her mind. He wasn't there. She barged into the studio, where the door to the darkroom was closed. She banged on the door.

"Jeez," he hollered. "What's the problem?"

"I'm home," she announced.

"That's good," he said.

"The poinsettia—" she started to say, and then hesitated, feeling petty. It was Christmas. Of course it was good she was home. What did it matter if he'd paid for the plant or not, he'd thought to bring it to her at the restaurant. That was sweet, wasn't it?

"Pretty damn cute, huh?" he said.

"Yeah," she said, deflated. "Are you coming to bed soon?" she prodded.

"No," he said, without even a tinge of feigned regret.

"I can thank you properly," she said.

"I gotta get this print right. See you tomorrow?"

"I work in the morning," she said stubbornly, feeling sorry for herself and guilty about feeling sorry for herself.

"Okay, then," he said. "Merry Christmas."

7

Between the free tourist map she'd picked up at the bus station and the numerous signs pointing down Loyola to Poydras to St. Charles to the French Quarter, Nevaeh was finding her way around New Orleans admirably, grateful to have the rolling cart. By midafternoon, the Quarter was unseasonably warm. The air reminded her of the nicest days of May when she was a child and red tulips stood triumphant along the driveway of their home. She was amazed that late into November, the iron balconies of the ancient Louisiana buildings were festooned with hibiscus and bougainvillea and that rose bushes overflowed with white and pink blooms.

On Royal Street a rag-tag group of people her age played bluegrass, featuring a skinny-legged woman on washboard. Down the street, a fellow with a red-brown beard played guitar and hoarsely mumbled a passable imitation of Dylan. She was drawn from one to another, deeper and deeper into the Quarter, caught up in their festive musical performances. The street musicians may have looked scruffy, but they weren't dirty; many seemed mellow, not aggressively high. Tourists stopped and smiled and listened and clapped, and reached in their wallets (in their front pockets, she noticed, remembering Tray's avocation) and dropped a dollar or fifty cents in open guitar cases or white plastic buckets. It was a little like begging, Nevaeh thought, to be so dependent on the kindness of others, but no matter—whatever these people were making from their music, they seemed happy and well fed.

As she approached the next corner, just before the spot on the map called Jackson Square, she heard a familiar sound, soft on the air like the coo of a morning dove. There, with a pushcart full of wineglasses, was "Phillipé, the Phabulous." She took a place behind the crowd.

Phillipé *was* truly fabulous. Thirtyish, he wore a three piece white linen suit with a white shirt and white ascot, and white canvas hightops. He had thick black hair, like a horse's mane, pulled straight back, and a bleached white stripe down the middle, like a skunk's. Even if he'd only been standing there, and not talking to the audience in mellow tones that blended perfectly with the music he was playing, people would have stopped.

Nearby he had a ten dollar CD for sale. When he finished "Amazing Grace," the dozen people around his cart appeared hypnotized, standing trance-like until the last vibrations faded away. Then they burst into applause. Four people bought the album, and Nevaeh watched as he helped one toddler wet his little finger and rub a glass, eventually eeking out a middle C. After the crowd dispersed, he reached below his cart and put a shirt cardboard over the "Phillipé the Phabulous" sign. In black marker, it read, "Back in Five." He gathered up his money and called out to Nevaeh.

"Newbie!" For a second she thought he'd divined her name. "With the pack! Would you do me a favor and watch my stuff while I run to the loo?"

"Sure!" she answered, as if they'd known each other all their lives. For a moment it was as if the musician were Tray. She missed him. At first she thought seeing him on every corner could give her courage, but then she thought it could also hold her back. Back in Iowa, she'd been confident that he would return to her, but now that she was in New Orleans, realistically, how could that happen? If someone left you, he left you and weren't you supposed to love him enough to let him go? Move on yourself?

She put her pack down, and rolled herself a cigarette. Usually she and Tray had rolled them in private so that they wouldn't be harassed by do-gooders and cops who didn't know a smoke from a smoke, but there seemed to be enough going on in the Quarter that no one would notice what one street person was doing. She'd rolled two cigarettes and was about to light hers when Phillipé flopped down beside her. He smelled sweetly of musk.

"Careful!" she cried, just as he said, "I'm Phil." She held out a cigarette. He passed it under his nose and put it between his lips. Silently, he took her pack of matches and lit first hers and then his. His eyes—one blue, one more like green—drilled into her.

"How long you been playing the glass harmonica?" he asked her.

She took a deep drag on her cigarette. "What are you, psychic or something?"

"A little," he answered, and picked up her right hand. He stroked the pads of her fingertips, and she was a goner. "You're new to town. You play music. You don't have a guitar case. The box says 'fragile.'" She looked to where she had, indeed, written "FRAGILE" in large letters on two sides of the carton. "It also says 'GLASS,'" he laughed. "In another life, I'm Phillipé, the Phabulous Psychic. But you can call me 'Phab.'"

She giggled. Emboldened by memories of what it felt like when she was with Tray, she said, "Gee, and here I was thinking of 'Louse,' as in 'Phab-U-Louse.'"

"My feelings are hurt! I save you from the streets and already you're talking back to me!"

"Saved? I'm sitting *on* the streets," she said, sipping on her cigarette. "And get used to it, I walk, I talk, I'm almost real. My name is Nevaeh and I talk back." She tickled his eyes with hers.

Phil stood up. "Come, play with me," he said with the lilt of Sinatra's, "Come, fly with me!" She jumped to her feet, positioned herself behind the second octave and together played the Pachelbel Canon, hardly missing a beat. A crowd gathered and Phillipé the Phabulous was into his rap. He played a solo, then invited her to play again, and then again. Without asking her, he assimilated her as part of his act, as if she were his missing half.

She played along, intrigued. There was this practical thing, her needing a place to stay, and this other thing, her wanting a friend. No matter how independent you were, everybody needed somebody—somebody who would help you lead a bigger, better life than you would on your own. Tray had done that for her, and then he'd left. Perhaps it was time, she thought, to move on.

Taking her hand and guiding one of her fingers around a glass, Phillipé demonstrated to a fascinated tourist the amount of pressure needed to make a continuous sound. You couldn't find that next person if you didn't give him a chance. It seemed rather random, his calling her out of the crowd like that, and she might have all the signals wrong, but he was good looking, and his voice was mellow and kind, and she'd never meet the next right guy if she didn't stay open to the possibilities.

They played for two hours, and as Phil closed up the rolling cart containing his musical glasses, he promised Nevaeh a massage for her sore shoulders and aching feet. She plopped herself on a nearby bench and began to untie her shoes.

"Not here," he laughed. She looked around, not sure why not. "At my place."

"Where's that?" she asked.

"Come, I'll show you," he said. "Will you stay with me? As they say, we can make beautiful music together."

"Well, I …" The truth—and he probably knew as much—was that she had no place else to go. And the truth also was, she was pretty bad about hiding her feelings. She was willing—more than willing, desirous, even—of going home with him.

"No pressure. I'm sorry. I shouldn't be so … I mean, come home with me, and meet my friends, and we'll get to know each other and see what happens. Does that sound okay?"

She rubbed her ankle, a little disarmed by his directness, but all the more positive of her response. "How far do we have to walk?" she asked.

He laughed again. "Half-a-mile. I could call the limousine."

"Yes, do," she said, getting to her feet.

Phil lived in a house just outside the Quarter, in an area known for "local" music. The two-story, four-bedroom house had been his grandmother's. She'd taken him in when he first arrived in New Orleans and died in her ancient sleep just a couple of years ago, at the age of 98. He said that to help her make ends meet, he'd rented rooms to other musicians, and they'd helped him entertain the old woman, who was stone deaf but too proud to admit it. Nevaeh was pretty sure that this whole arrangement benefited Phil more than the old lady, but she took his version at face value.

Although there'd been only four people living in the house when Grandmama was alive, Nevaeh would make number 10. Phil showed her his room upstairs, with a double mattress on the floor, covered by a navy-striped duvet in a disheveled pile. Two pillows were stacked together as if one person had slept there the previous night. The closet door was open, and she saw another white suit, just like the one Phil was wearing, as well as several white shirts. A pair of jeans and some tee shirts heaped at the bottom of the closet seemed to complete his wardrobe. There were two white dresses hanging at the far end of the closet. He saw her notice them.

"Long gone" he said, and closed the doors.

"Not coming back?" she asked, for a moment feeling disloyal to Tray.

Phil didn't answer her. "We can get you a chest of drawers," he said. "The Goodwill usually has stuff like that. For now, just anywhere will do."

She put her things in the far corner. They were all she owned in this world and she hadn't seen any of the other people who lived in the house. Could she trust them? Even if she were going to be with Phil, she knew that didn't count all that much if someone else in the house was desperate. She and Tray had been taken in by goodhearted souls before, but they themselves had not always been able to maintain their own ethical ambitions in the face of temptations like loose change and useful items which weren't locked up.

"No one will mess with your stuff," he said, as if again reading her mind.

"Don't want to make it too easy," she said, hoping she sounded lighthearted about it.

"This *is* the Big Easy," he said. "Come, let me introduce you to the thieves."

"I'm not that cynical," she said, realizing as she did that she was.

"Yes you are," Phil said. "You've been out there long enough to know there are no rules. You're not exactly a babe in the woods."

"Oh, stop!" she said. Again, he was telling her who she was, and while he wasn't wrong, she did find it annoying. Still, she'd been on the road long enough to know there were compromises to be made. If one of those was that if an attractive man just slightly older than you pretended he knew you better than you knew yourself, and if he wanted to give you a place to stay with a roof and running water, the expected answer was a grateful, "yes." So it was important to her to let him know she wasn't just passing through. She was staying because she wanted to, not because she had to.

"Stop what?" he asked, his tone curious.

"You don't know me well enough to tell me who I am."

He hesitated a moment, during which Nevaeh surmised that he wasn't used to being contradicted. Neither one of them moved, and then he bowed deeply, with a flourish of his hand, a salute from head to outstretched foot. "You're right, my love. I don't. But it will be fun to find out!" He grabbed her hand and led her downstairs.

Not everyone in the house was as together as Phil. Except for his buddy, François, a stubby and sixtyish astronomer, Phil was the oldest, the most talented, the most articulate. There was a couple in their early 20s who reminded Nevaeh of when she and Tray had first started traveling a year-and-a-half ago, he a bald painter and she a fortune teller with bulging green eyes. There was another, younger seer named Serena, a recent arrival. The longest term residents were a blue-grass band known as The No-Band, anchored by Skinny and Toby, whom she recognized from the afternoon. Skinny got her name from her toothpick legs. She played the washboard. Toby was her partner and played guitar. Two other musicians rotated in and out of The No-Band, depending on their inclination for work. Together, the four occupied the downstairs bedroom and dining room.

The communal living room had two old couches, a La-Z-Boy in the permanently lazy position, and a very large TV, a "present" from Phil to his Grandmama before she died, and paid for, Nevaeh guessed, with her own Social Security checks. Most of the original furniture, except for the once-grand, now marred mahogany dining table, had long since been replaced, Nevaeh surmised, with Goodwill, the profits going to food and wine and dope. The No-Band band was crashed around the big-screen TV. A pipe of something sweet was being passed around. They barely acknowledged Nevaeh when Phil introduced her.

"Heaven," the one named Toby said.

"Backwards," Nevaeh answered, but he'd looked away.

"I get it," Phil laughed. "I've got me a little bit of Heaven!" He put his arm around her and waltzed her out of the living room to the front porch, where he kissed her as if he had, in fact, wanted her all his life.

Around ten o'clock the next morning, after a wine and weed night of the promised massage and lovemaking and talking, Phil brought her toast and coffee on a tray, along with an orange. He'd been out for a run.

"You needed your sleep," he said. "Today we have to earn the Thanksgiving feast."

"We?" she asked.

"Women make more money on the streets," he said, peeling the orange and dropping the rind on the tray. She bolted upright in the bed, her heart racing with the memory of the farmer's warning, and held the sheet tight under her chin. "Sex sells, of course, but the tourists worry more about the women; if they don't sell their music, they might sell themselves, that sort of thing."

"Don't do that!" she cried.

"What?" he asked.

"You know. I would never …"

"You thought I meant sell sex for money?"

"People do," she said.

"Now you're insulting me! I'm a musician! Not a pimp."

"I'm sorry," she said.

"You're a musician, too," he said. "And you and I are in it together." He handed her a section of orange and popped another one in his mouth. "So, let's go do some duets, play some music. Then we'll stop around four, finish shopping for the party—bring your rolling cart—and start to cook. We have a lot of mouths to feed."

"Party?"

"Tradition. Meaning, we did it last year and it was a blast. Pretty much all the entertainers will come by. If they've got something to share they will. But I'm guessing we'll be long on booze, short on food."

"Weather?" she asked. When he didn't take her meaning, she added, "What's the temperature?"

"Oh," he said. "Warmer than Iowa, cooler than yesterday." He eyed her, almost suspiciously. He was already dressed in his white suit, which up close was a little dingier than it appeared in the sun. "Women in the South don't wear white after Labor Day, if that's your question. How many other choices do you have?"

"I was thinking of the tangerine peau de soie," she teased.

In her blue jean skirt with a tan "The Bluffs" tee-shirt, she felt underdressed for the occasion of her professional street debut. Phil said that she'd be part of his act until they got her a license of her own. His plan was to do a few sets so she could see how the act worked, and then watch her do one or two before he headed off to do the first round of shopping. He needed two 20-pound turkeys, one for the grill and one for the oven, and he needed them fresh since there wasn't time to let them thaw.

Nevaeh swelled with a sense of well-being. Fresh turkeys were a far cry from the community dinners for the homeless that she and Tray had attended back in California. While they hadn't gone to a soup kitchen on a holiday, they'd never scraped together enough money to have a party big enough for not one, let alone two turkeys, and fresh ones to boot.

With remarkable efficiency, Phil tuned his glasses, already mostly full and anchored to their spot on his rolling wooden pushcart. He played a few scales and then gave Nevaeh a chance to practice. It was just before noon, early for Phil to be out, but the streets were beginning to bustle with tourists, some walking off the night before, some working their way through the guidebook, heading to lunch at Antoine's or the Court of Two Sisters or K-Paul's. Two middle-aged couples stopped to watch Phillipé the Phabulous, and another small knot of a family stopped as well. Just like yesterday, he looked each member of his audience in the eyes and told the story of the glass harmonica. His voice floated in a sing-song that enchanted their loose change right out of their pockets. Three listeners dropped a dollar each in his tip box, an oblong of white ceramic with raised grape leaves molded into it, far more discreet than the guitar cases that gaped hungrily in front of other acts in the Quarter. Nevaeh recognized it as the bottom half of a cheesy tissue holder. He sold one CD.

Ten dollars for the CD, six dollars and something in change. In just 10 minutes! They could easily make 50 bucks in an afternoon!

It had taken her all day to do that at The Bluffs!

"Your turn," he said, and sat at the curb. Her stomach did a little back flip of surprise and panic.

"But I haven't performed solo before," she said. "I've just played for myself."

"It's not Carnegie Hall," he said, and lit a cigarette. "Do, 'Twinkle, Twinkle,' they love that."

She wet both her index fingers and added a spot of water to middle C to bring it up a notch. She began, concentrating so hard that she was unable to talk. She got through the tune perfectly, but no audience had gathered. She looked at Phil for approval, but his head was turned away from her, toward the next corner, where Skinny and the No-Band were faced off on one side of the street against a silver-coated mime on the other. Phil sprang to his feet and headed down the block in long and purposeful strides. She kept one eye on him and tried, "Twinkle, Twinkle" again, glancing at the harmonica as necessary. She watched Phil stop at the intersection and spread his arms like a Christ on the Cross, then saw Skinny shake hands with the mime, Skinny and Toby maintaining the intersection, the mime retreating a third of a block up the street. As Nevaeh finished her encore of, "Twinkle, Twinkle," Phil gave Skinny a kiss and a friendly pat on the rump, and Nevaeh busied herself again with her music, making more eye contact with the passersby and smiling all the while. This time a few people stopped, and she played, "My Wild Irish Rose," which yielded what she estimated to be $3.50 in coins. Not bad, she thought, for her first time. And it didn't even feel like begging.

"Talk to them, Babe!" Phil said, collecting her change from the tissue box. "Talk to them!"

They shared a cigarette by the curb before he left her, promising to be back in two hours. "Don't forget to take breaks, too," he said, "and talk to them. Tell them about the standing wave." He showed her how the water in the gigantic margarita glass in the front of his harmonica vibrated with mini-waves, and then pinned his street performer's license on her skirt. "Knock 'em dead."

She did three sets the first hour, each about 12 minutes long. She found her own pattern: a tune, a little talk, a demonstration, a tune, another tune, a request. *How are you doing today? Happy Thanksgiving. Have you heard the glass harmonica before? Have you ever played the glasses? Welcome to New Orleans. Anything special you'd like to hear today?* Nothing like the esoterica of Phil and his serious banter about the history of the instrument, but friendly. During the third set, a middle-aged woman from St. Louis stumped her with "Only You," and was so embarrassed that she started singing the tune to the hoots and hollers of her companions, and then dropped not one, but two whole dollars in the box and bought a CD.

"Oh!" A fiftyish woman in yellow cotton clam diggers pointed at Nevaeh. "We've been to The Bluffs! We conceived our first child there!"

"Honey," her red-faced husband said, and dropped a dollar in the box even though they didn't stay for a song.

Nevaeh found herself loving the attention and the edgy spontaneity of figuring out what kind of tune which people would like best, making up stories to satisfy their curiosity about a nice girl like her on the mean streets of New Orleans. "I was kidnapped when I was 10," she confided to one group. "I was on milk cartons for a while." Several in the audience thought she looked familiar. "Oh, my dear, how did you escape?" one grandmotherly type asked. "There was a shoot-out," she said. "On Valentine's Day."

"Shipwrecked," she told one group, who quizzed her in such detail about her sailing adventures that she had to admit it was a fib. "Truth is," she said, "my sister needs a bone marrow transplant, and I'm trying to raise money for her."

Dropped out of music school. Taking care of an aging grandparent. Writing novels. Whatever. It could all be true or not. The point was to entertain, and Nevaeh, her smile as wide as the Mississippi, knew both how to read people and how to entertain them.

She also knew how to protect herself. While she appreciated the opportunity Phil had given her, and the place he gave her to stay, and while it appeared that they might have something between them, a girl had to take care of herself. She'd learned at least that much from Tray. She took five dollars from the ceramic box and slipped it into her Bible, at the bottom of her backpack, in Luke's story of the Lilies of the Field.

The crowd began to thin around three thirty. She wheeled her pushcart a few yards to avoid the growing shadow, but she was afraid of encroaching on someone else's territory, so she put on a sweater, took another three dollars from the box, and played, "Jingle Bells," which got some attention from a crowd beginning to get into a holiday mood. Phil returned around four, picked up her forty dollars and gave her a kiss. "You did great, kiddo! I told you, sex sells!"

She would've liked to think her music, not her sex appeal or femininity, did the selling, but it didn't really matter. Phil thought forty dollars was great, and it was more like forty-eight. She'd done spectacularly well and loved the work. Her fingers tingled, and the tops of her hands felt stiff, as if she'd typed an entire term paper at one sitting, but she felt at home and at ease. At the end of her work day, as Phil covered the glasses with a blue tarp and secured his cart, she saluted the sun, wherever it was.

By the time dinner was served in the late afternoon the next day, Nevaeh was too tired, from working the street and chopping vegetables and baking pumpkin and pecan pies, too full from nibbling and tasting, and too smoked and liquored up from partying and being social, to claim any spot on the living room floor or porch for the purpose of actually sitting down and enjoying the Thanksgiving meal. As soon as she put the last of her pies on the buffet, she slipped upstairs, peach brandy in hand, glancing at Phillipé the Phabulous, who was wearing a black velvet top hat he'd found at a rummage sale for last year's party. He was giving some long toast/blessing over the feast. He'd crowned himself King of the Quarter, king of this krewe of lost-and-found of young musical lives. He toasted their good fortune in having each other, this house, this place. She smiled and blew him a kiss, which he may or may not have seen. It had taken only two days to figure out that Phil, like Tray, had this flamboyant, leader-among-men, devil-may-care public persona, and a private, less secure one. It was his night with his friends, and though he seemed in no great hurry to come up to bed with her, that felt right to her. It was like an acknowledgment that they had a long future ahead of them.

She woke up later when a body plopped on top of her. Actually, not one body, but two, both of whom appeared more startled than she was. She didn't recognize either one of them. Both were young, both wore jeans and tee shirts; both had spiky hair. Both smelled, not surprisingly, of smoke and alcohol. They rolled to one side—Phil's side—of the bed and passed out. She herself must have drifted off as quickly as she'd come awake because when she woke up a few hours later, it took a few minutes to reconstruct what had happened. By then it was midnight and she could hear music downstairs. The couple was gone. She felt better, so she smoothed her dress, brushed her hair and went downstairs.

"Been looking for you, sweetie-pie," Phil said when she ran into him—quite literally—in the kitchen. He had his arm around another girl, but it looked more friendly than girl-friendly, and Nevaeh would never act jealous of a guy like Phil. Tray had taught her that. The more willing you were to let them go, the less they went.

"I had too much pie!" she moaned.

"Coffee?" he handed her his cup.

She took a sip. "Yum!" she said. It must have been half Kahlúa.

"That's N'awlin's style," the girl said, and put her arm around Phil's waist. He peeled it off again and patted her behind. "Why don't you find François, honeybun?"

Disappointed and pouting, but too drunk to care, the girl wandered off. Phil put the coffee cup down, and wrapped Nevaeh in his arms, peeling her away just enough to rub her shoulders. "You give a good party," he said.

"I've been asleep," she said. "With two people who crashed on your bed without even introducing themselves."

"It happens." He picked up her hands and kissed her fingertips. "Everything happens for a reason."

8

At the beginning of the new year, Susan Stevens returned to the ten o'clock spot with a shorter, boyish haircut softened only by feathered bangs across the right half of her forehead. Instead of the soccer mom next door, she now looked like the CEO next door—and you'd better be damned sure your dog stayed on your side of the wrought iron fencing. Everyone in the newsroom noticed the haircut and had an opinion, but the unspoken undertone was the question of most interest to Dawn Ann McKnight: she'd had a little tuck, too, hadn't she? They'd shaved five years off Susan's talking-head, she thought, and while it set her back an equivalent amount in her own climb to the ten o'clock news, Dawn had to admit that whoever had done Susan's cut-and-paste had done a flawless job. Susan's forehead was as taut and smooth as a polished agate, but not so tense or fragile as to tear if she dared to smile. And that same whoever had sharpened her jaw lines to a youthful angularity, removing that extra pinch of flesh around her jowls. Reportedly, when the make-up girl asked her point blank, as a matter of professional interest, what all she'd had done, by whom, and for how much, Susan only smiled slyly. Susan's secretary, however, remembered that a Dr. Harvey had left a few messages "hoping things are okay." It took no serious investigative reporting for Dawn Ann to find out that Dr. Harvey headed the cosmetic surgery unit at one of the city's finest hospitals.

At a news meeting of the weekend team, Dawn suggested a weekend feature on the effects of weather on cosmetic surgery, and was a little surprised when the team went quiet. "Ha, ha," the producer finally said, deadpan. "Susan looks great. I think it was terrific of her to do what needed to be done, and to do it on her own initiative, time and money. We should all be so proactive when we get there."

"Of course," Dawn Ann said suddenly realizing the perceived insensitivity of her comment. Truthfully, *she* agreed with the producer: she saw nothing wrong with cosmetic surgery, it was *they* who were projecting *their* negative thoughts onto *her*. She was sincere: she wanted to branch out. Her idea was to report 15 second features, like they did on The Weather Channel, except shorter and less serious. She was thinking of weather wisdoms or interesting weather facts, and even an occasional longer exposé, like the effect of weather on complexions, dye jobs and nip-and-tucks. Such a daily feature would distinguish the Channel Three weather cast—*her* weather cast—from its rivals.

"Susan looks terrific, Doug," she said, as assertively as she'd ever said anything at the station. "And you bet I'm using her surgeon the second, the very nano-second that I need so much as a hangnail removed."

The producer shrugged. "Talk to me first, Dawn Ann. I'll set you up," he said, and Dawn Ann realized that Susan's surgery had not been voluntary, but mandated. Management had decided it was time to make Susan over the way they refurbished their offices every five years. What that meant was that management was not yet convinced that they'd found a suitable replacement for Susan. The good news was that they recognized Susan's aging appearance; the bad news was they didn't yet trust their hand-picked heiress.

At 32, Dawn Ann felt acutely that it was now or never. Thirty-two sounded still young, but 34 rang as old as 43. Thirty-two was early 30s; 34 was mid-30s, half of 70, almost dead. She was fighting off panic, trying to regulate her breathing, when the producer recaptured her attention. "But I like the drift of what you're saying, Dawn Ann. Kind of like the Bernard cat thing. People like that. It humanizes you. Sketch out some ideas, not so in-your-face, and I'll get marketing to work on a mark."

She'd never thought of herself as in need of "humanizing." In Madison, the reviewer had specifically mentioned how very likeable she was on camera, on top of her flawless appearance and delivery.

That night, over sushi she'd picked up on the way home, she asked Derek what he thought about her idea and immediately regretted it.

"Can't hurt to add a little intellectual heft to the broadcast," he said.

"I don't mean that," she said, frustrated that he would key in on the least personal, least emotional aspect of her story.

"Okay, more like 'Trivial Pursuit,'" he said.

"I mean do you think I'm not human enough on camera?"

"You're very human," he said, plucking one of her maki from her plate. "At least he didn't tell you to get a nose job."

"What do you mean, nose job?" she said, panicked. "No one's ever complained about my nose."

"I'm *not* complaining!" he said. "You wanted to know whether you looked so perfect on camera so as not to look human, and the answer is you look plenty human."

She didn't remember posing the question exactly that way. "I'm not trying to look human," she said before she realized exactly how that sounded. Derek had reworded the question so that she fell into his trap.

"Little Miss Perfect," he said in a tone that made her glad she'd never had a little brother.

"Nothing wrong with striving for perfection," she said.

"You'll drive yourself crazy," he said.

"My mother said we should try to be as good as we can be," she said. "To be our best selves."

"Your mother," he said.

"I know," she said, rushing to head off an argument. "She's not a great specimen at this point, but she taught me …"

"She's nuts, and you'll drive me nuts if you insist on some silly standard of perfection. We all must accept our human imperfection, even the daughter of the good doctor." She gritted her teeth for the rest of Derek's coming lecture. "Get over yourself, sweetheart. You'll be happier. *I'll* be happier."

Happier? She could've pushed him: was he unhappy now? Is that why he drank? Flirted with Trudy? Couldn't produce a satisfactory, albeit imperfect, piece of work? If she said something, they'd get into it, and she really wanted to focus her attention on the opportunity before her, not a petty argument with Derek.

She knew he was partly right, but the illusion of perfection was a necessary illusion in her business, not in his. If she took perfection as a standard, it was not out of vanity, but out of humility. This was a business where wrinkles became gullies and stray eyebrows forests. One had to pay attention.

Starting the next week, she was given 15 seconds in weekend broadcasts and five to 10 seconds in her daytime shows in which to try out her features. As a trademark for these segments, the station's marketing department had come up with "Puffs." They were going to put the fact or saying in a child-like drawing of a white cloud. Dawn Ann hated it. She said her idea had been to dignify the weather, not trivialize it.

"How about 'The Elements'?" she asked her producer.

"That's good, McKnight," he said, and she would have been delighted had he not sounded so surprised. "The Elements with Dawn Ann McKnight," he mused. "That can work."

She debuted "The Elements" on the last Saturday night in January.

For the standard weathercast, she had bad news to deliver: for at least three days, it was going to be single-digit cold. January had been a snowy month. In the outlying areas, the four- or five-inch snow blanket would remain, growing crusty and gray. The City was opening its shelters for anyone without heat and the police were letting the homeless warm up for a few hours at their precinct headquarters.

"January blossoms fill no man's cellar," she confided to the camera for the "Elements" feature, and explained that the up-side of a cold winter was that it would prevent an early thaw and the frosts that can kill winter wheat and other crops. As a parting consolation, she told her viewers that whereas the last ice age had lasted 700 million years and turned the entire planet into a snowball, this one wouldn't last seven days, and no new snow would fall.

"You could flirt a little more," was all her producer said, which sounded alarmingly like the kind of put-down that had been her mother's specialty. Her mother congratulated Dawn Ann on her As on tests but quickly followed with the query, "Did they give A+s?" Dawn Ann herself had been delighted with the tone of her first piece, casual yet informative. She hoped it sounded like an intriguing aside, as if she were drawing on her general knowledge—the kind of thing she might say if you were to meet her at a cocktail party and, foregoing politics and health, found yourself discussing the weather.

At home, Derek had gotten involved with a James Bond movie

and apparently fallen asleep on the couch. There was no evidence of any activity in the darkroom. Annoyed by being so ignored, she completed her nightly facial ritual and didn't bother to wake him. She left the next morning before she had to confront him, but left a note specifically asking him to watch—or at least tape—the show.

For this edition, she talked about the four times that Lake Michigan, 118 miles across at its widest, had frozen over: in 1936, 1963, 1977 and 1979. The upper Great Lakes, Huron, Superior and Erie, froze more regularly than Michigan, but still only once every 10 years. While it was cold outside, this was not a year the Lake would freeze solid, she predicted, and gave a warm and sunny smile for the camera.

"Better," her producer said, which was odd, because the material didn't lend itself to flirting, but she was enjoying herself, and perhaps that's what showed.

"Not bad," Derek said that night when she got home. He'd been watching a movie on TV and she'd had to repeat her story for him. "Where are you getting your material?" he asked.

"Books, mostly," she said.

Within a week she didn't need books. People at the station started foisting weather stories on her. She had a stack of photocopies viewers had sent, along with handwritten notes about their pets and what they did in certain weather conditions, like a cat's licking her fur backwards or a dog refusing meat (both predicting bad weather). At first she wished she'd just opted for weather photos like the lead weatherman on Channel Six. The crew at Channel Three called the Channel Six guy—tall, dark and handsome—Channel Sex. Flirting with the camera was his specialty. He didn't care whether he was right or wrong; he laughed and joked about the weather as if there were nothing else to be done about it, whereas Dawn Ann had opted for predicting and planning around it, managing it like a mischievous child or an errant boyfriend. Still, she realized that while she'd created a massive amount of work for herself, she'd also put herself at the center of the staff's interest in weather. Management was sure to follow.

The week after "The Elements" debuted, she received her first three invitations to women's service clubs: one after-lunch talk and two emcee gigs, one for a fashion show and one for community service awards. These appearances were wonderful PR for the station, her producer said, and for her. While they'd cut into her free time and her time with Derek, they would certainly serve to advance her career.

When she said it seemed a lot of effort to drive 45 minutes to Wilmette or an hour to Schaumburg for lunch with 50 women, her producer said, in a rather snippy tone, "That's how we build audience, Ms. McKnight: One viewer at a time." He was half her age in the business and had no right to lecture her on anything, but he wasn't, she understood, wrong.

The community relations department took her collection of facts and stories and staff-supplied research and wrote her not one but three different "light-hearted but gently informative" speeches that could be tailored for each group that asked her to speak. "The Elements of Surviving Chicago Weather," was basically about lightning on golf courses, small craft warnings, tornadoes and driving in blizzards. "The Elements of Climate" promised a look at the practical side of the Midwest's seasonal weather data and what it told you about the place at the center of the country: compared to Miami, for instance, how many sweaters were sold vs. how many bikinis, how many fur coats vs. how many tee-shirts, how many golf-balls and how many brats, and how many pizzas were delivered and the average outside temperature at the time of ordering. Lastly, there was a short talk on, "A Career in Television," which was the station's canned stuff for high school students. Everybody at the station had to do these career days, and as the junior person, she was sure to be assigned to some. But by making herself famous—an expert on "The Elements"—she'd put herself in demand for the schools as well as clubs. Community Relations said she should be prepared to do more than one career day.

She wasn't prepared for what happened next. The *Tribune* called and wanted to do a cover article on her for its *Sunday* magazine, with a 9 × 11 close-up portrait taken by one of the city's most famous society page photographers. At first, she'd thought they meant a story on the whole weather team, Susan, herself and maybe even Barry, a young chatty man who substituted on the odd day and covered big-time weather stories, like floods and tornadoes in the suburbs and collar counties. "Solo, sweetheart," the writer's voice trembled just enough to make her feel there might be some danger—flirtatious, ultimately harmless danger, but nonetheless a sort of titillating danger, in going to the shoot alone. Station policy was that she had to run the interview request by Community Relations. She was flattered, of course, and thought the station would be thrilled, but there were channels, as the *Tribune* writer understood. When she informed Patsy Fletcher in the PR department, Patsy readjusted the silk scarf draped just so over her left shoulder and said, almost believably, that she'd been working on getting the *Trib* to do this story ever since Dawn Ann had come to town. As she left Patsy's office Patsy called after her, "I'll talk to Susan for you. I'll make it okay with Susan."

Of course Susan would need special handling. It was good of Patsy to say she'd talk to her, in the spirit of one for all and all for one. Someone had to tell Susan that the *Tribune* was doing a "new kid on the block" story, so that her day would not be ruined the Sunday she opened her morning newspaper and saw Dawn Ann in the frame she'd assume was rightfully hers. Susan wouldn't scream at Patsy—Dawn Ann knew Susan was much too passive-aggressive for that. Instead, Susan would lunch with the General Manager and let him know that Patsy wasn't doing her job. Not only had there been no "new girl" story when *she'd* moved to town 20 years ago, but as far as she could see, there was no "anniversary" celebration in the works, either. Dawn Ann was sure that by the time the cappuccino was served, Susan would have squeezed her way onto half of her cover.

Dawn Ann dashed off to the far west suburbs to try out one of her speeches at a woman's Garden and Service Club. The Community Relations department had modified her talk to focus on "Spring, the Growing Season." The ladies, who'd enjoyed a glass or two of Chardonnay with their crab salad, were an appreciative, if opinionated, audience. She'd been good at sight reading in college and as she scanned the audience, making eye contact, she could see their heads bobbing like cotton balls, fascinated by her every word: that "solstice" means "sun stands still" and is counted by astronomers as the start of a summer that lasts 93.65 days, making the solstice either the beginning of the summer or the beginning of the end of summer. Meteorologists, on the other hand, start summer when the average daily temperature reaches 68 degrees Fahrenheit.

"Which day is that?" a voice like a basketball coach's called out from the back of the room. Dawn Ann scanned the tables and located a woman her mother's age, with gray hair tied back in a ponytail, at the rear of the room. Her mind went blank. She didn't have a clue.

"Well," she sputtered, and in a blessed instant remembered that she'd seen footnotes in her text. Glancing down, she saw, sure enough, that the question was answered in a footnote. "It's March 1 in Florida and July 1 in northern Maine. But here in Chicago, it depends. It's usually between June 15 and July 1, but later on the north side than on the south side, which, I suppose, makes June 21 as good an official average start date as any."

"Should we wait for summer to put out seedlings we started in the greenhouse?" the woman persisted. A few women at the front tables strained to see who was undermining the Garden Club's credibility by asking such a question. Dawn Ann took a sip of water and cleared her throat. It was just the kind of question that threw Dawn Ann for a loop, shaking her self-confidence in the same way that Derek sometimes did. She never liked to admit she didn't know something. Because the question seemed so appropriate—such a practical application of her meteorological knowledge—she was embarrassed not to have a ready answer.

"I'm not a horticulturalist," she demurred. "I'm just a city girl with a cactus on my desk. I'm sure you all know much more about that." There was a ripple of gentle laughter. Dawn Ann skipped the next two paragraphs of her speech, speeding to a conclusion. When asked if she'd take further questions, she declined, saying that she had to get back to the studio. The ladies didn't seem to mind, but all the way back into the city, in stifling traffic that made no sense in the middle of the afternoon, she felt a little deflated. She didn't think she knew enough about her subject matter to answer unvetted questions from the audience. As a result, her satisfaction at having performed well (up until the interruption) and being asked to star on the *Tribune's*

Sunday magazine was punctured by acute anxiety that she was about to be found out.

She knew that people like Derek—people much like her father, with only modest goals in terms of public recognition—might think she was terribly ambitious, but for some reason, she was plagued by the worry that they might also think she was out of her league. Was she good enough at what she did to merit her success? Did anyone really deserve all the success they had? Why couldn't she be satisfied with where she was in her career? Why should she doubt herself?

"You'll worry yourself sick," Derek said that evening. He'd reacted with surprising magnanimity to the news of her *Tribune* cover. He'd made dinner, which was nice of him, although he'd kept it simple—skinned chicken breasts, baked potatoes and broccoli.

"It's not worry, exactly," she said. "I just like to know my strengths and weaknesses, so I don't get blind-sided," she said.

"That means you'll spend a lot of time looking everywhere but ahead," he said. His voice had the authority of someone who was looking back over a long and distinguished career.

"What does that mean?" she asked, irritated that he would profess to know anything about her business.

"It means you play your own game and don't worry about what other people are doing."

"I *am* talking about me, not other people."

He sighed one of his pre-lecture sighs. "You're talking about yourself *comparatively*. Strengths and weaknesses. You mean, relative to others: strong*er*, bett*er*, pretti*er*-er, -er, -er."

"But that's what business is about!" she protested. Again, he was making her sound vain, and she wasn't. "There's a pool of talent, and only the bet-*ter* get ahead."

"And where's ahead?" he asked, putting down his fork. "See, that's another point. You're hustling so fast to get ahead, and you don't really know where that is—sure, it's the weeknight spot, but where is that?" He raised his hands palms flat out, the posture of a saint in an old-style holy painting.

"At least I know I'm going *somewhere*," she said, frustrated by his criticism. "You're a photographer. What do you know about managing a career?" What she meant was that for artists, there wasn't a clearly defined path to success.

"What do I know?" he exploded. "I know this!" He picked up his potato and threw it across the room at a large ceramic vase. His aim was dead on, and the vase skittered off its end table and shattered. "You think you're better than me? Huh? Do you?" He stood up, took his plate to the kitchen and dropped it into the stainless sink. Dawn Ann froze, hardly daring to breathe for fear of what he might do next. With relief, she heard him stomp off to the darkroom.

She knew better than to go after him. She'd provoked him, and to apologize now would inflame him again. When these things happened, (and this was the first since that afternoon when she was going to pose for him), he would slip into bed later, while she feigned sleep, and in the middle of the night, he'd tickle her and they'd make love, and the next morning she'd try to forget his tantrum.

She left her dishes on the dining table, ignoring the broken vase. In bed, she kept her vigil in a gray satin nightgown, and stared at the ceiling, feeling an uncomfortable and reluctant responsibility for his rage. Her success accentuated his failure.

But he hadn't failed, she reminded herself. He couldn't fail because he hadn't tried! He didn't network, wouldn't enter juried competitions or exhibitions, felt that he was too good for art fairs. He hardly had a portfolio that met his own standards. She didn't understand it. No doubt her parents would've diagnosed him as a narcissistic egomaniac, but she thought that he, like she, was consumed with self-doubt. He hid in his darkroom, petrified to show his real self—his art—to anyone, except sometimes, and preciously, to her, his truest friend. She shouldn't push him. Art takes time. That's what he always said.

She rolled asleep before learning whether or not Derek had relented. In the morning, his side of the bed looked undisturbed. When she finally struggled out of bed, she felt cranky. He'd started this. He owed her an apology. He had no right to punish her.

But what if something *had* happened in the darkroom? Passed out from inhaling those chemicals or whatever? Shouldn't she just peek in? She hated being put in this position. He was like an adult child, threatening to run away from home, so that if he did, it would be her fault. But she knew he'd be lost out there, without her. She had to help him, didn't she? She was his wife.

She pushed herself off the bed and crept quietly to the darkroom. She knocked, and when he didn't answer she slowly pulled the door open. A bottle of gin lay on its side, empty. Still in his long-sleeved white shirt, Derek lay collapsed in a fetal position on the floor.

She didn't deserve to be treated this way, but she didn't know how to stop him. Aside from the economics, she'd always wondered why women didn't have enough self-respect and dignity to leave men who didn't treat them right. Yet here she was, supporting a man who could emotionally beat her black and blue.

Silently, so as not to wake him, she closed the door, put some clothes in a canvas bag, and left a note on his pillow, "Have a good day! Home 3-ish. DA." Then she slipped into the living room, picked up the pieces of the vase and put them in a plastic grocery bag which she deposited in the trash chute on her way out.

She would shower and do her make up at the studio. What else could she be expected to do? Marriage counseling? Derek would ridicule her mercilessly if she mentioned that one. "If you meet the Buddha on the road, kill him!" he'd say, his way of avoiding being told anything by anyone, ever.

Derek only spouted spirituality, she thought crossly, the image of the broken vase fresh in her mind. He hid behind words she'd once found comforting but words that he could twist, she now saw, to justify whatever he wanted—or didn't want—to do, to absolve himself of responsibility for what was. No, she could hear him: he wouldn't consider "touchy-feely" counseling or therapy. He would say he was who he was. He wasn't neurotic. He expressed himself plenty in his art. He wasn't the one with issues.

Still, he holed up with a bottle when he was angry, and took it out on her. He didn't know even the rudimentary elements of self-expression—using nails and screws in still lifes hardly counted, she thought, as the productive use of anger in art. Her father, who'd treated several famous artists, had said that even as art, anger needed to be refined: admitted, understood, owned. Dawn Ann was finally beginning to understand what he'd meant. Unarticulated, Derek's anger lashed out randomly at those he professed to cherish most; worse, his outbursts were always someone else's fault.

She did her morning forecast, then had coffee at Walter's with Linda Livingston, where the morning staff recognized them both but gave them their space. Of the two, Linda was the more recognizable one, her face sharply defined by startling black eyebrows, wide-set deep brown eyes and shiny, absolutely straight, shoulder-length black hair, parted in the middle so precisely that a line of pink showed through. In contrast, Dawn Ann's looks were malleable. The make-up artist could dust her tan for an outdoorsy look or pale for a china-doll, fragile one. Week to week, she could tinker with her hair, reddish, brownish, yellowish. This week, it glowed with highlights of wild honey.

"Patsy's all atwitter about the *Trib*," Linda said, blowing discreetly over the top of her coffee. "Watch it, new pot."

Stirring sweetener into her coffee, Dawn Ann hadn't been listening to Linda. "Gin," she said. "Not pot. Not all the time. It's just that he gets so down on himself, you know?" She looked across the Formica table at Linda, who held a finger against her lips as if trying to follow a news tip being offered in another language.

"I said the coffee's hot, a new pot," Linda nodded the way she would to encourage an on-camera subject to focus on the question. "But I take it Derek takes his comfort in his gin? A little jealous of his star wife, so when she comes home with good news like the *Trib*, he spoils it by getting shit-faced?"

"Do reporters make up all their stories?" Dawn Ann asked in exasperated admiration. How had Linda come so close?

"Some stories keep repeating themselves," Linda said. "Sometimes I think we could do 90% of the nightly news with file footage. The Dan Ryan is still stalled. The State is still out of money. The West Side is still a dangerous place to wander alone. Husbands still beat wives; politicians still cheat, and businesses inflate prices, lay-off employees and lie about their profits. This is Linda Livingston, saying Good Night from all of us at Channel Three."

"Clear," Dawn Ann said, mimicking the director.

"So, tell me, Dawn Ann, which is it?"

"He doesn't beat me," she said, hoping to dispel any notion Linda might have that she had a dramatic story to tell. "He's a photographer and he just gets *very* frustrated. It's a difficult market out there for art prints. If he's having a bad day and I'm having a great one, like yesterday with the *Trib*, then it's particularly hard on him."

"Doesn't mean he should take it out on you," Linda said, as matter-of-factly as if she were questioning a state budget line item.

Dawn Ann shrugged. "It's just his temper."

"Are you sure he doesn't hurt you? Threaten you? Throw things at you?"

"He only hurts my feelings and only throws things across the room," she said, surprised to be revealing this much.

Linda folded her hands and leaned across the table. "You know, I just finished a story on battered women—on the north shore—wealthy, battered, intelligent, battered, beautiful, battered women, who stayed with their husbands and boyfriends despite the bruises, the threats, the intimidation."

"You sound like a script." Dawn Ann signaled to the waitress for more coffee.

"Listen to me, I'm dead serious," Linda said, shoving her cup to the edge of the table for a refill. "Men with buried anger and resentments, with frustrations like Derek's, men who turn to the bottle and throw things ... if he hasn't hurt you yet, he will. Maybe it will be rough sex, or wrestling, or daring you to do something dangerous. Don't defend him. Help him. Get him some help."

"He'd never go to counseling. Most of the time, he's fine. If something would happen for him with his photography, this would all pass."

"How can you be sure?"

"Forget I said anything."

"The problem usually doesn't go away. It escalates."

"Really, Linda. Stop imagining things. I didn't even bring this up, for god sakes. Some investigative reporter sunk her claws into me...." She gave Linda a full, for-the-camera smile. She had a new respect for her friend, one who'd made up a story so quickly and even elicited a confession, of sorts, from a wary subject. Linda was good, very good, even if, in this case, she was wrong.

"Thank you," she said finally. "I do appreciate that you're trying to look out for me, and that you care about me, even if you are dead wrong about Derek." Their conversation had relieved her of a gnawing worry, not admitted to anyone. Derek was not an abuser.

After her noontime broadcast, she returned to her office, surprised to find Derek there, his klieg lights set up on tripods.

"I thought we'd do a couple of shots here, and then move to the studio," he said.

"What are you talking about?" she said, pleased in a way that he was there and talking to her, and not looking too hung-over, his hair still damp, his face shiny and freshly shaven.

"Your cover, my darling! My cover girl!"

She walked around and sat behind her desk. Instinctively, she reached in her bottom drawer for a square, battery-operated make-up mirror she kept there, and began applying lipstick. If this was Derek's gesture of apology, she wanted to accept it, but she needed time to think, to compose herself. The *Tribune* would want to do its own shoot, wouldn't they? That would be an important part of the PR, her bonding with the photographer and the writer. Derek would be furious if they didn't use his pictures; but today he'd be furious if she didn't let him take them. Later, he'd claim she'd made a fool of him by sitting for photographs she knew wouldn't be used, but if she warned him now, he'd pout and accuse her of not giving him an opportunity. What would Linda say?

"I don't think I look my best, hon. I'm afraid there's not much even you can do for me today—I need a haircut, don't you think?"

"No," he said curtly. "Smile."

Smiling was one of her strengths. She gave him one of her better ones.

9

In the *Tribune* photographer's simple studio, Dawn Ann smiled and smiled again. She grinned ear to ear, wider than her wide-set eyes. She beamed, she giggled, she glowed, she triumphed, sparkled, rejoiced, teased, cheered, humored, encouraged, flirted, frolicked, flushed. André, the *Tribune's* photographer, shouted out a thesaurus of smiles and she did her best to run up and down the scales, teeth, no-teeth; tongue, no-tongue; lower lip out, in, bitten. Smiles as pouts and pouts as smiles.

"They love you, Dawn Ann," he cheered. "You love them. They applaud you. Wave to them. No, no, not with your hands, with your eyes. Lovely. Perfect. Hold it." André sounded like a parody of a high-fashion photographer, but in the midst of all his instruction to concentrate on herself, he made her forget about herself, so that she could smile with abandon, responsively, but without effort. She could forget about the last time she'd smiled for a photographer's camera.

It was also quite a change from when she was in grade school and her father would cajole, "Give a big smile for the camera," and she'd felt shy and exposed, as if the purpose of the picture was to create a person who would reflect the perfection of her parents' creation. A photograph that would be examined later for its revelations of character: a nose too big when seen from that angle, hips too wide by an inch, hair not quite full enough to properly frame the face. Her parents said, "The camera doesn't lie," but she'd learned differently in college. Make-up, lights, lenses, angles, editing. The camera lied. It made Dawn Ann, pretty though she knew she was, prettier. It gave her an image to live up to.

Her husband took pictures that often magnified the difference between her natural beauty and some impossible standard of perfection. The pictures he'd taken of her in her office made her look bloated, her pale face spreading into her hair rather than setting a firm line against it, her eyelids just short of fully open, her smile caught between ear-to-ear and up and down, a false surprise. Her nose cast a shadow like an oil derrick's. When she told him she hated how her nose looked, being careful not to blame the photographer, since it was her nose, after all, and the camera didn't lie, he'd said, "Yes! My new trademark. A Derek in every picture. Get it?"

"Get it. Don't like it," she'd said, laughing good-naturedly and ripping up the offending print. He'd come after her then, striking her across the face, full force. She threw her hands up to protect herself, and immediately his hands were on hers, pulling them away.

"You're okay, you're okay," he pleaded. "Honey, darling, I'm so sorry." His voice sounded desperate. "I didn't mean to. I meant it as a joke, to pretend. I didn't mean to." He pulled her to him, pressing her head against his chest, so close she could barely breathe. She pushed her fists against him, every muscle of her body tensing, but he held her even tighter. She could feel his body tremble, his heart pounding against her chest, so fast. Then, between beats, everything slowed, her vision sinking back in her head, so that Derek and then the walls of the room fell away from her, distinct and separate, but fuzzy, not real. She went limp, as if her legs wouldn't hold her, and he walked her to the bed, sat her down, and stroked her back and her hair, putting his hand under her chin and looking into her eyes, saying again and again, that he was so sorry.

"It's not funny," she said, folding her arms around herself. "It's never funny."

He promised to retake the pictures and she'd said maybe. That night, tickling and fondling, he coaxed her into making up and making love. He hadn't asked to retake the pictures.

She smiled at the *Tribune* photographer, and asked for a break.

"We're almost done, here," he said. He walked around his camera and without asking brought her a mirror and a comb. He touched her hair, circling her face with a long manicured index finger and let his hand slide down her arm in an absent-minded seduction. Then he positioned her chin, held her gaze in his beady brown eyes, and sighed. "Almost," he whispered, and she realized with a start that the man's flirtation was harmless.

"Aren't we going to do any shots at work?" she asked.

"In the field? I should hope so, but it's not my call. Evan Shaunnessy's doing the story. Maybe next week, at your place. Someone will let you know."

• • •

A happy and satisfied Dawn Ann McKnight, with nothing to hide, stared up at a fidgeting Dawn Ann McKnight, who, on a rare Sunday morning off, sat alone with her coffee in her kitchen's breakfast nook and brought the Sunday magazine as close to her face as she could without losing focus. Not unlike her parents, she determined to be objectively honest, to see every possible flaw. In Old English script, the word "Magazine" perched atop her honey-and-lemon hair like a crown, and her eyes flashed green like a cat's in the night. She thought that a couple of eyebrow hairs stuck straight up instead of lying flat, giving the arch a ragged—perhaps natural—look.

Her eyes, her smile, her hair, her complexion. She studied every element of her visage, trying, though she could not, to avoid serious scrutiny of her nose. Derek would say she was obsessed with her nose. The *Tribune* photographer had gotten it as right as anyone could. She ought to send him a thank you note for that, a bouquet. On the air, she had no control, and when Derek photographed her, he had no appreciation for her concerns. But here, staring up at her, her nose was almost acceptable.

The phone jangled and she shot out of her chair to answer it, hoping to grab it before it woke Derek, although he seemed increasingly able to sleep through anything and everything.

"You look gorgeous!" Linda gasped into the phone.

"Thank youuuuuu!" Dawn Ann eeked, like an adolescent just invited to the prom. "You sure I'm not too disheveled?"

"I'm sure," she said. "No false modesty. Bad form in this business, you know that."

"I hate to have to ask this," Dawn Ann said, but she trusted Linda and could say almost anything to her. "Have you read the article?"

"Too busy admiring yourself?" Linda asked with an assurance that conveyed she would've done the same thing. "Let me summarize it for you, until 'your people' get around to it. I think the story is, 'She's the sexiest girl ever to live next door and she actually seems to know a lot of stuff about the weather, even if her predictions are no more accurate than anyone else's, and she's got good graphics people and if all you want is the weather, then you could go to the National Weather Service, but wouldn't it be so much nicer to tune into Channel Three's newest star?'" Remarkably, Linda didn't even sound jealous.

"I'm scared to death to read it," Dawn Ann said. "I probably sound like an air-head."

"Not too bad, really," Linda said. "It sounds more like if you ever decide to leave Derek, Evan Shaunnessy would be happy to take you in."

"I'd never leave Derek," she said, just as he shuffled into the kitchen in his boxers and tee-shirt. "Hold on a minute, Linda, I'll need to reconsider that." She put the phone down and held up the magazine cover. "Good morning!" she squealed, but Derek squinted, grunted and reached in the cupboard for a mug.

"Gotta run, Linda, himself just woke up and he looks hungry as a bear."

Derek had the refrigerator door open and was pouring milk into his coffee. "No eggs?" he growled.

"Yes, there are eggs, and if you're nice, maybe even a cheese omelet in your future," she said brightly, getting up to give him a kiss. He closed the refrigerator without looking at her and turned to leave, his coffee in hand.

"Where are you going?" she asked.

"Shower," he said.

"Bacon?" she asked after him, but he didn't answer. She took one last glance at herself on the cover, then folded it with the rest of the Sunday paper and put the whole thing on the coffee table in the living room. Perhaps it was better not to rub his nose in it. She'd enjoyed the moment with Linda, and now she should try to make it up to Derek, whose career so badly needed the kind of boost that hers had just received.

Derek retrieved the newspaper from the coffee table and sat down to five rashers of bacon and a three-egg cheddar cheese omelet. One week of every month, Derek liked to do his food version of Atkins, like a purge.

"You're the best, honey," he oozed, and she accepted that as an apology. Derek rifled through the paper, searching, she knew, for the sports page. One by one, he tossed the unwanted sections on the floor beside him. She got up to get herself another cup of coffee, and out of the corner of her eye saw him pause over the cover of the magazine and then drop it, face down, on the pile of the unwanted sections. The phone rang, but Derek opened the sports, and sat motionless, transported, no doubt, to the 17th hole at Palm Something Golf Club or a power play at the United Center. Assuming that the call was most likely from her agent, she let it bounce into the message machine connected to the phone in the bedroom, so they couldn't make out the caller's message.

She didn't have to be at the studio until four. "What do you want to do today?" she asked.

"Sleep," he said. "I'm beat."

"You just got up!" she cried. "You can't go to sleep!"

"I could," he said. "Or we could go work out."

"Great idea," she said. Derek was always in better spirits after working out, as if he had burned all those negative, aggressive calories, and she herself liked to sweat, to push herself until she could feel the impurities beading out of her body, giving the camera no need to lie.

• • •

"Sixty laps?" he challenged her as they stretched their quads at the side of the Club's indoor-track. There were 20 people in motion on the track, mostly young, like themselves. Several lanky men set a marathon pace, as if they were in training, and two or three pairs, friends or couples, ran at a more leisurely but still cardio-healthy speed.

"You trying to kill me?" she said. "I was thinking three miles or 40 minutes, whichever comes first."

He shrugged. "See ya around," he said and sprinted off.

"Like two ships," she muttered, but there was no one to hear. Why couldn't he slow down, spend a little time with her? She didn't really expect that he would have the patience to read a whole four-page article about her success, but he'd seen the picture. He could at least acknowledge that, or say that he was proud of her. The pairs sailed by, seemingly able to talk or laugh to ease the tedium of 30 or 40 or even—if Derek had his way—60 laps. Scanning the track, she spotted Derek at the far end and eased into the outer lane. At her first half-lap, he passed her, slapping her bottom, "Giddy up!"

"I'll show you 'giddy up!'" she said, and doubled her stride. She was just behind him when he cranked up his speed and she fell back, winded. She walked a few steps and then forced herself to get back in the rhythm, her own rhythm. What a jerk her husband could be!

She finished 30 laps, pushed herself to 31 and walked another for cool-down. Then she stood on the sidelines and as Derek pounded by, she called his name and pantomimed a curl with free weights. She wasn't sure he saw her; his eyes were focused down his nose a few steps in front of racing feet. Above the jostling of his body, his head was still, like a raj sitting atop a divan. At times like this she wished Derek was less spiritual—if that was the posture he was presenting—and just plain nicer to her. This was her big day, and he was all but ignoring her! Even though he purported not to think comparatively, he was acting as if he were jealous. Okay, she thought. Let him take all afternoon at the club, lifting every weight they have, besting every machine. Just so he didn't take it out on her.

She finished her workout, showered and waited for him in the lobby. As she sat there, she noticed people noticing her, giving each other an elbow. Without make-up, she knew she looked different than the woman on the magazine cover. She wondered if that's what they were saying: see, she's not so pretty after all. Sitting there made her uncomfortable, so she stared at a golf game on the giant television. Derek was taking his sweet time—longer, it seemed to her, than normal, making her wait for him, as if he were the boss. When he finally showed up, he took her upper arm in what may have looked to others as a friendly gesture, but she winced under his pinch, certain she would find a bruise there in the morning.

• • •

The General Manager of the station slipped into the studio at the end of Dawn Ann's noon broadcast the next day and asked to see her in his office. She disconnected herself from her microphone and followed him to the second floor office overlooking Michigan Avenue. He gestured to the seat in front of him and poured a glass of water from a stainless decanter. He held it towards her, but she declined. He was, she thought, acting very seriously, as if there had been something in the article that he disapproved of. She couldn't imagine what. He drank half of the glass of water in one swallow and said, "We're putting you at ten. Are you okay with that?"

"Why, yes!" she said. "I'd love it!" She was thrilled, but something about the question felt odd. Why shouldn't she be okay with the promotion? That's what she'd hoped for, all along.

"Good. We'll start in two weeks. There'll be a lot of fanfare about Susan's retirement, *et cetera*, but you just let us handle that and you don't say a word to anyone that's anything other than 110% positive. In fact, don't say anything to anyone until we go public. This is NOT an age thing, or," he hesitated, "or a beauty thing or anything like that. Capiche?"

Although unsure of herself, she nodded. It had been her plan to unseat Susan, but the reality of this opportunity caught her off-guard. How is one supposed to act when one gets what one wants at another's expense?

"Don't you worry," he continued. "I'll take care of Susan."

He stood, walked around his desk and put his arm around her shoulder as he walked her out. "I knew from the beginning you'd be great for this station. I was right." He gave her a squeeze that felt more paternal than professional, and as she thanked him and walked down the hall to her office, next door to Susan's, she felt the first disappointment of an achieved goal: not much had changed. No more money (should she call her agent?); the same office, at least for now; the same time slot until some day two weeks off that would be then, not now, the culmination of her career. Probably the same reaction from her husband, who would toss out the announcement with the other unwanted news of the day.

She'd felt elated when she landed the Channel Three weekend position, even expected Derek—foolishly, she could see now—to give her an opening night party, but today, her ultimate goal achieved, she felt robbed of its satisfaction, as if André's portrait, not her own effort, was being recognized by the management of Channel Three. Did they understand that she really *did* know a lot about the weather? But, did she know *enough*?

She closed her office door and leaned against the heavy glass window, staring out and down at the Chicago River. At least a month early, two rowers in wet suits risked the still ice-cold water, racing their sculls in nearly perfect rhythm and harmony, one pulling marginally in front of the other for no visible reason. She stared for a long time. Her breath created a little patch of fog; she stepped back to see how long it would take to dissolve. Then she blew against the glass, almost close enough to kiss it, and again leaned back, waiting for the fog to disappear. She tried her experiment a third time, using her finger to trace a face with two dots for eyes but no nose or mouth. As the last of her drawing disappeared, she noticed one oarsman ever so slightly out of synch with the others, and tapped on the glass, as if to alert him. She didn't know how she was going to tell Derek.

10

Thanksgiving weekend was a big one in the Quarter, lots of folks in town. Phil, the other housemates and assorted guests slept in on Friday morning, missing the opening bell for the day-after-Thanksgiving Christmas shopping sales. Some stores opened as early as six, about the time the last of the revelers called it quits. Nevaeh was alone in the kitchen, making herself some coffee when Phil came bounding in, completely refreshed from the day before. It was noon. They made toast and loaded it with peanut butter from a four-pound jar as Phil surprised her by announcing they were going shopping.

"You need a white dress," he said.

"Are we getting married?" she laughed.

She noticed the slightest hesitation before he laughed, too. "For our act," he said. "I'm thinking Old English faerie sort of thing. You can take it as a business deduction."

"You report all your tips?" she asked, incredulous. Even at The Bluffs, she'd managed to hide most of hers (and certainly all of her self-serve gratuities) from the paymaster.

"Enough to get my Social in," he said, and she realized that Phil was far more organized than anyone she'd ever met on the street. He had a house, friends, a social security number, and a street vendor's license. He had a voter's card and a driver's license too, but not a car. He had a CD, a marketing plan, a routine and—Nevaeh suspected this was the major difference between Phil and Tray—discipline.

"And where do the hoi polloi shop?" she asked, returning the conversation to where they'd started.

Opening his hands like a statue of St. Francis feeding the birds, he intoned, "Come, follow me." He spun on his heel, and, like a drum major, led a parade of one through the house and down the porch steps, where he gathered her in his arms and kissed her as if indeed she were the bride and he the groom and they were in the Garden of Eden.

At the Goodwill, Phil headed straight to the fancy party dresses at the back of the store. The assortment was unlike any Nevaeh had seen at any other Goodwill store she'd visited—beaded dresses, feathered capes, satin shoes, even elaborate headdresses that harkened back to the Folies Bergère. New Orleans' hyperactive social scene, supporting charity balls, Mardi Gras, coming-out parties (both kinds) and the occasional Super Bowl, loaded the racks of the Goodwill with a dazzling array of cast-offs. Among the gold lamés and silvery satins and skimpy blacks, there were a surprising number of non-bridal, pure white formals.

"The innocents," Phil said, waving his arm along a rack of white and off-white dresses.

She laughed. Only someone with Phil's street savvy could think of dressing a fellow street musician with innocence. Quickly, he flipped through the hangers. "Too sexy," he said to one chiffon number with a plunging back; "too sophisticated" to a jacketed satin.

"You're looking for something wispy, wistful," he said, but she didn't bother to correct him—*he* was looking, *he* was taking charge. She felt like a little girl waiting for her mother to tell her what dress she wanted, except that her own mother had never shown such a sustained interest in any activity of her daughter's. Still, here she had to trust Phil's professional judgment; she knew he was looking for something that would make the audience open their wallets.

"I want them to see an angel," he said, and winked at her. "You should look like you've just received your degree in early music from some overpriced snot-school like Juilliard and are working the streets to pay back your student loans."

He held up a gauzy affair, full-skirted, square-necked, long sleeves tight to the elbow and then belled. The neckline and the sleeves were embroidered in a shimmery gold thread. A size 10, it was one size too big, but he insisted she try it on. It was a bit delicate, she thought, both for her taste and the street, but she took it to the fitting room and considered briefly that since there was no security camera she could stuff it in her backpack and no one would be the wiser. But this was Phil's store, and it seemed risky on a first visit. She pranced out to show him the dress. It was a little big at the waist and could use a tuck in the back to keep the neckline from flopping, but it was also only fifteen dollars.

"It'll be perfect," he said.

"I'm not sure I'm quite this innocent," she said, with an exaggerated twirl.

"Braid your hair and add some silk flowers," he said. "Buy it."

She curtsied to indicate her obedience to his wishes. With a start, she realized that, when he mentioned the taxes, he expected her to buy her own dress. She wasn't sure why she'd thought otherwise. He was giving her work, a piece of his street corner and a share of his bed. Even if she wasn't choosing her own clothes, she should at least buy them. Otherwise, she'd become a kept woman, and she'd never been kept—not by Tray, not by anyone. In the dressing room, she opened her Bible to the Lilies and took out a twenty dollar bill and a ten. After their purchase, she thought she'd further demonstrate her independence and treat them to something to eat.

Phil didn't want to eat a lot, but he said he'd let her buy them each a beer and they could split a sandwich. Without asking him, she chose a neighborhood joint. When the waitress asked what they wanted, she quickly ordered two Buds and a ham and cheese on rye. His mouth slightly open, Phil swallowed whatever response he'd been prepared to give the waitress. Nevaeh was pleased that he seemed to understand.

"Thanks for treating," he said as they were leaving.

Then they went by the house, changed into their costumes and unchained Phil's cart from the back porch. They made it to Phil's usual corner on Royal Street about three and found a young man with stringy hair struggling to accompany a teenage girl in reflective blue sunglasses who was screeching out Janis Joplin imitations that the Mercedes Benz people would've paid to terminate, had they known. Under a brown cardboard sign, "Tips Welcome," their open guitar case contained a lonely dollar bill and some change, including a smattering of pennies. Phil quickly noticed that neither was wearing a street musician's badge and strode up to the guitarist. Nevaeh braced herself for a brawl; if these two didn't understand the rules of the Quarter, they might not take kindly to Phil's request that they move up or down the block. She imagined, though, that he would be diplomatic. This was his intersection and had been for years. Being new, he'd understand if they didn't know, but now that they did, he'd expect them to move on. Quietly.

Nevaeh watched as the young man looked at her, then at his girl, then at Phil. Finally, he shook hands with Phil, stuffed something in his front jeans pocket and, scooping up his meager tips, closed the guitar case. The girl followed him listlessly. Several times the guitarist stopped and came back to get her, as if she were a lost puppy.

"No drugs in the workplace," Phil said to Nevaeh, his finger at her nose. "None."

"Depends on the work," she said lightly. At The Bluffs, an occasional joint, if she'd had one, made the work that much more palatable.

"No. Not on the street," Phil said.

"Gotcha," she said, even though she didn't like his telling her what she could and couldn't do. Besides, she was quite sure that Phil had palmed the interloper some cash—maybe ten dollars—and probably a joint or two. Without protest, the young man had withdrawn his hand from Phil's straight to his pocket. She hadn't lived with Tray Ashley for nothing. If asked, she could testify that Phil had specifically said no drugs on the streets. Never on the streets. But she was sure he'd paid the young man off.

Restored to their rightful place on Royal, Phil and Nevaeh played several improvised duets that drew a crowd and lots of dollars. Maybe it was because they played "Greensleeves" and "The Impossible Dream;" perhaps it was because Nevaeh did look like an angel from Juilliard; perhaps it was because they appeared to be innocent and in love. No one on the street was wholly innocent, Nevaeh knew, but no one anywhere was pure, and their advantage here was that they'd not descended as far down as many of the others, like, for instance, the ones they'd just displaced. And they were good. They were good musicians. They were good together.

The weeks flew by. In late December Phil repeated Thanksgiving's festivities with a party that started at eight on Christmas Eve and petered out sometime on Boxing Day. After a few days of recovery, Phil announced that New Orleans was too uncomfortably cold and damp in January to be a street musician, and that he always rested up for the Mardi Gras crowds by taking his vacation then. He asked Nevaeh to hitch along with him to Key West, where there was another glass harmonicist whom Phil had taught, who'd offered them a room in his two-bedroom bungalow. They stayed with "Stu" ("Phil's student, get it?"), although for the most part, Nevaeh didn't see him very often. Phil knew enough people—how, he didn't say—that they joined in a round of post-holiday parties that would rival fraternity rush week at the best party school in the country, the difference being that these parties featured hard liquor and harder drugs. At home, Phil and Nevaeh usually drank only beer or wine, and enjoyed a joint a few times a week. In Key West, they could claim vacation, not lifestyle, although for Nevaeh, the days and nights of parties, sometimes combined with fishing and boating, stretched and contorted in length like a watch in a Salvador Dalí painting. Some days they'd smoke in the morning and then go gallery hopping, adding their own distortions to the abstract paintings on display at some of the town's cutting edge shops. They'd walk the pier at sunset, tip the performers the way they themselves liked to be tipped and have their meal of the day at a neighborhood spot with a loud jukebox and a pool table. Phil, like many musicians, was good at geometry and angled shots, and he regularly picked up a little extra spending money. One night towards the end of the second week, Phil wanted to play pool but Nevaeh was too tired from too much grass and too much rum. It was only three blocks to Stu's house. He gave her a kiss and said he'd be home later.

Outside the night was warm and cozy. The Key West sky was clear, sequined with as many stars as the tree house in Iowa. Nevaeh was benignly drunk and stoned and tired, but grateful and happy.

To her surprise, Stu was home, watching a black-and-white movie on TV in the living room of his two-bedroom bungalow. There were no lights on, only the flicker of the picture. He had a bowl of popcorn and a bottle of Coca-Cola and was stretched out on the floor on one of two huge soft pillows.

"Hey," he said, his voice mellow. "You okay?"

"Fine," she whispered, not wanting to disturb his movie. "Phil's playing pool."

"Bogart. Wanna watch?" Stu asked.

"Sure," she said. She sat next to Stu on the floor. He was a nice guy, a simple guy, clean shaven, wire-rim glasses and a mop of curly light brown hair that looked so soft and fluffy Nevaeh had to stop herself from patting it. He wore jeans and a Maui Jim tee shirt. She didn't know Stu very well, but he was the sort of person you could be comfortable with right away.

"Coke?" he offered.

"Great," she said. "I've had way too much booze in this town."

"Yeah," he said. "It's an environmental hazard."

They watched for maybe half an hour in silence. During a commercial, Stu got up to go to the kitchen. "Need anything?" he offered.

"I'm fine," she said, but when he got back, she realized she needed to go to the bathroom, so she did. "Hold my place," she said.

When she got back, Stu had brought her another Coke. She took a big swallow and lit herself a cigarette. She offered one to Stu, who held her hand for a moment when she gave it to him. She could tell that, shy though he was, he liked her. She thought it was sweet when he rolled over and gave her a peck on the cheek. She was taken aback when he lifted a lock of her long hair and curled it around his finger in a curlyque.

• • •

Nevaeh was deep into a dream when someone turned on the bright lights. Phil knelt over her, holding her panties.

"What's this?" he sputtered. "What's this?"

It took a minute for Phil and then her underwear to come into focus. She had no idea what he was talking about.

He grabbed her crotch and she jerked away. She smoothed her skirt down, surprised to feel herself so exposed.

"Slut!" She curled into a fetal position, facing away from Phil, but he bent down and shouted in her ear, "How could you! I've taken care of you! You're mine!"

He threw the panties in her face. He started shouting for Stu. "Son-of-a-bitch! Stu!"

As if the sound were coming from a great distance, she heard the door to Stu's bedroom bang open, then punches thrown, men grunting, furniture scraping against a wood floor. Trying not to hear, she concentrated on the green and gray yarns of the shag carpeting which lay matted next to her at eye level, and stared senselessly at the haphazard, lazy way they paired up, intertwined one with another. The carpet was thin, and there were bare patches, little catch-basins for a sprinkling of sand and the shiny brown husk of a single kernel of corn. A little further away, she saw a wadded up mound the pale color of a latex glove. She heard Stu scream, and his voice, strangely high and frightened, seeped through her stupor. She remembered a cigarette, a peck on the cheek. She did not remember taking off her panties. She did not remember anything else with Stu. She felt a familiar, pleasant heaviness between her legs, as if she and Phil had made love. She replayed the evening: the crack of Phil's solid break, the tumble of a yellow striped ball in the corner pocket, the clatter of glassware, the bass vibrations of a barely audible jukebox music. She'd left Phil at the pool hall, enjoyed the peaceful walk home under Iowa skies. Then he'd barged in here and called her a slut. Her left arm tingled, as if she'd slept on it wrong. She felt so very tired.

She shook out her arm and the feeling slowly returned. Something had happened with Stu, but she had no memory of it, as if she'd been in some kind of black-out. Drugged? There'd been warnings on TV and in magazines about a date-rape drug, but since she never went to bars alone, always with Tray and then Phil, she'd not paid much attention. She searched her memory and remembered the cola Stu had brought her. She groaned in recognition.

The idea of the rape—she had no physical memory—made her feel filthy, out of control; stupid, unsafe, angry at herself and violated, but also somehow responsible for letting it happen.

She struggled to her feet, steadied herself in the doorway and stumbled to Stu's room. A table lamp lay strewn in pieces beside Stu's unmade bed. Overhead, a bare bulb swung on its cord.

"Stop!" she moaned at Phil.

He ignored her and took a swing at Stu.

"Stop it, Phil!" Her voice was hoarse, and seemed to be coming from a place way outside herself. Stu deserved a beating for what he'd done. But she didn't want Phil to be the one to beat him. She didn't want him to be hurt, but even more, she wanted to fight her own battles. She was also angry at Phil, for dangling her panties in her face, for blaming her. He hadn't protected her from Stu, which in a way made him an accomplice. He could have warned her.

Phil threw another punch and blood spurted from Stu's nose. Stu covered his face with crossed forearms, cowering against the closet door. Bare-chested, his jeans unbuttoned, Stu didn't look at her. He didn't fight back, only begged Phil, in a tiny, injured voice, to stop the pummeling.

"I didn't," she said. She hadn't consented. She wouldn't have consented. Phil was her boyfriend: He'd said "you're mine." She'd followed his lead and his guidance.

Up against the wall, with Phil's face inches from his, Stu whined, "We were high."

"I wasn't," Nevaeh moaned, but the men were not listening to her.

"I'm sorry, I'm sorry." Stu sounded like a school boy.

She stared at the vibrant blood spewing from Stu's swollen nose. She'd been raped. By Stu. Drugged and raped and she couldn't remember a moment of it.

She wanted to throw up. She limped across the hall to the bathroom with its stark white fixtures, leaned over the toilet and retched. She started to cry. The taste in her mouth was sour, stale rum and fried shrimp. She retched again and again, until only a thin strand of clear mucous hung from her lips.

She wasn't safe.

Gasping for the breath that might clear her head, she flushed, rinsed and splashed her face with ice-cold water. She felt wobbly, heavier on her left side than her right. Holding her palms flat against the walls of the hallway, she staggered into their bedroom and gathered her two tee-shirts, cotton skirt, cut-off jeans and sandals, cramming them into her backpack. She'd left a book, her brush and a package of roll-on deodorant on the bureau. Some spare change was there, too, and she figured it was hers. She started to reach for the coins and then yanked her hand back as if they were burning coals. Phil and Stu were still shouting and shoving.

To hell with both of them, she thought.

She strapped on her backpack and labored down the hallway. She was struggling with the heavy front door when she heard footsteps behind her. Phil reached over her shoulder and with his arm straight out, held the door shut.

"Let me go!" she screamed, stomping her feet and trying to kick him. The angle was awkward and he pressed his body against hers so that she couldn't move. She squirmed and twisted but couldn't break free. Finally, she stopped trying, hoping to make a run for it when Phil relaxed. Ever so gradually, Phil released the pressure, letting the silence grow between them.

"I'm so sorry," he said to the back of her neck. "Let me take you to a doctor."

His voice was so gentle, his touch now so tender, that she let him turn her around. He held out a white, scored pill. "He drugged you," he said, his voice cracking.

She stared at his outstretched hand, the little pill so innocuous, like an aspirin. "Sorry" was so insufficient. Both for what happened and for Phil's betrayal.

"You didn't trust me," she said, challenging him. It was the lesser of the two crimes, the easier to confront.

His face fluttered for a second, the canny street performer unprepared for that comeback. Finally, he said, "You're right. I didn't know if I could."

She tossed her hair back. Not to trust her was to imply she was a whore, giving him sex in return for food and shelter. Maybe other girls on the street had to do that, but she knew how to get by without a man in her life—Tray had taught her that, and she'd proven herself back in Iowa.

She knew who she was. She believed in serial monogamy, and had assumed, when Phil asked her to move in with him, that he did, too. She'd even asked, and whoever owned the dresses in his closet was "long gone." There hadn't been time or opportunity for either of them to be with someone else. Wasn't the real question whether she should've trusted him? Was it now just a matter of time before he left her, too, like Tray, or kicked her out? Perhaps she'd trusted him too much. It was time to move on.

"We should call the police," he said.

"No." She was surprised, really, that he would think to call the police, since he didn't like to draw that kind of attention to himself, and it meant something that he might turn in his friend for her sake. Still, she didn't want to face the police, answer their questions, suffer the scrutiny and judgment of their leering eyes.

"At least let me take you to the hospital," he said.

"What for?" she said. She imagined being probed and questioned and counseled, and since Stu had used a condom, she was pretty sure she was okay physically. There would be nothing in the police or the hospital documentation of her violation that would undo it. "I don't want to go to the doctor. I want to go to sleep."

"Not here," he said. "I'll get my stuff."

"I'll wait outside," she said. Even if she decided to move on, there was nowhere to go at this hour. For the rest of the night, at least, she needed Phil, if only for safety. On the porch, she lit a cigarette and stared at the night sky, letting the tears flow and wondering how she would salute the sun come morning.

11

That night, they went to a cheap motel that wasn't cheap, but gave them a day rate if they'd clear out by ten. The morning manager didn't know the difference, so they slept until ten and left at eleven. Phil treated them to three-egg omelets at the diner next door. Afterwards, they walked to the plaza. He asked if she would mind being alone for a little while, and she sat on a bench, watching their stuff and the pods of dolphin she thought she saw leaping on the horizon. She tried to replay the previous night, to determine the exact moment at which she'd lost consciousness, but she could not, and hypnotized by the rhythm of the sea, she slipped into a deep meditation. She was startled when Phil appeared, an hour later. Down on one knee, he handed her a single rose in a clear plastic cone with a red bow and a set of keys.

"Our own place," he said, "for a week. If you don't mind watching a cat."

"Do we have to walk it?" she teased, with the air of someone who was in a position to be fussy, but her eyes watered.

He hung his head for a moment, as if in silent prayer. Then, his face as serious as she'd ever seen it, he said, "I'm so sorry. I can never make it up to you." She fought back another wave of tears. "But," he jingled the keys, "friends of friends of friends are going out of town for a week, and all we have to do is feed the cat and make sure she doesn't go outside."

She swallowed hard. The food had helped, but her mouth was dry. If she hadn't been slightly drunk and high to start with, maybe she would've been more alert, noticed some warning sign, slapped Stu down when he pecked her cheek. She'd had a friend in college who as a sophomore had been raped at a fraternity party, not drugged, but drunk. Lindsay had contracted genital herpes, and didn't go out with men for the rest of her college career. People thought it was because she couldn't trust men, but she'd said to Nevaeh that she didn't trust herself. She knew all men weren't rapists; she just didn't know which ones were and which ones weren't.

Nevaeh wanted a beer to settle her stomach and her nerves and this tingling in her eye ducts that threatened to break the dam of her anger and shame and guilt and rage. She wanted a beer and a smoke and for her consciousness of the rape to go away.

"And there's a pool."

• • •

It was a small place, with a backyard overgrown with tropical plants and a small, in-ground pool tiled in rows of dark blue and gold and white tiles—a Grecian look—with several huge cement urns of towering red hibiscus. Phil and Nevaeh each claimed their respective chaise lounges and slept their days away in the sun and warm shade, reading occasionally, Phil a Clancy thriller and Nevaeh a biography of Eleanor Roosevelt. They barbecued fish on the built-in gas grill, and afterwards walked to a small park by the water where they could count the stars as they appeared. After, they smoked some dope and watched movies from their host's video library. Phil put his arms around her and hugged her and when she ended their kisses a few seconds later, he took the hint and did not ask for more. She was not a virgin, and she was not a prude, but the thought of Stu had so permeated her being that sometimes she felt she might not get over it until she'd sloughed off all the cells he had defiled. She had more sympathy now for her college friend. Despite her best efforts to think her way through it, she wasn't ready to distinguish among men.

"Get over it," she told herself firmly. Have a positive attitude. Be resilient. Let it go. She told herself she'd been violated but her life hadn't been threatened. She had no memory of the act itself, so she shouldn't torture herself by making one up.

The day before they left, they smoked a joint in the morning, and visited a secret garden behind one of the homes in the old part of town. It was overgrown like a jungle, with canopies of broad-leafed plants and palms and mango trees. Every so often along a winding path there were large cages with grand old parrots and cockatoos chattering and rattling the locks on their doors, "Help me out here, buddy, would ya?" Stoned, they answered the birds' questions and laughed like adolescents when they asked the parrot a question and got a plausible but ridiculous answer. Nevaeh asked a scarlet-tailed bird named Polly, "Polly want a cracker?" and Polly duly responded, "Hell, no. Pardon my French."

The birds were magnificent. Many were old or injured, which was why they were in this private refuge, but they were vibrant and spunky and cared for. Phil took her hand as they walked. She remembered that men had left her—her father, Tray—and she had survived. Something more had happened with Stu, but she would, again, survive. She could take refuge in Phil.

They shared another joint and strolled home in the afternoon heat. Nevaeh brought ice teas to the pool and without speaking, they left their glasses sweating on the wrought iron table while they stripped and dove in. They swam and then made love standing chest-deep against the side of the pool, and later did it again in the shower, and after a red snapper on the grill and a last walk with the stars, again in their king-size bed.

They'd avoided Stu in Key West by not going down to Mallory Dock for sunset, but back in New Orleans, living in a house where she could never be certain who would be sleeping in any of the bedrooms, or on the living room floor, she felt his presence everywhere. She peeked around corners before entering the kitchen or the living room; she moved the waste basket in front of the bathroom door while she showered. She couldn't bring herself to shampoo her hair. Every familiar house noise frightened her. She tossed and turned all night, despite Phil's attempts to hold and comfort her.

Gently, knowing it would be nearly impossible for Phil to understand her regression, she pushed him away when he rolled to her side of the bed. During these days, she dragged through their shows, putting up what she thought was an adequate front. She couldn't make herself feel light and airy, like the white dress she wore. She felt, instead, heavy and soiled.

At night, Phil's custom was to make some kind of dinner for whoever was there, asking each of them each to contribute a couple of bucks, if they had it to spare. He made stews and spaghettis and jambalayas, and there were always jugs of red wine and a half-keg of beer tapped in the kitchen. It was a pretty good deal, one that Phil tried to work on the honor system. Despite the serious temptation of the family-size Hellman's Mayonnaise jar on top of the keg, most of the time there was just enough honor among thieves to make ends meet. Nevaeh started putting in an extra dollar. Many of those first nights back in New Orleans, she fell asleep in the old La-Z-Boy in the living room, a cup of beer at her side.

After a week, on a night when she'd made it up the stairs to their bed on her own accord, Phil asked, "How much time do you need?" His voice hovered a tone away from bored contempt, as if he might be ready to toss her out. Well, let him, she thought bitterly, and started to cry.

"I don't know," she said.

"He's not here."

"I know. I know it's over and done with and I shouldn't dwell on it, and I'm physically okay and everything, but …" She couldn't finish. She clenched her fists and tried not to, but tears seeped down her cheeks. Next to her, Phil lay perfectly still, staring at the ceiling, his patience apparently used up.

"I want my happy, sunny, Nevaeh back," he said.

"She's gone," she whimpered. "I don't know how to get her back."

After a pause, he said, "We can't go on like this," his voice tired.

"I need time," she said, although she hated to sound like she was begging.

"No time but the present," he said. "You can't dwell in the past."

"I'm not," she said.

"I think you are," he said firmly.

She resented that authoritative tone, but she understood his point, and even agreed. She just didn't know how to get her feelings to follow his instructions. "I'll try," she said.

"Good," he said. "It'll be okay."

The next morning, just before noon, Phil brought a glass of juice, coffee and a plate of wheat toast up to their room. In the middle of the toast was a yellow pill.

"What's this?" she asked.

"A kind of vitamin," he said. "A mental vitamin. For your ailing spirits. To take the edge off."

"No speed."

"No, no. A relaxer, a pain-killer to help you enjoy the present."

She hated feeling as low and disconnected as she'd felt these past couple of weeks, but she didn't want to become a pill popper. Her mother had often mixed pills and alcohol, and Nevaeh knew the dangers. Still, she wanted to feel better. He'd said they couldn't go on the way they were.

Like a miracle, she began to feel better the next day.

"Where'd you get that stuff?" she asked Phil as they were packing up their carts on Royal Street. "It took the edge off."

"Talk to Serena," he said, the 19-year-old who'd landed at Phil's place around the same time as Nevaeh. "Don't get hooked, though. Promise me, you won't get hooked."

"Why are you so preoccupied with other people's intake? As I recall, not a day goes by that you don't have a little smoke for yourself."

"That's different. It's just weed. Like beer or wine or a daily martini."

"You're a naturalist?" she scoffed. "Very old argument."

"You smoke every day, too," he said, tossing their pitcher of water into a nearby urn of flowers.

"I didn't use to, before I met you," she said.

"You couldn't afford it before you met me."

"Well, that's true," she said. "But now I have to work just to keep up with it."

"Tsk. Tsk. What else you gonna do with all this cash?" He waved the day's take—it looked like 50 or 60 dollars—under her nose.

Playfully, she took a swipe at the wad.

He snapped it back. "Later, if you're good," and she felt a little jolt, like a metal door clicking shut. She was sure he didn't mean it that way, but she also understood, as she watched him close up his cart, that she was as dependent on him as she'd ever been on anyone in her entire life. And that worried her more than a pain killer or tranquilizer or whatever it was that Serena could offer. She figured she ought to develop a direct relationship with Serena, to eliminate the middle-man, as it were.

Phil made a big pot of spaghetti that night and 12 people, including guests, gathered around his grandmother's mahogany table. Half of them needed to eat and run to work. Three fortune tellers, including Serena, wanted to be in place around Jackson Square by eight for whatever straggling tourists and conventioneers might be on their way for beignets and coffee. Two painters who used spray paints and torches to create psychedelic renderings of the underworld needed to claim their spots on the sidewalks near the carriages on the Decatur Street side of the park. François, an eccentric old man who studied the stars was anxious to set up his telescope, claiming that that night the moons of Jupiter would be visible and he could charge three dollars a peek. Since Key West, Nevaeh had become more aware of the night sky. She thought she might accompany François one night if Phil wanted to go out to shoot pool.

Toby and Skinny, the other stable couple in the house, had been with Phil the longest. Between them they played banjo, guitar, bass, fiddle and washboard and played both their own gig and with others in The No-Band band. They were working on getting together enough money to do a decent CD, but in two years, they were still short, one thing after another interfering with their plans. Toby in particular was easily stressed out. If the tips were poor for three days in a row, he'd take to bed for three weeks. Skinny, an uncomplicated person who took things exactly as they came, would nurse him without complaint until they were nearly out of cash. Then she'd sit in with another group or do whatever she could to raise a few bucks. Eventually, Toby's spells passed, but Nevaeh understood that they got in the way of the band's success. Thankfully, Toby and Skinny were in a working phase.

"Never heard much about Key West, Nevaeh. How was it?" Skinny asked as she grappled with serving herself from Phil's huge bowl of spaghetti, already sauced.

Without warning, Toby produced a scissors and snipped Skinny's dangling strands. He grinned. "Here, Nevaeh, dig in and I'll cut."

The distraction was enough to let Nevaeh get away with, "Fun" as the answer to Skinny's question. There was no reason to say anything more. Some sadness came over her as she realized that despite Phil and housemates and smiling at and talking to hundreds of people in a day, she felt lonely. She needed a friend. Skinny, the natural choice, was preoccupied with Toby. Perhaps Serena, though a couple of years younger, could be that friend. Perhaps she could even help Serena and play the big-sister role.

"Can I come along with you tonight?" she asked Serena at dinner.

"Will you shill?" the girl asked.

"You won't read me for free?" Nevaeh was taken aback.

"If there's time," she said. "I'll go set up on Chartres," she said, and Phil interrupted her.

"Char-ters," he said. "You've got to sound native."

"Chartres. We did French in high school," Serena said, looking around the table. "I've been here three months. No one's told me different."

"Well, we didn't know you were staying," Skinny said. "Now that you are, Phil's handing you the keys to the city." Phil smirked, as if the three of them knew something Nevaeh didn't. Did Phil have designs on Serena? Is that how he knew about her pills? She stopped herself. She was becoming paranoid and distrustful, and she didn't like that in a person. Phil had shown nothing but concern for her since that horrible night with Stu. They were a duet and they made money together. She had nothing to worry about.

"Char-ters," Skinny repeated.

"There're a ton of these mispronunciations," Nevaeh said, warming up to self-appointed new role. "It's 'Or-leens Street,' by the way."

"Whatever." Serena wiped her mouth. "Do you know how to shill?"

Nevaeh shook her head vaguely enough so that Serena could sound knowledgeable in front of the others.

"If there's no one with me, you should stroll the block once and act like you're sizing me up. Stop in front of whoever's next to me, but look in my direction, that kind of thing. Then come up, act a little shy, and sit down. If I see a real prospect, I'll wind up and you can leave. Don't come back for 45 minutes."

Nevaeh, Toby and Skinny did the dishes. Phil said he'd take a boys' night out, and went off to play pool at the neighborhood bar. Toby said he'd join him later.

"She's actually pretty good," Skinny said, handing her the washed spaghetti pot, a string of suds still clinging to its sides.

Nevaeh raised her eyebrows.

"I mean, she read me, and I thought she did a good job. She's got the generalized-specific down pat."

"I've never been read," Nevaeh said. "I don't know what you mean."

"'I see a great change,'" Skinny intoned, feigning a voice reverberating through a tunnel. "Then there's always, '.You've been greatly hurt, a parent failed you,' that sort of thing. True of everyone who ever walked the planet and still, it's news when we hear it applied to us."

Nevaeh quickly scanned her own life; of course, her mother had failed her, and her father, too, wherever he was. Change? She'd come to New Orleans as one person, went to Key West with Phil as another, and returned changed, hurt, scarred. All life was change. Some good, some bad. Brilliant of Serena to know that at such a young age, when the aches of the present promise to last a lifetime and so many adolescents don't outlive their sorrows. This, too, shall pass, she remembered. Her mother had been on that kick during the week she'd gone to rehab, when Nevaeh was 12. This too shall pass. So had rehab.

"The trick," Skinny added, "is to sense which platitude to give which person. If you say them all, then they kind of get the idea you don't know what you're talking about, but if you can give them three good ones, that are really top of mind for them right then, they become believers. Will even come back tomorrow for a little more."

"I suppose it also helps if you give them one bad thing. If it actually doesn't happen, they won't be mad at you. They'll still come back next year."

Nevaeh knew these things, of course, but she sort of wished she didn't. She'd thought it would be fun to hear what Serena might say, but now it wouldn't seem as true. How ridiculous was that? Now that she knew the platitudes were in fact universal truths, what did it mean to think Serena's predictions wouldn't come across as being true? "I'm getting confused," she said. "I think I'll go shill. Something

I know how to do."

• • •

Jackson Square at night was different than during the day, at once more spiritual and more sinister. The carnival of music and tumblers and fire eaters and contortionists gave way to numerous tables devoted to the occult. Some readers wore black capes and displayed human skulls, but Serena's props only included a glass ball, though she didn't purport to read it, and half a dozen fat white candles. Her small TV-sized table was dressed in a black cloth with a pattern of white hieroglyphics.

Serena mostly read the Tarot cards and was learning palms, but she was best, for those who could trust in her innocence, at simply reading the person. She would examine their hands, and hold them loosely until she had a feeling, and then she would begin. Because she was only 19, and looked no more than 20, many trusted her not in spite of her youth, but because of it. They assumed one could not learn to con so convincingly at such a young age, that the experience of youth, being more limited, left more blank space for fresh intuition rather than the cynical stereotype of wisdom. Her name, Serena, avoided the nether-world image of others set up around the park and set her apart from *les faux* Madames l'Amusé, LeBourbannaise, and LaCondolet.

Serena set up near the corner of St. Ann and Decatur, a choice spot for its two-way traffic. Against a chill in the night air, she wore a bulky Irish knit cardigan over a black leotard and a colorful long full skirt of velvet and metallic braid. She'd pulled her hair back in a scarf tied behind her neck and in her small ears she wore not one, but three sets of huge silver hoops. Half an arm's worth of thin silver bracelets clattered when she moved even slightly. Beads of every description, some hand-painted and some like those thrown from Mardi Gras floats mingled around her neck, attesting, like Girl Scout merit badges, to her material success. Nevaeh studied her from a spot near a neighboring booth, where a guy in white makeup and painted arched black eyebrows studied cards and looked deeply into the eyes of two teenage girls with shiny, dyed-black ponytails, the sort to be easily impressed by his drop-dead serious declarations. Nevaeh made eye contact with Serena, who glanced down at her little table and slowly swept her hand across it, palm open, inviting her to sit. Because she was at that moment feeling shy, Nevaeh glanced in both directions to see if a real customer could be lurking, and, seeing no likely takers, she strolled over, stood at the table and pretended to inquire about the price. She reached in her pocket, where she had a 10 dollar bill, and slid it onto the table, with her hand obscuring the number "10." To Nevaeh's surprise, Serena put her hand on the bill, dragged it to her side of the table, and left in its place half-a-dozen yellow tablets. Afraid that someone might see, even though it was night and no crowd was hovering, Nevaeh immediately palmed the pills and put them in her pocket.

"Take 'em when you need to," Serena said. She picked up Nevaeh's hands and held them by her fingertips.

"Need them for what?" Nevaeh asked, even though she knew.

"Like instead of a smoke or a beer, to smooth out. I know you've been through a lot." She turned over Nevaeh's hands so the palms faced up.

Nevaeh stiffened, and started to pull her hands away. She hadn't told Serena anything about Stu. It wasn't his story to tell. She didn't want people in the house to know; it was none of their business.

Serena tugged back. "You've been greatly hurt."

Nevaeh didn't respond, but waited silently, giving the impression that the reading was continuing. She felt sheepish. "Greatly hurt" had been the words Skinny had used when they were doing the dishes. It was another universal truth: everyone had "been through a lot."

"Go now, and be well," Serena said.

Understanding Serena's signal, she said, "Yes" and added, "Thank you."

A middle-aged woman in a copper-colored wig came up right behind her. "Can I be next?" she asked, and Serena smiled a closed-lipped smile, swept her hand across her table, and said, "I see that you are anxious about your future, yes?"

12

Like a grateful client, Nevaeh whispered "thank you, thank you," over and over as she backed away from Serena's table, her cache of yellow pills in her pocket. She retreated to the steps of St. Louis Cathedral, and, her heart racing, stared across the walkway at the various fortune tellers. She was relieved to have this distance between them; as it was, she was obsessed by trying to read the reader, to figure out whether Serena's techniques were as good as Skinny said, or whether Phil had blabbed about what had happened in Key West by way of explaining his need for the pills. She fingered the tablets, rubbing one between her fingers.

"To smooth out," Serena had said. The one Phil had given her that morning had done that for her. She felt as if it were melting in her hand. She coughed and slipped it into her mouth.

Out of the shadows, a dark teenager in oversized jeans approached her and, standing too close, asked her for a light.

"No." she said loudly, with some vague hope that Serena would hear her, should she need help. "Sorry," she added and bolted down the steps to the corner, where a small crowd grew expectantly around a fire-eater. Although she'd seen his act a dozen times, she applauded the man as he leaned his head back parallel to the ground and sent a torch of fire straight down his gullet. Then she trained her vision sideways to the cathedral steps. Another kid came by and lit her potential assailant's cigarette. The two sat calmly smoking and looking the other way. She sighed and reached for another pill, afraid her anxiety was getting the best of her.

She was supposed to let 45 minutes pass and then see if Serena needed further shilling. She wandered over to the open-air Café du Monde, where she could treat herself to a café au lait and watch François sell the night sky.

He was set up just outside the café, his poster board sign frayed at the edges and in need of repair. "Heaven's Here," it said in large black letters like balloons.

"Good evening," he bowed, and accepted her offer to bring him a coffee. "Two sugars," he said, but she brought him four, knowing he'd use two and pocket two for later. She took a table near him and ordered beignets and coffee for herself and then put her backpack on the chair opposite, as if it were her date for the evening.

"Good stars in Key West," François said to her between customers.

"Beautiful," she said, and for the first time since coming back to New Orleans, her anxiety lifted.

She raised a beignet to her lips, a fried pocket of sweet dough that felt as heavy as a lead ball. She'd worked hard during the day, and she was suddenly so tired. It was like crashing.

An hour later, the waiter, an older man with a cinnamon-dusted terry cloth towel over his shoulder, shook her by the arm.

"Your coffee's cold, miss. Pack it up and move on." She stared up at him without recognition, but slowly became aware that she was sleeping in a public place, not at home in the comfort of Phil's double bed. She wrapped the last two beignets in a napkin to take with her. Her mouth was dry and her tongue scratched her cheek like sandpaper. Cold or not, she gulped the coffee.

On the sidewalk, François was finishing up with a customer. He caught her eye. "Clouds are coming in. Wait for me and I'll take you home."

"You don't have to do that, Francy. It's close enough. I can do it." Her words sounded very far away. She took another long, slow breath and stretched her hands over her head, not as elegantly as a salute to the sun, but with the abandon of a body that knows no pain and can't remember itself.

• • •

Back in bed at Phil's house, Nevaeh was still half-asleep in her clothes at noon the following day when Serena plopped down next to her.

"Now who's the newbie, heh?" she giggled, stretching out and propping herself on her elbow. "You okay? Francy and Phil and everybody, they're worried about you! You were a mess last night. What'd ya do? Take 'em all?" When Nevaeh didn't answer, she continued, "I guess I should've warned you. 'Take as directed. May cause drowsiness. Don't operate heavy ...'"

"I get it, Serena," she yawned, disgusted with herself and the whole situation. "I overdid it. *Mea culpa*. Why don't you do something useful, instead of lecturing me and waking me up? Like get me a glass of water? Some aspirin?"

"I can do that," she said, and propelled herself into a vigorous sit-up from the bed. She came back half a minute later and sat next to Nevaeh's immobile body.

Nevaeh sat up and took the glass without saying "thank-you."

"If I were you, I'd get up and move around," Serena said, her voice innocent and worldly at the same time.

"Where's Phil?" Nevaeh asked, ignoring her.

"Not my day to watch him," Serena said. Nevaeh could see that Serena was trying hard to be lighthearted, to be a friend. "Francy brought you home, and Phil walked you upstairs, and then, I dunno, he came back downstairs for a while. Toby and Skinny were jamming a little. It's after noon now, so I suppose he's out doing his thing."

"*Our* thing," Nevaeh said, surprised to be on the verge of tears.

It was after two in the afternoon by the time she found Phil, for some reason not at their usual corner. It was the beginning of Mardi Gras and he had a fairly good crowd. He was playing "Amazing Grace," probably for the sixth time that day, but it was just the tune she needed to hear. The glasses vibrated, giving her courage, and as the crowd parted, she went up to him.

"Sorry," she said.

"Me, too," he said, and adjusted the pitch of middle C with an eyedropper of water.

"Don't see why you're so huffy. You started me on 'em," she said.

"I thought you were a responsible adult," he said. "I'm not going to talk about it here." He made eye contact with a couple of middle-aged tourists and began his rap. "Have you heard the angelica before?" He played the first few notes of "To Dream the Impossible Dream," and they stopped. The two women, in polyester slacks (one navy and one green) with matching light spring windbreakers, stepped right up to the cart, leaving their husbands 20 feet behind them.

Ignoring Nevaeh, who stood to the side, Phil didn't bother with his usual patter, but engaged the women in conversation as he played random notes in an improvised harmony. They were from Texas, here with their husbands to visit relatives; it was their fourth trip to New Orleans.

Nevaeh watched Phil hook them both with his eyes, then take one woman's hand and dip it in the water, showing how to make a sound, and then got the other to build a chord with her. The husbands, inching closer, dutifully pulled their cameras out of their front shirt pockets. Phil put his arms around both ladies for a parting shot; each bought a CD and one put a few extra dollars in the ceramic holder to boot. The tip apparently made her bold enough to ask if his white stripe was natural or dyed.

"As true as true is," he answered, and they left, chattering with each other as they walked away.

"It's no big deal, Phil," Nevaeh said, trying again to coax his forgiveness.

"I have rules," he said. "You disobeyed them."

"Rules?" Her face burned.

"Not to abuse. Not to get hooked."

"Hooked? On a few pills? Let me get this straight," she said, feeling the adrenaline of anger rush through her, as if Phil himself had been her rapist, and her survival depended on fighting him off. "You think you have the right, one, to issue me rules, and two, to *punish* me if I don't follow them to the letter?"

Deliberately ignoring her, Phil greeted the next passerby. "Good afternoon, ma'am. Welcome to the Big Easy."

Lying, self-righteous son-of-a-bitch. His hair was dyed, and he wasn't taking this little incident easy. How dare he make rules, and how dare he try to tell her how to recover from her pain! What could he possibly know about it? He wasn't a woman. She didn't need his rules; she knew how to take care of herself. She had, and she would. Because people, even those who love you, aren't that dependable in a pinch. Maybe she *had* become too dependent on Phil. She'd put an end to that. She could get by, on her own, like a lily of the field.

Without a word, she started home and didn't look back. For half a block, she could hear Phil, playing water music, as beautifully as he'd ever played, and he was playing for her, wasn't he? Stroking the glasses with his fingertips, beckoning her. At the corner, she passed by the Silver Man, frozen in mid-stride, tipping his top hat in a jovial pose: "Hats off to you, girl!"

On the next block, a man named Johnny made marionettes dance to scratchy recorded honky-tonk music. She stopped for a minute, to help him gather an audience, and thought about the other performers she'd come to know over the past few months. A couple of them, like Michael the magician who could make a dollar bill, signed by an audience member, appear in a grapefruit, had places of their own and would probably take her in for a night or two. But that would embroil them in her relationship with Phil, and there was no need for that. They'd have to live with him, if only as King of the Quarter, long after she was gone.

She didn't understand Phil's attitude. His house had an open keg and known pot-heads crashed there regularly. Serena had a supply of pills. He himself had given Nevaeh her first one. Why was he so down on her for taking one little pill too many? Was he afraid she'd never get over it?

Arriving at Phil's, she ran up the stairs to their room. She took a deep breath and made a decision. She still had the card from those people at the bus station. She would pack and then call them. Because of the harmonica and her garbage bag of assorted household items, plus a few more clothes than she arrived with, she hoped they'd pick her up. No matter how hard a person tried not to, you just seemed to attract stuff, like metal filings to a magnet. In gift and souvenir shops on Decatur Street, she'd seen some desktop objects that were just that, magnetized metal pieces that could be sculpted by a flick of the hand, like a three-dimensional doodle pad.

Stuff accumulates. Stuff clings. She promised herself she would do a rigorous sort-out before calling those people. She'd have to consider whether to take her white dress, or whether she should leave it behind for Phil's next fantasy. She hadn't promised him fidelity or sobriety, and he had no right to expect either or to punish her. She wasn't a pile of metal chips to be pushed into shape by whoever offered her the warmest bed. If she had to listen to a few Jesus lectures to preserve that much of herself, she would do it. Tomorrow she could decide where to go. With the exception of Tijuana, Prairie du Chien, and Key West, the world was hers to discover and explore.

• • •

The garbage bag, with the camping stove, shower, and coffee pot, felt heavier than before, due, perhaps, to the winter clothes she had kept. She debated taking the white dress, but finally, liking the statement it made, laid it out just so on Phil's bed, to look as if it were sleeping. She wrote, "Honor truth above friends," and tucked it in the bodice.

Making two trips, she lugged her garbage bag and then her backpack downstairs. She found a stack of old newspapers in the kitchen and took them to the back of the house, where her harmonica lay silent under a clear tarp. Sadly, she began to empty, dry and wrap each glass. It was getting dark and she had to work fast, in case the Hummers—that was their name—had a closing time. She also didn't want to see Phil, if he came home early.

Finishing the glasses, she felt winded, so she went inside and, without warning, retched what little she had in her stomach. She couldn't let the Hummers and their Lilies of the Field Transitional Living Center see her like this, so she reached into the pocket of her patchwork blue jeans skirt and, with the kind of discipline Phil claimed to be proud of, took a single yellow pill, her first of the day, just to take the edge off.

Outside Leo's, the neighborhood bar and hangout, she dried her face on the sleeve of the man's shirt she wore over a tee and shoved her face between the pocked metal sides of the phone booth. What would she do if Phil saw her and left a fresh rack on the pool table, dropping on his knees at her feet and begging her—really begging her—to stay? The thought replenished her tears. She didn't want to go to the Hummers in this condition. She broke another yellow pill in half.

• • •

Cheryl pulled up outside Leo's in a white van with large, iridescent pink, orange and lime green daisies on its side and rear panels. It almost looked like a tub-and-tile van, with the legend "Lilies of the Field" appearing in miniscule type on the front doors. Nevaeh was comforted that no one inside Leo's would probably give it a second thought.

"I remember you!" Cheryl squealed as she got out of the van. "That hair!" Nevaeh held out her hand and introduced herself again as Jane, not sure if "that hair" was a good or a bad thing. For a sad moment she was almost grateful that if Cheryl was so bold as to touch it, she wouldn't find Tara nestled there. "Too much vanity for you and too much temptation for the street. Tomorrow, first thing, we ought to trim it up for you." Nevaeh gasped, but Cheryl bustled her way to the back of the van, where she opened the rear panel doors and started praying.

"Oh, Lord, help us," she exclaimed, slapping her hand over her heart when Nevaeh bent over to lift her harmonica box from the bottom. "Oh, Lord."

Nevaeh heaved the box into the van, Cheryl stretching her arm to steady the box, as if trying to look helpful without putting forth a lot of effort.

"Thank God you're strong," Cheryl said. "I've had a terrible cross to bear with my back, and I have to be very careful."

"I'm sorry to hear that," Nevaeh said. She put her garbage bag next to the box.

"It's God's will for me," Cheryl said cheerfully. "His way of telling me to slow down, not do so much."

"You must be very busy."

"God only gives us what we can handle," Cheryl said, taking Nevaeh's measure up and down. She should've crashed, just this one night, with one of the street performers.

"His will not mine be done," Cheryl intoned, and slammed the van door shut. At first they drove west from Nevaeh's familiar neighborhood towards downtown, although she soon lost track of where they were relative to Phil's. Panic gripped her as familiar antique shops and restaurants became a mix of dingy houses and used-furniture stores.

It was impossible to exit the moving vehicle, and even if she followed her instincts and threw herself out at the next light, she couldn't leave her harmonica and survival bag behind. Within 10 minutes, they arrived at a three-story brick building that seemed to be on the edge of the central business district, its stucco a flat shade of lemon yellow.

They parked in front of the narrow building and Harold came out to greet them.

"Welcome and God Bless You," he said. He bit his lip when Cheryl opened the van and saw the box and the garbage bag.

"They're not heavy. Only awkward," Nevaeh said. She slid the box out and carried it to the threshold, where Harold caught up with her, fumbling with his keys before unlocking the door to let her in. The door squeaked as she pushed it open. She left the box in the entry hall, and retrieved her backpack and garbage bag on two more trips.

"Dorm's on the third floor," Harold said, pointing up the stairs. "There's a locker there for your things," he added, then looked to Cheryl for help. Nevaeh listened, but didn't hear any sounds—no televisions or radios or conversations coming from the upstairs.

"Well, for now, the box could go just here, in the group room," Cheryl said, pointing to the large, wooden-floored living room on her left, where blue-vinyl couches faced each other in a square. Two of them had wide strips of silver tape across the seats, as if they'd been slit.

"Okay," Nevaeh said. She shouldered her pack, picked up the garbage bag and headed up the stairs. She saw a look pass between the Hummers, and she again felt a twinge in her stomach.

"Is anyone up there now?" Nevaeh asked.

"Oh, yes," Cheryl assured her. "It's mandatory quiet time. Group will be at seven thirty. Put your things away as quietly as you can and then we'll meet down here."

"Okay," Nevaeh said, feeling numb. She didn't know if it was the pill or terror.

"You'll be in the dorm on your left," Cheryl said.

She was on the fourth step when Cheryl called after her. "Oh, I almost forgot. I do need to inspect your things." Nevaeh turned around, startled and insulted. Even if she didn't know their last names, she was sure she could find some street performers back at Jackson Square yet tonight, if she could get there.

"For the safety of the other girls."

Nevaeh smiled weakly. "Of course." What if they wanted a urine sample? Well, she'd give it, Nevaeh thought. She'd be out of this place by the time the lab could analyze it. She trudged down the stairs, sat on the first one and started to undo her pack.

"In here," Cheryl said, and they settled in the living room. "Just a routine precaution."

"I've got nothing to hide," Nevaeh said, carefully laying out her things on the low flat table in the middle of the square of couches, her tee shirts, her journal, a blue plastic coin purse. On the wall to her right was a giant mural of Jesus suffering the little children to come to Him as He read from a book (not a scroll), and the lambs, each leashed to a child's pink hand, were white as snow. The painter had used way too much yellow in an attempt to portray Jesus' halo and its effect on the children, but the result was to render their faces looking bilious.

"A Bible!" Cheryl clutched her heart when Nevaeh placed it next to the rest of her things. Nevaeh hoped that the book would divert Cheryl's attention when she put the can of Five Aces Blend in the back of her pile of possessions.

"You'll need to read the rules, honey," Cheryl said. "No smoking."

"That's cool," she said.

"No drugs."

Nevaeh fingered the pills in her pocket. She had no joints with her. "Just loose tabacky," she grinned, popping the top and holding the can for Cheryl to smell. She recoiled as if from rotten eggs. In a stroke of genius, Nevaeh opened two bottles of vitamins for her keeper's further inspection.

Cheryl patted down the pack, apparently satisfying herself that Nevaeh carried no knives or weapons. "Okey-dokey," she said. "Now, run upstairs and come back in 10 minutes. Don't be late."

Upstairs, in the bunk room to the left, door ajar, four girls lay flat on their bunks, leaving one bed unoccupied. Trying not to disturb them, she rested her backpack against the hallway wall and opened her garbage bag, every crinkle of the heavy plastic sounding louder than a cellophane candy being unwrapped in a silent theatre. The sounds of storing her stove, cook kit and household items away in the narrow metal school locker got louder and louder the harder and harder she tried to do it quietly. She could feel her roommate's eyes upon her, feigning sleep but taking inventory of her possessions. With her own lock and key, she secured the locker, ignoring the used and reused combination lock that had been provided. Christian trust was one thing, foolhardiness another.

"Praise the Lord and pass the ammunition," a harsh voice behind her said, loud enough to wake anyone who was really sleeping.

"The marshall searched me coming in," she said, hoping to sound as tough and experienced as the owner of the voice.

"She doesn't know what to look for," the voice said in a mixture of disdain and tease.

"Hi, I'm Jane Shane," Nevaeh said, glancing around. She'd always liked Tray's approach: Meet the challenge straight up, then deliberately turn your back to let them know you're not afraid. People usually don't attack from behind. The voice came from the lower bunk closest to the lockers, where, in a flowered skirt, blue jean jacket and an unpolished version of black army boots, sat a diminutive girl with short spiky maroon hair and a diamond chip in her left nostril. She appeared to be 15 or 16.

"Watch yourself," the girl said.

"You bet," Nevaeh answered. She didn't want to say more, for fear that would suggest she needed help or friendship.

After a pause, the girl asked, "Where you from?"

"Around," Nevaeh said. It wasn't like her to be so unfriendly, but she needed to be tough. Still with her back to the girl, she walked out to the hall to retrieve her pack. She paused, staring down the stairs, blinked quickly to clear her eyes of threatening tears, and then swallowed the other half of the pill she'd reserved back at Leo's. She turned back to the dorm and allowed herself to look at the girl who'd warned her.

"Where are *you* from?" she offered.

"Around," the girl said, and raised an eyebrow to punctuate her half-smile.

If only she could get through this night, Nevaeh thought, tomorrow she would find a job, a real job and a real place to stay. Cheryl's place was clean enough to greet the Christ himself, and Cheryl was herself a happy person and meant to do good, but the whole thing, the dorm, the artwork, the prescribed schedule, just wasn't her. The words "Transitional Living Center" were kind and inviting, but didn't hide the fact that in other times, Cheryl and Harry would have used "Home for Wayward Girls." Nevaeh was not wayward. She knew her way around. Though she'd been thrown off kilter, she would find her way. She promised herself her life as a lily would be short.

13

Dawn Ann watched the rowers on the Chicago River until they were out of sight. She was finished for the day and by all rights should be rushing home to tell Derek her good news or call her mother, but she couldn't get the right pictures to play in her head. She imagined telling Derek she'd been promoted to the ten o'clock spot, but saw him totally preoccupied with his own concerns, setting up a still life of hammers and screwdrivers, assorted nails and screws, and, lately, melons and bananas, barely responding with a "hmm" while readjusting his lights. Her mother, of course, could no longer comprehend or appreciate her success.

The sculls reappeared, having reversed someplace down river. One shell was several boat lengths ahead of the other. The water was dark like rolled steel and the day encased by a dreary, gray low ceiling and she felt as if she were sitting in a damp cave, the buildings stretching up like stalagmites, the clouds like overhead rocks. The dampness seeped into her body, blurring the lines between it and the moisture of the air. If this were a cave, she would chisel her way out, hammering the rock to dust until she could break through. She needed blue sky, dry air, crisp distinctions between herself and the rest of the world. She scratched at her office window, her nails sliding like fake diamonds against the solid glass.

She decided she would tell Derek not of a promotion but of a change in her schedule. She would have no expectations. If he wanted to recognize the change as a promotion, he would. If he preferred to see it as simply a change in schedule, then so be it. This was *her* success. She wasn't going to let anyone ruin it for her, not even her husband.

"So we'll have weekends, again, but I lose you for five nights a week," Derek said that evening over his favorite carry-out ribs she'd picked up on the way home.

"But, I can sleep in!" she said, as if that were the most significant thing. "I figure I'll work, say, 3:00 to 11:00."

"Phew!" That was as close as he came to sympathy. "When will we have dinner?"

"Like seniors," she said. "We'll have our 'big meal' at noon. It's healthier."

He laughed, and she was relieved, but found herself unable to relax, as if at any moment the full import of her success would hit him and ricochet off him with the force of a rock off a slingshot. They made love that night, with enthusiasm and energy, and it was like in Madison, when she was working towards early success and he was being supportive. They'd been a team, then; she the player, he the coach, and he'd watched her rehearse and praised her strengths, without taking any of the credit for her success, staying on the sidelines, cheering, letting her become a star in her own right, as her own person. Since coming to Chicago, though, he'd backed off entirely and, far from relishing her success, now ignored her career the way he ignored ice-dancing, sumo wrestling, and synchronized swimming.

• • •

Derek started drinking before noon on the day of her first regular prime-time assignment.

"Bloody Mary?" he asked, although she never drank before a broadcast, even if it were five or six hours before she would be on air.

"Der-ek!" she said. Still in her plush white terry robe, she'd come into the kitchen for a refill of coffee.

"Don't want to drink alone," he said, pouring an extra shot of vodka into a tumbler. "You won't be here for happy hour, will you? Now that you're Miss Prime Time!"

She shrugged. "It *is* a big deal," she said in self defense. "In fact," she made a quick decision, "I'm going in early today. To go over some things."

"What am *I* supposed to do?" he said.

"Today?" she asked. When he didn't answer, she pitched her voice to sound like a kindly school teacher, giving the most obvious of orders, time to stand in line, hold hands, go outside. "You are supposed to play with me during the day and work in the darkroom

3:00 to 11:00. It's perfect, when you think about it. We both get to enjoy the sun while it's out, and then when it's dark, in the winter, especially, we work. The best of both worlds."

"I'll never get anything done," he said in disgust.

"But it won't be my fault," she said, "'because I'll be out of your way." She meant it as a playful, almost sexual tease, but as soon as she said it she stepped backwards.

"You self-righteous bitch!" he spat, and threw his drink at her, bloodying the front of her fresh white robe.

"Dammit, Derek! I didn't mean anything!" She stood rigid, her face flushing, splotching red.

"Dammit yourself."

"Screw you, Derek. I didn't!"

"Hell you didn't. 'Not my fault,'" he mimicked. "Then whose fault is it?"

She swallowed hard. He was like a towering storm cloud, a super cell of anger that could uproot her at any moment. She hadn't meant to provoke him, honestly, she hadn't, but to say anything more in self-defense was to risk making it worse.

She put her coffee mug down on the counter as gently as she could. Her right hand was shaking, but she didn't want him to notice. "I'm sorry," she said, and backed out of the kitchen. In her room she threw on jeans and a light sweater, grabbed the oversized handbag that held her make-up and took her on-camera outfit from the closet. She held her breath, unsure if she heard Derek following her or not. All was quiet, but she braced herself for a possible eruption.

She knew that her success was hard on him, but he'd entertain neither consolation ("The art market's lousy right now") nor encouragement ("You have to keep trying, we know you'll make it") nor favor ("Linda knows someone who is starting a gallery over in River West") nor plain old commercial work ("The theatre on Halsted needs publicity stills.") It was impossible to help someone who wouldn't help himself, so what was she supposed to do?

She knew her success only made him mean and reckless, like a frustrated two-year-old who couldn't get his own way. Did he want her to choose? Her success or his ... his what? There *wasn't* a choice here between her success and his. He hadn't had any, and it wasn't, she repeated to herself, her fault. It wasn't. Still, she shouldn't have said anything about his productivity. Art was not like weather; it didn't just happen. That's what Derek always said. If she loved him, she would understand that.

She poked her head in the kitchen, where Derek was at the table with what looked to be a fresh drink and the newspaper. Attempting conciliation, she said, "I'm off, honey. Wish me luck."

He didn't look up. "Yeah."

"Okay then," she said, as brightly as she could muster. "See you later."

In fact, she'd told Derek a little white lie. "Going in early" today meant going first for a facial and manicure. When she got to the salon, though, what she really needed was a massage. Luckily, Mike could fit her in. Working his hands into her back with aromatic oils that evoked a cool pine forest, he kept instructing her to relax. "Your muscles are like stones," he said. "Are you nervous about tonight?"

"No, Mike, really I'm not. I'm doing the same thing I always do, just at a different time." Precisely. So who was overreacting here, her or Derek?

"But you are so tight, so tense! What has you in such knots?"

"I'm okay," she insisted.

"I didn't mean to pry," he said, although she was certain that he did. Wouldn't that be a story for the gossip columns, that the rising star at Channel Three was a basket of nerves!

"Really, Dawn Ann, honey, you've got to relax," Mike said, warming more oil between his palms. He gripped her shoulders firmly and apologized when she jolted. "Are my hands cold?" he asked.

"No," she murmured. "They're fine." But they were large hands, a man's hands, and she felt small and vulnerable beneath them.

By the time she got to the station, she felt as good as could be expected. The woman in make-up was most solicitous, and the weather for the middle of April as predictably changeable as ever. You've gotta love a city, she thought, that snows on its daffodils and jumps from 30 degrees one morning to 70 the next afternoon, like a giant mood swing. Like Derek. Most of the time he loved her, he did, and she loved him. Most of the time.

She turned her attention to the last details of her charts and the latest weather updates, then took her seat on the far end of the anchor desk for *The Ten o'clock News with Felicity O'Neal and Alberto Beltran*. For the majority of the broadcast the camera was tight on those two, but at the promos for the weather or sports, the camera pulled out for a long shot of the four of them, including Ed Hayes, the substitute sportscaster. That spot was up for grabs, the regular having jumped ship for the chance to do more play-by-play at ESPN.

Spring in Chicago was always fitful and April, she reminded her viewers, was the "cruelest month." She wondered how many of her audience would even catch the reference to T.S. Eliot's "Wasteland." Last week, when she'd used Emily Dickinson, "A little Madness in the Spring/Is wholesome even for the King," she'd received a dozen e-mails telling her what a wonderful way she had with words. For her debut as the new permanent ten o'clock weather person, she had rain to predict, and cold, icy rain at that. She refrained from chirping about the good that Eliot's April showers could do, breeding lilacs and all, but delivered her bad news in a no-nonsense fashion followed by "The Elements." She had no hope that the computer model was wrong—Bernard, her cat, was on a tear at his birch log scratching post, so rain was definitely on the way.

On her way home from the broadcast, she had no great expectations about Derek surprising her in any joyful or conciliatory way. He hadn't done anything for her first broadcast in Chicago and he wouldn't think to do it for this one either. It was a little disappointing, but she could understand. She knew that the achievement of any goal involved some measure of disappointment, a little of the baleful refrain, "Is that all there is?" This was her goal, achieved, and this was her disappointment. A husband might be expected to temper failure; what was his proper response to success? To say it didn't matter? To say, like her mother would've, "Do more?" To rob the giddiness of the moment by warning of the hangover to come?

"I would've loved you anyway," seemed as good a response as any and Derek, before the jealousy kicked in, had convinced her of that the way no one else in her life ever had—certainly not her ambitious mother and not her father, who often said there was only one star in the family—his renowned wife. But that night, as she turned the key in her door, she hoped without words that her husband had passed out cold. She felt ambushed by her own success. Sometimes she felt like the best days of their relationship were gone forever. If Derek didn't sell a photograph soon, or get some kind of professional recognition, they may never recapture those early days when even cruel months like April had seemed full of promise and possibility.

If their best days were all in the past, Derek apparently didn't notice; in fact, he gave her intermittent hope, sprinkled like spring rain. As she grew into her prime time spot, she spent less time at the station, regularizing her hours to what she'd initially promised, 3:00 to 11:00. Sometimes, Derek would be in the darkroom when she got home, sometimes he'd be passed out on the living room couch, and sometimes he'd wake before her, coffee in hand, playfully stripping the bed covers off and urging her to get up and go for a run with him. Some days she'd come home to a bunch of tulips in a vase on the vanity in her bathroom. Other times, his dirty laundry would be piled in the middle of the kitchen floor, waiting for her to put it in the washing machine. Some days, if she was feeling lovey-dovey and made an advance, he'd sweep her off her feet and they'd make love with all the passion of their first months together. Alternatively, he might push her away with a snarl. He was, like a flash flood or microburst or spring itself, totally unpredictable.

The randomness of his behavior made her crazy, but it inspired her, made her feel she could salvage her marriage. She felt certain that there was a pattern to Derek's actions, only she hadn't yet discerned it. She reciprocated his kindnesses with her own: his favorite sushi, a massage, free tickets to concerts and sporting events, even if she couldn't go with him. From day to day, she accepted his rages as somehow deserved and his love as earned, and she threw her best efforts into forecasting his moods, pleasing him or avoiding him, giving him his artistic space, tiptoeing around him, coddling him, receiving his passions, making his cruel world as perfect as she could.

14

Nevaeh lay on her bunk at Lilies of the Field for a few minutes, just to test it. It reminded her of college. No better, no worse. It was as if none of these people, neither university administrators nor operators of homeless shelters, appreciated the therapeutic value of a good night's sleep. Even though she'd gone to a good mid-western university with a huge endowment, the joke had been that the rats in the psych lab had better sleeping conditions than the students. At the thought of Tara, she closed her eyes in a little prayer. It would've been hard on Tara to be homeless, and for the first time in her life, Nevaeh herself felt homeless. She set her jaw and fought back a sob.

Just before seven thirty, she joined the parade down the stairs to the house meeting. Including her, there were 11 girls in all, ranging in age from the girl in army boots, who looked to be 15, up to 28, all without make-up, most sporting shoulder-length or shorter hair, the older women dressed alike, in chinos with permanent-press, long-sleeved shirts that had lost some of their press but appeared clean. Three or four bulged. Two stared at the floor, sullen; a couple cowered meekly, like injured baby animals. Only one or two smiled at her, but without curiosity.

Cheryl opened the meeting ritualistically, "A moment of silence, girls, for all of the lilies of the field," and then read from the gospel—Luke 12:22—and instructed them to bow their heads again in silent prayer.

"Girls, we have a newcomer tonight," she bubbled. "Nevaeh?"

"Hi," Nevaeh said.

"And?" Cheryl prompted her.

"And, uh, hi!" she said.

"You're here to ask for help, right, Nevaeh?" Cheryl asked, as if Nevaeh should have intuited somehow that this was what was expected of her. "Tell them how we met at the bus station months ago."

"Cheryl met me at the bus station when I arrived last fall," Nevaeh said, looking around at the other girls, none of whom seemed particularly interested.

"You never know when your good works will come back to you, girls, if you cast your bread upon the waters, Song of Solomon, 11:1," Cheryl concluded, then gave a "house report," including the schedule of service projects for the next few days—serving soup at a homeless shelter, environmental "monitoring" (picking up litter) at a local park, polishing pews at Cheryl's and Harold's church.

The rest of the meeting was devoted to "check-ins." Each girl was to say something good about herself (an "affirmation"), something she'd done that day to improve herself (an "act of hope"), and some sin she'd committed that day (a "confession"), for which she was to ask forgiveness, which seemed to be Cheryl's to dispense. The girl who'd challenged Nevaeh in the dorm room went first, reporting that she'd been friendly and welcomed the new girl, whose name she'd forgotten, that she'd done two hours of school work assigned by Mrs. H., peeled potatoes for dinner, and that she'd had impure thoughts about sucking her boyfriend's—. Cheryl abruptly raised her hand and admonished the group that describing evil and filthy acts, even when asking the Lord for forgiveness, was itself evil and filthy and offensive to the Lord and a defilement of the tabernacle, and if she persisted in having such filthy thoughts, words and deeds the Lord would vomit her out, Leviticus 18:25. During this tirade, the girl dipped her chin but stared unflinchingly at Cheryl, who began to squirm.

Although Nevaeh felt the need to be on guard against any brainwashing, the dynamics of the meeting made for fairly entertaining theatre and she readily imagined what she might say when it was her turn. She'd given a dress away to the needy, obviously had done something to improve herself just by calling Lilies of the Field, and her sin was ... what? Sleeping until noon with a drug and alcohol hangover? Skipping work? The extra twenty-five dollars she'd lifted from Phil's house money jar? If she said she'd stolen from the beer and drug money, that would put Cheryl in a bind, wouldn't it?

But Cheryl didn't call on her. Instead, they read from the Bible about investing one's talents, Luke 19:11–21, and then she asked Nevaeh if tomorrow she would tell the girls her story.

"Like a lead at an AA meeting?" Nevaeh asked.

"I've not been to an AA meeting," Cheryl said, sounding insulted. "But I understand they do something like that. A confession."

"I went to a couple when I was a kid," she said, and Cheryl gasped. "You poor child!" she said.

"When I was 10," Nevaeh explained, "my mother went for a week."

Cheryl peeped, "Oh!" and sighed in apparent relief that it was the mother, not the daughter, who was the alcoholic. This surprised Nevaeh, who'd always heard that growing up with an alcoholic could screw you up as much as being one, and had hoped her revelation would squeeze some sympathy out of Cheryl.

Nevaeh remembered that stories she'd heard at AA had been funny; at least, the people there had laughed. Some had cried. What she remembered most was that people kept telling her mother that AA had no rules, only suggestions, but her mother wouldn't listen. By any name, she'd hated rules, especially the most important one, "Don't drink."

Still, Nevaeh felt her experience of the world and of meetings gave her an edge on Cheryl, who disapproved, with equal vigor, of sex, beer, marijuana, cigarettes, swearing, dating boys, R-rated movies, talking loudly, being late and not clearing your plate at dinner. Nevaeh had read the rules posted in the dorm. Cheryl wasn't a leader, like the ones at AA meetings, who'd risen from the ashes to share their personal experiences, strength and hope with others; apparently, Cheryl felt herself assigned by direct message from God to impose her peculiar brand of help on these homeless weeds of women. How could someone who'd never lived on the streets tell someone else how *not* to?

"Sure, I can tell my story," Nevaeh said. "Happy to." She was happy to agree. It occurred to her that she probably wouldn't be there to follow through.

• • •

None of the girls seemed particularly eager to talk to Nevaeh and she was too tired to reach out to them. She fled upstairs, and since no one was in line for the two stalls, took a long and steamy shower, her hair tied on top of her head with a long scarf.

After her shower, Nevaeh dressed in underwear and a tee shirt and tucked her backpack under the covers of the bunk, against the wall, putting her arms around it, reminding her of Tray. After Key West, she slept on her back, side by side with Phil, but she and Tray had spooned, and the feel of the backpack in her arms was familiar, comfortable, bittersweet. She didn't care what it looked like to the girl in army boots, she had to protect her pack. Besides, she didn't want to risk making too much noise later, opening her locker to make her escape. Wake up call would be at seven, but she'd be gone long before that. She stared at the slats of the top bunk, then closed her eyes to avoid conversation as the girls straggled in.

"She won't be here long," she heard one girl say.

"Cheryl'll be after her with a chainsaw," another said.

Nevaeh bit her lip. It was seven hours until 4:30 a.m. She closed her eyes and thought "four thirty, four thirty" over and over, programming her inner alarm clock.

When she awoke, it took a minute to get her bearings. A nightlight glowed at the baseboard in the middle of the room, and there was a clock on the wall. She sat up on her bunk and froze, letting the squeak settle. None of her dorm mates stirred. She stood and took a step towards the clock. It was 4:15. She took a step back, retrieved her pack and in three giant steps made it to the hallway. She took her skirt from the top of the pack, pulled it on and let her eyes adjust. She resented that she would have to leave her household possessions behind, but it would make way too much of a commotion to open the locker and repack the garbage bag. Maybe she could come back for them. Or not. It didn't matter. They could be her donation to the other lilies.

Slowly, she made her way downstairs, the building full of little popping noises, water clanging in the pipes, refrigerators humming in the kitchen, wood swelling or contracting. In the group room, she found her box of glasses, unmoved, and smiled to herself. She unlocked the door, turned the handle, put the box on the front stoop, and closed the door behind her.

She grabbed one quick breath, darted down the stairs and then lifted her box. Neither left nor right looked familiar, but she thought left perhaps had a bit more of the city's loom to it. Sooner or later, she would have to find a major street so that a bus driver could point her in the right direction. Towards wherever she was going.

Whenever she found herself on the early side of a new day, either the long way (being up all night) or the short way (waking up early), she was surprised by how relatively noisy a city, as opposed to her tree house in the country, could be. She heard the whir of air conditioners kicking in and turning off, cats screeching in heat, the rattle of trash pails near bars closing late or restaurants opening early. There might not be many people out and about, but the ones who were, towered, as if expanding to fill the available space. Although there would be less traffic, she expected there would be garbage trucks clearing away the previous day and delivery trucks greeting the new one with the morning's bagels and news. Here—wherever she was right now on the edge of the business district—not even that much was going on. There was a newspaper box on the corner, but it was still empty.

She heard a muted noise, like rubber soles on cement. A dog? It wasn't close; perhaps across the street. She quickened her step. Several blocks ahead there was a street light, a beacon of hope that she was near a major thoroughfare. She didn't feel unsafe, exactly—Cheryl and Harold Hummer weren't the type to put the girls, or more importantly, themselves, in an unsafe neighborhood—but she was alone, and if she'd learned anything from her time in Key West, it was that you were never safe. No matter what.

On the next block, she passed plate glass windows protected by chain links or wrought iron bars, a trophy shop, a money exchange, a legal aid office. Clenching her teeth, she thought she saw a white curtain streaming from a window like a ghost. Next door, a pink-shuttered coffee shop was locked up tight. At the corner, under the street lamp, the green street sign was inexplicably crushed in on itself, but there appeared to be a bus stop at the next corner to her left. She couldn't see a bus coming, but on her right, she heard an eerie humming. She whipped her head around and her heart froze. Crossing the intersection, coming towards her, was a tall and muscular man, holding a white dress. It took a full, terrifying second for her to recognize the tuft of white on the man's head, the stripe of a skunk.

"You forgot your dress." Phil held out her white concert dress with one hand and a long-stemmed red rose with the other.

She didn't reach for either. Her emotions rolled somersaults. Here was the scene she'd wanted with Tray, but he'd never chased her down. But here was Phil, and she realized she was surprisingly joyous. She felt herself saved.

"You forgot you loved me," she said.

He lowered his arms, the skirt of the dress gathering on the sidewalk.

"No, I didn't. I just didn't want to talk about it then."

"What *it*?"

"You and pills."

"You gave them to me. I took too many, by mistake. Can't you give me a break?"

"I don't know. I over-reacted. I'm sorry." He held out the flower. "Will you forgive me? Can we start over?"

"No," she said. "We can't start over. Everybody knows you can't start over, like nothing ever happened. Stuff has happened!" She took the rose in one hand and held out the other for the dress. She waited while his face contorted in disappointment. "But we can start again."

He bowed the princely way he'd bowed the day they'd first met. "Semantics," he said, and held out his arms for a hug. She took a step in his direction and started to weep. "Perfect pitch," she said, and accepted his hug. They stood like that, huddled together, for what seemed like at least five whole minutes. Then, holding hands, they waited five more for a bus to arrive. The driver looked at them suspiciously as he opened the door, apparently not used to riders at this hour.

"How did you know where to find me?" she asked when they were seated, at the very back of the bus.

"That's where they all go."

"Who, 'all'?"

He put his arm around her so she couldn't get away. "All the wayward girls," he said, and kissed her.

• • •

For the next few weeks, Nevaeh started her day with a salute to the sun and a yellow pill, and Phil and she made love in the morning and again at night. Things were a little slow in the Quarter right after Mardi Gras, but then spring breaks and Jazz Fest followed and finally May, one of the sweetest months in the city. A few more acts bloomed on the streets. Skinny and Toby recorded half of their CD in a week. Phil got Nevaeh her own harmonica cart. Then, he led a two-day spring cleaning at the house. He was in a wonderfully expansive and generous mood. Nevaeh was feeling better and better, half a yellow pill in the morning and half at night, and all seemed delightfully right with the world. Phil's rejuvenated charisma drew new people to the house, as did a weekend post-clean-up celebratory bacchanalia that defeated the initial purpose of the evening. He spent much of his free time helping the new ones get settled in the city, which always meant feeding them, and often meant letting them sleep on the floor in the living room until something better came along. He was, in every way possible, as generous as the Hummers, but without their rules or Christian rap.

One day, in a new location in front of St. Louis Cathedral, their backs to the wrought iron fencing around Jackson Square, they were playing "Greensleeves" on their harmonicas, an enchanted cacophony, when Phil missed a note, then suddenly fell behind the beat. Nevaeh looked at him and saw that he was playing, but was obviously distracted. She smiled at her side of the crescent crowd that had gathered around them and then turned back to Phil. His head was turned away from hers and his hands had stopped moving. A tall thin woman with long black hair as straight and coarse as a horse's tail stood a yard away from the crowd, her huge dark eyes locked on Phil. She wore a white sleeveless blouse carelessly unbuttoned to reveal the top of a pink lacy bra pushing her substantial breasts up and together and towards her obvious target. Her cut-offs revealed nearly all of her thigh; her brown legs were long and slender. The shorts were slung low, beneath her belly button, and their top button flapped open suggestively. In profile, she was breathlessly exotic, Nevaeh thought, a page out of a glossy men's magazine, but she wore four-inch black patent leather stiletto heels that made her look like a hooker.

Phil backed away from his harmonica glasses and walked over to the black-haired girl—Nevaeh guessed she couldn't be more than 25. She bent her head to her music, certain that looks—his, hers, the whole scene—were deceptive. She finished with a flourish, and graciously accepted the applause with a little curtsey. She smiled routinely, hawked Phil's CD, answered a few questions—from Chicago, self-taught, nothing particularly special about the glasses—then made change and thanked her audience again, keeping her peripheral vision trained on Phil.

Phil and the woman turned away and Nevaeh saw what might be the source of Phil's interest. Just like Phil, she had a white streak of hair all the way down the left side of her otherwise perfect black mane. That could not be coincidence. Were they related? He'd never mentioned a sister. But it could be. The same hair. The obvious familiarity.

If it was his sister, Nevaeh wanted to be introduced, but the pair disappeared through the gates into the square, and she couldn't very well chase them down, without looking jealous or suspicious. They'd probably want some time alone together; there was obviously something important going on. He'd introduce them later, at the house.

There was nothing to do but press on, and she did, number after number, lost in her music, until she realized it was after four thirty and time to wrap it up for the day. Phil had been gone more than an hour. She'd made 50 bucks. By herself. Without him.

She began to tidy up her cart, leaving the water in the glasses but tossing the bowl of tuning water on a planter at the corner as they always did. She did the same for Phil's instrument, securing it for the push home. By five, she was ready to go, but Phil hadn't returned. It didn't seem like the biggest risk in the world to leave his instrument unattended for 40 minutes, while she pushed hers home, and then came back and got his. She could ask someone to keep an eye on it. Or she could take his home, and leave hers at risk. A glass harmonica didn't have a lot of value to a person who didn't play it, but for someone who had nothing, it might have "reward" value. Then again, there could be a few jealous types who wouldn't mind inconveniencing Phillipé just the slightest bit. She was just debating what to do when Skinny and Toby came by, guitar cases, washboards and tin whistle in hand.

Of course they asked where Phil was, and when she told them, Skinny counted to six on her fingers, put down her guitar case and hugged her. "Oh, honey," she said. "I know how you must feel. But it will be okay." Nevaeh was afraid she'd left the wrong impression, and she peeled herself away. "I'm okay. It was just a girl, like his sister, or an old friend or something."

Toby, searching frantically for a cigarette, found one and lit it and after a stern look from Skinny, offered them each one as well. "Tell her," he said to Skinny.

Skinny put her arm around Nevaeh and guided her to the cathedral steps. The three of them sat on the top one, where Nevaeh had a view of the green canopy of the square but couldn't see Phil, if he were still there. She couldn't imagine what could be so serious that Skinny couldn't just say it.

"You'll get over it," Skinny said. "They all do." She took a deep breath. "Look, honey, I know you love Phil. Everyone does. I do," Skinny continued. "He's just a terrific human being and he's saved so many people, been so helpful and generous and good and kind, but ... but ... he ..." She signed and tried again. "He ..."

"Can't save himself," Toby finally finished her thought.

Skinny took a deep breath, and her undershirt stretched against her breasts, revealing more cleavage. "What's gonna happen now," Skinny said, "is that he's gonna go off with her for at least a week, to give you time to clear out. He'll probably find Toby later and give him some money to give to you, and maybe a little note or whatever."

Nevaeh smoked her cigarette in long, pensive drags, trying to piece together the precise meaning of what Skinny was saying. Her heart was racing, and she flicked her ash repeatedly to try to conceal the slight tremor in her hand.

"This has happened before?"

"He tries to shake Ophelia, but he can't. This has been going on for eight years."

"Man, he's one crazy dude," Toby said.

Skinny bobbled her head in agreement. "The first two times, he went after her. Okay, fair enough. The last three, she's just shown up, after three months and reclaimed him. Now, this time, she's been gone," she counted on her fingers again, "six months, and Phil had met you, and everyone thought you were it and he was finally over that bitch and…"

"Maybe that's what he's telling her right now!" Nevaeh insisted.

Toby punched his right index finger through a circle made from his left thumb and left index finger, probably intended for Skinny's eyes only, but Nevaeh was on full alert, and she understood his crude reference to sex. She felt her own desire for Phil kindle a warmth between her legs. She loved him. She didn't want to give up on him, but she wasn't going to share him, either. She glanced over at a glassed-in case on the outside of the cathedral and read the title of the coming sermon, "He Was Lost, and Is Found, by Reverend J. Huston Prieur, (Luke 15:22–24)."

"Prodigal pussy," Skinny said.

"I hate that word," Nevaeh said reflexively, and felt her desire for Phil drain sadly, reluctantly away. She didn't want to believe she'd again been left by a man, or that—shame on her—Phil had led her on for months, all the time knowing that he couldn't kick his addiction to Ophelia. He'd conned her into almost forgetting Tray, into thinking that their whirlwind romance was not, as she'd imagined, the passion of two kindred spirits blending their music and their souls. No, she thought bitterly, it had been hormones and convenience.

Sure, she'd gotten something out of the relationship, beyond a place to stay, just as with Tray she'd learned a bit about resourcefulness. Phil had taught her about street performance. She'd arrived with 25 glasses and he'd taught her the 37 note glass harmonica. Plus, she was a better survivor today than before. Still, in an odd way, his leaving her was more of a shock than Tray's. Tray was always spontaneous and on the move; Phil was seemingly settled in his house and his role and his routine.

She tossed back her hair and looked Skinny in the eye. "Thanks for telling me straight up," she said. "You know, I'm a sucker for BS." She nodded towards the street. "Can you help me take the carts back?"

Toby jumped to his feet and piled his guitar cases on top of Phil's cart. Skinny took Nevaeh's, as if she were a widow and her cart the coffin, and the three of them walked home in silence, Nevaeh grateful for the stash of pills that would get her through yet another betrayal.

Just as Skinny had predicted, Phil did not come home that night. Nevaeh didn't care. She took a couple of pills before dinner and was ravenously hungry for the spaghetti and meat sauce Skinny threw together at the last minute. With Phil not there to organize, to cook, or to preside over the operation, Skinny rose magnificently to the occasion, the huckster turned earth-mother.

Spaghetti was Nevaeh's favorite comfort food, and she was in just enough of a fog to be totally preoccupied by the game of twirling her fork enough times to get the plump linguini to her mouth. A half-gallon jug of red wine went around and around the table—there were 10 or 12 there that night—and she drank it like water. No one spoke of Phil. Skinny must've told them, because everyone was being oh, so nice, to Nevaeh, who was oh, so sleepy.

She didn't help with the dishes, but dragged herself to the living room, where Skinny and Toby jammed for a while. Nevaeh quickly fell asleep on the prized old leather recliner that the others had left for her.

She woke up mid-morning, hung over, alone in Phil's bed, miserable. She was still in her clothes from the night before, a full-length flowered skirt from the Goodwill and a tee shirt, and had no idea how she'd gotten upstairs. She lay there, crying for she didn't know how long. Phil was gone for good, and it was up to her to be gone, too, but she couldn't begin to figure out how. Phil owned the Quarter. If she wanted to perform, she'd have to see him, become his ex-girlfriend friend, the one who was dumped, not the one who'd dumped him. Phil might start over and over and over with Ophelia, but she would have to start her new life in New Orleans again. Perhaps because of her night at Cheryl's, she wasn't sure she was up to it.

15

Skinny's big green eyes bulged as she hung over the side of the bed while Nevaeh slowly came to in a daisy-yellow room she didn't recognize. Skinny's voice sounded far, far away, as if from across Farmer Jones's field.

"Wakey, wakey," Skinny whispered.

"Where am I?" Nevaeh asked.

"Charity Hospital," Skinny answered, not waiting for the entire question. "You've been asleep for—how long, Toby, would you say? Uh, two days."

Nevaeh licked her lips and started to lift her head, but Skinny gently held her back. "What am I doing here?" Nevaeh croaked.

"Drying out," Toby said, although his voice came from a corner of the room Nevaeh couldn't see.

"It's a long story, honey," Skinny said.

"Tell me," Nevaeh asked. She grasped at the blanket as if to ground herself, and studied Skinny's eyes. She saw herself reflected in Skinny's pupils, her head against a white pillow, her hair kinky and caught up in an elastic band on top of her head.

"I'm so, so sorry," Skinny said, over and over, but it was unclear to Nevaeh what Skinny was sorry about.

"Just tell her," Toby said, sounding nervous and impatient. Gently, and without recrimination, Skinny then told Nevaeh what Nevaeh herself could not exactly remember: that she'd stayed in bed at Phil's house for a week, feeling miserable. After the first day, the yellow pills had stopped working. She took more, and learned that if she chewed them, she'd get faster relief. She'd asked Serena for more, which she'd provided, but by the end of the week, when Nevaeh asked yet again for more, Serena said she should be more efficient with the ones she had and showed her how to crush a pill and snort it. Nevaeh had snorted and then come down to the group dinner where she drank red wine and picked at her food.

"You weren't breathing," Skinny said. It was risky, Skinny said, because Phil didn't like to draw attention to the house, but Phil hadn't returned home yet. Skinny'd called the Fire Department, and two paramedics rushed Nevaeh to the hospital. Listening to Skinny's apology, Nevaeh imagined their faces, pupils wide, beads of sweat at their hairlines, lips sealed with fear and disgust, assuming she was a degenerate drug addict.

"We shouted fire!" Nevaeh heard Toby chuckle, but didn't understand the humor.

"The bad news is," Skinny whispered, "they're gonna keep you here for a while."

"I don't have insurance."

"It's a public hospital. I think they have to take you."

"I don't want to be here," she said, sitting up, aware for the first time of the soft restraints, the bars on the side of the bed, the IV drip in her right hand and a clear bag hanging on a pole. "I want out. I want to go home."

Skinny looked at Toby, and straightened. She put her hand on Nevaeh's left hand.

"Phil came back," she said. At the mention of Phil's name, Nevaeh's legs jumped off the bed, startling Skinny, whose eyes widened as if she'd seen the devil himself.

"Kicking the habit," Toby said. "It's part of withdrawal."

Nevaeh closed her eyes and sank back on the pillow, studying the acoustic tiles in the ceiling.

"How would you know?" Skinny turned to him, but Toby shrugged. Immediately Nevaeh craved every comfort her body had become accustomed to: alcohol, tobacco, oxy. She felt ice cold, as if back in Iowa, the gooseflesh raising the fine hairs on her forearm like frost on the fresh wood of her tree house.

Skinny stroked Nevaeh's hand. "The point is, honey, that this might be a good for you until we can find someplace else for you to go."

"It's only good if you want to go straight," Toby said. "It's a total clean-out. NA, AA, the works."

Skinny shot him a look. "So, when you get out, you'll be back to normal, you know. You could still drink and everything, you just wouldn't overdo." Skinny's voice was reassuring, maternal. "Don't you worry, we'll find you a place and you can still be one of us."

Toby got up to leave. "Oh," he said, but he didn't sound spontaneous. "Phil wanted me to give you this." He handed her a sealed, business-size envelope. Nevaeh took it and held it up to the light, to see if there was any money in it. Satisfied, she had him stick it in her backpack. It didn't matter what words Phil'd written inside; she needed the cash.

The next day a social worker, just about Nevaeh's age, came to her room and told her, with genuine, well-meaning and misplaced excitement, that they'd found a residential program that would take her in for 21 days of intensive treatment. Nevaeh, despite what she'd told Cheryl Hummer, didn't know that much about AA or addiction or treatment, and didn't know what it had to do with her. But she had no other place—no physical place—to go for the next 21 days.

"Free?" she asked.

"Totally," the social worker bubbled. "It's a really fabulous place."

Nevaeh flinched at "fabulous," at this girl in her thin white sweater-set who thought a "place" could be "fabulous," even if it wasn't home, your friends weren't nearby and you were there not because you wanted to be but because you had no place else to go.

"So, do you want to go there and get help for your addiction?" Because the question was combined, Nevaeh mumbled "yes." If, in order to put a roof over her head, she had to admit she was addicted—to what, wine? A little yellow pill she'd only taken for a matter of weeks?—then so be it.

She heard herself say, "hey, sure, it'll be a gas," which reminded her of Tray, but she wasn't Tray, and she found herself afraid of saying anything but "yes" to these people who'd found her a place to stay. "Yes," Nevaeh said.

A woman from the treatment center picked her up that afternoon. Her name was Barbara. She was older than the social worker by 10 or 15 years, sported a broad smile and a confident handshake, and dressed in pressed jeans and a white golf shirt. She had no strained-back issues to complain of or prayers to offer as she easily gathered up Nevaeh's box of glasses and led her to her plain old car, a gray, Buick LeSabre. They drove a little ways out of the city to what looked like a converted roadside motel. There was a low brick wall around the place and a gated driveway.

Barbara pointed to one end of the yellow brick building, "That's the dining area, meeting rooms and meditation center. On the other end we have a little physical fitness area and a community room. We're four to a room in between."

Barbara unloaded Nevaeh's things into a room labeled "14" (all the rooms were even, no odd numbers, apparently for the purpose of avoiding unlucky 13) and introduced her to two young women who were lying on their bunks and reading. Vicky'd been there 10 days, Ellen 14.

Vicky was black, dreadlocked, almond-eyed, elegant and gaunt. Ellen was husky, like a girl who'd thrown shot put in college, and had tattoos up and down her left arm, green and pink bouquets on sharp black stems. They both sat up, Vicky barely making eye contact, Ellen staring straight at her. To Nevaeh they both seemed fragile, soft, vulnerable. She knew exactly how they felt.

There was a meal at five and a community meeting, and then the counselors left and a few alkies and drug addicts from the city appeared and Nevaeh found herself in one of those meetings where she was supposed to say she was an alcoholic but she didn't think, honestly, that she was, so she just said her name. She held her chin up and one of the women said, "Welcome," and since they thought this was her first meeting ever in life, they went around in a circle and all 16 people told a little bit about how they came to be there. Towards the end, Vicky talked, as honestly as Nevaeh had ever heard anyone talk, about the pain and pleasure of shooting heroin and turning tricks and getting beat up by her pimp and thinking it was her fault and how she was only clean this time for 10 days, but now she was willing to do whatever it took, because before when she'd quit for three months, she stopped going to meetings, and four months later, she was back at it, worse than ever. "My disease was doing push-ups," she said, "Just waiting for me."

Nevaeh felt both sleepy and jumpy at the meeting. She didn't like everybody directing their comments to her and telling her that she was the most important person in the room simply because she was the newest. She scratched at the top of her left hand until she dug shallow tracks like chalk marks.

At the end of the meeting, they held hands and said the "Our Father," out loud while Nevaeh mumbled along. Then Vicky gave Nevaeh a coin that said something about "one day at a time" and told her she didn't have to decide that day whether she was an alcoholic or an addict or if she wanted what they had, but that she should just not drink or do drugs for 24 hours and see what happened.

"They make it easy here," Vicky said. "There ain't no booze or drugs." The women laughed knowingly.

Nevaeh smiled weakly, shuffled back to her bed, and slept until mid-morning. She felt physically beaten. During the meetings the following week, they called it "surrender," but Nevaeh was a fighter and a survivor. She'd made it across the country and back, and up and down the Mississippi, and she'd be damned if she'd admit to being beaten by a pill and a jug of wine. The rest of "treatment" blurred. She was given appointments with doctors and nurses and counselors and it took a few days before she told any of them the truth about how much she drank in the Quarter, and a few more days before she mentioned that her mother was an alcoholic. Halfway through, she told a counselor about Key West and then one night she told the group. "A friend of my boyfriend put drugs in my cola and raped me without my knowing it," she said, as evenly as she could manage. She also told them about the pills, and about Phil and Ophelia, and about the note he'd sent that said, "Thanks for the sweet memories. Have a nice life!" but she didn't tell them about his gift of $200, because she was talking to a bunch of addicts and who knew how badly any of them might still need a fix. The residents and the alky visitors smiled sympathetically, laughed at themselves for trusting men, and shook their heads at Serena for getting Nevaeh involved with pills in the first place. They hugged her after each meeting until she'd thought well, maybe she *was* an alcoholic because, with the possible exception of Tray, all these other alcoholics seemed to understand her better than anyone ever had.

On day 17, Barbara asked to meet Nevaeh in her office to talk about "after-care," and how she might manage the first few months on her own.

"You really shouldn't leave here without a plan," Barbara said.

"I thought you all wanted us to stay in the moment," Nevaeh shot back. Since spilling her guts to the group, she'd been feeling pretty good but the thought of leaving treatment shoved her off what the counselors called the "pink cloud." She had no place to go.

"Most people go home to their families," Barbara said.

"Ha!" Nevaeh said. "I haven't lived at home since I was 18."

"We all need to do humbling things in order to stay sober," Barbara said.

"It's not that," Nevaeh said. "But she drinks." There was no way Nevaeh would go home to her mother, and she knew her mother's drinking would convince Barbara that going home wasn't possible.

"Well, you think about it, and I'll see what there might be in the way of half-way houses," Barbara said.

Nevaeh thanked her and left the interview in somewhat of a panic. No way she wanted to go back to Lilies or to any half-way house, but she could see how returning to her crowd in New Orleans, even if she could get over the problem of Phil, would make it difficult for her not to drink. Maybe she could just drink on weekends, although all the alkies who came for meetings every night said that didn't work, and almost all her friends in the Quarter drank at least a little, every day.

That night she had a dream. When she started taking the yellow pills, she'd stopped dreaming entirely. Now, as their residue left her system, her dreams, snippets of them, were returning with a colorful vengeance. That night her dream contained an image of a gingerbread house with thin pastel mint shingles and spearmint leaf jelly evergreens and a pathway of red pinwheel peppermints. A sweet house. Sweet home. Sweet Home Chicago. Who did she know in Chicago? Who did she have for family? She couldn't go home to mother, and it might be embarrassing to have to go to her cousin's, but maybe her aunt?

The next morning, she told Barbara about her aunt in Chicago. Barbara located Aunt Jacqueline's number, and dialed it for Nevaeh.

"Aunt Jacqueline?"

The voice on the other end of the phone sounded ancient. Her aunt was supposed to be some brilliant psychiatrist, but she sounded clueless as to who Nevaeh was.

"Call Dawnie," the old woman said. "On TV."

Nevaeh gave this information to Barbara, who with a few strokes of the computer keyboard quickly located Dawn Ann, was impressed enough by her fame to approve of her as a guardian of Nevaeh's nascent sobriety and listened while Nevaeh made the call.

"Hello," a cheery voice picked up on the second ring.

"May I please speak with Dawnie?" Nevaeh heard the hesitation, as if Dawnie had changed her name, or she wasn't willing to admit who she was. "This is Nevaeh Thera."

"This is Dawn Ann," she replied. She didn't seem particularly pleased. Barbara nodded encouragement and spun her index finger to keep Nevaeh going. "Hi!" Nevaeh said, trying to sound sunny. "Remember me, your cousin? My mother is Star Thera, your mother's sister, which is kind of how you got your name, and your mother is my Aunt Jacqueline," she lowered her voice for the imitation, "—not Jackie," then rose, "from Winnetka?"

"Nevvy?" Dawn asked.

"I'm really, really glad you remember me," Nevaeh said. "How've you been?"

"Fine, Nevvy. Fine! Uh, married, and doing the weather here." She gave her own commercial in an announcer's voice, "'The Elements, Weeknights at Ten with Dawn Ann McKnight.'"

"Way cool! I used to have a boyfriend who wanted to be in TV. He went to law school instead."

"Well, it's a tough business," Dawn Ann said. "And you, where are you?" She sounded curious as to what Nevaeh could possibly want, and Nevaeh took a quick breath in anticipation.

"At the moment, I'm in New Orleans, but they won't let me out, I mean, I'd like to leave, and I'd like to move, like, home, but you know, my mom, she's not well, and I was wondering …"

"What's wrong with your mom?" Dawn Ann said

"Uh, the usual," she said.

"I don't know what you mean, Nevvy," Dawn Ann said.

"Glug, glug."

"Oh," Dawn Ann murmured. "I didn't know."

"Doesn't your mom?" she asked. "You know, that stuff runs in families, I'm told." She laughed a little, and Barbara knit her eyebrows as if to suggest it wasn't a laughing matter.

"My mother is not very well, but it's more of an old age thing."

"Oh. You're lucky, then. Listen, I need to ask a big favor. I came down here to play music and that worked out for a while but now I kind of need to move on, and you know, Chicago is kind of home, and a great town for music, and I wondered if I could stay with you for a few days, just until I get on my feet and get a place of my own."

Without hesitation, Dawn Ann said, "Of course, honey. That would be wonderful!"

Nevaeh exhaled her relief and hung up. Barbara congratulated her on asking for help, and offered her a few extra days at Grace Place. Then she drove Nevaeh to the train station, where they hugged and promised to stay in touch.

On the train, Nevaeh had the seat to herself, almost the entire car to herself. She had 25 glasses, a backpack and $540 that no one knew about. She'd been clean and sober for 30 days and when she wasn't dead tired, she was crawling out of her skin. She started to cry. She remembered Tray and Tara and Key West and Phil, and, dwelling on the goodness of Skinny and Toby, she let herself cry all the way to Hammond, Louisiana. One thing she'd learned in treatment was that she needed to get all that sorrow out so that she could hope to leave it behind.

She was starting another phase of her life, clearing her slate for the next chapter. Tray most likely would not be part of it, and she would have to let that specific hope go, along with Phil and Stu and almost everything before. Her plan was to stay with her cousin for a week or so until she could find a job and a place of her own. The idea of looking for a job in the next week was as far ahead as she'd been allowed to think for a month. In treatment they'd concentrated on the *day*, sometimes the *hour*, as if it were the only one that would ever be—"The only thing we're sure of," Cindi, the curly-haired counselor used to say. Nevaeh couldn't imagine looking for a job; she didn't know what she might be qualified to do, despite her college degree, and there wasn't that much of what people called "work" that she found interesting. She thought maybe she could write, but who would pay her to do that? She had no clips or past experience to show. An office job of some kind? Secretary? Maybe she could fake it. Answering the phone? Boring. Selling clothes? Not her thing. She tried to put those thoughts aside and let the countryside drift by her.

The counselors said not to have any expectations, but as she approached Chicago, Nevaeh felt herself feeling younger and younger, less and less in control of her future, more and more apprehensive. The nine year difference between 23 and 32 was not nearly as great as the nine-year difference between seven and 16, but even six years ago, at Dr. McKnight's funeral, when Nevaeh'd been 17 and Dawn Ann 25 or 26, Dawn Ann had been worldly and elegant, and Nevaeh gangly and awkward. Nevaeh took a deep breath and wiped her damp palms on her cotton skirt. She'd have to put all those past images aside and just try one day at a time to be whoever she was now, no matter what age.

• • •

Dawn Ann hung up the phone in amusement. "You never know," she said to herself. She hadn't thought about Nevaeh in years—not since her father's funeral, when Nevaeh's appearance had been brief and mandatory. She remembered her most vividly and fondly as a friendly seven-year-old, who, with curly hair down to her knees, had followed Dawn Ann around the entire day she'd spent getting ready for her junior prom, and how she'd feigned being pestered by all of the girl's admiring questions, but had, in fact, felt like a princess or celebrity, relishing, more than she could ever admit, the adulation and attention.

Odd that she would call, but flattering as well. It wasn't easy to make a career in music or the arts, Dawn Ann knew that, and it made her feel good to potentially mentor someone trying to make it. Of course, Derek was trying to make it, too, but he never accepted help from anyone. Woman to woman, it would be different with Nevaeh. At the thought of Derek, she cupped her mouth. She prayed he'd be okay with having a visitor—it could go either way: he could see it as an invasion of his space, or he might welcome the company. It was only a few days. He liked music, and liked hanging around with other artistic types. Maybe they could take photographs together, or he could take photographs of her playing music—what was it again that she played? Guitar probably. Derek would like that.

She told Derek when she got back from the gym at one o'clock and Derek was having a cup of soup at the kitchen table, still in his boxers.

"That's cool," he said, and for a moment Dawn Ann felt like a relic. She rarely said "cool," unless she meant the weather, and here her own husband was using the term, sounding just like her younger cousin Nevvy. Maybe both of them were "cool" or "hip" or whatever you were supposed to be and she wasn't. Nevvy would think Derek was cool, and Derek would blossom under such adoration, and before you knew it, Dawn would feel like a third, uncool wheel in her own house. No, she thought. Nevvy was just a girl, not a grown woman. Dawn Ann fluffed her hair, exasperated with herself. Once she'd made prime-time, she'd expected never to feel self-doubt again. She'd expected, she guessed, to in fact be cool.

Mostly, she was relieved that Derek took the news of a house guest so well. "She can use the hide-a-bed in my office," she said. "I'll get her a key from James so she can come and go as she wants. You won't have to entertain her," she said.

"Naw, I'd be happy to," he said, looking up from the sports page. "We can do some clubs while you're working."

She nodded. "That would be really nice of you," she said, and realized that there was something unfamiliar about his attitude. It was pleasant not to have to battle to get him to do the right thing, but a little unsettling, too. Still, he was a great guy when he wanted to be and she imagined Nevaeh's arrival as incentive for her husband once again to be that wonderful guy she'd married.

16

Nevaeh's train from New Orleans was late arriving at Union Station in Chicago and, tired from the constant jostling of the past 20 hours, she immediately sought a coffee shop where she could sit still and gather her thoughts. When Nevaeh had called a second time from New Orleans to give Dawn Ann the specifics of her arrival, her husband Derek had answered the phone. He said you never knew when Dawn Ann was going to be home and when she'd be off doing "TV star stuff." Nevaeh couldn't tell from his flat tone whether he was proud of Dawn Ann and trying to be humble or rancid with envy. But he was nice enough and said he was always home and would be there that morning when she arrived. It was eleven thirty before she decided to call. She was about to hang up and try later when, on the sixth ring, she heard the phone being lifted off the receiver and clunking against something hard, followed by a cough, a muffled curse, and finally a dull, "Hello?"

Nevaeh gripped the phone as if it were a life preserver and rushed head-on, "Derek, Derek, is that you? This is Nevaeh," she said.

"Yeah, it's me," he said. "What time ... oh, hey, guess I overslept. Where are you?"

"I'm at the train station," she said.

"You got any money?" he asked.

She wasn't destitute. What had Dawn Ann told him about her? "Ye-ah," she said, as if his question was the dumbest thing she'd ever heard.

"Then take a cab," he said, "and when you get here we can go get some breakfast." He gave her the address, which of course, she knew. "It'll cost you six dollars or so, and you should give the guy a buck tip."

Did he think she was a child or some hick off the farm? She'd grown up in Wilmette and while in high school she and her friends had spent a lot of Saturdays taking the local Metra train to downtown Chicago, going to the art museum, shopping and in general trying on the world. She'd taken all sorts of cabs, four girls in back, one in front, hugging the door, and they'd each kicked in two dollars so they could make the five thirty train back home, as promised. She was a college graduate, for heaven's sake; she knew how to tip.

"Yeah," she said.

In the back of the cab, Nevaeh tried some of the breathing exercises she'd been reminded of in treatment, staring straight ahead at the Plexiglas divider between herself and the cabbie and breathing in, "hello," and breathing out, "let go." The cab had a new-car smell, and a small TV screen which displayed welcome messages and ads.

Silently, she "hello, let go-ed" her way across the Loop to Michigan and Wacker, where the bridge was up and she could see a flotilla of 20 or so sailboats making their way down the Chicago River to Lake Michigan. She hadn't seen the river since high school and hadn't seen Dawnie since Dr. McKnight's funeral—what, six years ago? She'd been a senior in high school, she remembered that, and Dawnie was on TV in Wisconsin, either Madison or Milwaukee. At both the funeral and the luncheon at Aunt Jacqueline's club afterwards, Nevaeh had been in the throes of self-consciousness, without a clue as to how to behave or whether or not to cry, because she didn't know her uncle all that well, and because her mother was a mess before they even left for the church.

She remembered being in awe of Dawnie's composure. Her blond hair was perfect, tied back with a broad black satin bow. She wore an elegant black silk suit with gold braiding around the collar and cuffs. At the church, Dawn Ann had spoken from the pulpit, reading from large index cards, and made her audience both laugh and cry, then nearly applaud. It was a masterful performance. At the time, it had seemed so grown-up and Nevaeh couldn't imagine ever feeling that kind of command and self-assurance. She'd concluded it wasn't part of her DNA, and had consoled herself, as now, with her other qualities—resourcefulness, for instance.

Ahead, the bridge slowly knit itself together in the middle and the first cars sped across. *Trust.* While New Orleans hadn't worked out so well, she'd learned some things, and had this chance to start again. She was about to be reunited with her cousin, which was kind of cool, and she need to trust her instincts and herself. A couple of joggers and bikers wove among the street traffic on the sidewalk, their bare legs lightly tan in the sun. Everyone looked so healthy. She had a vague picture in her head of Dawn Ann as a generic, blond TV star, but she had no guess about Derek. A photographer who slept late: she imagined a full head of long, curly hair, purposefully in disarray, and dark, impenetrable eyes. A photographer should be known by his eyes, she thought.

Her ride, with the extra wait at the bridge, was $6.30, and she gave the driver $8.00 because she didn't have any coins and was too embarrassed to ask for seventy cents in change. She remembered a few times in New Orleans when a tourist had placed a dollar in their box and carefully took back two quarters. She'd thought that was kind of cheap.

Dawn Ann's doorman was extraordinarily polite, more polite than many of the shopkeepers in New Orleans, who always assumed the street performers were shoplifters. He called up "Mr. Baldwin" and told him that "Ms. Thera" was there to see him. Then he took a white handkerchief from his pocket and opened the inside door for her, offering to take her box. She declined his help as he repeated, "2503, to your right off the elevator." She thanked him and he bowed slightly, "It's a pleasure."

It was a swank building, two concrete towers on the outside but warm wood paneling, blue-gray carpets and crystal chandeliers inside, even in the elevator. Derek opened the door before she knocked. "Hey," he said, sweeping his arm across the shiny dark gray marble of the entry way.

"Hey," she answered. "I'm Nevaeh," she added, but then thought of course he knew that. "Duh."

"Yeah," he said. "Dawn Ann said you should dump your stuff in her study." He looked around her. "That's it?" he asked.

"That's it," she smiled. "I travel light." Derek shrugged and she laughed, "I'm not moving in."

"Got that right," he said, and signaled to her to follow him down the hall to her left, to a room carpeted in furry white shag. She hesitated for a moment, inspected the bottoms of her shoes, and finally dared to step foot into her new room. The outside wall was all window, from the waist up, very urban and sophisticated, and Nevaeh suddenly felt older and more mature than she'd ever felt.

Derek led her to his studio. She stared at the back of his head, hair not particularly curly nor in terrible disarray. He was of average build and nondescript looks. She needed for him to turn around so she could check out his eyes; when he'd opened the door, they'd been only half-open.

"This is where I work," he said. His voice was friendly, cadenced like a big brother on his best behavior. He flipped on the lights in his darkroom. "Here is where the magic happens," he grinned. "Do you do any photography?"

"No," she said, and she realized that Derek was treating her as if she were his wife's best friend. Good thing she hadn't told Dawn Ann the whole story. When people knew you'd been in treatment for alcohol and drug addition, they tended to treat you like a two-year-old, a ticking package ready to blow at any moment. She was glad she'd kept her story to herself. She really wasn't as bad as most of the people who the counselors called drunks and addicts, and besides, wasn't a blank slate what a new beginning was supposed to be about? The counselors had said that as much as she shouldn't repeat her past, she shouldn't forget it either, but it occurred to Nevaeh that she was the only one who had to know she was "starting over." As far as Dawn and Derek were concerned, she was a blank slate.

"So what's your thing?" Derek said.

She finally got a chance to see his eyes, dark, but kind. Perhaps a tad too close together, more vague than impenetrable. Serious. Not merry like Phil's or affectionate, like Tray's. "I want to be a writer," she said without hesitation, "but lately I've been playing music."

"Cool. What do you play?"

She studied Derek, leaning haphazardly against one of the fancy rolling cabinets that he said contained his negatives and prints. "Angelica," she said, hoping to dignify her art in the face of his, "and piano, too, although I haven't played in a while." With any luck, he wouldn't question her about the obscure instrument and she could change the subject.

"Glasses?" he whooped. He struck an imaginary baton against a row of imaginary glasses. "Or bottles?" He rolled his eyes back in his head and pantomimed blowing into long-necked cola bottles.

"So, you play, too?" she asked, not wanting to acknowledge that he was making fun of her.

He furrowed his brow and looked out at her from the top of his eyes. "Dawn Ann said you were a musician, not a carney act."

"That would be a no?" she said, and started to walk out, prepared to start unpacking in her room.

He put his hand on her shoulder and she flinched. Firmly, he turned her around, "I asked, which," he said, his tone not exactly threatening, but demanding.

"Glasses," she said, wetting her finger and tracing a circle in the air.

"How many?"

"I own 25," she said, "although I've played a 37."

"Could I photograph them sometime?"

She was oddly relieved by such an ordinary request. She reminded herself that Derek was almost family.

"Of course," she said. "Although I don't know that they're much to look at."

"But *you* are," he smiled, and she laughed nervously. With uninvited familiarity, he hung his arm around her shoulder, "Come, let's have lunch."

She squared her shoulders, uncertain of the intent of Derek's touch, though he seemed casual enough. They walked to Walter's Round-the-Clock, the diner where Channel Three's employees hung out, and two sound guys, a cameraman and an assistant producer said hello to him as they took a table in the window. A frizzy-haired waitress waved.

"Hi, Trudy!" Derek shouted, with the flair of Phillipé the Phabulous greeting his subjects in the Quarter. Nevaeh had only a little change purse with her, and it felt odd to be without her pack in a new city. Even at Phil's, she'd usually had it with her on the street, although she'd left her clothes in his closet.

Trudy bounced over and gave Derek a pat on the hand that lingered long enough for Nevaeh to notice. "Hi, honey," she said, and then "Hi, ya," to Nevaeh.

"Two Buds?" Trudy asked.

Nevaeh hadn't prepared for that. It was lunch-time, and Derek was older, and a serious artist, working in an air-conditioned apartment, not on the hot streets. She'd thought Chicago would be different from New Orleans, where people were always schmoozing and partying, eating and drinking. In treatment they'd made a big deal about not drinking in the morning or at noon or every day and how "just one" always, always, for people like her, led to more. She quickly did the calculus, and while she was sure she'd be able to drink again some day, today she wanted to be absolutely certain that she didn't screw up meeting her cousin. She looked up and with more insistence than the situation required, said, "Could I have a Coca-Cola instead?"

Trudy nodded and looked to Derek, who said, "Yeah, two Buds. Might as well."

Wondering what the counselors would suggest she do now, Nevaeh looked out the window at the four wide lanes of mid-day traffic, unlike so many of the Quarter's quaint, winding and narrow streets, and just as she was thinking what a big and anonymous city Chicago was and that no one would know if she had a beer at lunch, a woman walked by on the sidewalk, waved to them, entered the diner and approached their table.

"Hi, Derek," the crisply dressed woman said. "This must be Dawn Ann's cousin?" Linda Livingston, a reporter and sometimes anchor weekend at Channel Three introduced herself, breezing through the formalities and seating herself next to Derek. Linda had a relatively large head on a precise, small body, but her features were perfectly proportioned and she wore a light blue linen jacket with the kind of gold buttons that flashed "expensive." It took Nevaeh a good 10 minutes to figure out that she was being interviewed. As Derek attacked his iceberg lettuce and tomato salad and drank down the first of the two beers Trudy had placed in front of him, Nevaeh could see that the big difference between the two of them was that Linda, for whatever reason, was actually listening to Nevaeh's answers. Linda talked to her the way someone talks to a person they'd like to get to know for her own sake, not because she was somebody's relative. It was a very fine line, totally subjective, but if Nevaeh'd learned anything on the street, it was to go with her gut. Linda was a good person, despite her nosiness about Nevaeh's college major and where in New Orleans she'd lived and with whom and how much money a person can really make as a musician.

"Did you play in clubs or on the street?" Linda asked. There was no sneer in her voice when she said "street;" if anything, there was a slight lilt, a hopeful vote for street.

"Jackson Square, mostly," Nevaeh answered. "Sometimes Royal." As far as Nevaeh was concerned, if you had a more-or-less fixed location, that was just as good as a club. It surprised her that Linda would come so close to asking how much money she made; she'd been brought up to think that question was rude. Besides, Phil always said he played for the love—not the love of playing, but the applause. Nevaeh herself was a realist: she needed money to live, so she needed to play for applause.

"How much can a typical street musician make in a day?" Linda asked. "I'm not asking how much *you* made, just ballpark."

Derek jumped in. "I'm sure Nevaeh was not typical," he smiled at her, a curl to his lip that Nevaeh interpreted as, 'it's okay, I'm going to save you.' "Being related to Dawn Ann McKnight, I'm sure our Nevvy here was a *star*."

Nevaeh laughed. Derek's tone was snotty, but it saved her from having to answer Linda's question, one she didn't want to answer because they might think that she could afford her own place and might kick her out before she'd even settled in.

"No, I was thinking more for your sake, Derek. Maybe you could sell some work on the street, like they do in New Orleans." As she turned to him, Nevaeh saw that Linda had a perfect profile, smooth forehead, high cheekbones, lovely sloping nose, a strong jaw. From Tray's television studies, Nevaeh knew enough about photography and film to recognize that Linda's angles would catch the light well and cast only gentle shadows.

"That's a great idea," Nevaeh said. "All the best artists in New Orleans show their works at Jackson Square, and they get to be outside instead of holed up in a loft somewhere."

Derek slammed his palm on the table. The silverware clattered and the water sloshed from his stubby glass.

"Screw you, Linda."

"Oh grow up, Derek. All I meant was maybe you could create a market here, like they have there. I didn't know you were limiting yourself to the Whitney." She turned back towards Nevaeh, done with Derek, as if he were a gnat she'd brushed away. "So, Nevaeh," she began, but Derek grabbed Linda's wrist like a handcuff. She immediately tried to pull it away, but Derek hammered it down like the victor in an arm-wrestling match. "You're a royal bitch, Linda," he said. "You all are." He gave her a shove with his elbow and let go his grip. "Get out of here."

"With pleasure," Linda said. "Listen, Nevaeh, I think the world of your cousin. If there's anything I can do to help you settle in here, please, please call me. Come by the station sometime and we can have lunch."

"You," Derek said, jabbing his finger at Nevaeh. "This is Chicago. You know nothing about getting along, *capiche*?" Her stomach flipped.

"Ignore him," Linda said lightly, and Nevaeh braced herself, but Derek was slugging back his beer and must not have heard.

"Thanks," Nevaeh nodded to Linda, with what she hoped was the right amount of enthusiasm, because she liked Linda and her open, honest style, but didn't want to appear to be taking sides in the spat between her and Derek. When she was eight, before her father'd abandoned them, she'd been in the middle all the time, like the center ball in one of those desk toys with the five metal balls hanging on strings, the ball at one end causing the one on the other end to fly rhythmically out of position, and the one in the middle hanging steady, absorbing the hits and transferring all the power from one side to the other, until the balls at either end were either worn down or restarted. She never wanted to play that role again.

"Bitch," Derek muttered as she left, then smiled at Nevaeh as if nothing were wrong and he was again her big brother. Nevaeh took a huge bite of her cheeseburger. He stared at her, and, still chewing, she stared back. She couldn't get a handle on Derek; she felt like she'd seen at least three different personalities so far—the big brother, the flirt, the jealous husband—and maybe more—the noontime alcoholic, the woman-hater. She would be on her guard, and in a week or so she would have her very own place. For now, she would go along with whatever game he was playing. She watched him down his second beer, straight from the bottle, and, without taking his eyes off of her, hold it out. Trudy swooped by, dropped another sweating brown, long-neck at the table and grabbed the empty in as smooth an exchange as an Olympic relay. "So, Nevaeh, what are we going to do with you?" Derek asked, just as smoothly.

She would've liked to give him back some of his own and tell him that he didn't have to do anything with her, that she was self-sufficient, had lived by herself in a tree house, had survived on the streets of New Orleans, and didn't need to take hand-outs. But Tray had taught her early on to stay focused on the goal, not to get goaded into or embarrassed out of whatever it was they were after. In this case, that meant trying to make sure she didn't aggravate Derek the way Linda had, that she play little sister to his big brother,

"I hope I won't be in the way," she said. "I'm going to start looking for a job tomorrow, and hopefully find a place to live. How's the job market here?" she asked, and then, because of all that nastiness with Linda, added quickly, "for someone like me? I mean, I've never worked—except at the library in college—and well, my degree is in writing. Where should I start?"

"I dunno," he said, running his fingernail down the label of his bottle like a razor blade. He kept picking at the label until only the glue clung to the bottle like old wallpaper paste. He sighed. "Dawn'll have some ideas. She's good at that ambition stuff." He held out his beer and passed it to Trudy, who obliged with another fresh one.

"She's coming in," Trudy said.

"Dawn?" Nevaeh asked.

"Her Highness," Derek answered. Dawn Ann beamed as she sailed through the restaurant, greeting her public with a little "hello" for each. She was trim and fit, not an ounce of fat on her, but not emaciated either. Dawn Ann's blond hair was redder than Nevaeh remembered, and fluffier, framing her face like the filigree around a gilded mirror. In a short-sleeved lime green shell and a flowered skirt, Dawn looked, as Derek had said, like a star.

"Nevvy!" she squealed, like someone who suddenly was a teenager again, not the queen of Channel Three weather.

Nevaeh jumped up, happy to see her and happier to be free of Derek's growing surliness. "Long time, no see!" she managed, as tongue-tied as the awestruck seven-year-old she once was. "My, how you've grown!" Dawn Ann said, laughing in mimicry of a generic old-maid aunt. "I'm so glad you're here. Really," she said. She sat down next to Derek, who'd barely looked up.

"Seat's warm. Who was here?" she asked.

"Your friend, Linda," Nevaeh said quickly, failing to forestall Derek, who spat, "That bitch" on top of Nevaeh's reply. Dawn Ann ignored him.

"He really loves her," Dawn Ann confided. "He loves a woman with balls."

Derek grunted. "I must," he said.

Without being asked, Trudy brought Dawn Ann a cup of decaf, who stirred an ice-cube from Derek's untouched water into it. "So," she said, "what's going on?"

They caught up, after a fashion, with a quick overview of Nevaeh's college years and an expurgated version of the time since then. Treatment didn't come up; Phil did. She mentioned Tray and Iowa, left out Key West. Dawn Ann laughed and sympathized and agreed that at her age, there were lots of men in Nevaeh's future. Nevaeh said she wanted to make Chicago home. She didn't say she had to sober up. She said she was ready to start a career, but when Dawn Ann asked her what she wanted to do, Nevaeh giggled and blurted out, "Find one?"

Dawn Ann, as sweet and genuine as anyone she'd ever known, said, "You take your time. It's important to find something that you're passionate about." Gently, she put her hand on Derek's, and he accepted the gesture. "You can stay with us as long as you need to. I'm sure that you and Derek, being fellow artists, will have a great time together."

Derek smiled, the fourth beer, or perhaps the presence of his wife, finally leeching the tension out of his body, making him seem almost mellow. "I always wanted a little sister," he said wistfully, and although Nevaeh winced at being cast in that role, it seemed at that moment the safest one available.

"It's a great city," Dawn Ann said. "You'll have a wonderful time."

17

Undaunted and spring-like in her lime and pink floral outfit, Dawn Ann went off to the station and Derek perked up enough to suggest a walk up Michigan Avenue. Because she'd been a street performer, Nevaeh thought she'd seen just about everything there was to see on the street, but within a few blocks she realized how different Chicago was from New Orleans. In New Orleans, there'd seemed to her to be a clear distinction between the gawker and the gawked-at. There, the tourists and shoppers looked their parts, whether they were businessmen from Atlanta in navy blazers and khaki trousers, or tourists from Iowa, in town for a party in their hibiscus shirts and newly-purchased plastic beads. But here, in broad daylight, she saw skinheads with pierced lips in three piece suits, dirty and unshaven men guarding their shopping carts while opening Federal Express packages, ladies in St. John suits with Gucci hand bags and cardinal-red hair. They all huddled at the "Don't Walk" sign, oblivious to each other but creeping *en masse* into the intersection as if their collective will could change the signal to "Walk."

There seemed to be a lot of people who didn't work, or at least didn't work during the day. She wondered how they supported themselves. She liked the idea of a creative job like Derek's, work you could do as the spirit moved you, the proceeds of which would sustain you until the next spurt of imagination or creativity or whatever divine energy it was that turned paper into art and gave you time to walk up Michigan Avenue during the day.

They sat on a bench in the park across from the historic Water Tower, one of the few buildings to survive the Great Chicago Fire, and watched the parade of personalities streaming by, Derek apparently content to be a gawker. It occurred to her that writing and photography were a little less demanding in terms of your time than other sorts of jobs. You could do them whenever, wherever, and even walking up the street or sitting on a bench could be termed working, as in "gathering material." On the other hand, if you were a musician, you had to show up every single night at a club or restaurant, waiting for your big break.

As if to prove her point, a tall bearded man in a shirtless tuxedo jacket, fishnets and patent-leather high heels, strolled by, walking a white dog the size of an old fashioned muff. Nevaeh elbowed Derek. "You should've brought your camera," she said.

"Don't you start with me," he said meanly, and jumped to his feet.

At first, she had no idea what she'd "started," or why he was abandoning her. Maybe he didn't want her to visit after all. She watched in slight terror as he headed out of the park and down the Avenue, swinging his arms forward and back in giant arcs around his hips, as if to mark his territory.

Nevaeh felt glued to the bench. She appreciated spontaneity as much as the next person—of course she did, she'd lived with Tray and with Phil—but theirs was a free and joyful spontaneity that surprised you, like an extra rung on the ladder, or a plastic baby in a King cake at Mardi Gras. Derek's mood swings were random and disconcerting, if not frightening. If he weren't so successful and married to her cousin, she might suspect that he was one of those alcoholic personalities the treatment counselors were so fond of describing: impulsive, self-centered, dramatic, insane. Impulsive and dramatic could be fun, the way Phil and Tray were fun: the self-centered part could be forgiven. It was the insanity, the unpredictability of it all, that telegraphed "danger." She looked up at the limestone turret that topped the relic water tower, closed her eyes and breathed out, "hello, let go." A pigeon dropped a white splatter on the sidewalk in front of the bench. She heard busses trudging their way down the Avenue, taxis beeping friendly honks at one another, a cheerful but off-key rendition of *The Flintstones* theme song. She was surprised when a body plopped down next to her.

"Whatcha doin'?"

"Nothin'" she said, even before she turned to her accuser.

"Nothin's okay. Doesn't hurt anybody," Derek said. She was surprised he'd returned so quickly. He stretched his arms over his head in a yawn. "Why is everybody so goddam ambitious, so goddam busy all the time? Dawn Ann and Linda, now you, thinking I need to take my camera everywhere I go, as if I don't have eyes without it."

He leaned back on the bench, using his arms as a headrest, and gazed at the tower.

"Do you?" she asked.

"Do I what?"

"See differently with the camera than without it?"

"I am the camera," he said. "But it's not as good as I am. I get pictures in my head, but they don't look the same on paper."

"Even digital?" she asked, and realized, as she said it, that she was taking him way too literally. She shied away slightly, afraid she may have tripped the wire of his wrath.

He pushed back his sunglasses and gave her a withering but amused look.

"I am full of it, aren't I?" he said, and flipped his glasses back down.

"I didn't say that," she said. "I think I know what you mean—like when I have a memory of a note on my harmonica, and then I play the sound, and it's not quite the same, or a glass breaks, and the note on a new glass is just ever so slightly different, at least to me. Probably no one else knows, because they don't know what I remember hearing, or *what* I hear, for that matter." She bit her lip, afraid that she'd said too much. To show him she wasn't trying to out-think him, she rubbed her index finger up and down on her lips, making a vibrating nonsense noise. In fact, her own thoughts were getting too complicated to keep track of.

"You're alright," he said, grabbing her hand and yanking her up from the bench. She accepted his boost, but was relieved when he dropped her hand, and they strolled back to his apartment in a comfortable silence. Every so often, he'd give her a jab with his elbow and nod his head in the direction of some particularly entertaining walking work of human art: green hair, blue hair, white hair with black velvet eyebrows and purple lips. She didn't let on, but she enjoyed a lot of what he called "visual detritus." She was dressed the way she always dressed in New Orleans—a pale olive green cotton tee-shirt, scoop-necked and an Indian-print long full skirt, with elephants and urns in shades of beige and rust, the kind that easily conceals dirt or stains, and tells a story if you stare at the pattern long enough. She wore her sandals with white socks. Except for her feet, she felt she looked like the others—students and waitresses, she guessed—who Derek didn't single out.

"Make yourself at home," he said when they got back to the apartment. He pulled out the sofa bed for her and told her that Dawn Ann would be home around eleven thirty. "I'm gonna do some work," he said. "See you tomorrow."

"Thanks," she said. "For lunch and everything." He nodded and closed the door to his studio. She heard the tumbler lock, which struck her as odd, given that he was in his own home. Another Derek eccentricity.

She flopped on the bed. Not perfect, but far better than the bunk at Lilies and better than treatment. She laughed at herself. She was lying in the lap of luxury and thinking the mattress could be just a little firmer, when just a few days ago, she'd had no place to go! Now, she'd landed with a rich and famous woman who was actually willing to take her in and help her get started and she was picking nits.

Dawn Ann made perfection seem so easy: the confident and efficient way she walked, acknowledging all the people in the restaurant who knew her; the way she smiled with her chin dropped just a tad, so her eyes stayed wide open and sparkled; the way she seemed to understand Derek and bring out the best in him, with just a touch of her hand. Dawn Ann gave you hope, made you feel good about yourself, that she'd take the time to be with you.

She drifted off, and was surprised that it was after nine when she awoke. The apartment was dark and eerily quiet. She turned on the desk lamp in her room, then stuck her head in the hall. No light leaked from under Derek's door, no sounds of work. She flipped the hall switch and then went to the living room, where the city shone in through the wall of southern windows.

In the kitchen, she peeked in the refrigerator. On the top shelf, six cartons of low-fat yogurt, a half-gallon of skim milk, an unopened brick of low-fat Swiss cheese and an almost-empty bottle of Bloody Mary mix. Below that, a carton of eggs and a loaf of bread. The bottom shelf was divided in two: on the right at least a dozen cans of Budweiser and on the left, an equal number of bottles of spring water.

Nevaeh shook her head, amused. They looked like two armies facing off, the forces of good and evil, light and dark, life and death. She pulled open the crisper drawer at the bottom and found a stack of individually-sized bags of baby carrots. The shelves in the door had a bottle of ketchup, a tub of margarine and four bottles of white wine.

She opened the freezer side on her left, home to a lone frozen chicken pot pie and two frosted bottles of vodka, one of them opened, inviting. She recognized the brand from billboards. At Phil's house, they'd only bought cheap vodka, Phil being of the opinion, shared by Tray, that vodka was vodka. Without thinking, she took the bottle, unscrewed the top and inhaled deeply. It was supposed to smell like citrus, but she wasn't getting it. She put her finger over the top of the bottle and tipped it, and then held her finger to her nose. A little, distant essence of lemon peel. She licked her finger, enough to taste, not enough to swallow. She screwed the top back on and replaced the bottle in the freezer. She wanted to stay awake and sober for Dawn Ann.

She turned on the little TV on the kitchen counter and sat at the small round table in the breakfast nook, munching her way through two bags of carrots and a bowl of Special K with skim milk. She watched the news on Channel Three and The Elements with Dawn Ann McKnight. Dawn Ann predicted a beautiful five days ahead, but a hard beat into the wind for anyone cruising up-lake that coming weekend. Then, "on a personal note," she welcomed all the summer tourists to Chicago, especially her cousin, Nevaeh, who must've brought this "heavenly" weather with her, wink, wink. It was pretty cool to know someone—actually, two someones—on TV. Linda was substituting that night for the usual anchor, and Nevaeh was mesmerized by the two of them. Beautiful, intelligent, articulate, friendly, casual, confident. Their very presence on TV made Nevaeh feel a little stifled, as if she were stuck at four feet two while all her friends were growing to five seven, five eight. No wonder Derek was so intimidated! Not that he'd admitted he was intimidated, or that he should be—he was a successful photographer, wasn't he? It was highly unlikely that as a creator he'd ever be the household name Dawn Ann might become as a reporter, and maybe that pissed him off a little. It would annoy anyone with creative ambitions.

"It pisses me off," Derek said. She hadn't heard him in the hall. Now, he shuffled into the kitchen, his hair tousled, his shirt open, his eyes blurry. "You're one print away from perfection, and you run out of effing paper." He was talking to himself and didn't even seem to notice she was there. He reached in the freezer, took the open bottle of vodka and left without noticing her.

If Derek was intimidated by being married to Dawn Ann, Nevaeh couldn't help but wonder how Dawn Ann felt about being married to a powder keg. On the one hand, Dawn Ann seemed to have a calming influence on him, as she'd witnessed at lunch, and she seemed to adore him. Still, she must know how he treated Linda—Linda hadn't seemed surprised by his behavior at all. Had Linda started it with that line about the Whitney, or had she been trying to improve Nevaeh's stature as a street performer? Whatever, Nevaeh didn't want to get caught in the middle of such a skirmish. The sooner she could find her own place, the better.

When Dawn Ann came home an hour later, she grabbed a bottle of water from the refrigerator for each of them, turned off the TV and sat down at the table, beaming at Nevaeh as if she were her own daughter, recently returned home. Bernard jumped up on her lap and Dawn Ann scratched under the cat's chin until he purred.

Nevaeh had to keep reminding herself that Dawn Ann knew nothing of Nevaeh's past except what she had told her; she could jettison the bad and embellish the good. Not that she regretted all the experiences that had brought her to Chicago. "Learning experiences," she could hear her mother say. "Effing growth opportunities." During the rare spells when her mother had been sober, she'd spewed a few such pearls of wisdom that had stuck with Nevaeh and served her well. Especially now. Her censored past was obviously fascinating to Dawn Ann, even in the cleaned-up version, which made Nevaeh feel like she had something to offer in return for her hospitality, in the same way she'd spiced up Judith Scott's life by virtue of applying for a library card.

"How was your day?" Dawn Ann asked. "Did Derek behave himself?"

"We had a great day," Nevaeh began, understanding immediately why half a truth could be socially desirable.

"Sometimes, he can be a little temperamental." As if on cue, Bernard jumped down from Dawn Ann's lap, his appetite for affection apparently satiated.

"Everybody has moods," Nevaeh said, not admitting that she'd witnessed his explosion at Linda and that she, herself, had been, if not exactly threatened, at least warned off.

"Everyplace has weather, too, but Derek can have four seasons in an hour!" She laughed nervously. "So if tomorrow you see a sudden rise or drop in temperature, just stay clear. Agree with him, whatever it is, and eventually, he'll come around. He's kind of like a two-year old sometimes," she said, "but I know he's really happy to have the company."

"I appreciate your letting me stay here," Nevaeh said. "After all these years! I feel a little bit like the long lost relative who shows up the day you win the lottery."

"I know that happens," Dawn Ann said, and reached for Nevaeh's hand. "But that's not this. I'm glad you're here, even if I didn't win the lottery."

Just then Derek materialized in front of the refrigerator. "The lottery," he snarled, swinging open the freezer. "You want more money? I'm not providing enough for Her Highness? You want more? Do you? Do you?"

Dawn Ann gripped her water bottle so hard the plastic buckled. Derek struggled to keep his balance, then bent to the bottom shelf, loaded two beer cans in the crux of his left elbow, and slammed the door shut. "Ungrateful bitch," he muttered.

Dawn Ann sat as still as stone. They heard the door to the studio clatter shut.

Without looking up, Dawn Ann said, "He doesn't mean anything by it. He's probably been working in the darkroom and maybe had a few. He gets that way—sometimes—when he drinks."

Nevaeh didn't say anything. Why was her cousin making excuses for her husband's behavior? They hadn't even been talking about him, unless he'd been eavesdropping earlier. Still, there was no reason for his outburst.

Why did Dawn Ann take this? In New Orleans, even when she'd had no place to go, Nevaeh had left Phil and his house rather than have him tell her how to run her life. Her cousin had a beautiful apartment and all the money in the world and could have any man she wanted, so why did she allow Derek to terrorize her so? Because she *was* terrorized, Nevaeh could see that. Dawn Ann's lips were tight, her breath imperceptible, and her eyes so wide and white that stillborn tears filled the corners, fixed like raindrops on a rose.

"Then you should make him stop drinking," Nevaeh said, her voice low and confidential. "You shouldn't have to take that kind of verbal abuse."

Dawn Ann let go of the water bottle and cocked her head like a big sister wanting to explain the ways of the world to a grade-schooler. Quickly, as if readying herself for the camera, she touched her hair into place. "He doesn't mean anything by it. He loves me, I know he does. So don't you worry about it. We'll be fine," she said.

"I can't believe you'd let a man treat you like that," Nevaeh insisted.

"It's different when you're married," Dawn Ann said. "You'd have to be married to understand."

Something in Dawn Ann's voice warned Nevaeh that she shouldn't challenge her. She wasn't married. Perhaps she didn't know. "I don't understand," Nevaeh said. She meant that she didn't understand marriage as an excuse for abuse, but apparently Dawn Ann took it as apology for butting in.

"I just want you to take your time here in Chicago and find the right job and the right apartment and, you know, the right friends and all."

The next morning Nevaeh woke up about ten. Dawn Ann had left a note near the coffee machine in the kitchen saying that she was at the gym, and had drawn directions if "anyone" wanted to join her. She planned to be back at noon. The door to Derek's studio was closed; the door to their bedroom half-open. Nevaeh couldn't bring herself to peek in. She couldn't hear Derek and didn't know if he'd gone to the gym or not. She wondered if Dawn Ann and Derek had made up last night before they went to sleep. It was possible, she supposed, that Dawn Ann had gone to bed and awakened without having to speak to him, depending on how late he worked in the darkroom.

    The invitation to the gym did not appeal to her. She didn't much see the point of running in place and lifting artificial weights for no constructive purpose. What she needed was a job, so she could go back to being independent and not have to deal with Derek's drinking and mistreating Dawn Ann. She opened the newspaper to the want-ads. They were arranged alphabetically, and while she knew most people her age were searching on-line and finding dream jobs that dropped into their laps like electronic manna, she rather liked the image of reading the help-wanted ads at the kitchen table, circling the promising ones with a ballpoint pen and drinking her coffee. Just opening the newspaper, folding it in half vertically and then again in half horizontally, made her feel grown-up, as if she were already riding the el or bus to work. She read the first column—junior accountants and bookkeepers—and then got up and made herself a piece of toast. She was somewhat heartened that the A's included "Activism," including an ad for a summer job with Greenpeace working with "Great People!" which would "Protect our National Forest!" and pay $300 to $500 a week. But even at the top end of the range, she wasn't sure she could live in a big city like Chicago on $26,000 a year. She read the second column of As—administrative, advertising, auto mechanics and auto sales—and Bs, Cs and Ds—banking, bartenders, canvassers, chemists, computer-everything, construction, dental assistants, drivers—and had a second piece of toast. At "General Office" she paused to consider her skills: she could type fairly well and knew enough about word processing for most office needs; she had sufficient personality and presence to be a receptionist and certainly could master a phone system; she could probably manage an office, too, but the fact that she'd never worked in one was probably a strike against her.

    She smirked at an ad that read, "Models: Dancers, centerfolds. No nudity req'd. Can earn up to $500/day." She circled it and placed a question mark next to it. Not that she thought she was a beauty like Dawn Ann, but if they were looking for a certain type, it might be easy money. She'd worked on the street. People had taken her picture.

It would be okay. Better than restaurant, sales associate, telemarketing—an alphabetical jambalaya of jobs where even computer matching would be difficult.

She was still imagining her answers at a job interview—"self-employed musician," "staying with friends," "couldn't afford grad school anymore," "happy to work overtime," "good team player,"—when she heard a key in the door and Dawn Ann came in, as energetic as if she were going to her work-out, not returning.

"It's invigorating," she announced. "Did you get something to eat? Have you seen Derek?"

She said yes she had and no she hadn't.

"Ta da!" Derek swooped into the kitchen and grabbed Dawn Ann around the waist from behind. He started nuzzling her neck, "yum, yum, yum," and Dawn Ann laughed and wrestled free to give him a morning kiss, which he obliged by bending her back in a tango flourish and then threatening to drop her as he looked up. "Oh, hi, Nevaeh," he said, with a calculated inflection of surprise. Dawn Ann struggled to a squat and then stood, draping an arm around her husband and thoroughly confusing Nevaeh. "How about I take you lovely ladies to lunch?"

There was a bistro and outdoor café a few blocks from their apartment. Dawn Ann didn't even bother to change out of her work-out shorts and tank top or to put on makeup. Nevaeh swept her hair up with a decorative stick and the three of them held hands, Derek in the middle, as they strolled down the street. Derek and Dawn Ann were in high spirits, which rubbed off on Nevaeh, who was, after all, being saved from the further press of business on her first full day in Chicago. At the restaurant, Nevaeh followed Dawn Ann's lead in every regard; Caesar salad with shrimp, no rolls, ice tea with two packets of sweetener. Derek had a light beer and a half-pound burger with bleu cheese and cottage fries.

Nevaeh eyed the beer, but quickly decided she didn't need it. She'd seen how it could change a person—how Derek had turned against his wife the day before because of it. She would try on this new, non-drinking, healthier lifestyle, and see how that fit for a little while. Sitting at this café on a perfect al fresco afternoon, she realized that in her own case, maybe things had gotten a little out of hand in New Orleans. On a day like this, with Dawn Ann drinking ice tea and not even noticing when people on the sidewalk nudged each other and pointed to the famous person who was Nevaeh's beautiful cousin, if Nevaeh had a choice, she'd choose Dawn Ann and ice tea, any day. Drinking, Derek was like a shapeless blob of conflicting storms formed miles away from the moment and as likely to dissipate as to surge into the storm of the century. Even the weather in Chicago was more predictable than Derek on a binge, that was for certain.

18

By the end of the first week of her stay, Nevaeh was nearly convinced that Derek's tantrums—first with her in the park and then with Dawn Ann over "lottery"—were aberrations, as uncommon as snow in May—possible, but not the daily norm. Nevaeh and Derek both slept later than Dawn Ann. When Dawn Ann returned from the gym or errands or a P.R. engagement, the three of them would often have lunch together the way they might've shared dinner, had Dawn Ann been in a different line of work. Then Derek would invite Nevaeh off on some special adventure, a boat ride on the river to see the city's architecture, a walk to the aquarium, a bus ride uptown to the vintage clothing shops and record stores he thought she'd like. With Derek's help—although he'd never worked in an office, either—Nevaeh bought an "interview outfit," a long black linen skirt cut on the bias so it had a little swirl to it and a shiny red, black and white jazzy-patterned blouse that Dawn Ann thought didn't go with Nevaeh's wild and curly auburn hair when she wore it down. It would, however, work just fine if she tied her hair back and off her face. But she found nothing to interview for. Over the course of the week, the classifieds didn't change much—accounting, administration, air conditioning. Nothing sounded right for her. She thought briefly about applying for a street performer's license and making herself a new rolling cart for the glass harmonica, but she wasn't a carpenter, and where, in a city apartment, did one work on such projects, anyway? She figured she could hunt resale shops or pay someone at an art or trade school to make one, but she didn't want to admit to her secret stash, let alone dip into it. Besides, it was one thing to play an occasional solo or take a set from Phil, but it was quite another to be a solo act all day, every day.

At the end of the second week, Nevaeh hadn't been on a single job interview, in fact, hadn't sent a resume to any potential employers. Dawn Ann and Derek didn't seem to mind. Dawn Ann started asking her to do household errands, picking up dry-cleaning or milk or buying a book of stamps with money she'd leave her or taking Bernard to the vet for his allergy shots. Nevaeh came and went as she pleased, often with Derek, sometimes not. If in the evening he shut himself up in his studio, Nevaeh would go out, sit in a coffee shop or a book store or watch a movie in Grant Park. Between readings and festivals, there were plenty of free things to do, and she didn't mind being by herself. She'd been free of alcohol and marijuana and oxy for two months now, and her body was beginning to remember itself, how she used to feel living in the tree house, when wine and weed were for weekends and her worst vice was a hand-rolled evening cigarette or two. So it set her back when Dawn Ann came home one evening and popped a bottle of champagne. She'd won a "Reader's Choice" poll for the best weathercast in Chicago! In the living room, Dawn Ann filled three delicate flutes. Derek came out of the studio, with a print to show them both. They clinked their glasses and toasted to their respective successes. Derek put his arms around his wife, and then around Nevaeh, and the celebration felt real and inclusive and full of joy, and it never occurred to Nevaeh not to drink to such a special occasion.

    Nevaeh sprawled out in a leather wing chair that reclined like a La-Z-Boy. They finished the bottle and Derek opened another. Dawn Ann protested, but not strenuously enough to garner his attention and on her third glass, Nevaeh felt a little of the old familiar buzz and teetered between the elation of victory—she was fine again, normal—and defeat, her new-found sobriety lost to an emotionally high moment of forgetfulness. But she'd never promised herself she wouldn't drink again; she'd been hooked on pills, if indeed she'd been hooked on anything, and she was young and a glass or two of wine certainly wasn't going to kill her. So, victory it was, and she toasted Dawn Ann again and Derek poured her another glass.

    In the morning, still in the wing chair, her neck was stiff from the sagging weight of her head that had drooped chin-to-breastbone for the better part of the night. Two empty bottles and three glasses lay strewn on the glass coffee table. An inch of pale, flat liquid lay in the bottom of the flute closest to her. She yawned and felt the linings of her cheeks crack. She picked up the old champagne, swirled it around like mouthwash and swallowed hard. She stood and faced the sun streaming through the southern windows, but didn't salute.

She didn't know what to feel. It wasn't the end of the world. It was just a little hangover, and she'd get over it. The odd thing was that she didn't remember falling asleep.

Behind her, she heard Derek's bellowing, big-brother voice. "Gotta learn to hold your liquor," he said, and when she turned to see him, he handed her a beer. "This'll take the edge off," he said.

"Oh, I, what time is it?" she asked, remembering that much from treatment.

"Depends on where in the world you are," he said lightly. "Hair of the dog." He tipped his can and took a long swig. She hesitated. "You got a problem?" he said, his voice now stern, as if she were questioning his authority.

She couldn't say "yes." They didn't know she'd spent some time in rehab; it hadn't even been her choice. She'd not been going to meetings in Chicago, so they had no reason to suspect she had a habit she was trying to break.

"Bow wow," she said, and took a sip. She sat back down on the wing chair.

"Herself is running it off at the club." He sat on the couch opposite her and put his boat-sized, scruffy leather tennis shoes up on the glass table. "I'm so relieved about you, though," he said. "I was beginning to fear you had no vices."

She laughed, at first astounded and then suspicious that he was reverse-psychologizing her into spilling all. She took another drink from the can and looked out the window, slipping into a very still meditation, like a lizard in the sun.

After a while, he said "Don't move," and she immediately turned towards the noise of his voice. "Don't move," he commanded again. He got up and left the room. He came back, minutes later, with a tripod and a camera.

"What?" she started.

"Shush," he said. He clicked a few shots from a half-dozen points on a clock around her, and then approached and, without asking, unbuttoned the top four buttons of her shirt, then the fifth and draped the right side of the shirt off her shoulder. He pushed her bra strap off so that it hung carelessly. Then he took her hair and twirled a curl in his fingers and placed it on her breast, letting his hand linger there. She held her breath, frozen in place. With his index finger, Derek pushed her chin up and hard to the left, then traced a line down between her breasts.

"Beautiful," he said, and went back to his camera. He clicked, the camera whirred. There was a long pause where it seemed that Derek wasn't doing anything but staring at her. She hoped that if she didn't move—if only she could hold her breath long enough, like a prey playing dead—he would lose interest and move away.

The key turned in the lock, and Nevaeh panicked. Quickly, she closed her shirt and buttoned up. Derek smiled a devilish smile, like someone who'd been interrupted this time, but promised to come back to finish what he'd started. He moved to the door.

"Morning!" he called.

"You're up?" Dawn Ann said in benign surprise.

"Taking pictures!" he exclaimed. They came into the living room.

"Hey," Nevaeh said. "Sorry I fell asleep on you all."

"I think you passed out, honey," Dawn Ann said, assuming a confidential tone. "It happens when you're not used to drinking."

Nevaeh nodded. Passing out, not remembering, drinking drinks brought to her by Derek. Suddenly her behavior seemed reckless. Hadn't she learned her lesson in Key West?

Dawn Ann noticed the beers. "Oh, Derek," she said, but she didn't sound angry. "It's so hot outside, if I didn't have to work, I think I'd even join you."

"Have a sip," he said.

Dawn Ann licked her lips, and waited a beat before taking it. "Thanks. This once."

Dawn Ann went off to work, Derek to the darkroom and Nevaeh to her own room, to nap. At five or so she woke up, took a long and leisurely hot shower, shampooed her hair and dressed in her new long black skirt and an olive shirt. She wiped the fog from the mirror and studied her face: pale, slightly freckled, brown eyes. Lots of hair. When wet, the curls were very tight, but as they dried, they'd bush out some and she'd have this mass, down to the middle of her shoulder blades. She was eager to see Derek's pictures, and a tad anxious about what they might reveal. The modeling thing might work, for the Gap, or Eddie Bauer or Sears or someone like that—real people, earthy, that would be her niche, not glamour. She wasn't being vain. Lazy, perhaps, she said to herself, smiling a test photographic smile at her image in the mirror, but certainly not vain. She was relieved when she emerged and Derek was still in the darkroom; she went by herself to Walter's, the Channel Three hang-out, for something to eat.

• • •

Handing her a menu and pouring some water, Trudy was friendly enough, although she kept looking at the door as if she expected Derek to arrive at any moment. Nevaeh didn't bother to open the menu, but ordered a grilled cheese with potato chips. Trudy sighed and finally asked, "Where's Derek?"

"I think he's in the darkroom," she answered.

Trudy shrugged. "I'd like to get him in a dark room," she muttered and sauntered off.

Nevaeh couldn't imagine how Derek would respond if Trudy actually were to proposition him. Was he all tease, the way he'd played her that morning before Dawn Ann came home, or did he tease to shift responsibility, to make seduction the woman's irresistible fault? Seducing a friend's boyfriend was at the top of the short list of things Nevaeh had always said she'd never do, and Dawn Ann was not merely her hostess and friend, but her cousin, the closest thing she had to a sister. Her hormones were raging and Derek was stoking the fires, but she promised herself she would stay clear of Derek Baldwin, no matter what. He could be charming, but something about him seemed to be pure trouble. While in the past she'd rather enjoyed the drama that Tray and then Phil had brought to her life, she'd been told in treatment that drama was something she could ill afford if she wanted to get herself on a nice, serene even keel and stay there.

"Alone?" Nevaeh jumped at the sound of Linda's voice. "Mind if

I join you?"

She didn't mind; she was flattered. They were only nine or 10 years apart, both adults, but the gap between them seemed as wide as the difference between their looks and their careers. Linda's ebony hair was as black and straight as Nevaeh's was auburn and curly; Linda's features, particularly her meticulously-shaped eyebrows, were so precise they made Nevaeh feel undefined. Still, those differences were only physical, and although Nevaeh was quite certain that she'd experienced a broader range of life than Linda, Linda clearly had been the more successful one. She resolved now to defer to Linda (and to Dawn Ann, for that matter), on everything important about the life she was trying to grow up and into.

"Where's Derek?" Linda asked.

"You, too?" Nevaeh laughed. Linda shook her head, as if she didn't understand. "Just that Trudy asked me the same thing," Nevaeh said. "It's not my day to watch him!"

"Good one," Linda said, and Trudy brought her a cup of coffee.

"He went into the darkroom this afternoon and stayed there," she explained. "I wanted to get out. So I came here." she said.

"Oh, of course. I'm working on a special report tonight, and I just needed to get out of the newsroom for a little while. You'll always find somebody you know here."

Linda's segment was on battered women.

"Not really news, is it?" Nevaeh said.

"It hasn't gone away," she said simply. "In fact, we keep finding out how widespread the abuse is, and how many women, even in upper socio-economic echelons, put up with physical and emotional and verbal abuse for reasons as ridiculous as main floor opera seats and as well-meaning as the kids, although I can't imagine how it benefits the kids to see their father beat up their mother."

Nevaeh's father had never beaten her mother. He'd left one night after a drunken battle between the two: broken bottles, a police escort, a packed bag, a fistful of bills thrown at her mother and thrown back. His tweed jacket unbuttoned, his auburn hair unruly and windblown, his white shirt splotched with coffee-colored stains, her father had stood at the door, then spotted Nevaeh sitting on the stairs. He kneeled to hug her, sent her back up to bed, and assured her it would all be okay. He was just going out for a little while. He'd be back, he'd said, although in retrospect she couldn't remember whether he'd looked her in the eye as he told that final lie. He hadn't come back, and while she'd missed his toothy laugh and his amateur magic tricks—a foam ball behind her ear, a string of silk scarves from his mouth—it had been a quieter, safer place.

Linda pushed aside the water glasses and leaned towards Nevaeh, elbows flush with the table. "Does Derek hurt Dawn Ann?" Linda asked, her eyes trained like interrogation lights on Nevaeh's.

"No!" she recoiled. "Why would you say such a thing?"

Linda held her ground, as if she knew, as Tray used to say, that the first answer to an unexpected question only bought time to manufacture a lie that might point inadvertently to the truth. Linda didn't explain or query further. In the background, Trudy's twang punctuated the mild clatter of cups and saucers being cleared into a rubber dish tub, a barely audible canned laugh track, a cell phone's "1812 Overture" ring. Between Nevaeh and Linda though, there hovered the silence of a school principal extracting a truth from a stubborn child.

Nevaeh looked out the window, across the street and down the block to the Channel Three studios, where a small crowd of teenagers was gathering, as if waiting for a celebrity.

"Silence is assent?" Linda asked.

"What silence?" Nevaeh said, letting her voice rise in annoyance. "I said, 'no.'"

"Okay, then," Linda said, her tone crisp and dismissive, her eyes hard.

"What do you want me to say?" Nevaeh asked, feeling herself about to break down under Linda's steely insistence. There was something determined about Linda that was conveyed, not with words, but with the set of her jaw and her absolute refusal to blink. "He has a temper, but he doesn't hit her, if that's what you mean."

"Maybe you haven't seen him hit her," Linda said, as if evaluating the credibility of the witness before her. "But has he held her, pushed her, pinched her?"

Nevaeh ripped open a pink packet of artificial sweetener and thought back. "Maybe," she mumbled. She didn't like the position into which Linda was cramming her and turned around to see if Trudy might come to her rescue with a pot of coffee.

"'Maybe' is not an answer," Linda said.

"Why are you asking me, Linda?" Nevaeh squirmed. "I've only been here a couple of weeks. I can't imagine Dawnie would stay with Derek if he hurt her." Linda leaned back and accepted another round of coffee when Trudy came by, splashing some into her cup. Nevaeh went on, "He's only been charming to me."

"Watch yourself." Trudy looked straight at Nevaeh as if she knew something Nevaeh didn't.

"Mind your own," Linda started to say, but Trudy was down the line to the next booth and didn't hear her, or didn't acknowledge that she did.

"I'm just watching out for my friend, is all," Linda said, whispering now. "I know Derek can be terribly charming when he wants to be, but it's got to be awfully frustrating for him to have her be such a success and him ... well, so, unknown. From all my research—oh, hell, my own experience—he seems like the kind of guy who constantly needs to feel and act superior, even though he denies it. He could explode, and Dawn Ann is the kind of woman who would likely understand and forgive him! But, it's unforgivable, and down inside, Dawn Ann knows that."

Linda's right hand trembled and Nevaeh noticed that she used her left hand to force it down to the table top. No wonder she rarely held notes when she reported, the slight tremor would suggest that the cameraman was wobbly. It occurred to Nevaeh, that this was a subject of more than mere ratings interest to Linda, more important to her than "The Elements" segment was to Dawn Ann. Something in Linda's persistence made the story seem deeply personal.

"All I'm asking, Nevaeh, is that you let me know if anything like that happens, to Dawn Ann, or"—a look of horror crept across her face—"or to you, when you're alone with him. Don't hesitate to call me. That's all I'm asking."

It was nice of Linda to want to help, but it still seemed creepy, and a bit paranoid, voyeuristic and just plain nosey.

Linda got up. "Watch my story tonight," she said. "Let me know what you think."

Nevaeh thanked her and after one more cup of coffee and a complimentary piece of rubbery chiffon pie, a backhanded gift from Trudy, who said it hadn't been ordered by anyone all day. She wandered home. James recognized her and held the door open for her, saying, "It's a pleasure."

Nothing had changed in the apartment in the few hours she'd been gone. She went into her room and closed the door. She marveled again at the furry white carpet, the orderly white bookcases, the expansive windows—the sheer luxury of her new life. She turned on the television, keeping the volume low so as not to disturb Derek.

Even if she didn't believe everything Linda had to say, she didn't feel like being in the middle of something as confused and volatile as her cousin's relationship with her husband. The luxury would have to go: she'd better find a job, a place, and a life of her own, sooner rather than later.

19

Three weeks into Nevaeh's "visit," Dawn Ann found herself humming on the way home after her final broadcast of the week. Derek had been in the darkroom almost non-stop for the past week, but two nights ago he'd tickled her awake in the middle of the night, and that very morning, they'd made love. After, he'd made Denver omelets for the three of them. Nevaeh'd been so sweet and had done the dishes and had had the sense to stay home and read the want-ads while she and Derek went to the health club and had lunch together, just the two of them. Conventional wisdom had it that house-guests were supposed to stink like fish after three days, but Nevaeh wasn't just a house guest, she was family. Dawn Ann liked having her around; her presence seemed to have a calming effect on Derek. Since Nevaeh's arrival, their marital skirmishes had been minor and he seemed to have a new energy, showing Nevaeh around during the day but still attending to his art at night. Dawn Ann was dying to see what he was working on so diligently.

It was good to be in such a good mood, an antidote to another of Linda's special segments, which had been graphic and depressing. Dawn Ann had found it surprising that the producers would head into a weekend with such a dark story, about the frightening numbers of middle- and upper-class women who were treated each year in emergency rooms in posh suburbs for injuries reported as accidents which in fact had been inflicted at the hands of their spouses. Linda insisted that it was a weekend kind of story, arguing that that's when many of the worst beatings, mental and physical, took place. She said maybe this weekend, because of her story, one of those women would get help—report her CEO husband to the police, call a lawyer, file for divorce, get an order of protection, take her children to a safe house. Linda told Dawn Ann and the producer that 30 per cent of all women murdered were murdered by their husbands or boyfriends. Linda was all fired up on the subject. You'd think she'd been abused herself, but she wasn't even married.

All the lights in the apartment were on, and Dawn Ann heard music in Derek's studio. Usually, if he were in the darkroom, the hall would be as dark and silent as a cave. She dumped her briefcase in the foyer and called, "Hi guys, I'm home!"

No one answered. The door to the studio was half-open, so she stepped in, repeating, "Hey, Derek, I'm home!"

"Shush!" Derek said without turning to her. "Get out." He was behind his camera, and Nevaeh was on a stool, bare-shouldered, draped like a statue in an almond-colored sheet. Her hair was stuck up in back and a couple of loose ringlets bobbed at her neck.

"No," Nevaeh said. "She can stay, I don't mind."

"I do," Derek said, pushing up the sleeves of his white shirt.

"That's not right," Nevaeh pleaded.

"Shut up!" Derek screamed. "Both of you!"

"Okay, okay," Dawn Ann said and pointed at Nevaeh, putting her finger to her lips, signaling for Nevaeh not to provoke him. "Sorry to bother you," she whispered.

She went to the kitchen, poured herself a glass of white wine from a bottle that was half-full and went to the living room, where she picked up a news magazine and the paper, slipped off her shoes and put her stockinged feet on the coffee table. The section of the paper in her hands contained the want-ads, and a couple of them were circled. Although she'd miss her when she was gone, she was glad Nevaeh was looking; it was the right thing to do. But she couldn't focus on the paper. In the studio, Derek obviously had posed Nevaeh just so. He'd arranged the lights. He'd draped her. Dawn Ann put down the paper. What was Nevaeh wearing underneath the sheet? How long had it taken him to arrange each fold? Had his hand brushed her flesh? She took a long drink of her wine, holding it in her mouth while she tried to evaluate her suspicions. She swallowed and pushed aside her thoughts. Nevaeh had said "come in." She was her cousin and had nothing to hide.

Dawn Ann picked the paper back up and forced herself to focus on the job listings. Perhaps Dawn Ann could find something that Nevaeh might've overlooked. Someone—Nevaeh, certainly—had circled a couple "general office" listings, but then Dawn Ann saw,

"Models: Dancers, centerfolds. No nudity req'd." Was that what they were doing in there? Trying to get Nevaeh a job? Derek should know better than to help her get a job like that. Nice of him to want to help, but totally misguided. "No nudity req'd" didn't mean it wasn't *requested*, or that there wasn't more money in it, or that partial nudity, near nudity, might-as-well-be nudity wasn't what was called for. How could they be that naïve?

She finished the last of her wine and poured another half glass to accompany her nightly cleansing ritual. She emerged from her bathroom 15 minutes later, relaxed, and called "good night," before tucking herself in and closing her eyes. Surely Nevaeh, brought up on the North Shore and a college graduate, could find something to do other than stripping. What had Nevaeh said she'd done for work in the French Quarter? Dawn Ann's eyes sprung open. Maybe *she* was the one who was naïve.

• • •

Dawn Ann slept fitfully until ten and woke up grouchy. She'd exhausted herself tossing and turning, fighting the demon of Nevaeh's unemployment as if it were here own. Would Nevaeh be willing? Had she undressed for Derek? Is that why Derek was such a changed man? Having his cake, as it were, his mistress supported by his wife? She reached out and Derek wasn't there. On his side, the sheets were cool. What a fool she could be!

She smelled something burning and then the smoke alarm went off. She struggled out of bed, stumbling down the hall, nearly tripping over a retreating Bernard. In the kitchen, Nevaeh, dressed in a short white terry robe Dawn Ann had loaned her, was standing on a chair holding a wet towel to the smoke alarm and Derek, bare-chested but in blue jeans, was reaching up as if to hold her. Nevaeh took the towel away and the thing resumed its screeching. She smothered it again and Derek put his hand on her waist. Neither one of them seemed to notice Dawn Ann until she opened the kitchen window.

"You like your bacon crispy?" Nevaeh giggled.

"Morning, princess," Derek said, coming over to give her a peck on the cheek.

"What are you two doing?" she asked.

"Making you breakfast!" Nevaeh cried, still holding the towel tight against the alarm. Without make-up and without special lights, her face was young and trifling, not seductive. Her sunny disposition deflated Dawn Ann's suspicions.

"It's not our cooking," Derek said. "The smoke alarms are super-sensitive."

Nevaeh hopped off the chair, as Derek jerked away from Dawn Ann, startling her with his urgency to protect Nevaeh. Nevaeh cinched her belt and tossed her hair back. Dawn Ann, her emotions twisting, plopped herself down at the kitchen table. "I'd settle for a cup of coffee," she said. Nevaeh quickly poured one and brought it to her.

"Thanks," Dawn Ann said and then looked at Derek, who stood over the stove now, considering the blackened bacon. "So, honey, what do you want to do today?"

"We were thinking …" Nevaeh began, then stopped abruptly. Dawn Ann smiled to cover her dismay. Had they, indeed, become a threesome? Had her suspicions been right, after all?

"I was thinking I'd take Nevaeh out to the Pier, do some outdoors work. What do you think?"

Dawn Ann started to answer when she realized that Derek wasn't asking her. Nevaeh didn't answer either; she was looking at Dawn Ann. For what? Permission? Understanding? Help? Did Nevaeh want to pose in public like that? What would she wear? Was this Derek's idea or hers?

"Yes? No? Anybody?" Derek drained the hot grease into a coffee can and Dawn Ann held her breath, as if the question were more momentous than it appeared to be.

"Whatever you want, Derek," Nevaeh said. "I don't have any plans for today, so it's up to you two." Dawn Ann found herself in a whirligig of emotions that had little to do with her cousin and everything to do with her husband—a monstrous, self-serving tormenter who seemed to get sadistic pleasure out of seeing her squirm between her polite, good-hostess reflexes and her raw, jealous-wife reactions.

"Why don't you do that, then, and maybe we can all have an early supper and catch a movie?" Dawn Ann said, pitching her voice to sound nonchalant, as she imagined an older sister—even an older cousin—would sound. "I have a bunch of errands," she added, although she couldn't think of anything other than taking her pink linen pants suit to the cleaners. "Okay," Nevaeh said. "What's playing?" She picked up the unopened newspaper from the kitchen table and found the weekend section. "You choose," she said to Dawn Ann, and read off the list of summer movies.

Nothing appealed. "Just dreck," Dawn Ann said. "How about some music?" Dawn Ann turned to Derek, hoping to gather his approval of that idea, but he was breaking an egg into the scorched pan. If he was making an effort, and trying to be nice by making her a fried egg, well then, she'd eat it, pretending, if need be, that it was like a charcoal broiled rib or a blackened marshmallow.

"Music," Nevaeh repeated, and started reading out those listings. "Lots of choices," Dawn Ann stopped her. "We don't need to decide right now. We can play it by ear."

"Good idea," Nevaeh said, much too enthusiastically.

Dawn Ann looked at her and then at the newspaper. "I saw the want-ads you circled," she said. "Don't answer any modeling ads until you've talked to me," she said.

"Oh yeah, I put a question mark on one of those," she said.

"Obviously, it's okay to model for Derek," Dawn Ann began.

"She doesn't need your permission," he snapped.

"Of course not," Dawn Ann retreated. "I just don't want her to get involved with the wrong sort of photographer. You know what I mean, honey."

"Honey," he mimicked, but she couldn't imagine what she'd said that was wrong. She let it go, though, because she didn't want to appear to Nevaeh to be jealous. She knew, in her heart of hearts, that Derek loved her.

•••

Nevaeh dressed in a long print skirt and a peasant blouse, and she and Derek carried Derek's camera equipment to Navy Pier and its on-going festival of *a capella* singers, stilt-walkers and balloon artists. While that part of the Pier was fun, Nevaeh liked the end of the Pier the best, where it turned into a semi-circle surrounded by the Lake and where there was always a good breeze. She imagined the pictures Derek would take of her there, her hair streaming in the wind as she looked thoughtfully out to what might pass for a sea. Maybe that wasn't very original, but it was the picture she wanted for herself, all hope and secret thoughts. The image calmed her even as the morning's events churned inside her. She'd gotten in the middle of something between Derek and Dawn Ann, and she hadn't meant to. She resolved to treat him just like a brother.

It was a hot and muggy day, the humidity so thick it was a struggle to lug Derek's camera, tripod and spare lenses the half mile to the sculpture park at the entrance to the Pier. They took a break and sat on a bench, watching a fountain of water spouts jumping high in the air from dozens of holes arranged in a square in the cement plaza. Derek said the water was treated so that it would hold together in the air like a column and not break up until it landed with a splash at the base, but then he settled into a pensive silence. Running between the water spouts, a dozen children squealed in half a dozen languages, drenching themselves. Nevaeh smiled as the children shouted with surprise, unable to figure out the random order of the jumping water. She felt herself near melting in the beating sun. The hair around her face hung limp and wet, as if she'd run a distance.

Without a word, Derek stood and started fiddling with his tripod. He set up his equipment as if he were going to take some pictures of the kids.

"Get up," he said, and she stood. He gave her a teasing smile and a little shove. "Get in there."

"What?" she asked. It was one thing for kids to play in the water, but yesterday, in Derek's studio, he'd made her feel more sophisticated than that, beautiful even. She'd look ridiculous among the kids. And terrible, too. Like a wet poodle. Dawn Ann had straight hair, she could pull it back and look stunning, but Nevaeh's unruly curls would look like a wet mop. She didn't want her picture taken like that.

"Go," Derek pushed her.

"No, I'd feel silly," she laughed, and started to sit back down, but he grabbed her wrist and squeezed so tight she cried out. "Ouch!" He twisted harder, the little hairs on her arms pulling away from her skin. "Derek," she said in a low, trembling voice. "Please stop."

Before she knew what was happening, he had her arm behind her back and was walking her to the fountain, where he brushed aside her hair and nipped at her neck, his breath hot against the perspiration that gathered there. "You'll be beautiful. Free and beautiful," he whispered harshly. "As beautiful as Dawn Ann, more beautiful, even, a free spirit. Show me." He pushed her to the center of the fountain and stepped back to his tripod.

The water splashed on her back, then exploded on her breasts, then plopped hard on her head, bullets of water shooting randomly at her face, her arms, her legs. The children shrieked, and ran to the edges, towards their mothers, their playground domain invaded by an adult. But Nevaeh didn't feel like an adult, she felt humiliated. Within seconds, her hair was dripping, her clothes were heavy, and her nipples, hard from the shock of the stinging, cold water, were poking through her thin blouse. It all seemed so crass, so ridiculous.

"Derek!" she yelled, but he hollered back, "Stay there! Look up! Lift your skirt! Higher! Hold it out, spin around!" She lifted her skirt out to both sides and then gathered one side at her waist, showing only the side of her leg. Part of her understood that Derek was going for themes of spontaneity and freedom and *au natural*, but the photograph struck her as trite and exhibitionist. She was afraid of him, afraid not to do what he said, and here she was, wet, cold and dizzy, looking like a homeless girl without a shower of her own or a change of clothes. The mothers around the fountain were tsk-tsking in their disapproving languages and she hated Derek even as he shouted, for all the world to hear, "Beautiful!"

"Hey, lady!" A gruff voice, not Derek's, shouted, "Get out of there now!" Two uniformed Chicago police officers, neither of whom appeared to be amused, pointed their billy sticks in her direction. Immediately she scurried out, pulling her wet clothes away from her body and wringing the water from her hair. She stood as close to Derek as possible without dripping on him or his camera bags.

"And you, buddy, you got a permit?"

"What for?" Derek asked, swerving his camera in their direction and clicking as if they were models.

"What the hell!" the tall one said. There were beads of sweat glistening on his forehead. "Cut the crap, buddy."

"Public place, I can take pictures in a public place," Derek was skipping around the two now, taking pictures with the hand-held.

"When you use a model or do anything commercial, you need a permit," the other one said, waving his hands. "Wrap it up and we'll let it go." Click, click. The power advance whirred. "Now," he shouted.

Derek stopped, bowed facetiously, and pulled the camera up over his head. Nevaeh held her breath, hoping his stupid gesture was enough to satisfy his bruised ego and that he'd back down and pack up his things. The tall officer strode past him and the other one followed, looking Nevaeh straight in the eye the way the beat cops in New Orleans had looked at street performers, striking the deal that says, "I know you, I'm watching. Let's stay out of each other's way." She gave him her most innocent smile, as if she really were a commercial model, not a homeless addict ridiculed by an attractive but dangerous man whose attentions, once brotherly and welcoming, had become bizarre and threatening.

Remarkably, Nevaeh's exchange with the policeman was enough of a distraction that the officer never made eye contact with Derek, who was clearly itching for a fight. Neither officer acknowledged him when he said, tauntingly, "Effing pigs, she's no model."

20

That night the three of them ordered in Chinese and Nevaeh insisted on paying. They sat on the living room couch, Derek in the middle and watched a movie. Derek brought out a joint during the opening credits and, after taking a deep and meaningful drag, passed it to Nevaeh, who didn't think twice about whether she should or shouldn't take a hit. She'd had a stressful day and she'd already had some red wine with dinner. Getting high for the movie seemed natural to her and perhaps a way that both Derek and she could forget what had happened at the fountain. Much to her surprise, Dawn Ann took the joint from Derek and took a short hit, too.

At some point in the middle of the movie they all lost interest. Derek started telling Dawn Ann about the cops and the fountain and how they wanted him to have a permit because they thought Nevaeh was some high-paid model. Nevaeh tried to laugh, to let them know that she had no real ambitions as a model. Truthfully, she'd never compared herself that favorably to strikingly beautiful women like Dawn Ann or that Ophelia woman who'd shown up and taken Phil.

"Don't quit your day job, sweet pea," Derek cautioned, cackling as if that were hysterically funny. He pushed himself off the couch and left the room. Dawn Ann hit the pause button. Nevaeh had no idea how long the two of them sat staring at the frozen image, but a flash of bright light brought them both back to life.

"Let's do some family shots," Derek said. "I'm beginning to see the resemblance."

Dawn Ann moved next to Nevaeh on the couch and draped her arm around her shoulder. Dawn Ann smiled at the camera, a poster-girl smile, from what Nevaeh could see out of the corner of her eye. Not to be outdone, she looked straight at Derek and gave him a matching center-fold grin.

"Good," he said, "good, good," a parody of a photographer at work, but friendly, so unlike the afternoon at the fountain.

"Derek usually doesn't work with people," Dawn Ann said. "Usually it's screws and nails."

He ignored her. "Profiles, now," he said sternly. "Look at each other. Nose to nose."

"Oh, not my nose," Dawn Ann said. "Not my nose."

"Yes, the nose," he said, his voice suddenly as commanding as it'd been that day when he'd twisted Nevaeh's arm. "Oh, look at that, a matched pair. How about tip to tip?" The command in his voice was gone; he sounded amused, coaxing his subjects into relaxing before the camera, like a professional working with children.

High and goofy, Dawn Ann and Nevaeh went tip to tip, giggling like eight-year-olds.

"Great!" Derek said, his enthusiasm mounting. "Great, oh, yes, great! Now tongues."

They were both laughing so hard, it would later be difficult for either Nevaeh or Dawn to say why they did it, why on Derek's command each stuck out her tongue, and let Derek click a picture, their noses and tongues tip to tip. At the time, with Nevaeh feeling all the warmth and giddiness of a sisterly pillow fight—silly for the sake of being silly—they continued the pose as Derek's powered shutter captured six frames when Dawn Ann, too, forgot who and where she was.

The next day Derek and Dawn Ann went sailing with Linda Livingston and a friend of hers. Nevaeh read the Sunday paper, took a long walk, stopped for a beer and a burger out at Navy Pier and listened to a free live concert at Grant Park. She got home after ten, and the apartment was dark, Derek and Dawn Ann apparently asleep.

When she woke up late the next morning, Dawn Ann had already left. It was raining outside, as had been predicted. The coffee pot was on. She was startled when Derek came in to the kitchen, barefooted. His hair was wet and he smelled pleasantly of soap. He was wearing blue jeans that hovered around his hips and an open cotton shirt.

He handed her a Bloody Mary. "Good morning, my dear," he said. "How've you been?" He sat down at the kitchen table and gestured to her to do the same.

"Me? Fine." She held the drink, and then, because Derek's look was so insistent, joined him at the table and took a sip. It burned as if it were half vodka, but she wouldn't give him the pleasure of knowing he'd shocked her. "Heard a great band yesterday in Grant Park. Blind Boys of Alabama."

"Did you get a CD?" he asked, his voice rising in apparent interest.

"No, I didn't," she said. The truth was that she'd spent $173 in the past three weeks and she couldn't afford to be frivolous. She wasn't desperate yet, but she was getting there.

"Maybe we can go out later and get one," he offered. He sounded kind again, like a big brother.

"I can't buy anything until I get a job," she said.

"So get a job! You've got some modeling experience now," he said.

"Have I? I haven't seen the studio photographs," she said, hoping to tease him into showing her the pictures they'd posed in the studio, the ones with the sheet. She'd just as soon not see the fountain shots. Despite his threatening behavior at the fountain, Derek must think she has some potential or why would he even mention modeling again? And this morning, he wasn't acting mean, as far as she could tell. "Don't I need to have a portfolio, head shots or something?"

"Yes," Derek said, slapping his hand on the table. "Yes, dammit, you do! Drink up! We'll begin today." He sounded like someone ready to get down to serious business.

"That would be great, Derek!" she said and took another sip of the Bloody Mary. "Let me take a shower first, while you set up." She wished she hadn't said "shower," for fear it might remind Derek of the fountain and start him off in the wrong direction. Derek didn't react to the word one way or the other, and Nevaeh realized that Derek carried no residual embarrassment or animosity from two days ago: if he was conscious of his misbehavior at all, he obviously forgave himself and forgot it with ease. Today would be different, a professional sitting not just for practice, but for real.

She locked the bathroom door, as she always had since Key West. In the shower, she let her mind wander. What she was trying to do, ultimately, was to get a job that would permit her to be independent and maybe get back to what she'd gone to college for. Modeling wasn't a career, it was just a step towards financial freedom, and the freedom to write. In college, she'd looked down her highly educated nose at models, but now, in a very different place, she limited her disdain to the pouty, underfed, six-foot stick figure variety.

Today, modeling didn't seem so far-fetched. She had a cousin in a related business, her cousin-in-law was a photographer and he saw her potential. Hadn't she once had a dream of "pulchritude?" She wouldn't call herself drop-dead beautiful, but she was photogenic enough and she immediately cast herself in ads for student loans, Fannie Mae mortgages, health clubs, first cars, vitamins. The girl next door.

She put on an old flannel robe that Dawn Ann had loaned her and stuck her nose in the studio. "Tee shirt and jeans okay?" she asked.

"Come in," he said. "Stand facing the curtain there." The corner of the studio was draped in black curtains that could be opened to reveal a blank wall or pulled closed, as now, for a softer background. Derek had set up the lights to create a super-bright spot in the center. Without her permission, he'd opened her box of stemmed glasses and arranged them randomly along the hem of the curtain, some straight up, some on their sides. Her favorite cobalt blue stemmed flute was on its side, next to a gold-rimmed balloon, neither one fine glass but she remembered exactly where they were on the right side of her harmonica cart: second row, second from right and first row, center.

"Facing?" She thought it was an odd pose—she'd thought they were going to take head shots—but when he didn't answer, she obeyed, back to the camera. He was silent and, unable to see him or figure out what he was doing; she felt very vulnerable.

She held her breath and tried not to think. Lapsing into a near-meditative trance, she stood there silently for five minutes. Then she felt Derek's hand arranging the robe off her shoulders. A little chill went up her spine and she shivered. He massaged her neck. "Relax," he said, and stepped back.

She felt a moment of relief, but was still uncertain. She remembered that first week, when Dawn Ann said Derek was a windstorm, and that she shouldn't provoke him, she should let him be. He wasn't forcing her to do anything, she told herself. She was fully covered. She should just let him do his job and she would pretend she was doing hers.

She heard the camera click, click, click, then stop. Suddenly, Derek was behind her again, untying the belt of the robe, pulling it off her, letting it drop to the ground.

She didn't move a muscle. His finger slowly traced the middle of her back, the tip of his fingernail cutting a thin line, lower and lower and down the crack between her buttocks.

She wanted to pull up the robe, run to her room, pack her things and escape. She could run to Linda, tell her "yes," now she was frightened. But she felt frozen in place.

Derek backed off and returned to the camera, adjusted the lights, and then came up behind her again, gently rearranging the robe at her feet, adjusting her hair. Nevaeh tried to relax. This was Derek, being a photographer—for all she knew, treating her like a professional model. Perhaps, she'd been overreacting.

"Turn around," he said, startling her.

"Turn around," he said again, his voice a mixture of coax and threat.

Reluctantly, she turned, brushing her hair forward over her nipples and fanning a hand in front of her crotch. As she turned, a glass fell over next to the robe. She bent to right it.

"Leave it," he said. "Stand up." Slowly, she straightened.

"Hmmm," Derek said, and sighed. Unable to look at him, she chose a spot to his right, near the door, where there was a smudge on the beige wall, like a splash of coffee or perhaps the shadow of a dent caused by a thrown object. The camera shuttered. What was he doing? Immediately, she bent down to gather the robe around herself, but Derek shouted, "No! Don't!" Then suddenly he changed his mind, saying, "Okay, stay there like that a minute." and he took a series of pictures of her crouched like a dog, on her haunches, a mass of shaggy curls hiding most of her face, hiding from the abusive camera. Her right foot began to tingle so she stood, shaking the sleep out of it while holding the robe in front of her.

"Derek," she managed to say. "Derek, I really don't feel comfortable doing this."

"It's not about your comfort," he said, knitting his eyebrows and staring at her eyes as if he hadn't even noticed her undress. "If you think you're turning me on, huddled there like a newborn calf, like some goddam embarrassed Presbyterian, you're only insulting me. Drop the robe," he commanded.

"I'm an artist," he continued, the camera working. "I happen to find the human body beautiful. Even in its lesser forms." He pranced in an arc around her, his camera humming, aiming at her knees, her breasts, her bellybutton: the camera's Cyclops prodding and prying everywhere. She felt totally helpless. She thought about Linda and her warnings. She'd been right about Derek's superiority and his ploys for control: he'd been friendly to her, sometimes flirtatious, sometimes ignoring her, but underneath it all, almost always suffused with a hint of danger. He frightened her. She prayed she would be safe. She would get through this without getting hurt.

"I know it's about the art," she whimpered. "But I'm not pretty enough for that."

"You belong in art if I say you belong in art."

"I think you could find someone prettier. Dawn Ann ..."

"Shut up! I'm feeding you. Giving you shelter. The least you can do is try to earn your keep, Cousin Nevvy." He took a dozen more pictures and finally grunted, "That's it. You can go."

"Okay," she said, grabbed the robe, and hurried out, grateful Derek hadn't gone further, turned violent. It was difficult to fully grasp, but Nevaeh thought for a minute that she understood then the source of Derek's power, not just over her, but over his wife: one moment he was charming and loving and considerate, and the next he was debasing, insulting, and physically intimidating. Random. Unpredictable. Making a mockery of Dawn Ann, who paid for their private lives by making public predictions.

She rifled through her backpack, making sure that it was stocked with all of her survival necessities, including the Bible where she hid her remaining money, then quickly dressed in jeans and a tee shirt and a long-sleeved blouse and brushed her hair so vigorously it stood out over her shoulders like a tent. She rearranged the sheets and pillows on the day bed so that if later Dawn Ann came home and peeked in, she'd think Nevaeh was asleep and wouldn't investigate further. Nevaeh wasn't certain where she was going or what she was going to do, but she needed to cover all her bases, just in case. In the kitchen, she found an apple and a bottle of water, and scooped up loose change someone had left on the counter. Then she turned back to the refrigerator and grabbed a can of beer and slipped it into her pack. As quietly as she could manage, she shouldered her pack and left, the adrenaline thumping in her chest the way it had the night she escaped from Lilies TLC. She stood in front of the elevator, praying for it to arrive before Derek might burst into the hallway and drag her back inside, kicking and screaming, with no one to hear her distress.

• • •

When Dawn Ann arrived later that night, neither Nevaeh nor Derek was there. The door to Nevaeh's room was closed and when she knocked, no one answered. The light was on in Derek's studio, the door to the darkroom open. One of his two computers was humming. When she touched the key pad it woke up, and instead of the swirl of Derek's psychedelic screen saver, the image of a woman came up, a nude photographed against a black background, the pose awkward at best, its emotional tone mixed. The model seemed to be deliberately avoiding the camera, about to crouch down.

"Ohmygod," she said. "Ohmygod." She bolted from the room, as much afraid of being discovered as she was horrified by the image. Under her own nose! How could she! How could he?

What else had happened? She wasn't stupid: she knew very well what had happened.

Derek she could almost understand. Not forgive, but understand. Nevaeh was young and beautiful and a free spirit; of course a man would be attracted to her. Nevaeh's naïveté was an act, a ploy. Derek must've been seduced. Dawn Ann should have seen this coming; her work hours and her trusting nature had given them lots of time together. She pounded again on Nevaeh's door, then pushed it open and flicked on the lights.

"Nevaeh!" she hollered. She marched to the daybed, tossed

back the sheets and threw the pillow down on the floor, kicking it. Nevaeh's clothes—rags, all—were still in the closet. Where was she? Where were *they*?

Dawn Ann's heart raced so hard she felt her stomach churn, like a runner who bends over at the finish line and vomits a bile of spent adrenaline. She didn't know what to do. If she could put the photo out of her mind, she might be able to calm down, think, rehearse, address the matter in a mature manner, but she was frantic. Every insult Derek had ever lobbed her way, every transgression she'd ever forgiven him—miniature poinsettias, bedroom rapes, verbal insults—exploded again in her head.

She had to leave the apartment, for fear they'd return. It was almost unbelievable that they'd left together. Where would they go? Nevaeh didn't have a place to go, she couldn't even go to her mother's—the only person in Chicago she'd had to move in with was a cousin she hadn't seen in years. What was the real story there, anyway?

She grabbed a sweater and ran to the elevators.

They might've gone to a hotel, if Derek had taken his credit card with him. Wouldn't that be something? She'd get the bill for his infidelity!

But who would support them? Neither one of them had a marketable skill, unless you counted rubbing your fingers around wet glasses or hawking pictures of screws or … She hadn't noticed if anything was missing from Derek's studio. But how would she know? He kept his photographs to himself, the prints, negatives, and CDs stored in the locked rolling cases. She rarely saw any of his work.

There could be a market for the pictures of Nevaeh, that kind of stuff. She was breathless. Before Nevaeh, Derek had done dozens of nudes of her! Worse yet, the pictures he took last night! Silly tongue-to-tongue pictures—if they were made public, she'd be finished. He knew that. He could blackmail her for the rest of her life!

She pounded on the elevators, fighting back her tears. She didn't know where she was going, except far away from the possible return of Derek before she could form a plan. She could pretend she hadn't seen the screensaver, but she was in no condition to pull that off, not until she calmed down. She called Linda Livingston on her cell phone.

When Linda answered, she heard the clatter of restaurant noise.

"Are you at Walter's?" she asked.

"Good guess. What's up?" Linda said.

"Is Derek there?" she asked, holding her breath.

"No," Linda said. "You sound frantic. What's wrong?"

"Just wait for me," she said, beginning, at last, to cry. She flew out the revolving lobby door and jogged the half-dozen blocks to the restaurant.

• • •

Linda sat rigid and stern-faced in a corner booth at the window, her coffee growing cold as Dawn Ann choked out her story.

"So, what do I do?" Dawn Ann pleaded.

Linda propped her right elbow on the table and rested her chin in her hand. She stared at the Formica and picked at the scallops of her white paper placemat.

"I'm no expert," Linda said. She picked the whole left side of the placemat flat. "We could call a hotline."

"NO!" Dawn Ann said, so loudly that a couple two tables away looked up. "This absolutely cannot get out," she said. "I don't know the whole story yet," she said.

"Stop that," Linda insisted. Before Dawn Ann figured out what Linda meant, Linda added, "Stop making excuses for him. This is emotional abuse and you know it. Even if in some perverse, artsy-fartsy way this project is legitimate, he should have told you, up front, what they were doing, not leave it on a screen-saver. Isn't that your answer, honey? Art goes in a frame, porn on a screen-saver."

Stunned, Dawn Ann nodded.

"Okay, we don't know what to do. So let's take the high road. Call. Leave a message that says "Linda's got a huge guy-problem" and that you're staying with me tonight. That'll buy us time. Tomorrow, we can see where we stand." Linda handed Dawn Ann her cell phone, already speed-dialed.

No one answered, and Dawn Ann left her message. "Love you," she finished, out of habit.

"Good cover," Linda reassured her. "Remember, he doesn't know you know."

"Oh, yeah," Dawn Ann said, slightly relieved. In her mind, she and Derek had already had the knock-down drag-out fight, words and dishes flying recklessly, Bernard hiding under the bed. She hadn't pictured herself winning.

21

As she stepped out of Dawn Ann's apartment building, Nevaeh felt the same terror she'd felt on the stoop of Lilies of the Field. Back in New Orleans, she'd had a network, some loyal friends. The only people she knew here were Linda, who was probably working, and Trudy, who was not the sort Nevaeh would think to go to for advice, even if she could screw up enough courage to ask anyone for advice. It was hard to have courage without trust. Hard to trust without a plan. Despite the Scripture about the lilies, Nevaeh couldn't help but feel that without a plan, courage was mere bravado, loud and boisterous but essentially useless. She needed a plan.

First, though, she needed clarity, and that meant time and a place of peace and relative quiet. She looked up; the afternoon sun was scorching the city, its heat rising off the sidewalk in silvery mirages. That night the weatherman at Channel Six would probably try to fry an egg on the cement, to win back viewers lost to her cousin. She shouldered her pack and headed east on Ohio Street to the lakefront.

Old men played chess at stone tables in the park that led to the beach. Down below, on the sand, nannies watched their charges while retired couples huddled under colorful umbrellas. The lifeguard sat in a boat at the outer edge of the swimming area, a water shepherd tending his flock, although most of the bathers stood knee deep in the water. Nevaeh perched on the ledge and considered the possibility. If she wandered out there, fully dressed, would the guard rescue her, diagnose her as mad, and call the paramedics who would drop her at an emergency room, where she could act crazy enough to be kept overnight for observation?

She reached in her pack and brought out her vinyl Bible, marked at Luke 12:22, but she couldn't open to that page without revealing her wad, so she went to the page before, and at the beginning of Luke, 12, found the warning to be vigilant against hypocrisy: "Everything that is now covered will be uncovered, and everything now hidden will be made clear." Her heart nearly stopped. " ... what you have whispered in hidden places will be proclaimed on the housetops." She saw Derek's rude pictures of her tossed from the rooftops to the winds, picked up and fingered by strangers. She had to go, immediately, and find Dawn Ann, and tell her exactly what had happened. Putting her Bible in her pack, she headed back under Lake Shore Drive. In the hollow of the tunnel, a saxophonist played the opening bars of "When the Saints Come Marching In" over and over again, propelling her west on Ohio Street to Channel Three.

It was now late afternoon, and in the shadow of the television studio building, Nevaeh stopped and took a deep breath before presenting herself to the security guard. She tried to rehearse what she might say to Dawn Ann, to "play it through," as she'd been taught in rehab. When she envisioned telling her cousin, she imagined Dawn Ann lunging at her and then at Derek, and Derek striking back and Dawn Ann clawing at him before he crushed her to a quivering mound on the floor.

She could also see it going another way: Derek pleading with Dawn Ann for forgiveness, trying to put the whole thing off on Nevaeh, "that little hussy," who wanted to earn fast money by modeling for up to $500/day, *"no nudity required"*—better that Nevvy get to see what that might actually feel like in a friendly environment like his studio, because he only had eyes for Dawn Ann, and after all, he hadn't touched her slut of a cousin, had he?

Nevaeh turned away from the oval security desk and its bank of security cameras and video loops of Channel Three promos, including one for "The Elements" with Dawn Ann McKnight. "I'm sorry, I'm in the wrong building," she said, and outside once again, she knew that the best thing for everyone would be to pretend it hadn't happened. But then what?

She headed over to Walter's, thinking at least to get a sandwich and maybe a beer. In a short black jeans skirt and a white shirt unbuttoned far enough to reveal the top of a lacy pink bra, Trudy served her a patty melt and fries without a lot of chit-chat and brought her a second beer "on the house." Two Channel Three sound guys came in and, seeing Nevaeh alone in a booth against the back wall, asked if they could join her. She welcomed their company and was disappointed that both wore gold wedding rings and were simply being friendly, exchanging info on movies and concerts and other entertainments going on around town. When they left, Trudy brought her another beer and sat down for a minute, keeping one eye on Lizzy, the manager at the front of the restaurant.

"So, where's the rest of the fam?" Trudy asked.

"Dawn Ann's working," she said, perhaps too quickly, as if she had something to hide. "Don't know about Derek. Last I saw him, he was in the darkroom." Close enough, she thought.

"How long you gonna stay with them?" Trudy asked. "Or is it a threesome?"

"This is probably my last week," she answered, ignoring the glint in Trudy's eye. "I haven't told Dawn Ann, yet," she hurried. "But I'm close to getting a job." She had no idea why she was lying to Trudy, except to make her forthcoming disappearance seem credible.

"Where will you live then?" Trudy asked.

"I don't know yet," she said.

"My roommate's moving out," Trudy said. "Moving in with her guy." She stood up suddenly, as if Lizzy had caught her eye. She picked up Nevaeh's empty bottle. "A one-bedroom, but real nice, up near Irving Park. You can have the hide-a-bed in the living room. Whadya say?"

Quickly, Nevaeh considered her options and grabbed the lifeline. "Um, that would be great, Trudy, it really would. I mean, I want to get my own place and all, but for a month or two, it would really help me out."

Trudy beamed. "I could show it to you after my shift," she said. "Come back around eleven o'clock."

Nevaeh checked her watch. She had four hours to kill. She didn't want Trudy to know her entire situation, so she left a tip as she would for any waitress, took her check to the cashier, and walked a few blocks to a bus stop. When #151 groaned to a stop, she got on. She rode for three hours, seeing parts of the city she'd not seen before, until neighborhoods became a blur of lights. Then she dozed a little, but fitfully. If she missed her appointment with Trudy, she'd be riding the bus until morning or wandering from all-night diner to all-night diner, drinking coffee until some drunk harassed her into moving on. At least, that's what she imagined for herself, even though she knew that on a hot and boring summer night, it could become much worse.

Returning to Walter's just after ten o'clock, she quickly scanned the room, relieved that Derek wasn't there. In a corner TV, Dawn Ann was waving in the weather with a graceful scoop of her arms, and Linda was sitting in for Felicity. Dawn Ann looked like her usual self, not a hint of anxiety about her. Nevaeh had to keep reminding herself that she didn't know about the pictures Derek had taken just that afternoon. Dawn Ann also didn't know yet that Nevaeh was gone. She didn't want to worry her. It occurred to her that she couldn't call the apartment without risking the possibility that Derek might answer, so she borrowed Trudy's phone and left a message on Dawn Ann's personal number at the station, saying that she was spending the night with a friend.

Trudy wanted to stop for a drink on the way to her place. Even though Nevaeh was as tired as she'd ever been, drained emotionally from Derek's abuse and weary from her wanderings around the city, she had no choice but to tag along. They took the bus up to Trudy's neighborhood, a few blocks of three-story limestone buildings converted to three-flats and grimy brick U-shaped buildings divided into 12 units. They walked two blocks to Cornerby's, a tavern with a 4:00 a.m. license. Trudy knew a small group of men and women gathered at the long dark wooden bar, dressed in jean shorts and mini-skirts. Although there were five different beers on tap, they were drinking martinis from giant glasses like the ones used in upscale downtown hotels. They'd ordered a pitcher, and the bartender put down two more glasses, each with three olives on a plastic sword. Someone poured them each a drink and Trudy introduced Nevaeh.

"She used to live in a tree house," Trudy said proudly, which obliged Nevaeh to describe her place on Farmer Jones's property and answer the questions that Dawn Ann had been too embarrassed, she guessed, to ask: about the toilet arrangements, mostly, and bird droppings, and spiders and squirrels and what she did for ice. As she talked, she found herself homesick for those times, when she and Tray lived day-to-day and enjoyed each other and she made beds at The Bluffs and sometimes she harvested a real tip, like ten dollars, and a little handwritten "thank you" with a loopy daisy for an exclamation point. She put five dollars on the bar when the group ordered another pitcher and accepted one refill, and then another. She watched Trudy flirt with each of the three guys at the bar, throwing her arms around them when they told jokes and resting her hand on their butt while they listened to someone else's story. At three thirty, having kicked in for two more pitchers, the group was down to Nevaeh, Trudy, and a skinny but clean-shaven and good-looking friend of hers whose name she thought was Steven. The three of them were drunk, and Nevaeh knew they were drunk, and she was on that precipice when she didn't know how much longer she'd know it.

"Shouldn't we go home?" she asked, and Steven put his arm around her and said, "Yes, my dear, we should," although he was in no condition and Nevaeh shook him off a bit more forcefully than she intended. He didn't seem to notice, and draped his arm over Trudy's shoulder instead and the three of them headed out into the cool night air. It was three exhausting flights up to Trudy's apartment. Trudy tried her key four or five times before the tumbler clicked and the three of them spilled into her tiny living room. In the dark, Trudy pointed to the couch, and Nevaeh immediately sprawled out on it. Steven followed Trudy down the hall as though he lived there.

"Thanks so much," she managed to mumble.

It was nearly noon when Nevaeh opened her eyes and studied the white speckled ceiling, her body flattened on the corduroy couch. In a sleeveless tee, her arms were bare and she vaguely remembered that she'd left Dawn Ann's with a long-sleeved blouse on, but it was gone. Her neck hurt, presumably from having used her backpack as a pillow. "Demon booze," she said out loud. "Why do I do these things?"

Trudy came in, wrapped in a towel, her ruby red hair hanging in heavy wet strands like linguini. She had darker circles under her eyes than Nevaeh thought someone under 30 should have.

"To escape our shitty lives," Trudy said. "You can shower after Steven."

"Boyfriend?" Nevaeh asked.

"Kinda," Trudy said. "Needs a place to stay." She tossed a blue towel at Nevaeh.

"Thanks," Nevaeh said again. She hadn't thought of it last night, when they'd all been drinking, but she was relieved that Trudy hadn't brought home a stranger, no matter how good looking. Lying back on the couch, she didn't move. Her stomach churned and she hoped she could hold off vomiting until Steven got out of the shower. She heard the water pinging against a plastic stall.

The three of them drank warm Coca-Colas from cans. Both Trudy and Nevaeh looked away as Steven wolfed down three pieces of toast smeared with peanut butter. Trudy gave Nevaeh a key and asked her to make a duplicate. Trudy had to work that night from 2:00 to 11:00, Steven from 3:00 to 10:00. They planned to meet up again at Cornerby's. Nevaeh said she was going to go back to Dawn Ann's to get the rest of her stuff.

"You never said when you're going to work," Trudy said, downing a second can of Coke.

"I need to find out," Nevaeh said.

"I mean, you do have a job, right? You can pay your share?" Trudy crossed her arms.

"I can pay," Nevaeh said. "But you never said how much." She wanted to add, "for a couch in a room with cheap blinds, no drapes, no air-conditioning, and an extra roommate," but the reality was she needed a place to stay. Besides, Steven seemed nice enough, and while she'd been wrong about friends' roommates before, Steven seemed more likely a protector rather than a threat.

"Half would be almost $400," she said and Steven choked. Trudy threw him a killer look and he said, "swallowed the wrong way," then turned towards the sink. "Can you kick in $300?"

Grateful for Steven's signal, Nevaeh didn't answer right away.

"Utilities included," Trudy offered.

"Yeah, sure, as soon as I get my first paycheck," she said.

James was working the day shift and said it was a pleasure to see Nevaeh when she returned to Dawn Ann's in the early afternoon.

"Derek home?" she asked him.

"I haven't seen him this morning," James said. "But Arnie went home sick and I didn't come in until noon."

"Oh, that's too bad," she said.

At the door to their apartment, she took a deep breath and held it, as if she were about to jump off the high dive. As quietly as possible, she opened the door, closed it behind her, left her backpack in the marble foyer, and tiptoed to the Oriental runner in the hall that led to her room. She heard a clock ticking, maybe two clocks. Then the air-conditioner kicked on, causing her to expel all the air she'd saved. The door to the studio was closed. She prayed that Derek was still asleep or holed up in the darkroom.

She ducked into her room, removed her blue jean skirt, her interview clothes and her new pair of dressy flat shoes from the closet. Her harmonica glasses were missing, probably still in the studio. Quickly, she decided not to retrieve them; they could be replaced.

Back in the foyer, she noticed Derek's wallet on the decorative side table, next to his keys. She held her breath, Derek was probably home, most likely in the darkroom, making it imperative that she leave as noiselessly and quickly as possible. She set her jaw and, despite the risk, reached out and opened the wallet. Thick with twenties, it looked like he'd been out to the bank. She took $120, stuffed it in a front pocket of her backpack, and left the rest. Then, she thought to get a plastic bag for her clothes, and having come this far without being discovered, she turned to go into the kitchen.

Without warning, she slammed into Derek, who grabbed her shoulders, shouting, "You bitch! Thief! Goddam slut!" He loomed over her, his face too close to hers, his eyes raging. His breath was warm on her face, the fumes of alcohol stinking between them. He slammed her full force against the wall. Then he stepped back and struck her across the face. When she raised her hands to protect herself he grabbed her left hand by the wrist and wrenched it away, striking her again, and again, a blow for each word, "Dawn! Ann! McKnight!"

Struggling to get free, she screamed "Stop! It's me! Not Dawn Ann!"

He laughed.

His spit sprayed her face, and she could feel a trickle of blood sliding past her lips. He was so close, so ugly in his fury. With all her strength, she shot her knee up into his groin and he fell away, writhing. She grabbed her backpack and fled into the hall, but was afraid to wait for the elevator. She headed down the fire stairs. She ran down five flights, and then entered the floor hall, where, panting, she pressed the button for the elevator and rested against the wall. It was taking forever, so she hit the button over and over until it arrived.

She was alone in the elevator and at the mercy of whoever might get on at another floor, but the elevator didn't stop. In the lobby she ran past James, who was signing for a Fed Ex delivery. When a look of alarm crossed his face, she answered his unasked question. "I'm fine," she said. Outside, she stood coughing and choking and gasping for control of her breath. She glanced back briefly to make sure Derek hadn't followed her, but afraid that he might, shouldered her backpack, and headed away from the building as fast as she could. Her breath came in giant waves and in the troughs she had fragments of panicked images, one after another. The floor in Key West, the hanging bag of fluids in the hospital in New Orleans, the flowers on the Lilies of the Field van. She heard footsteps behind her and quickened her pace. At a stoplight she turned right just to keep moving; out of the corner of her eye she confirmed that Derek was not following her. Still, she did not feel safe. She found herself heading towards Walter's.

There, she aimed straight for the ladies' room. There, she inspected the damage to her face without recognizing it as her own. It was red and puffy and she could see where the bruises would rise later in the day. Her nose had stopped bleeding, but blood was caked on her upper lip. Her left eyelid drooped and she started to cry. She shouldn't have taken the money from Derek's wallet, but she'd intended to pay it back, if she ever got on her feet again, and she wouldn't have had to take it if Derek hadn't made her pose the day before. Even so, he had no right to hit someone like that. She felt a spasm up her back as she replayed the horror of his hitting her, again and again. The gleam of satisfaction in his eyes. It wasn't only that he couldn't help himself or manage his anger; he'd been enjoying himself.

She splashed cold water on her face to help prevent swelling, but it stung, so she took a paper towel and ran it under hot water and used it to soothe her aching cheeks. The door to the ladies' room opened, and Nevaeh bent further over the sink to hide her face, but the woman came up next to her and leaned over. "Nevaeh? Is that you?"

Nevaeh recognized Linda's voice. She lifted her head, but when Linda reached out towards her face, she recoiled.

"My God, what happened?" Linda drilled her dark eyes into her, demanding the truth.

The enormity of the question—what and how and why everything had happened—was too much. Nevaeh sank to the floor, sobbing.

Linda knelt down next to her. "Did he do this to you?"

Nevaeh didn't answer.

"Derek?" Linda insisted.

Nevaeh handed the warm paper towel to Linda, and she stood up and got a fresh one, handing it to Nevaeh. "Do you want to go to the hospital?" she asked.

Nevaeh shook her head violently. Hospitals, treatments—they'd only gotten her into more and more trouble. She would fend for herself.

"We need to call the police." Linda reached into her purse for her cell phone.

"NO!" Nevaeh moaned. "No, please. It would be bad. Dawnie would be mad."

"It *was* Derek!" Linda said, triumphant. "That bastard." She flipped open her phone and started to dial.

"NO!" Nevaeh struggled to her feet and grabbed Linda's phone. "Don't! It's none of your business!"

"It *is* my business," Linda said. "It's my business when my best friend's husband goes around beating up women! He did this to you; he could do this to her! He probably already has."

"I made him mad," Nevaeh said, vaguely aware that she was defending him.

"He's always mad," Linda said.

"I took some money," Nevaeh said.

"That doesn't give him the right to beat you," Linda said firmly and reached for her phone. Nevaeh swung it behind her back.

"Please, please don't!" she cried.

"Okay, Nevaeh, okay. Give me my phone and then let's go out and have some coffee and calm down so we can think more clearly about this." She held out her hand and Nevaeh gave up the phone. She let Linda carry her pack as they tried to sneak into a booth in the very back of the restaurant. It was almost two o'clock; Trudy was due at work soon.

Linda ordered coffee for herself and a bowl of chicken soup for Nevaeh. "You'll need your strength," she said, handing the menu back to the waitress. She sat silently, as if to give Nevaeh time to collect herself.

When the soup came, Nevaeh crumbled two packages of Saltines into it, using her spoon to drown the pieces one by one.

"Eat," Linda said. Obediently, Nevaeh lifted a spoonful to her mouth. She winced as she sucked in the warm liquid, swallowing hard to get it past the lump in her throat.

When the bowl was almost empty, Linda signaled to the waitress for a coffee refill, and then leaned across the table. In a calm and reassuring voice she said, "You must file charges."

Nevaeh fixed her eyes on her, not comprehending.

"We need to call the police and you need to charge him," she said.

"I can't, Linda, I just explained that to you." Nevaeh looked underneath the booth for her backpack. She needed to get away from Linda; there was no way she could call the police without implicating herself in her own crime.

Linda reached across the table and put her hand on Nevaeh's arm. Nevaeh looked at her, alarmed by being touched against her will.

"You have no place to go, Nevaeh. First the police, and then you can come stay with me for a few days. Derek wouldn't dare try anything at my place. He can't get past the front door."

"I do have a place," Nevaeh said, withdrawing her arm from Linda's grasp.

"Hey, roomie!" Trudy walked by, just about to clock in for work. "My God," she leaned in towards Nevaeh's face. "Hey, we had a hard night, but not that hard. What the hell happened?"

Linda shook her head. "Derek."

"No," Trudy said. "You and Derek take a roll in the hay? A little love-wrestling get out of hand?"

"He. Beat. Her," Linda said, pausing between each word.

Trudy looked at Linda, and then Nevaeh and then Linda again. "I don't believe it," she said. "What did you do to make him that mad?"

"I took," Nevaeh started, but Linda cut her off.

"He beat her," Linda said again. "It doesn't matter whether he was angry or not."

Trudy shrugged her shoulders as if she didn't agree but would think about it. "So you want to go home now? You've got the key, right? You can use my bed." Trudy hurried off, hips swinging, promising to call when she got off her shift.

Linda watched her go, a little curl to her lips. "Please, Nevaeh, won't you just call the police and then I'll take you up to Trudy's, wherever that is, if that's where you want to stay." She reached in her purse.

"Thanks anyway, Linda. I know you're trying to help, but I'll be okay."

"I can't make you," Linda said. She pointed her phone at Nevaeh's face. "But just let me take this picture, in case you change your mind."

Nevaeh didn't have the energy to stop Linda, or even the energy to smile. For the third time in two days, her picture was being taken with her knowledge, but not with her full and free consent. All of these images could be used against her—to ruin her relationship with her cousin, to ruin her chances of getting a job or even to land her in jail. She thanked Linda for the soup, hoisted her pack and left, alert to the possibility that Derek was either in the restaurant or waiting for her outside. She turned her head to check behind her and saw Linda scooping up the plastic wrappers from the Saltines and signaling to the waitress to clear the table.

22

On the train to Trudy's, Nevaeh feigned sleep so as to avoid the inquisitive gaze of a couple of teenage boys who obviously were ditching school, and several middle-aged women who were carrying shopping bags and who would've stared disapprovingly, had Nevaeh met their gaze. At the first stop, one of the women leaned down and handed her a card for a women's shelter. "You have a choice," she said, and disappeared. Nevaeh quickly put the card in an outside pocket of her backpack; it was a cardinal rule of urban survival not to let your fear show. When she got to Trudy's stop, she checked to make sure that Derek wasn't following her and then walked at a near-run the few blocks, then up the stairs. She double-locked the door, dragged a wooden chair in front of it and one against the back door and then took one of Trudy's washcloths, warmed it under hot water, and, lying down on the living room couch, covered her face. She couldn't sleep and finally tears came again. She sat up and pressed the now-cool cloth on her eyeballs until she saw red and the tears stopped. She was fidgety and unable to calm herself. She went out to Trudy's kitchen in search of comfort. In treatment, they'd said alcohol would not make things better, but what did they know? Had any of those happy, happy counselors been raped or beaten? Had any of them lived with a guy who left her in a heartbeat for another woman who didn't love him enough to stay around more than six months?

In the freezer she found an unopened bottle of vodka. She recognized the frosted label as an expensive brand, probably a present. Since there was no beer or wine in the refrigerator, she thought Trudy would understand her need for a painkiller, and would be willing, if not happy, to share.

She poured a good amount into a glass and sprawled on the living room couch, idly opening one of Trudy's celebrity magazines. The women were beautiful and their lives perfect, but there was a one-page story about a starlet who'd been beaten by her boyfriend while he was coked up. He reportedly was in rehab now and all was forgiven.

The next thing she remembered was the phone ringing around ten o'clock. Trudy said she and Steve were going to Cornerby's and they wondered if she wanted to join them. She wanted to, but she couldn't face the five-block walk in the darkness, every shadow a potential rapist, every doorway a hunter's blind. She didn't want Trudy to know that she was frightened, so she just said she was tired and needed to rest. Trudy understood.

Nevaeh flipped the TV on, hoping to see Dawn Ann, fresh and beautiful and smiling that wonderful smile of hers. It was summer. It had been warm and sunny. The TV reporters would be delivering their stories outside. Seeing Dawn Ann on TV would be reassuring. Derek wouldn't hurt Dawn Ann; he'd only hurt Nevaeh because she'd stolen from him.

A young man stood in for Dawn Ann McKnight. Nevaeh sat up straight, her nose pressed to the TV, as if she could make Dawn Ann materialize. Why wasn't she at work? Had Derek gone after her, too? Nevaeh got up and, feeling like a caged animal, paced in circles around the room. What to do? She didn't dare call Dawn Ann's apartment, not at this hour. What would she do if Dawn Ann weren't there? She'd have to talk to Derek, who would be angry, might even figure out where Nevaeh was hanging out. Reluctantly, she called Linda.

"Where's Dawn Ann?" Nevaeh asked, not even bothering to say "hello."

"Nevaeh, is that you?"

"Yes, do you know where she is?"

"I think she had a benefit gig tonight," Linda said. "Why do you ask?"

"She wasn't on TV," Nevaeh said, feeling a little foolish for her panic.

"This is why you should report him," Linda said.

Surprised that Linda should make such a connection, Nevaeh said, "Please don't bug me about that," and promised Linda she'd call her if she needed anything. When she hung up, Nevaeh poured herself another vodka, shocked to find the bottle half empty. Her life was spinning out of control. She took the bottle to the sink and filled it with enough water to make it look like she'd only had a drink or two—Trudy might not notice, or perhaps not even remember whether the bottle had been opened. She gritted her teeth. She resolved to stop drinking as soon as this whole ordeal was over.

She decided that tomorrow she would have to have a long talk with Dawn Ann. She should tell her what happened with Derek before Dawn Ann found out on her own, and then she should confess about the money and return it. She hadn't wanted to pose nude; anyone should be able to tell that from the pictures. So, if she could just talk to Dawn Ann, after the shock wore off, then maybe they could be friends again. She would call mid-morning and see if they could have lunch together. Her treat.

Before Nevaeh was fully awake the next day, Linda called. She said she was coming over and would be there in 10 minutes. Although it was almost noon, Steve and Trudy were asleep and Nevaeh was just getting out of the shower when Linda buzzed up. Nevaeh was wrapped in a towel when she let Linda in.

"Oh, Nevaeh," she sighed. "Don't you own a robe? Get dressed, for god sakes, and I'll make some coffee."

Nevaeh didn't quite understand why Linda sounded so peeved, but she grabbed her Indian skirt and a tee shirt from where they were piled at the end of the couch and went back to the bathroom to dress. The charred aroma of strong coffee filled the kitchen when she joined Linda.

"You can see how people might get the wrong idea," Linda started. "Dawn Ann thinks," she interrupted the coffee maker long enough to pour half a cup for Nevaeh and hand it to her, "maybe you provoked Derek in some way."

"You talked to Dawn Ann?"

"This morning."

"I asked you to stay out of it."

"She's my friend."

"Well, maybe she's right." Nevaeh was angry again with Linda. She opened the refrigerator door, looking for milk. "I told you," she said into the largely empty shelves. "I took a few bucks from him.

I'm taking them back today."

"That's not what I meant. She knows about the pictures. She didn't know he hit you until I told her. She doesn't know about the money, I don't think. She thinks maybe you teased him or went after him, and he was only defending himself."

Not finding any milk or creamer, Nevaeh shuffled back to the kitchen table. She couldn't drink the coffee. Her stomach churned.

"She's my best friend, Nevaeh, but she's crazy when it comes to Derek. She makes excuses for him, defends him, forgives him the unforgivable. I think the only way to get through to her is for you to press charges."

"So she can get on the stand and say I hit him first? I didn't! She wasn't there. It's his word against mine, and no one's going to believe me. Not when I'm up against Dawn Ann McKnight! Are you nuts?"

"Nevaeh, I know it sounds like I'm hanging you out to dry to save my friend, but don't you see? Derek is dangerous—to all women. You have the chance to stop him. Or if not to stop him, to make Dawn Ann see the truth. Would you at least go visit the Women's Advocacy Center? Get their advice?"

"I don't know anything about it."

"They advise women who are the victims of crimes like this. For free. They could assess the possible actions and outcomes—better than I can."

"I want to talk to Dawn Ann first."

"They'd help you decide what to say to her."

A wave of nausea gripped Nevaeh's stomach. "I'll be right back," she said, and ran to the bathroom, where she ran the water in the sink to cover the sound of her retching. When she was finished, she splashed her face with water and looked at herself in the mirror. Her eyes were bloodshot, although she knew it was not just the trauma to her head. The bruises were fully purple; she looked, she had to admit, as if she'd been beaten up. She'd seen that look occasionally on young men who came to Phil's in New Orleans, seeking a place to stay.

"Okay," she said to Linda, who was wiping the kitchen counter with a bright yellow sponge. "Let's go now. I want to settle with Dawn Ann today."

To Nevaeh's surprise, Linda had left the cab waiting—an extravagance that showed Nevaeh how eager Linda was to get her to go the Center. The cabbie drove them about a mile, to a storefront on Lincoln Avenue. A bell tinkled as they entered. Inside, everything seemed to Nevaeh designed to calm shattered nerves: a small Zen fountain bubbled in one corner; subtle, meditative music played over hidden loudspeakers, and some form of aromatherapy—incense or a candle—filled the room with a mixture of bay and lavender. The large glass window on the street was shielded from intrusive eyes by faux tapestry drapes in mint green and mauve. A young woman, dressed in the same gauzy type Indian-print skirt as Nevaeh, introduced herself as Rosemary.

"I like your sandals," Nevaeh said, pointing to the woman's woven leather shoes.

"Super-comfortable," Rosemary said. "Did you want to talk to an Advocate?"

Nevaeh marveled at how quickly Rosemary put her at ease.

"Yes," Linda answered for both of them, as Rosemary smiled at Nevaeh.

"Just a minute," she said, "and I can take you back to Tray. He's interning with us this summer."

"Isn't there a woman intern available?" Linda asked, a little rudely, Nevaeh thought. The name Tray was comforting, and while she was beginning to feel she was in the right place, she felt a pang of sadness for her lost Tray.

"No, not today," Rosemary said cheerfully. "Just Tray."

"I heard my name," a male voice said. He started to hold out his hand, but he stopped mid-sentence. "Ohmygod," his voice shot up.

"Oh, no," Nevaeh said. The last she'd seen Tray, he'd been splayed at the bottom of the tree house ladder, passed-out drunk. It had been almost a year. He'd cut his hair and buttoned up his shirt. He had a nice tan, not as deep as when they lived in Iowa, but healthy, and he'd clearly gained a few pounds. In a gray pinstriped suit, he looked prosperous, almost adult, not like a starving student.

"I thought law school was like three years or something," she said. She wanted him to know she wasn't cowed by him just because he was wearing a tie.

"It is, but during the summers there are internships."

"You're going to practice on me?" she asked, hoping she sounded insulted. She knew she looked pretty bad, and was aggravated that after all these months Tray would see her like this.

"I'm going to help you, if I can," Tray said and she thought she heard his voice crack ever so slightly. He cleared his throat. "Who did this to you?" he asked.

"You!" she almost shouted. "You left me!" The hell of her life had started with Tray's leaving her. Now, she was supposed to think he could help her? She grabbed Linda's elbow to steady herself.

He grimaced. She expected him to say that it wasn't his fault she'd gotten beaten up. Instead, he said, "I shouldn't have."

"Damn right you shouldn't have," she said, raising her chin and shaking back her hair. She grabbed Linda's arm more tightly, and Linda had the good sense to not say a word, obviously trying to figure out what was going on.

"I don't know what possessed me," he said, so far choosing all the right words, as slick as ever. Then he surprised her again: "I came back, you know, but you were gone."

"No, I didn't know. If I was gone, how was I to know?"

He shrugged, then nodded his assent. He regained his composure and held his hand out towards Linda.

"I'm Tray Ashley, a legal intern here, and, I guess it's fairly obvious, a former boyfriend of Nevaeh's."

"I'm Linda Livingston, her friend."

"From TV?"

"Yes." Linda seemed pleased to be recognized. She wasn't a star like Dawn Ann—the station didn't put her face on the sides of busses, but she was on TV a lot. Nevaeh wondered for the first time whether Linda was ever jealous of Dawn Ann.

Tray had a cubicle with high gray felt walls which implied, but didn't guarantee, privacy. His metal desk was clean and orderly. Leaning against a wall were a couple of black binders with white stick-on labels that said, "SA Manual," "Health and Risk Assessment," and "Intake Procedures." There was a black phone with lots of buttons and he hit one that caused a red light to go on, presumably to kick the incoming calls to the front desk. No other clients were in the office, and Nevaeh began to feel that she had nothing to hide. She was the victim—in the eyes of this office, anyway—not the criminal. Still, she let Linda do the talking, asking Tray the questions to which she apparently wanted Nevaeh to hear the answers. Again, Nevaeh understood that Linda was not only smart, but knew exactly where her line of questions led. Tray and Linda agreed that Nevaeh should press charges. Tray seemed to agree, most likely because Linda was so positive, that the press could be handled; that Dawn Ann's career wouldn't suffer.

"Did he force you to pose for him?" Tray asked.

"Yes. Not at gunpoint, if that's what you mean. But he was so—" she hunted for the right word, "so volatile."

"Was he physically threatening?"

"Sometimes. Mostly he teased me; sometimes he pushed or pinched me. But he was totally emotionally abusive to Dawn Ann and he threw things at her."

She blinked back tears. "It will become public, Dawn Ann will hate that. Won't it make things worse between her and Derek?"

"Sometimes, people won't change unless they're in a lot of pain," Tray said.

"You could be putting her in danger," Nevaeh said.

"Precisely our point!" Linda and Tray said in near-unison.

"It sounds like she's in danger right now," Tray continued, "but she's in denial. We need to break through that denial. If you press charges, you could help her to see ..."

"I can't," Nevaeh said.

"You can," Linda insisted.

"I can't decide today," Nevaeh finally said. "Let me think about it."

"That's fine, Nevaeh. Of course. You should take your time. I have my notes, as proof of what happened. Also, let me take a picture or two." He took a few shots, full face and two profiles. "Take a day and think about it."

"A day," Nevaeh shook her head in disbelief and got up. Linda pumped Tray's hand, thanking him profusely. She turned to leave.

Tray and Nevaeh faced each other, almost alone.

"Could I call you sometime?" he asked.

"It's a free world," she said. "No law against it." All of her anger at him for leaving her, at Stu for raping her, at Phil for running off, came rushing back to her. She could almost understand why someone like Derek got angry enough to do what he did. She turned on her heels and followed Linda, imagining Tray standing there stunned and aching, and hoping secretly his pain was enough to make him change his mind, too, and come back to her, once and for all.

• • •

Linda dropped Nevaeh back at Trudy's, Nevaeh deciding she was too worn out to talk to Dawn Ann that afternoon. Upstairs, she crumpled onto Trudy's battered couch and cried. She pulled the afghan over her head and didn't move, except for the necessary trip to the bathroom or refrigerator, for the rest of the day and most of the next. Trudy and Steve each went to work and maintained their usual schedules, including their nightcap at Cornerby's. Steve left her a bagel each morning, but she only nibbled at them like a lethargic mouse. Trudy left her a bottle of cheap tequila.

She slept, but she didn't dream. She tried to retrace her steps, to figure out how she'd gotten herself into such a mess. On the whole, she'd done okay since Tray'd left her. She'd gotten along, had been pretty self-sufficient in New Orleans, worked her street schedule like a regular job and contributed to Phil's house and her own upkeep. She hadn't written anything, the way she'd planned to when she and Tray had started their adventure, but she'd gathered material. She'd *lived*. Had even *outlived* a rape, a brush with addiction and an encounter with a horrible man who'd terrorized her and demeaned her and struck her in the face. He'd led her back to booze and, in a ludicrous twist of fate, she'd become his victim. If she reported his crime, she'd be reporting her own, too, plus she'd be hurting her cousin's career. If she didn't, Tray and Linda were convinced Derek would hurt Dawn Ann next. And if Dawn Ann wanted to defend Derek, and blame Nevaeh, Nevaeh might become the criminal, the provocateur. She'd posed nude for Derek—and who was to say that it wasn't willingly?—and she'd stolen $120 from him and delayed reporting the alleged battery for days. Under an intense legal inquisition, the most impeccable of lives, let alone her own, would not bear up. Once a TV station displayed her picture as both an accuser and an accused thief, would The Bluffs recognize her and remember her petty crime spree there? Would Hope Abels remember the night she'd brought Nevaeh home from the library? Would they find out about the drugs and rehab and how she was drinking again and make it all her fault? Would they all testify against her? Would she be sent away to prison, where guards would grope her in corners and surly women with arms the size of tree trunks would leer at her in the showers? Would she be able to sleep on a metal cot, fresh air and sunlight dosed out in one-hour increments? She felt the world lose its color.

Estranged from any family, her face splotched purple by Derek's beating, humiliated by his pictures of her and ashamed of having left Dawn Ann alone with him to fend for herself, she felt the overwhelming craving for pills and the balm of obliteration again.

On the third day, the tequila gone, Trudy sat by Nevaeh on the couch, her eyes piercing her with their concern. "I'm not going to get you pills," she said. "You can't go on like this."

Something in Trudy's tone, a sound of alarm and concern, reverberated inside Nevaeh like a single tear plummeting into a well and she cried out, "You've got to help me! I don't know what to do!"

"Linda knows what to do," Trudy said. "Why not do what Linda says?"

"I feel like everyone, even my cousin, thinks it's my fault; that I provoked him."

Trudy looked over at Steve, who was standing by the dining table, spreading peanut butter on a bagel. "I don't get it. The guy beat you up. You report him. Period. Why are you offering him a defense?"

"How many times do I have to tell you, Steve? If I report Derek, Dawn Ann will be publicly embarrassed and Derek will hurt her."

"If you don't report him, he just gets a free pass to hurt her anyway," Steven's hectoring voice suggested to Nevaeh that she was being extremely stupid.

"You must've been in jams like this before, haven't you?" Trudy said, hurrying as if to keep the peace between the two of them. "What did you do then?"

Without intending it, Trudy had struck the chord by which Nevaeh had lived most of her life. The words from Luke, 12, sang in her head. "Consider the lilies of the field …" She knew what she'd done before, when things weren't going her way: she'd trusted in herself and her ability to keep moving through. She had also, on many occasions, relied on Tray and a change of location, or, more recently, too many shots of tequila, too many painkillers. The results for both approaches had been mixed. The romance of living like a lily, without a selfish concern for one's self, had, at times, led to reckless irresponsibility. There were too many weeds in the lily field, so many false or self-justifying signs.

Now she decided to trust herself, rather than Linda or Tray or Trudy or Steven. She would follow her own first instincts: call Dawn Ann, tell her everything that had happened and make sure she never saw Derek again.

Holding hands, Steven and Trudy went off to their jobs, while Nevaeh dialed Dawn Ann at the station. She hoped they could meet at Walter's, but Dawn Ann's secretary would not connect her and would only take a message. Reluctantly, Nevaeh stuffed her things in her backpack, adjusted her crinkly Indian print skirt and took the el down to the station. She'd just have to wait until Dawn Ann would see her.

Nevaeh arrived there at three o'clock. As always, the building was secured like a fortress, the oval desk in the middle flanked by guarded turnstiles that wouldn't turn unless the visitor obtained a bar-coded card from the uniformed attendant. The man at the desk dialed a number, announced "Nan Thera," and then told her that Ms. McKnight was unavailable. "Tell her I'll wait," Nevaeh said. "Oh, and it's Nevaeh—heaven, backwards."

Nearing the end of his shift, the guard yawned and pointed to the gray marble benches on either side of the desk, near the windows.

Not knowing for sure whether Dawn Ann was actually in the building, Nevaeh waited until the guard's shift ended, rehearsing what she might say to Dawn Ann, then losing track and staring out the window at the passersby. Neither the old guard nor the new one would tell her for sure, but the promo for the ten o'clock news promised, "The Elements with Dawn Ann McKnight," so she had some hope that if nothing else, Dawn Ann would have to go home afterward. Then, as she'd learned in rehab, she would tell Dawn Ann her story, starting with Tray and Iowa and most of what happened in New Orleans and Key West.

She'd nearly dozed off when, around seven, Dawn Ann and Linda came out of the elevators and slid through the turnstiles, Dawn Ann in a floral skirt with a tangerine blouse, and Linda in a tailored navy pantsuit with a light blue-striped shirt. Dawn Ann saw Nevaeh and sped up, but Linda grabbed her friend by the elbow, and Nevaeh jumped to her feet. She heard Linda say, "You should talk to her."

"She's a slut," Dawn Ann replied.

Nevaeh caught up to them. "No! Dawnie, please, no. Please, hear me out."

Jabbing Linda's elbow, Dawn Ann stiffened and looked over Nevaeh's head.

"Not here," Linda said. "Ladies, let's go to Walter's. I'll referee." She took Dawn Ann's arm and led her out the door, leaving Nevaeh to follow. They walked briskly, one dark and all-business and the other casual and light. In her drab olive tee shirt, Nevaeh fell behind, feeling like an ignored child. She didn't understand why Linda seemed to be taking Dawn Ann's side.

Linda and Dawn Ann were already seated at a booth in the back when Nevaeh joined them. Trudy, who apparently didn't know what to make of the three of them being there together, silently poured coffee into three white mugs gathered in the middle of the table.

"Something to eat?" she asked, pushing a mug towards each of them. Dawn Ann said, "No" simultaneously with Nevaeh's "Sure." Nevaeh bit her lip, suddenly aware that she hadn't been eating well and was famished.

"Bring two clubs," Linda said. "We'll share around." Trudy

hurried off and Linda nodded at Nevaeh. Dawn Ann's jaw was set and she avoided Nevaeh's gaze.

"I want to tell you what happened," Nevaeh began.

"I saw," Dawn Ann snapped.

Why did Dawn Ann insist on thinking the worst of her? It was as if Dawn Ann couldn't think well of Nevaeh without thinking poorly of herself. "I just wanted pictures for a modeling job, but Derek got real crazy, and he threatened me."

"You didn't look frightened in the pictures."

"I don't know what I look like in them. I haven't seen them. I just know he took them, and I didn't want him to."

"Did he hit you?" Linda coached.

"Not that day. I spent the night with Trudy. I knew I needed to move out. I went back the next day to get my stuff." Nevaeh hesitated, but Linda glared at her to go on and she did, telling about the money and Derek slamming her against the wall. Dawn Ann looked away, as if she'd heard it all before and thought Nevaeh was lying to her.

Nevaeh looked at Linda, begging for help. "C'mon, Dawnie," Nevaeh said, anger growing within her. "Why don't you believe me?"

"I did some digging," Dawn Ann said, her voice triumphant. "You're not the only one, Linda, who knows how to do investigative reporting. I have a few connections of my own. Turns out my cousin here is not just a thief, but a drug addict, too. With quite a history of seducing men and blaming them when she's gotten what she wants out of them."

"Where do you get off?" Nevaeh shouted, but Linda slapped her hand over hers. Nevaeh yanked her hand back and rifled through her backpack for her Bible. "Here," she shoved a fistful of money across the table. "Here's Derek's damn money."

"Keep it down, Nevaeh. We're here to work this out," Linda said.

"She had me investigated!" Nevaeh cried.

"You lied to me!" Dawn Ann shot back.

"Ladies!" Linda commanded. "Everybody, deep breath!"

Trudy plopped two club sandwich platters in front of them and three small plates. Nevaeh attacked a quarter sandwich and a handful of fries. Linda put a quarter triangle on a plate for Dawn Ann, and one for herself. Dawn Ann busied herself, removing the toothpick and the middle slice of bread from her sandwich, then stabbing the toothpick back in. Linda ignored hers altogether and began speaking in measured tones.

"Okay, so, let's ignore the *ad hominems*. Or better yet, let's just assume the very worst case." She held up her hand to silence Nevaeh's objections. "Let's assume Nevaeh is a felonious thief, a drug addict, a seductive whore. Does Derek have a right to beat her up?"

"He didn't." Dawn Ann stared coldly into Linda's eyes, as if Nevaeh weren't there, wasn't worth looking at.

"Dawn Ann, honey. Look at the girl. Where do you think she got those bruises?"

"How would I know? Who knows what pimps and low-lifes she hangs around with."

"Dawn Ann! She walked into your apartment looking fine and walked out looking like this. Worse. You can't deny that."

"Can you prove that, or are you just taking her word for it?"

Linda caught her breath. "Dawn Ann. I am your best friend. I would take your side in almost anything. But this, this is indisputable. Proof? How about James? Or the building's security cameras? Or this?" She held out her camera phone.

Nevaeh nodded enthusiastically.

"She provoked him."

Linda squinted. "You don't believe that."

"Don't tell me what to believe, Linda. Derek is my husband. I know him. He doesn't get angry except when he's provoked."

"Well, duh!" Linda said. "Listen to yourself! What does that mean? I don't get angry either, except when I have a reason, but I don't go around hitting people!"

"It's none of your business."

"Yeah, that's what I thought, Dawn Ann," Nevaeh said, and for the first time, Dawn Ann looked Nevaeh straight in the eye. "It's between me and Derek and that's why I just thought I'd move out. I'm sorry I posed for the pictures. Maybe I should've stood up to him. I was scared and I didn't know what to do. Linda wants me to go to the police. The guy at the Women's shelter wants me to go, too, but I don't want to file charges. I don't want Derek to get provoked and take it out on you." Nevaeh thought she detected a flicker of recognition in the quick blink of Dawn Ann's beautiful eyes.

"I can deal with Derek," Dawn Ann said, touching the short string of pearls at her neck. "What I can't deal with are friends who want to put my husband in jail."

"I just want you to be safe," Linda said.

"Then butt out," Dawn Ann barked.

"At the shelter," Nevaeh said, "this guy, who knows about this stuff, said you should also move out and make Derek take some anger management courses or something like that."

"That does it," Dawn Ann said. She got up, shook off Linda's outreached arm, and stomped out.

• • •

Nevaeh and Linda looked at each other, Linda leaning on an elbow and covering her mouth with her hand. Nevaeh had no clue as to what Linda thought they should do next. She grabbed the remaining sandwich plate and started to eat.

"She's so stubborn," Linda sighed. "Why can't she see what's going on here?"

Something in Linda's tone sounded a warning. Linda wasn't going to let go of this. She was going to insist on butting in.

"Tomorrow, you're just going to have to press charges," she said simply. "That's the only way."

"No, I told you. I'm going to respect Dawnie's wishes."

"Then I'm going to file a report of some kind. Something that will at least make the police go over and scare him." She looked at her watch. "I gotta get going, too. I'll call you tomorrow." She scooped up Nevaeh's stolen money and handed it back to her, leaving twenty dollars on the table. "That ought to cover it," she said.

"Thanks," Nevaeh said. After Linda left, Trudy came by and plunked herself down.

"What's up?"

Nevaeh waved her off. "Linda, worrying about everybody and Derek hurting Dawn Ann. Crazy stuff," she said.

"Yeah, he hurt you, not her," Trudy said, then seemed to rethink herself. "It's possible he could hurt her. If any guy ever hit me, or so much as even raised his hand—he'd be outta here," she said, "I'd never put up with that. Never. Not even from Derek." Trudy got up, and started to clear one of the sandwich plates.

"Leave it," Nevaeh said, grinning. "Derek's treat," she mumbled to herself.

Trudy picked up the twenty. "See ya later."

"Yup," Nevaeh said, but she knew she was lying. She'd had an idea and with a good meal in her, was ready to act on it. She reached in her pack for a pen and a piece of paper and wrote Trudy a note, thanking her for her hospitality and telling her not to worry. She said she was going back to New Orleans. She knew Trudy would understand: she's the one who'd just said, "outta here."

It wasn't completely dark when Nevaeh left Walter's and it was still safe enough to walk the five long blocks over to Halsted, where she could catch a city bus that would take her to the regional station with only one change. She knew it was unlikely she'd find a bus going anywhere she'd want to go at that hour, but it was all she could think of to do. Tray Ashley was going to be a good lawyer and might be able to figure out a way to help her and keep Dawn Ann safe, but Linda was going to do what Linda was going to do, and since Dawn Ann was never going to be friends with Nevaeh again, the best thing for Nevaeh to do was to get "outta here."

With the entire bench to herself at the front of the bus, Nevaeh felt terribly adrift and alone. She grew sad. Dawn Ann would probably be fine, she had enough sway over Derek, between money and sex and their history together. It was for herself that she felt sorry. She was finally recognizing in herself a little let-down and she hadn't even acknowledged that she'd had her hopes up to begin with. But she had. She'd wanted Tray back.

How could she want Tray back? He'd left her and her life had gone to hell. Even if that was coincidence, he'd come back into her life because Linda had inadvertently put him there, and now his ideas and Linda's big mouth were combining to exile her. She stared at her reflection in the window of the city bus, her face still swollen and blotched. She sniffed back insistent tears. There were no two ways around it. She loved him, and always would, but starting over was as unlikely as anything that had ever happened to her and a lot had happened to her. She wiped her eyes on the shoulder of her tee shirt.

In the waiting room, she studied the schedules. There was a bus leaving yet that night, just after 1:00 a.m., for Iowa City. A good choice; she had a place to stay nearby. She gave the clerk three tens and a twenty, taped in half. Without comment, he gave her a ticket and eight dollars change and told her to have a nice trip. She thanked him and took a seat in the waiting room. Feeling like a fugitive from the law—although she was wholly innocent, especially now that she'd attempted restitution—she buried herself in an abandoned, day-old newspaper.

A dozen sleepy passengers boarded the bus, one to a row. A mother and two young children, one asleep over her shoulder, the other wide-eyed and worried-looking, clinging to his mother's hand. Then a brown-skinned young man in military fatigues, his eyes scanning right to left, right to left, as if on look-out for an ambush. Next, a shriveled, gray-haired woman who needed the driver's help up the stairs. Nevaeh took a seat in the middle of the bus, separated by several rows from any of her fellow travelers. She stared out the window as the bus fled the city, and fell asleep as it reached a steady cruising speed through the farmlands of western Illinois. She awoke when the bus driver's voice announced their approach to Iowa City. As the bus turned into the terminal, she saw a young couple, each with over-stuffed backpacks, waiting to board the bus in the next stall. They reminded her of when she and Tray had started out on their adventure, and how far she'd gone, only to come home again. But now she was stronger, more resourceful. She didn't need Tray and she didn't need Phil. She was tough and independent. The sad part was that she was, in many ways, on the lam, starting all over yet again and again alone.

She washed her face in the ladies' restroom, and brushed her hair.

There was a local bus heading south out of town at seven thirty. She went to a diner around the corner from the station and had three eggs, three strips of bacon and three pancakes with coffee, for $3.99. She ate every last bit of the meal as if to fortify herself for the weeks ahead. Then she took the bus, got off at the town closest to Prairie du Chien and walked a mile to the highway to hitch the rest of the way. Herb, of Herb and Grace's Mobil On The Run, stopped a quarter mile past her and backed up along the shoulder, genuinely excited to see her and hear about her adventures since leaving town.

"Heard about Tara," he said. "Sorry. Old Lundgren can be such a lout."

"I guess he didn't realize," Nevaeh said, and she felt herself near tears again. It was so sweet of Herb to remember.

"How long you staying this time?" he asked.

"Don't know," she said.

"Need a job?" he asked.

She wasn't sure she'd heard him right. Of course she'd need a job. She hadn't thought of that; she'd just run out of Chicago as fast as she could, before Linda caused any more havoc.

"I do," she said.

"I told Grace I'd get her a little help," he said.

"Wow," she said again.

"Won't be paying no fortune," he said. "Seven dollars an hour, free sodas, one donut per day."

"Wow," she said.

"You gonna be out at the old place?" he said.

"Yeah," she said.

"Start tomorrow," he said. "Five thirty."

For an instant she hoped he meant in the afternoon.

"It takes Grace a little longer to get going in the morning," Herb said. "But you're young. You can be up with the birds."

After Herb dropped her by Farmer Jones's Creek, she walked up past the second downstream bend to the third oak. The rope ladder, weathered and gray, hung straight, secured at the bottom as she'd been instructed by Tray's diagram. She gave it a tug. Satisfied, she left her things on the ground and climbed to her house. It was much as she had left it, the two old tennis racquets propped in a corner and a quarter bottle of tequila on a wooden crate near the bed. Of course, the house needed a good spring cleaning. Remarkably, neither squirrels nor other vermin had settled in, but the Donald Duck shower curtain that served as a window had blown out along one side, and leaves and twigs had gathered in the orange shag and on her bed.

She stepped to the doorway and felt a warm breeze on her face. She stared down the length of the ladder and her stomach did a little flip, as if she were standing on a steep precipice. Slowly, she turned back into the house, picked up the tequila bottle and unscrewed the top. Then she stood again at the doorway and emptied the bottle, watching it puddle at the bottom of the ladder. Although it was noon and the August sun was overhead and only filtering through the oak's leaves, she saluted the sun, for the moment, home again.

23

Furious with Linda and Nevaeh, Dawn Ann stormed out of Walter's, her teeth clenched, her face flushed, her eyes dilated. Fixated on the minutiae—gum wrappers and cigarette butts in bas relief on the sidewalk, a bright red newspaper box, a purple neon sign with only the letters "Dry" left in "Dry Cleaners"—she bumped into a pedestrian.

"Hey," a familiar voice said. It was Derek, who'd probably gone out of his way to bump into her—an ordinary pedestrian would've avoided the mild collision. "See that new Jaguar?" he pointed. "What do you think? Time to trade in the old jalopy?"

"Um, oh. Where?" Dawn Ann knew she sounded flustered. She worried that Derek would suspect that she's found out about the pictures; she wasn't ready for that discussion, his insults hurled at her artistic insensibility, her false modesty. He'd understood when she stayed over to help Linda with her "guy" problems; he'd hardly mentioned Nevaeh in the four days she'd been out of their house. "Rude not to have left a note," he'd said, but that was all. She'd been grateful for the calm.

"Lighten up, honey. We don't need to decide today." There was an offbeat pleasantry to Derek's remark, as if he'd just won the lottery and his only decision today about the car was what color—or colors—to buy. "Come in with me." He took her elbow and steered her back inside.

"I need to be at work soon," Dawn Ann said, forcing herself to sound normal. Of course she was normal. Why wouldn't she be? She'd over-reacted to the pictures of Nevaeh and Derek didn't even know she knew about them. More to the point, Nevaeh was gone now, not able to seduce him into making such a mistake again.

They took a booth on the opposite side of the restaurant from where she'd just left Linda and Nevaeh. She was mindful that Nevaeh and Linda could still be in the back corner but hoped they'd left. A waitress came by with a coffee pot, and Derek said, "We want

Trudy. Tell Trudy we want her to wait on us." Dawn Ann wished Derek hadn't drawn attention to them that way, but the waitress only sighed heavily, as if she'd been made to walk a mile for no good reason, and left.

"Bitch," Derek smiled.

"Der-ek," Dawn Ann said cautiously, as if to a naughty child on the verge of tantrums. He shrugged.

Trudy flounced over. "You want me?" she leaned towards Derek, a short jeans skirt stretched across her buttocks and aimed in Dawn Ann's face.

"Trudy," Dawn Ann began, but Derek slammed his hand on the table as the silverware clattered. Dawn Ann closed her eyes, hoping if Linda was still there, she hadn't heard the commotion.

"Shut up, Dawn Ann."

Trudy gave a little wiggle of her rear end, as if Dawn Ann would appreciate that, and tears welled in Dawn Ann's eyes.

Derek gave Trudy a pat on the cheek. "Thanks, honey," he said, and off she went.

Derek spread his hands in a gesture of dismissal. "Gotta spread it around," he said, with a twitch of self-effacement.

"Oh, Derek." Dawn Ann was still rattled from her conversation with Linda and Nevaeh, angry that he was ignoring her when she had just defended him so vigorously.

"Oh, Derek, what?" Derek mimicked.

"You're so confusing, sometimes. So nice to me one minute, and then flirting with Trudy the next. I don't get it." It was as close as she could come to challenging him the way Linda and Nevaeh wanted her to.

"A guy's gotta stay in shape," he said, grabbing the long-neck from Trudy's tray as she came towards their table and waving her away. "What if you left me 'cause I was such a jerk? Wouldn't you want me to find a new girl?"

"Jerk?"

"Don't start with me," he said.

"Your word," she said, running her finger around the rim of her ice water. She felt as if she were sinking into quicksand; soon she wouldn't be able to breathe.

"That's different. The question is, don't you want me to be happy?"

Her skin prickled. She dared not look, but she felt the gooseflesh rise on her forearms. If Derek asked, she'd say she was chilled from the air conditioning. But even as that thought occurred to her, she resented the fact that she would even have to concoct a lie about such a thing. Derek could twist words around to the point where she didn't know what was her fault and what wasn't. Right before her eyes, with her unsuspecting participation, Derek had just turned his inappropriate flirtation into her selfish insecurity: *her* not wanting *him* to be happy.

She remembered how she'd admired Derek when they first met. He was an artist, a free spirit. He didn't sully himself with social conventions or petty concerns about money or status or achievement, all the things that had preoccupied the Doctors McKnight and that her mother, in particular, had demanded of Dawn Ann. It occurred to her now that Derek was her adolescent rebellion—the high school drunk, the missed curfew, the ditched school day she'd never had. "It's a good thing I have to go to work," she said evenly, "or I might actually try to argue with you."

"Don't do that, honeybun. You know what happens when you argue with me."

"What happens?"

He shook his head from side to side. "I get angry."

She stretched her lips into a forced smile. Her stomach churned. "Wouldn't want that, sweetheart," she managed. "See you later."

"Yup."

She blew him a kiss with two fingers and headed up the street.

"Bitch!" she heard a man's voice and reflexively turned, expecting to see Derek following her, castigating her about something, but he wasn't there. Ahead was a convenience store, the sort that robbed high-rise dwellers and hotel visitors in need of a late-night pint of ice cream, bag of chips or six-pack. In front of the store, a stiffly coifed, platinum-haired woman in white linen capris and a matching short-sleeved top with gold buttons stood between two shopping bags, Neiman's and Ralph Lauren. Her husband, in a navy blazer and yellow striped tie, faced her, his jaw set, his hand around her forearm. Wearing dark wrap-around glasses, the woman moved her chin slightly from side to side, as if concerned that they were being watched. "Bitch!" the man shouted again. Dawn Ann shook her head, assuming the woman had overspent. As she watched, the woman stiffened and picked up her bags, trying to shake off her husband, but he held on. Dawn Ann was startled to see bruises on the woman's forearms. Her stomach tightened, fully expecting to see the man slap his wife. Praying it wouldn't come, she felt her heart race against her chest. How humiliated the woman must feel! Even if she had spent too much, the sidewalk in front of an all-night store was not the place for them to discuss it.

Dawn Ann studied the pavement as she slinked by the woman, not wanting to make eye contact, even so much as to suggest that she understood. Once past the woman, her muscles relaxed as in a meditation exercise, and she took a deep breath. It had been an ugly scene, but a vaguely familiar one.

She could barely concentrate on the weather news, radar screens and web alerts from the U.S. Weather Service as she prepared for her on-screen weathercast, the scene at the store and Derek's "I get angry" playing over and over in her head. Was he joking, making fun of himself for his short temper? Or threatening her? "*Bitch.*" She'd thought for a moment that it had been Derek, daring to yell at her in public like that. Had that man hit his wife? Had Derek hit Nevaeh as a warning? *Had* he hit Nevaeh? What had Nevaeh done to provoke him?

She was obsessing and to distract herself for the half-hour before showtime, she turned on her lighted make-up mirror and started to pluck her eyebrows. With her light coloring, she had to use a brown pencil to darken them for the camera, but still she found the perfectionism of tweezing satisfying. When she was younger, she'd had them waxed every two weeks; now, her everyday routine included a quick pluck here and there; she never needed to suffer the yank and rip of waxing. Some women waxed their under arms, their inner thighs, their legs. "Ouch!" she said out loud, having pinched her skin instead of an errant hair. Even tweezing hurt. Sometimes, after spending five minutes selecting the exact offending hair, the one that refused to lay flat, arch into place, blend in with the others, it would take her a full 10 seconds to gather the courage to actually pull it out. In 20 minutes, she managed to select and weed out four or five hairs, and to forget, as if in a black-out, all the hurts inflicted by her husband.

As the ten o'clock newscast ended, her producer Stanley Watkins caught up with her just off the set. "Great show, Dawn Ann! You were really on tonight! No one can flirt with the camera like you can!"

She scowled. "Same old, same old," she said. She wasn't begging for more compliments; she was surprised that she'd come off so well when she'd been so preoccupied with all the events of the afternoon and evening—Nevaeh, Linda, the shopping bag woman.

"Naw," he said. "Not same old. A little extra juice."

She shook her head.

"Like pornography, honey, I know it when I see it," he laughed, and Dawn Ann stiffened. "Never mind. Whatever it is, just keep doing it or not doing it or whatever. You're terrific, honey."

For a moment, she watched him go. Was he making fun of her? It was just the weather, after all. She loved the weather, loved being on TV, but it *was* just the weather. She was good at it, and she could put aside her personal feelings and do her job with the best of them. That's what Stanley was saying, wasn't he? *Extra juice*? Was it the challenge of forgetting that sweetened her performance?

Linda sidled up to her, as if nothing was wrong. "You still mad at me?"

"I don't want to talk right now," Dawn Ann said.

Linda ignored the rebuff. "Some story in West Chicago, eh?"

That had been Linda's big story: A woman in a far suburb had been taken into custody late the night before for shooting her estranged husband. The woman lived in a trailer park with four kids under eight years of age. Neighbors said that there'd been trouble at the couple's home and the police had been called two or three times over the last six months. The man had voluntarily moved out two weeks ago, but had come back the previous night and kicked one of the younger children, the kindergartner. That afternoon, the woman had asked her brother if she could borrow his gun to protect herself and her children. Then she'd waited in the parking lot for her husband's shift at the plastics factory to end. It was there that she shot him. While witnesses said it was in cold blood, Linda said the woman's defense would likely be battered woman syndrome, a hybrid version of "heat of passion" and "self-defense." The woman had been beaten by her husband several times in the past year but had never pressed charges or sought a court order of protection. During Linda's report, Dawn Ann had felt a certain disgust. Why did women take such abuse? Why couldn't they just leave? Linda, ever the intrepid reporter, had shoved her microphone in front of the woman's younger sister, who lived with them in order to help with the kids.

"Oh, she really loved him," the sister had said. "He wasn't a bad guy, at all. Sometimes, he just got frustrated that he couldn't give the kids and us all he wanted, and it made him angry. But he really, really loved us. I can't believe she'd kill him over it."

"Let me know before you buy a gun," Linda added, patting Dawn Ann's shoulder.

Dawn Ann recoiled. "Oh, for god sakes," she said, still angry with Linda for taking Nevaeh's side in things.

"You don't think he deserved it?" Linda asked. Linda detested Derek, obviously. She didn't understand him the way Dawn Ann did, or even the way Nevaeh had. Dawn Ann had been so happy that Nevaeh and Derek had gotten along, that Nevaeh'd seemed to appreciate Derek the way she herself did—it must be something about that musical-artistic temperament. Sometimes Dawn Ann was just too uptight and it must frustrate someone as unconventional as Derek. That's why Dawn Ann forgave him his abuse. She quickened her step, as if she'd said the word aloud. She'd never used that word to describe Derek, even in her most private thoughts, and now it felt disloyal, and not wholly accurate. Not abused or battered, like the woman in Linda's story, but bruised, like the lady with the shopping bags.

"I don't want to talk about it, Linda. Please mind your own business." She crossed one arm over her chest and rubbed her upper arm.

For an instant, Dawn Ann pictured her mother, huddled near the door to her apartment, listening for noises, thieves, rapists, murderers. The woman who once insisted on conquering the world, the woman who succeeded by every conventional measure and held her daughter to the same punishing perfectionist standards, now protected herself from her own imaginings by refusing to go out. Her mother, a doctor of the mind, who had never acknowledged fears, not even her daughter's fears or childhood insecurities—a big test, or a speech or a tryout. "Rise to the occasion," she'd tell her daughter. The harder the challenge, the longer the odds, the greater the thrill.

Dawn thought, too, of Nevaeh's mother, also isolated from her own encounters with the world, stinking of booze, even in the morning, as she had at Dr. McKnight's funeral. Neither woman faced reality. Only Nevaeh's mother fought it, even though she took her courage from the bottle. Dawn Ann imagined what a scene Derek and Nevaeh's mother would have made, a thrashing, boozy fight, broken bottles. Nevaeh herself, scrappy though she was, hadn't fought with Derek. No, she'd posed for him! Anger rushed to Dawn Ann's temples, pounding. Surely, Nevaeh could've avoided that! Why hadn't she just said "no?" Did she really think Derek was violent and would have hurt her?

Nevaeh should have said "no." She should have! She was a petty thief and a hustler, and she didn't deserve the sympathy that Linda tried to drum up for battered women and others who couldn't stand up for themselves.

As she approached the station building door, Linda finally interrupted Dawn Ann's thoughts.

"I know you're not going to go out and buy a gun," Linda said lightly, "but I do wonder what you're going to do to protect yourself. I don't want to get a call …"

"Linda, let me say this once and for all, for the sake of our friendship. Stay out of my marriage. And don't believe everything my cousin tells you." She turned on her heel, and left the building. As she walked by the glass windows, she didn't look back in. For once, she'd have the last word, and she wouldn't have to see the concern on Linda's brow or the superiority of her raised chin. It was none of Linda's business.

Linda wasn't even married, for god sakes. How could she know what it was like to live with a man, to assume another person's disappointments as your own? Derek was a challenge—she wasn't saying he wasn't. He was sometimes abusive—if people like Linda insisted on that word—but she, his wife, could help him, because he loved her, and, despite it all, she loved him—didn't she?

When Dawn Ann arrived home that night, she felt, in an odd way, a little bit as she did on the night of her first broadcast, when she'd gingerly opened the door in anticipation, hoping for a big surprise; tonight, turning the handle, she felt the darker side of surprise, a dread of the unknown.

After the commotion of the newsroom, the silence in her apartment should've been comforting, but it wasn't. She called to Derek, but if home, he didn't answer. She realized that she hated not knowing whether or not he was at home; it made it seem like his place, not hers or theirs together. She had an idea: they should have a secret sign, like a door knocker in a certain position or an entry way vase turned in a particular direction, to let her know if Derek was in, so she wouldn't have to tiptoe into her own house, or be startled out of her mind when he popped up behind her in the kitchen. The door to the darkroom was closed, but he didn't answer when she knocked. In her bathroom, she opened and closed cabinets, hoping to alert Derek to her presence. If he knew she was there, perhaps he'd come out and they could talk or make love or do whatever normal couples would do in their circumstances. She filled her basin with water, massaged her face with a cleansing foam, sighed into a towel and sprayed herself with a toner, eyes closed. She dabbed the toner off and squinted, hoping to see Derek. Convinced then that he was not home, not awake, or possibly fooling with her, she scurried to their bed, pulled a summer blanket up to her chin and exhaled. She heard a series of creaks and groans, and again held her breath, but Derek didn't appear.

The silence of their apartment was filled with noise, if she chose to hear it: the joints of the building, the upstairs neighbors, the street life below. To block out the cacophony, she reviewed her show, wondering exactly what it was that her producer found so "wonderful." She'd lied to him, actually. She *had* felt particularly "on" tonight, energized. It was hard to explain, in the midst of all the disturbing events of the week—in her personal life, as well as the news—but she thought it was a sign of her professionalism that she could rise to the occasion and still be "wonderful." Though she could hardly admit it, it did give her a little thrill.

24

About eleven o'clock Saturday morning, Tray got an angry call from Linda. She'd called Trudy's and Trudy had read her Nevaeh's note. "What's with New Orleans?" Linda spat. "It's hotter than hell down there this time of year."

"She's got friends there," he said.

"She should stay and help her friend here."

Tray yawned. For personal reasons, he agreed with Linda, but she sure was judgmental, telling everybody what they should and shouldn't do.

"Let her go," Tray said. "Maybe that's the best. You can't save everyone single-handedly, Linda. You've done what you could. That's all you can do." He heard Linda sigh, and added, "That's more than most people would've done, so I applaud you for it." He was beginning to feel like an advocate, mediator, peace-maker. He could be good at this lawyering thing, he decided. He liked the sound of his words, and they seemed to soothe Linda.

"Thanks, Tray," she said.

Tray promised to call if he heard anything and hung up. "Damnation, Nevaeh. Now I gotta drive to Iowa!" He showered, talked his friend into loaning him his car for fifty dollars, and was on the road mid-afternoon, headed west, out of the city, to the corn and soy fields of western Illinois and the Mississippi Valley.

An hour into the drive, around Joliet, home of the state prison, he joined the procession of 18-wheelers barreling west and began to worry that by chasing Nevaeh to Iowa he was breaching some professional ethic. Surely, his supervisor would say he was getting too personally involved in his work, that he needed to keep more distance. But he felt it was now or never for Nevaeh and himself.

The sun was not yet directly in his eyes, still high enough to reflect off the distant white farmhouses that punctuated the flat landscape like exclamation points. He knew Nevaeh hadn't gone back to New Orleans. What future would she have there? She'd told him—surprisingly, now that he looked back on it—that the guy she'd been dating in New Orleans had run off with another woman, a woman who'd left him repeatedly. If Nevaeh'd gone back to New Orleans, Tray would never find her again, and why would she return to someone who left her?

Tray realized that *he* had left Nevaeh, too, but that was different; it had been an accident. He'd fallen out of a tree, become afraid that he'd always be living in a tree, and understood that Nevaeh would never push him to be more than just what he was. He'd been scared of that kind of love, that kind of commitment. But now, he'd had some time, had grown up, and he was still in love, and they wouldn't have to live hand-to-mouth. He, too, had gone straight. He no longer drank or smoked or picked pockets. He vowed he never would again, if only Nevaeh were home in their tree house.

It was almost nine when he pulled in to Prairie du Chien, the town tucked in for the night, the Perseid meteors showering the western sky. He drove out the road to Farmer Jones's and parked the car on the side of the road where the creek trickled into a culvert under the pavement. He didn't want to frighten Nevaeh, so he stopped about 10 yards from the third oak up and yodeled, "Ne-Vay-Ah, Ne-Vay-Ah!" up to the night sky. He felt like he was playing a scene in a high school production of Romeo and Juliet, but he didn't know how else to wake her without scaring the bejesus out of her.

A circle of light, as from a flashlight, scanned the ground in front of him. He walked straight to the spot, so that she'd be able to identify him immediately. "It's me, Tray."

"Here I thought it was Romeo," she said.

"I need to talk to you. Can I come up?"

"I don't know. Can you?" she giggled. "Last time you were on that ladder ..."

"I know," he said, climbing the ladder in his stocking feet.

Out of habit, he reached the top, put his arms around Nevaeh and kissed her. They kissed until she pulled away, then took his hand and brought him inside where a candle flickered under an overturned mayonnaise jar propped up to act like a hurricane lamp. She kissed him again and he was certain he felt a little tug towards the double air mattress in the corner of the tree house that had been their bed. Then it was as if they'd never been apart, and they made love and held each other and made love again. Tray slid open the skylight he'd devised for just such moments, so they stared at the Milky Way and talked. She told him everything about New Orleans, and then pillowed her head on his chest and fell asleep there. Then he knew, even as he closed his eyes, that he held in his arms everything he really cared about in the whole wide world.

• • •

The pre-dawn symphony of Iowa's songbirds didn't wake Nevaeh, who came to with a jolt just as the sun traced the horizon, panicked that she was late for work on her very first day. She shook Tray, who smiled without waking and reached for her, but she was up and dashing down the ladder to the shower.

"Get dressed!" she called up to him. "You've got to take me to work!"

Tray appeared in the doorway and pushed aside the plastic. "Work?" he echoed. "On Sunday?"

"At Herb and Grace's," she said, drying herself and then wrapping the towel around her head. As she scrambled up the ladder, he caught her in his arms. She gave him a quick kiss. "No time!" she said, proud of herself for the discipline. She was determined to act like this was her new life, the life she needed and wanted, together again with Tray.

Tray pulled on his crumpled jeans and button down shirt and Nevaeh ran her brush through his hair. Before she could object, he grabbed her toothbrush from the plywood counter and made his way down the ladder, jumping off the second-to-last rope rung.

She watched him go and for the first time in a week, felt the tug of real hope. Not that she needed to be rescued by a prince charming, she told herself, but frankly, she *was* a damsel in distress and any help would be appreciated.

He drove just at the speed limit all the way into town, one hand on the wheel, one hand on her thigh.

"Aren't you taking this law thing a little too seriously?" she asked, tapping the clock on the radio dashboard.

"Can't be too careful," he said. "Listen, we need to talk."

"At my break," she said. Talk, she knew, would shatter her illusions about her return to Prairie du Chien. As much as she wanted to, she knew she couldn't start over, pretending Tray'd never fallen off the tree house ladder. Even starting again would be difficult. She didn't want to feel like a fugitive all her life, always running from something, not towards anything. There couldn't be peace elsewhere unless she was comfortable in her own skin. She'd learned that much from being raped, hadn't she? The strongest drugs she could find had only worked for short spurts of time, and ultimately stopped working, causing more pain than comfort.

"Now," Tray said, and pulled into the empty parking lot behind the hardware store, within sight of Herb and Grace's. "Look. Derek's obviously a lunatic. He hit you and he's probably going to hit Dawn Ann, if he hasn't already. She hasn't got the gumption to leave the guy, and she's not going to unless he hurts her badly enough. The only alternative I see is that something else jars her loose. If you charge her husband with assault and battery, she's going to have to face the music. She'll get a lot of pressure from the Station—they've invested in her face, you know—and from her adoring public. And you, the gutsiest woman I know, will be doing the right thing—for yourself, too. You should do this for you, even more so than for Dawn Ann."

Nevaeh sat silently for a minute, not meeting his eyes. The hardware store was dark; sales signs and stickers blurred in the windows. "For me?"

"You don't deserve to be treated like that. It occurred to me driving out here that Linda and I have been talking to you about filing charges as if the point were saving Dawn Ann or, for that matter, all battered women. We didn't talk just about you. Now, I am."

She was touched that he was thinking of her, not of a cause or a headline. "I'm okay. I'll survive." There were two machines in front of the store, one for cold drinks and the other for bait. There were lots of ways to survive, she thought, if you stayed open to the possibilities.

"Of course you will," he said.

"I think I've learned my lesson. I'm on the straight and narrow from now on."

"You're not to blame for Derek's behavior."

"But I don't like my own behavior, Tray." She looked out the passenger window at three pyramids of mulch and one of small stones. "Booze and pills and free-loading—"

"You can change that."

She shrugged.

"I'm trying, too," he said. He stroked her hair, and then turned the key in the engine. Finally, she put her left hand on her knee, and he covered it with his.

They pulled into Herb and Grace's Mobil On The Run 15 minutes late, but Herb wasn't bothered.

"And who's this?" he asked, his hands on his hips. He blew a low whistle. "He's pretty near cleaned up. Wouldn't have recognized him."

"Tray's going to be a lawyer," Nevaeh said proudly.

"Deeper pockets," Herb said. "Well, Nevaeh, you going to work or what?"

"Yes!" she said, but Tray shook his head.

"If it's all the same to you, Herb, I think Nevaeh needs to come back to Chicago with me." He started to put his arm around her waist, but she wiggled free. "To take care of some business."

"No, Tray. Please, no. Let's stay here!"

"Why should she go with you, boy?" Herb asked, clueless.

She hoped Tray didn't go into the whole mess with Herb. There was no need for him to know.

Here was her choice: to work for Herb and live in the tree house, without Tray, or to trust him and go to Chicago to file those charges, reclaim her rights, and maybe even save her cousin.

"So we can get married," he said. She felt a tingle up her spine that nearly lifted her off her feet. She felt light, like a balloon, and unburdened. Because he was standing closer to her, she threw her arms around Herb.

Herb stood as stiff as a fence post while Nevaeh hugged him, then gently put his arms on her shoulders and pushed her away.

"Well, I'll be," Herb said, and Nevaeh danced away from him, laughing at herself and him and at the whole ludicrous situation. She pirouetted into Tray, who caught her and dipped her over in a deep tango-like bend.

Herb offered a celebratory donut and made the coffee. He took care of his first two customers of the day, each of whom looked disturbingly like the lout Farmer Lundstrom who'd murdered the innocent Tara, and at six thirty, they said their good-byes. They drove back out to the tree house and gathered up Nevaeh's things, fewer in number than the first time she'd left Iowa. As a souvenir from their reunion, they wrapped the mayonnaise jar and candle in a tee shirt, and hit the road again.

They were in the car for about half an hour, driving 65 mph between walls of dark green, tasseled corn, when, without warning, Nevaeh burst into tears.

"What?" Tray asked, touching the brake and causing the trucker behind him to blow his horn in one long angry blast. "What's wrong?"

She was bawling so hard she thought she'd choke, and when she opened her mouth to tell him she didn't know, she couldn't catch her breath.

"Shall I pull over? What? What?" Tray's panic made it worse, and she shook her head in violent convulsions.

Finally, and it seemed to her like half-way to Chicago, she whimpered, "I'm okay," but Tray had already put on his blinkers and was pulling off at the next exit. Tray stopped the car on the shoulder, yanked off his seat belt and put his arms around her. "It's okay, Nevvy, it's okay."

"No. No, it isn't," she said, wiping her tears. "What's going to happen to me? They'll find out I'm a thief and someone will find out about the drugs, and then I won't be able to find a job, and if something does happen to Dawn Ann, everyone will blame me!"

He cupped her face in his hands. "We'll get through this," he said again. "It'll be okay." She didn't believe the words, but she felt exhausted, as if she'd been sprinting for a finish line that kept receding in the distance. Her knees tickled, as if they'd given out under her. Beaten, she nodded tentatively and tried again to catch her breath.

After a minute of silence, Tray buckled his seat belt and eased the car back on the highway. He cleared his throat. "Haven't you had a dream or something? Don't you usually get your messages in dreams?"

She stared at the thread of gray highway stretching before them. "Sometimes," she said. "But I dream more when I'm alone than when I'm with someone."

"That's probably not true," Tray challenged. "You probably just listen better when you're alone."

She wasn't sure he was right about that, but it didn't matter. "When you left me, that first night, I had a one-word dream," she said. "Pul-chri-tude. Can you imagine?"

"I don't know what it means," he said.

"Neither did I. I had to look it up, which is how I lost Tara." She described the whole long story and when she finished he said, "So, what's it mean?"

"Big word for beauty," she said, squeezing her eyes shut to remember exactly. "Physical beauty comma comeliness."

"Better wait for another dream," he said. "What else you got there?" he nodded towards her backpack.

"Wanna play random Bible verse?" The idea lifted her spirits. She drew out her Bible and it opened, as always, to her money. There, opposite the lilies, she read out loud, in humorously sonorous tones, "When you see a cloud looming up in the west, you say at once that rain is coming, and so it does. And when the wind is from the south you say it will be hot, and it is. Hypocrites! You know how to interpret the face of the earth and the sky. How is it you do not know how to interpret these times?"

"Well, that's for Dawn Ann," Tray said, glancing in his rear view mirror and then changing lanes to pass an Isuzu pick-up truck. "Duck," he said, and she did.

"Remember Mexico?" he laughed, and she gave him a slug in the arm.

"Husband abuse!" he cried in false pain and then turned to her, dead serious. "How is it that our favorite pulchritudinous weathercaster can't admit her husband hit you?"

"I don't get it either," Nevaeh said. "She has no perspective on him at all. If he yells at her, she assumes *she's* done something wrong, that his bad moods are *her* fault. It's as though she can't admit he hit me, because then she'd have to realize he abuses her even more, and she must somehow rationalize that she needs him. For what, I don't know."

"Is it wrong to need someone?" Tray asked, reaching for her hand.

"Both hands on the wheel," she said. "No, it's not wrong, unless that robs you of your own faith in yourself."

She could see his jaw working on that, as if it pertained to the two of them. Which, she told herself, it didn't. They didn't "need" each other, in that sense. Tray had gone off and succeeded all by himself, and she'd gotten along quite well without him, all things considered. She—they—wouldn't be in this jam if Dawn Ann had stood up to Derek a long, long time ago.

"Growing up, Dawn Ann was always so perfect," she said. "Her family always seemed to be so orderly—Dr. and Dr. Reasonable and Responsible, as opposed to my house, Mr. and Mrs. Drunk and Disorderly."

"So you learned to take care of yourself and Dawn Ann learned to people-please," Tray said, "except that a person can't please enough people to make herself feel completely good about herself."

"They teach psychology in law school?" Nevaeh asked, thinking if they didn't, they should.

"Street smarts," Tray said, and winked.

"I don't know about 'taking care of myself.' I thought I could just be a lily of the field," Nevaeh said. "Look what's happened after all."

"Yeah, well, you gotta do the footwork," Tray said.

"A little late now."

"Not really. You can take a first step any time. You can change direction."

Cornfields gave way to suburbs of suburbs and in a matter of minutes the traffic slowed through the western business corridor, a sprawl of mid-rise business towers in various shades of blue, brown and green reflective glass. They drove a few miles in silence. "Oh, jeez," Nevaeh sighed. "I'm scared." She started to close the Bible on her lap, but at the end of the page with the passage meant for Dawn

Ann there was another: "Why not judge for yourselves what is right? For example, when you go to court with your opponent, try to settle with him on the way, or he may drag you before the judge and the judge hand you over to the bailiff and the bailiff have you thrown into prison. I tell you, you will not get out till you have paid the very last penny."

When she read it to Tray, he scowled. "Sounds a little bit like, 'The first thing we do, let's kill all the lawyers.'"

"Not all of them," she said, blowing him a kiss.

"It takes two," he said. "One lawyer would have nothing to do."

"Ha, ha," she said.

"Maybe there's something to that, Nevvy. Maybe Dawn Ann just doesn't believe you'd file charges. She knows you've got some history you'd rather not broadcast and she knows you don't want to hurt her career. She doesn't believe you'll file the charges. What she doesn't know is that you're strong, Nevvy, and you have the capacity to be honest and to face and speak the truth." He assumed a Biblical tone. "You can judge for yourself what is right."

25

Bernard jumped on Dawn Ann's bed, causing her to spring upright, her heart shocked from its loping rest. Her sleep had been as restless as if she were a tightly set alarm, coiled to spring at the slightest jostle. Now, she was suddenly, rudely awake. She raised her hands to protect herself, but her room was empty, except for Bernard, who was tiptoeing over her covered legs. Relieved, reached out her arm, curling her index finger to get his attention. She was sure only Bernard was there. The house was quiet, and Bernard usually didn't jump on the bed—Derek had playfully evicted him from their bedroom every day for a week when Derek and Dawn Ann first started sleeping together. As a result, the cat steered clear of Derek now. Dawn Ann listened, irritated that she didn't know if her husband was home, and more irritated still that if he wasn't home—locked up in his studio or his darkroom—then he was out and had been out, all night. What legitimate excuse could he have for that?

Bernard plopped himself on her feet, his weight pleasant and solid. At the same time the cat trapped her there in bed, waiting to hear what she would hear and working up the courage to get out of bed and confront either Derek or an intruder. If Derek was home, he was no doubt hung over, sore from having spent a night on the darkroom floor. If he wasn't yet home, he would be barging in at any moment—the clock said eight thirty—probably frustrated and angry over something that she couldn't do anything about, or possibly, but less likely, embarrassed and eager for her understanding and forgiveness. In either case, Derek would be volatile; any little thing could set him off—screaming and swearing at her, or worse. She would need to tread lightly around the landmines of his terrible whims.

She waited. She listened. Nothing.

Then, a tick of the clock, the cough of the air conditioner, the grunt of shifting gears down on the street. She felt paralyzed, on the brink of hopelessness. If she was afraid to venture from her bed, it was her husband's fault. She was a hostage in her own home.

She reached out and took Bernard in her arms, then slowly swung her own feet to the floor and straightened herself out of the bed, deliberately and quietly, as Bernard would if he were hunting in a field. She inched her way to the door, Bernard's purr vibrating against her breast, his eyes closed. She turned the knob and the button popped out; she was surprised that she had locked herself in. She took a breath and moved into the hall, glancing into Derek's studio, straining to confirm that he wasn't there. A small tripod on a table pointed towards a splash of industrial-sized screws, nuts and bolts in front of a tall can of Planters Peanuts. She frowned. She didn't understand Derek's art at all.

She cleared her throat in warning to any intruder and then, with longer steps, headed into the kitchen, where she dared a short whistle. Hearing no reply, no sudden vibration or creak from a footstep, no muted breath or swallow, she walked into the vast living and dining area with its teak tables, cream leather couches, thick gray carpeting, a peaceful and empty room.

Bernard roused himself and squirmed to be let free. She knelt and eased the cat to the carpet, where he stretched out his front paws, his head lowered in a relaxed yoga pose, his long, wide tail thumping the floor. Dawn Ann felt her muscles tense and remembered Derek's cavalier warning yesterday at Walter's. "*I get angry.*" As if that explained everything. As if he was entitled to his anger. As if his anger was more special than hers, or Linda's or anyone else's. Everyone was angry, at some level, about something. Husbands about too much shopping, women about too many kids, couples about too little money. Singles about being dumped or not getting lucky or not being loved enough as a child. Reporters about deadlines and other peoples' miseries. Everybody was angry about something, or worried or afraid. But that didn't mean you beat up the people you supposedly loved. She was dangerously close to arguing with Derek, was, in fact, arguing with him in her head and recognized that she *did* know what would happen if she argued with Derek, either about sleeping in the darkroom or about not coming home. If she argued, she knew what would happen. He would get *angry.*

She immediately felt the need to get away from the apartment, not to be there when he woke up or when he returned.

Quietly, again, but more quickly, she made her way to the bedroom, pulled on some jeans and a pastel tee shirt, and tossed her purse into her gym bag. She laced her running shoes with a double knot and headed for the door. From the living room, Bernard trotted to her and wound himself around her legs.

"Of course, my lovey," she soothed. She went to the kitchen and opened the cabinet. "Salmon, chicken or beef?"

She opened the can of salmon with the pop-top ring, forked half of it into Bernard's bowl and then poured him some fresh water. While he lapped up his food, she sat at the table in the kitchen alcove and wrote a short note to Derek saying she was at the gym and then running errands and that he should call her cell when he woke up. She immediately realized her error and scratched the potentially judgmental "when you wake up" in favor of "when you have a chance." She scratched that too and then furiously wadded the whole thing into a ball. Keys clattered in the front door lock. She took a deep breath and, with her gym bag over her shoulder decided to go to the hall as if she hadn't heard the sound of the keys.

She opened the door and acted pleasantly surprised to see Derek there, his keys in one hand, a newspaper and coffee in the other. Dawn Ann felt Bernard rub against her leg and felt a dose of affection for her bedraggled husband. "Hey, honey, you were up and out early!"

Hair uncombed, eyes cracked with webs of red, a puzzled look flew over Derek's face, followed by a furious one. So as not to be in his way, she stepped aside to let him through the door. Without any warning, Derek took a step forward with his left leg and let go with his right, lifting Bernard up off the floor and smashing him full force into the handle of the front closet door. The cat crumbled with a deafening, sickening thwack. Dawn Ann screamed.

"Son-of-a-bitch!" Derek shouted, and strode down the hall towards his studio.

Trembling, Dawn Ann crouched over Bernard and placed her palm on his chest, feeling for his heartbeat. As always, his fur was comforting; he looked as if he were asleep, but the throb of his heart was faint. She tapped his chest lightly. "Bernard?" she asked, as if expecting a reply. "Bernard? Are you okay, honey? Bernard?" Bernard didn't move. Dawn Ann felt herself rise to the occasion, inhaling deeply to calm her own panic so that possibly she could save Bernard. She put one hand under Bernard's slim neck and the other under his hindquarters, forming a gurney. Her gym bag slid down her arm, an uncomfortable, awkward weight at her elbow, but she held her arms steady. She couldn't feel Bernard's breath on her outstretched arm; but she thought she saw his chest heave ever so slightly. There was no blood. "You're gonna be okay. You're gonna be okay."

The elevator was empty. At the ground level, James held the door open and without comment rushed to the street to hail a taxi.

"I hope he'll be okay, Ms. McKnight," he said solemnly as he moved the gym bag back up on her shoulder and closed the cab door. Her elbows began to ache, and she hunched over to rest her arms while Bernard lay silent on her lap.

"Please hurry," she told the cabbie, who agreed, "no problem" in a sing-song Caribbean accent. He had the good sense not to ask if the cat was sick, just beeped and swerved his way through the relatively light Saturday morning traffic to the address she'd given him.

Gently, so as not to disturb him, Dawn Ann slid her right hand out from under Bernard's hips. His firm, rounded chin seemed at peace under her left palm. His ears stood characteristically tall and erect, high on his head. She studied his chest and stomach and thought she saw the slightest movement. She set her jaw in the firm belief that Bernard was still breathing, just knocked out. The vet would confirm that cats were lithe and flexible and could withstand falls like this one—hadn't Linda once done a story about a cat that had dropped 10 stories out of a window and survived? She put two fingers against Bernard's body. His wavy fur, thinning because of the summer molt, was still thick. She couldn't detect any movement except the blood pounding in her own fingertips. Despite the fact that both her parents were health professionals, she'd had no aptitude for medicine and didn't know how to raise a pulse. She touched the pad of his front left paw, soft but tough, like a fine leather, but she couldn't feel a thing. Still, Bernard had to be alive.

She knew Derek hadn't meant to hurt Bernard. But Derek had looked angry and she couldn't fathom why. They'd had dinner at Walter's and that had been pleasant enough, and he'd flirted with Trudy, who seemed happy to flirt back, the way she flirted, truth be known, with all her customers. Dawn Ann had done her show, and then it had been so very quiet at home. She remembered Linda's story. The sister said that the dead man—the one who'd beaten his kids and his wife so often that the woman finally had pulled the trigger on him—wasn't a bad guy, just somebody who felt frustrated.

I get angry. Alone in the back seat of the cab with her injured pet, Dawn Ann began to cry. She couldn't find a pulse or a breath, but that didn't mean Bernard was dead. There could still be time.

"Hurry, please!" she said to the cabbie, who smiled shyly as he looked into the rear view mirror. "Yes, Ms. McKnight. At your service." The cabbie leaned on his horn and blasted through a yellow light just as it turned red, then screeched to a halt at the curb, jumped out and took Dawn Ann's gym bag off her arm, helping her keep Bernard steady. He walked ahead of her into the clinic, as if clearing the way for a celebrity. The receptionist paged the vet and showed them into an examining room, the cabbie following Dawn Ann as if he were her husband or the cat's father. Dawn Ann was focused only on Bernard. "Careful," she said to the pony-tailed assistant who took Bernard from her and put him on a stainless steel table in the middle of the room. Dawn Ann remembered to pay the cabbie only when he made a move for the door. She opened her gym bag and found twenty dollars in her purse.

"Thank you," she murmured.

"No problem," he answered.

The vet, a Dr. Harrell who knew Dawn Ann and knew her cat, ran into the room. Putting his hand to Bernard's throat, he said, "Poor thing!" Then he looked at Dawn Ann. "What happened?"

For a moment Dawn Ann froze. What could she say that didn't implicate her husband?

"Did he fall?" Dr. Harrell coaxed.

She fixed her eyes on the doctor's. "My husband kicked him against a door," she said, her voice cracking. "He was angry," she said.

Dr. Harrell nodded and turned his attention to the cat. With his stethoscope he listened for Bernard's breath. He didn't smile as if he'd found it, but he didn't shake his head in despair, either. He moved the scope to the cat's neck, then placed his fingers at the neck. He held the cat's paw, stroked it, and gently placed it back on the table. He put his thumb on the cat's forehead, as if in prayer, then raised his chin to his assistant, who put her arms around Dawn Ann's shoulders.

"I'm sorry, Dawn Ann," the vet said. "I'm sorry."

"But ..."

"A broken neck, probably extensive internal injuries. We could autopsy if you want, but I don't see a real need for that."

Dawn Ann stood motionless, knowing what she didn't want to know. Her husband was, as Linda said, a vicious abuser. Nevaeh had been telling the truth.

"We can make arrangements here," Dr. Harrell said and Dawn Ann nodded.

The assistant removed her arms from Dawn Ann's shoulders and squared them. She was young, like Nevaeh, and her eyes were green and earnest. "Cruelty to animals is a crime, Ms. McKnight. It's a crime that should be reported to the police."

Tears welled in Dawn Ann's eyes. Reporting things to the police didn't change reality. It wasn't her style. She didn't seek that kind of retribution, and she abhorred the publicity that would ensue. A crime report or not, Bernard was dead. She would rise to the challenge and suffer that loss on her own.

"I need the ladies'," she said, and the assistant led her down the hall to a door decorated with a decal of two perky kittens in a white wicker basket with pink bows at their necks and underneath the word "kitties." She sat on the commode and covered her face with her hands, rocking back and forth with each fresh wave of agony, for her pet, for her marriage, for her cousin, for herself. She lost track of time, but when she felt herself spent, she stood at the sink and splashed cold water on her face. Tentatively, she raised her eyes to the mirror. Her hair was stiff and clumped, worse than the wind tunnel look the station had given her so long ago. She obviously hadn't brushed her hair before Derek had come home. She had bags under her eyes; not gray, but red and inflamed, swollen from her tears. She looked horrible. Not as bad as Linda's cell phone picture of Nevaeh, all bloody and bruised, but horrible nonetheless. Her deepest hurt didn't show at all. She called Linda. It was after noon; of course Linda would be up; she hoped she'd be home and not out doing errands or working out at the gym.

Linda picked up right away, and Dawn Ann managed only to say, "Hello."

"What's wrong?" Linda asked, sounding panicked.

"Bernard," Dawn Ann started, but was choked by a fresh round of tears. Linda didn't say anything. Dawn Ann took a deep breath to compose herself. It was one of her professional skills: converting a complicated meteorological situation into a few sentences delivered in a handful of seconds. Finally she said, "Bernard is dead. Derek kicked him. Can I come over?" It wasn't a question, really. Where else could she go? She'd called only to make sure Linda would be there.

Linda didn't hesitate. She said she'd come get her and Dawn Ann said no, it would be faster if she took a cab. The vet's assistant asked her to fill out some paperwork and then walked with her to the sidewalk, where she hailed a cab and opened the door for Dawn Ann. She felt like a widow leaving a funeral. A fresh wave of tears overtook her in the back of the cab; her lap felt empty and she could almost feel the weight of Bernard's small body on her knees.

Linda had a fresh pot of coffee ready and a tea kettle whistling. She'd set a plate of chocolate-covered graham crackers and chocolate-covered marshmallow cookies on her coffee table in the living room. "I keep these for emergencies," she said, as Dawn Ann began sucking on the corner of a graham. "Tea or coffee?"

"Tea, with honey and lemon," she answered, sinking into Linda's overstuffed couch.

Over three graham crackers, two pinwheels and three cups of tea, Dawn Ann told Linda what had happened. Linda took it all in, her face squirming every so often when she wanted Dawn Ann to hurry up, but Dawn Ann appreciated that Linda didn't pepper her with questions or probe for details, but let her explain exactly what Derek had done. Linda didn't express shock or call Derek a bastard, but Dawn Ann knew she not only was being listened to, but heard. She wasn't sure anyone else had ever listened to her as fully as Linda did now.

Linda cleared her throat. "Are you going to press charges?"

"The Vet's assistant mentioned that. I don't know what good it would do."

"I guess the idea would be to stop him from doing it again."

"I won't be getting another pet." She made a fist.

"You're staying with him?"

Dawn Ann was startled. This was something else she'd known as she was holding Bernard in the cab, but she hadn't yet formed the thought into words. "Right," she said, stretching her fingers and running her hand through her hair. "Probably not."

"What, probably?"

"I mean, probably, yes, but I never thought I'd get a divorce, so it's a new idea I need to get used to."

"People get divorced all the time. Over much less serious stuff," Linda said, her tone both matter-of-fact but tempered with sympathy. She stroked Dawn Ann's hand.

"It will be so complicated," Dawn Ann said. She was thinking of the practicalities, all that would have to happen to disentangle Derek: the apartment, her salary, their savings, his precious photographs.

"The lawyers will deal with the complications," Linda said. "The hard part is the emotional." She looked away briefly and then faced Dawn Ann squarely. "Derek will not take it well. He may become more ... violent." Dawn Ann pursed her lips at the word.

Linda continued, "But you will have support from your friends. I'll be here for you." She gave Dawn Ann's hand a squeeze and poured another cup of tea for each of them, as if to change the subject. "There's a lot going on right now, but I have to ask this. What about Nevaeh? Shouldn't she press charges for what Derek did to *her*? That might stop him from beating up another unsuspecting woman."

"You don't stop, do you?" Dawn Ann asked, putting down her tea cup and staring at Linda in disbelief. "I don't think I have that kind of strength, Linda," she said. "I'm not as strong as you want me to be."

Linda held her gaze. "On this one, it would be Nevaeh who would have to be strong. You would just need to back her up."

"It's more than that, Linda." She folded her arms across her chest. "You, of all people, should know. The press would be all over it, and how foolish would I look? I can hear the columnists now: a weather caster who didn't have the sense to come in from the storm; who couldn't see which way the wind was blowing."

"Oh," Linda said, as if finally understanding Dawn Ann's true concerns. She scratched her forehead, then brightened slowly. She bit her lip. "If that's the big reason—that you don't want people to know—then maybe, and I'm just thinking out loud here, maybe you could actually use that to … you know … inspire others."

"Become a poster child for wife abuse?" Dawn Ann stood and walked to the window, her back to her friend.

"Not that you have to become the leader of some kind of movement, but you could be up-front about it. Do a little public speaking, to women like yourself. Help other people seek the help they need."

Dawn Ann shook her head and moaned. "You're too much of a crusader."

"You don't need to decide today. If I may say so, I think you should let Nevaeh tell her own truth to the police, so that other women will be warned about him."

"Warned," Dawn Ann said in disgust. "People don't pay attention to warnings. People do what they want to do. You say, 'tornado warning' and people go out with their video cameras looking for the funnel." She whipped around to confront Linda.

"People run yellow lights all the time, too. They take cold medicine and operate heavy machinery. Caution: This coffee is hot. This knife is sharp." Linda chuckled. "I agree we're over-warned, but sometimes the dangers aren't obvious, or we think they don't exist because they didn't happen to us. Awareness of the problem, an honest look at it, lays the groundwork for the warning that might possibly, someday, get through. We really only hear a warning when it's too late: we've already taken the wrong job or married the guy."

Linda bit her lower lip.

"Okay," Dawn Ann said wearily. She hadn't heeded Linda's

warnings; she hadn't even believed Nevaeh when it happened. "If you really think it necessary, you can tell Nevaeh that I'm okay with her reporting Derek to the police. I'll get a place of my own where he won't be able to find me. I'll be alright."

"I heard this morning that Nevaeh's left town. But I'll tell Tray, in case they're in touch and I'll tell Trudy to have her call if she hears from her."

"Left town? She had nowhere to go! That's how she ended up with us in the first place." Dawn Ann thought for a minute and was flooded by a fresh spate of tears. "I could've warned her."

"You did the best you could at the time. Now, knowing what you know, you and Nevaeh together will warn others," Linda said, her voice smooth and calming. Linda opened her cell phone, dialed Tray's number and spoke into an answering machine, then flipped the phone closed. "So, nothing more for us to do on that score." She cleared her throat. "So, what do you want to do? Would a hot tub help? A run?" Dawn Ann seemed lost in thought. "Double-stuffed deep-dish pizza?" Linda asked.

"Yes," Dawn Ann said, wiping her nose. She'd been friends with Linda for a long time. "All of the above."

• • •

Tray had a small studio on the north side of the city where they quickly deposited Nevaeh's things on Sunday afternoon before returning the car to Tray's friend. They walked back to the apartment, dodging teenaged boys on skateboards and razors. On the nineteenth floor of a high rise, the living room looked west and had a fine view of the North branch of the river.

Remarkably, Tray's place had the feel of their tree house in Iowa. It was sparsely furnished—a bed, two bookcases made of cinderblocks and cherry-stained planks, a slightly scratched teak table and four chairs, and an off-white, coarse linen couch with a couple of Indian blankets draped over it, presumably to hide stains or rips. Two huge corn-plants towered in one corner, a ficus in the other. An array of smaller potted plants soaked up the sun on the window ledge.

"What do you think?" he asked.

Just to tease him, she considered saying, "beats prison," but she didn't. "Feels like home," she said.

"Home? Like the tree house?" Tray laughed. He swept his around the room. "Of course! We could add more plants, maybe hang some from the ceiling?"

"You have enough plants," Nevaeh said. "You know, the tree house wasn't my goal in life, it just sort of happened," she said. "It was fun while it lasted. I'm thinking this might be the next phase."

"Just until I'm out of law school," he said. "Then we could probably get something a little bigger, maybe one with a balcony."

"Maybe the first floor, with grass," she said.

He laughed, guessing her concern. "I could go with that," he said. "Welcome home."

The light was blinking on his message machine. He listened patiently, deleting three recordings in a row. Then he frowned and put the phone down carefully while turning to Nevaeh.

"Dawn Ann's changed her mind," he said. "Says you should report Derek if you want to."

Silently, Nevaeh sank onto the couch and sat perfectly still, fighting the surge of adrenalin that shot a deep heat all the way from her stomach to her throat. Finally, she swallowed hard and said, "That's a change. How come?"

Tray joined her on the couch and put his arm around her, holding her shoulder tightly as if he needed to bolt her down. He told her what Linda had said about Bernard.

Nevaeh remembered Tara, and how she had wailed, lying on the public library floor, and the satisfaction in Farmer Lundstrom's eyes. The horror of losing your pet, your best friend, your most loyal fan. She could imagine Derek, drunk and mean and frustrated with himself and having to take it out on someone or something, and Bernard, rubbing his body across Derek's legs, and then, a swift kick with the point of his boot, and Dawn Ann, helplessly witnessing all of this, unable to stop the one and save the other.

She started to cry. "Now, it is about you and Bernard, and about his hurting other women. It has nothing to do with Dawn Ann."

He held her even tighter.

"What about the money?" Nevaeh asked, her last bit of resistance to calling the police. It was no longer Dawn Ann's safety or career that would prevent Nevaeh from doing what she should do; it was her own culpability.

"The bottom line is, you didn't take it in the end, so it's more like attempted theft—and pretty petty theft at that. Besides it's his word against yours as to whether you were stealing it or about to leave a note that you'd borrowed it or …"

"Stop!" she said realizing she was being fed her cover story. "Now you really do sound like a lawyer!"

"It'll be okay," Tray said, holding up his hands as if he'd been arrested. He waited, but Nevaeh made no move from the couch. "Shouldn't we call Linda now?"

"I'd rather just talk to Dawn Ann," Nevaeh said. She played with her fingers, knitting them and unknitting them.

"I bet she's with Linda," Tray said. He dialed the phone, asked for Dawn Ann and held it out to Nevaeh. He stood facing her, like an encouraging coach.

"Dawnie? This is Nevaeh," she said, remembering her first call to her cousin from the New Orleans rehab.

Before she could say more, Dawn Ann broke in, "I'm so sorry, Nevaeh. I'm so sorry I didn't believe you. I should have warned you. I just didn't.…"

"Yeah, I know. He could be such a nice guy," Nevaeh said.

"I'm leaving him, Nevvy. I hope we can be friends again. Is there any way, any way we could start over?"

Nevaeh was touched by the change in her cousin, her new humility. That someone like Dawn Ann would even want to be friends with someone like herself. She stared at Tray and her eyes filled. "I've been known to say 'you can't start over,'" she said. "Although I do believe you can start again."

"What's the difference?" Dawn Ann asked.

Nevaeh took a deep breath, noticing that she felt, for once, not like Dawn Ann's little girl cousin but as an equal, with something to say. "Starting over always sounds to me like you're going to repeat yourself. To me, it's the difference between pretending the past didn't exist, that you have a fresh slate, when, in fact, there is a past, and when you start again, you start with all that experience."

• • •

A few weeks later, Nevaeh and Tray were sitting up in bed, reading the want ads and a book about careers Tray had brought home from the library. Despite everything they thought they'd learned during their adventures about spontaneity and going with the flow and overcoming the unexpected and the adverse, they were now trying to figure out a plan for Nevaeh's future. Tray would finish law school and then work for the Center, or another legal aid clinic. Nevaeh was looking for a simple job that would give her time to write enough to finish her master's degree, now that she'd gathered so much material. And then maybe she could get a job as a writer, maybe writing stories for someone like Linda.

At ten o'clock the news came on, and Felicity O'Neal and Alberto Beltran announced the headlines, and welcomed back Dawn Ann McKnight, who'd been on an extended vacation. When Dawn Ann appeared, in a teal pantsuit, she seemed to Nevaeh to have a new energy. Her eyes sparkled and her hair was, as always, perfect. There was a new moon, she said, that very night. "And I'd like to thank my cousin, Nevaeh Thera, for reminding me of tonight's 'The Elements' segment. Technically, the new moon is not the sliver we often think of as the new moon, starting its cycle over. The true new moon is when it's dark. You can't see it, but you know it's there."

About the Author

PHOTO: BARBARA NITKE

Mary Hutchings Reed is the recipient of the "Champion for Justice" award from the Legal Assistance Foundation (LAF), and is particularly pleased that *Saluting the Sun* is the inaugural publication under Ampersand's **"Good Reading"** imprint. All books sold under this imprint benefit a charity selected by the author. Mary has pledged 10% of the proceeds from the sale of this book to LAF, the largest provider of *pro bono* civil legal services to the poor and underserved of metropolitan Chicago. Over her career Mary has been active with many legal and social service not-for-profit organizations, including Lawyers for the Creative Arts, providing free legal services to emerging artists and arts organizations.

Although she practiced intellectual property law in Chicago for almost 39 years, Mary has always wanted to be a writer, and remembers fondly a toy printing press with handset type on which she wrote her first poem. After leaving the full-time practice of law at Winston & Strawn, Chicago, and becoming Of Counsel, Mary devoted much of her time to writing fiction—her thirteenth novel is in progress. *Saluting the Sun* is the third to find its way to print. Her first, *Courting Kathleen Hannigan,* (Ampersand, Inc.) was published in 2007. *Warming Up* was the second in print (She Writes Press, 2013). It was a top finalist in three national contests and was a runner-up in the Illinois Library Association's "Soon to be Famous" Author Project. Her musical, *Fairways,* has been produced three times in the Chicago area. Mary's short fiction has appeared in *ARS Medica, The Liguorian, The Tampa Review* and *The Florida Review* (forthcoming). She writes *Amicus Scriptor,* a bi-monthly column on fiction writing, for the *Chicago Daily Law Bulletin*.

Mary was named "Best Advertising Lawyer in Chicago" in 2012 and 2014. She is a graduate of Brown University (1973) with a combined bachelor's degree in public policy making and a master's degree in economics. She earned her law degree in 1976 at Yale Law School. Mary lives in Chicago and Walworth, Wisconsin, with her husband, William R. Reed.

• • •

www.maryhutchingsreed.com

SAFETY ALERT
Are you in an abusive relationship?
If you are in danger, call 911
or the 24/7 U.S. National Domestic Violence Hotline:
1-800-799-7233   TYY-1-800-787-3224

Be sure to access these sites from a safe computer:

The National Domestic Violence Hotline – 24/7
http://www.thehotline.org/

The Hotline is a national service available to anyone. Advocates can talk through specific situations, provide feedback and connect callers to vital resources. Their goal is to help survivors and their family members and friends understand the dynamics of power and control in abusive and unhealthy relationships. They also help create safety plans, or outlines of what to do in certain situations, that are both practical and effective for someone experiencing abuse.

U.S. Department of Justice,
Office on Violence Against Women
http://www.justice.gov/ovw/domestic-violence

Domestic violence not only affects those who are abused, but also has a substantial effect on family members, friends, co-workers, other witnesses, and the community at large. Children who grow up witnessing domestic violence are among those seriously affected by this crime. Frequent exposure to violence in the home not only predisposes children to numerous social and physical problems, but also teaches them that violence is a normal way of life, increasing their risk of becoming society's next generation of victims and abusers.

At this site you'll find access to local resources as well as a wide range of programs designed to guide victims to safety.

Safe Horizon
http://www.safehorizon.org/index.php

Safe Horizon is the largest provider of domestic violence services in the country. Collaborating with the criminal justice system, Safe Horizon offers innovative programs that provide women with support throughout the complex process of leaving violent relationships and building safe futures. For survivors of domestic violence, stalking, rape, and sexual assault, Safe Horizon offers services that help them and their children move toward safe and independent violence-free lives.

Questions for Book Club Discussion

1. Would you like to live in a tree house? What thoughts do you have about living in a tree house?

2. Is Nevaeh just naïve when she thinks she can live as a "lily of the field," trusting in the goodness of the universe? Why would Nevaeh believe that she could live as a "lily of the field"?

3. Do you know anyone in a relationship like Dawn Ann and Derek's? Why do you think Dawn Ann and Derek are in a relationship?

4. Is Dawn Ann too forgiving? Why do you think that Dawn Ann allows herself to be abused by Derek?

5. When one partner is publicly recognized as successful and the other not, it often strains the relationship. How can a couple best handle that situation?

6. Why is Linda pushing Nevaeh to report her situation? How could a friend help someone like Dawn Ann?

7. What must an artist do with his or her work in order to be deemed "successful"?

8. In what ways are Phil and Tray alike? How are they different?

9. What do you think makes Phil repeatedly go back to Ophelia?

10. What is the difference between starting over and starting again?